RYDEVILLE ELITE BOOK TWO

TWISTED
Betrayal

USA TODAY BESTSELLING AUTHOR
SIOBHAN DAVIS

Printed by Amazon
Paperback edition © August 2019

ISBN-13: 9781686312137

Editor: Kelly Hartigan (XterraWeb) editing.xterraweb.com
Cover design by Robin Harper https://wickedbydesigncovers.wixsite.com
Photographer: Sara Eirew
Cover Models: Cover Models: Anthony Desforges and Hélène Bujold
Formatting by Polgarus Studios

AUTHOR'S NOTE

Although this book is set in a high school environment, it is a **dark bully romance**, and it is not suitable for young teens due to mature content, graphic sexual scenes, and cursing. The recommended reading age is eighteen+. **Some scenes may be triggering.**

CHAPTER ONE

Abby

A light breeze ghosts over my legs as someone rolls the covers back and lifts my nightdress. Pressure bears down on my lower body, and a whimper escapes my mouth. I try to blink, but my eyes refuse to cooperate, happy to live in the hazy space I now call home.

"She'll be fine," an unfamiliar male voice says, as I attempt to sit up in the bed. But my limbs are like my eyes. They won't function the way they're supposed to, and I'm screaming, but no one can hear me because the screams remain locked up inside me. "Give her plenty of fluids, ensure she eats a varied diet and takes her vitamins and medication. I'll be back to check on her next week."

The sounds of retreating footsteps spur me into action. Forcing through the dark, hazy fog in my head, I extend my arm out from under the covers. "Wait!" My voice is raspy from lack of use and barely louder than a whisper. "Help me! Help my baby!"

The footsteps falter, and a hushed conversation pursues, but I can't hear the words, can't detect the voices, and my stupid fucking body won't move. Silent tears leak out of my eyes. "Help!" I croak again, but it's futile.

Images flash through my mind, and the worst pain imaginable slices through me, like a finely sharpened sword gliding easily through skin and sinew and muscle and bone.

"Shush, now, Miss Manning." A cool hand sweeps across my cheek before lowering to my arm.

"No!" I cry out as he flicks my skin with his fingers, readying me for the shot. "Please, stop!" The sharp prick stings, and cold liquid instantly seeps through my veins, numbing everything.

"It'll be okay now, Abigail." His fingers brush against my cheek again. "Sleep, pretty lady."

My eyelids grow heavy again, and my body feels like a dead weight on top of the bed. I fight the darkness, like I do every time, but I always succumb, and this time is no different.

Time loses all meaning for me, and I don't know how much passes as days and nights blend and I exist in some alternate cloudy realm. Lucid moments are rare. Until one day, I wake, and my limbs feel lighter, the fuzzy darkness in my head has almost fully disappeared, and I can move.

My movements are sluggish as I haul myself upright in the bed, slowly blinking. Blinding light dazzles me, and I shutter my eyes again, gradually opening them, a bit at a time, until I'm accustomed to the bright space.

I glance around the strange, well-lit room. It's sparsely decorated and furnished. On my left is a wooden desk and chair. On my right, a small closet and a dresser. A lamp sits atop the table by my bed. Drab gray walls lacking artwork add to the overall depressive feel of the room.

I look over my shoulder, locating the only window in the room. It's a small square with steel bars running vertically along the entire width. Slivers of dull daylight slip through the gaps, confirming it's early evening.

Gingerly, I slide my legs out the side of the bed and stand, clutching onto the table when my legs buckle, threatening to go out from under me. Bracing myself, I take one careful step at a time, walking toward the side door that I'm hoping leads to a toilet because I badly need to pee.

I stumble into the small bathroom, sinking gratefully onto the toilet. Stinging pain accompanies my urine, and I wince, rubbing a hand across my stomach as I relieve myself. When I'm done, I walk on shaky legs to the sink, inspecting my reflection in the mirror.

I could use some color in my cheeks, but apart from that, I look fine. I don't look like a kidnapped girl taken who the fuck knows where. I don't look like a girl whose entire world came crashing down around her that fateful night.

But appearances are usually deceiving. I learned that lesson a long time ago.

What a pity I didn't remember that the second Camden Marshall entered my life.

I may have spent most of my time here in a numbed-out state of ignorant bliss, but flashes of memories were enough to remind me he's the reason I'm here. Wherever the hell *here* is, because I've no clue if I'm still even in the US.

All I remember is waking up on an airplane, with Louis's smug grin in my face as he gleefully stabbed me in the arm with a motherfucking monster of a needle, and I passed out again.

The next recollection I have is waking up in a cold sweat, in an unfamiliar bed, with my screams bouncing off the walls.

And after that, it's one giant blur.

I turn the shower on, strip out of my nightdress, and step under the warm water.

I notice my enlarged breasts for the first time as I'm soaping my body, staring at them in puzzled amazement. I know boobs usually get bigger during pregnancy, but I wasn't expecting them to grow that fast or grow so big. I cup my hands around them, and they feel heavy and sore to the touch. I guess I will get used to a lot of changes in my body as my pregnancy progresses.

I flatten my palm on my flat stomach, wondering when I'll start showing.

I didn't ask for this, and I hate how my baby was conceived on a lie, but I'm not unhappy about it. My lips curl into a smile as I rub my hand back and forth across my tummy. The thought this tiny little being is growing inside me blows my mind, and I cling to my vow to do everything to protect him or her.

A frown replaces my smile as anxiety creeps up my throat. I don't know how long I've been here or what they have done to me, and a sliver of fear raises its head. If he's done anything to my baby, I will murder him with my bare hands.

I think about it logically, attempting to bring my crazy heart rate back down.

Father kidnapped me to keep me away from Kaiden and Atticus, because if I give birth and I don't marry my baby daddy, then my shares in Manning Motors automatically transfer back to him. Which is what he's always wanted.

So, my baby is safe.

For now.

Thinking of our child raises everything else to the surface, and I tilt my head up, closing my eyes and letting the water flow down my face as my mind wanders back to that night.

I can't believe I didn't make the connection.

That I didn't figure out Camden Marshall was actually Kaiden Anderson. My brother's best friend when we were kids. Son of my mom's best friend. Someone I enjoyed playing with. Until my mother's affair with his father ended her friendship with Emma Anderson and ultimately ended up costing both women their lives.

All the revelations from that night weigh heavy on my mind, and I sag against the wall, exhausted and tired—both mentally and physically drained. I finish washing my hair and my body, and I stagger out of the stall, tucking a towel around myself and switching off the water.

A shriek escapes my mouth when I return to the bedroom to discover my father standing by my bed with a strange man wearing white scrubs. All the tiny hairs on the back of my neck stand to attention.

"You shouldn't be up." My father casts a quick glance over me. "Get back in bed."

I flip him the bird. "Fuck. You."

He moves like lightning, and my head jerks to the side as he slaps me across the face. "I thought I'd beaten that insubordination out of you, but you share the same stubborn streak as your mother." He grips my chin painfully, and water drips down my back from my wet hair. "And the same lousy taste in men," he adds, shoving me, none too gently, at the strange man.

The man helps me to bed, pulling the covers up under my arms and smiling. He's in his twenties, I guess, with pale skin, dark eyes, and dark hair. I narrow my eyes, instantly wary. "I'm Wyatt. I'm a psych nurse assigned to look after you."

That *so* gives me a warm and cozy feeling. Not.

"I guess you're the one I have to thank for my drugged-up state." I glare at him, putting the full extent of my hatred behind it. He may not have given the order—I'm guessing that honor goes to Daddy Dearest—but he sure as shit acted on it.

His smile fades. "It was in your best interests, Miss Manning."

"Spare me the bullshit," I hiss.

"I need a few minutes alone with my daughter," my father says, and bile travels up my throat as I spot him clenching and unclenching his fists at his side. I turn panicked eyes on Wyatt, beseeching him not to leave even if I don't like or trust him either. I don't want to be left in here with my father on my own. I don't trust him not to hurt me.

"Sir." Wyatt nods reverently, ignoring my obvious terrified expression, before quietly slipping out of the room.

Pushing my fear aside, I pull myself upright, lifting my chin and planting a look of false bravado on my face as my father stalks toward me, sitting on the edge of the bed. "Why do you have to be so difficult? Why can't you be more like your brother?"

Thoughts of Drew do little to reassure me.

Atticus Anderson outed him to my father, confirming he'd played a part in breaking into his safe and stealing his confidential paperwork, including the real will which states that shares in Manning Motors will transfer to me and my twin after we both turn eighteen. Unless I'm married, and then my shares go to my husband. It's why my father has been so keen on marrying me off to one of the elite. "Where is Drew?" I ask.

"Drew is at home, where he rightfully belongs. Unlike you, he knows the meaning of loyalty."

I hide my surprise, wondering what Drew has said to extract himself from the hole he was in.

"Why am I here? Where am I? And what *is* this place?"

"You are here because I cannot trust you to do the right thing." He grips my chin hard again. "Atticus Anderson will not get his hands on you. He thinks he has it all worked out, but that pathetic drunk always underestimates his enemy."

A malicious grin slips over his mouth, and I want to ram my fist into his face until he bleeds. He digs his nails into my skin, and I grind my teeth hard. "As do you, stupid girl." He sneers, and panic bubbles up my throat. "Kaiden Anderson will not lay a finger on you again, and you will pay for your disloyalty."

He lets me go, standing, but I hold on to my breath, waiting for the pièce de résistance. "You will remain here, focusing on your studies, ensuring you graduate early, by the time of your eighteenth birthday. Then, and only then, will I permit you to return home, on the day of your wedding. You *will* marry Charles Barron the Third and he *will* sign over your shares to me. You will be a dutiful wife and do nothing to disrespect him or any of the elite. At a time of my choosing, you will give him an heir."

He's fucking delusional.

I would rather die than live that life.

And it hasn't escaped my notice that he hasn't mentioned my baby in his plans. *Has Charlie agreed to raise my child as his own, or how does my pregnancy fit into his plans?* Acute fear holds a vise grip on my heart as I consider all the horrible things he could do to my unborn child. "I won't do it." I fold my arms across my chest. "You can't force me."

His evil laughter wafts around the room, sending chills tiptoeing up my spine. "I think you'll find that I can, and I will." He removes an envelope from his inside jacket pocket, tapping it on the back of one hand as he smirks at me. "Your naivety has left you vulnerable, Abigail, which only adds to my disappointment. I taught you better than that, but you're just like every other useless female. Weak and ruled by her emotions."

A look of disgust crawls over his face. "You will do what you're told, because I have the power to take *everything* from you. Starting with this." He places the envelope on the bed beside me. "This is just the beginning. Think of all those you love. Your rebelliousness puts every single one of them at risk. You can test me if you like, but I wouldn't advise it, although I'd enjoy ticking every name off that list."

"You sicken me."

"The feeling is mutual." He leans down into my face, and his sour breath turns my stomach. "If I didn't need you, I'd have squeezed the life out of you the second you were born."

A messy ball of emotion clogs my throat, and I work hard to maintain a neutral expression. I've always known he's hated me, and if he was capable of anything even close to love, I wouldn't want to be on the receiving end of it. But to hear his disdain spelled out so bluntly hurts.

But it also motivates me and helps keep me focused, so I should probably thank him for his indifference, because it ensures I never lose my determination.

I don't want to let my emotions get the better of me, because then I'm just proving his point. So, I do what I always do to deflect my feelings. Concentrate on something unemotional. "Why do you need me?" I pierce him with hateful eyes. "My marriage to Charlie doesn't help with your auto-drive program, so why is it so important?"

He narrows his gaze at me, and I notice the fine lines at the corners of his eyes are no longer there. My father is forty-six, but he doesn't have a wrinkle on his tight face, because he's long been an advocate of cosmetic surgery and a regular visitor to Doctor Gunning's Rydeville clinic. His vanity and arrogance know no bounds, and he spends an inordinate amount of time—for a man— on his appearance. Dying his hair as soon as any gray appears at his temples. Working out for two hours a day without fail. Eating a carefully calorie-controlled diet. Getting weekly manicures and facials.

I guess those women he fucks in his sex den expect their men a certain way, and he doesn't like to disappoint them.

Or he's just that vain.

Bile floods my mouth again, and looking at him makes me ill.

"The reasons are none of your business. Your job is simple, Abigail. Look pretty. Smile. Speak only when spoken to. Open your legs whenever your husband demands it, and run an orderly house." He smooths a hand down the front of his custom-made navy suit. "Surely, even you can manage that."

I want to tell him to fuck off, but I don't want another slap, so I settle for glaring at him instead.

"Read the letter." His cold, inhumane eyes penetrate mine. "And remember you forced me to do this, Abigail. This is on you, and your behavior will decide whether it warrants further action. Cooperate and I'll consider the matter closed. Disobey me, and your loved ones will continue to pay the price."

He stalks out of the room without a backward glance, leaving me clutching the envelope in my trembling hands.

I know what's in this letter has the power to destroy me, and I'm tempted to ball it up and throw it in the trash. But knowledge is power, and wallowing in a pit of denial won't help.

I've already decided my father is dead to me.

And it's not just enough to run away now.

I want to fucking bury him. To end his life as he knows it.

Metaphorically speaking, because death is too easy for a psychopath like him.

I want him to suffer, and I'll make him pay. I don't know how. But, someday, he is getting what's coming to him.

I open the envelope, unfolding the letter with sweaty hands and a heart that's trying to beat a path out of my chest. I draw deep breaths, trying to prepare myself, but nothing could prepare me for these words.

Pain infuses every cell in my body as I read, my teardrops soaking the page and blurring the ink as silent tears cascade down my face. Choking sobs clog my throat and the weirdest noises escape my mouth as I die inside.

I know he's a monster, a psychopath, but this... This goes beyond that.

There are no words in the English language strong enough to describe him.

The letter floats to the ground as I curl into a ball, clutching my arms around myself, as gut-wrenching sobs birth straight from my soul. Agonizing pain rips through me, and it's like I'm being beaten up from the inside out. Wave after wave of pain batters me from all sides, and I scream and scream, over and over, until my dry throat rebels and I can't make another sound.

Time ceases to have meaning again, and I rock myself to sleep, absorbed in inner pain, vowing to make him suffer.

CHAPTER TWO

"*Abby.*" *Her soft voice whispers in my ear, and cool hands brush hair back off my brow. I whimper, leaning into her hand, her voice affecting me even in sleep.*

"*Mommy!*" *I cry, reaching for her.*

"*It's okay, sweetheart.*" *She cups my face, pressing a soft kiss to my cheek. "I'm here, and I will let no one hurt you ever again.*"

The memory returns full force as I bolt upright in the bed, holding a palm to my cheek, as if I can magically conjure her soft touch. "Mom!" Tears leak out of my eyes as I cry out to the dark, silent room.

It's no surprise I've dreamed of her.

Not after last night.

After she passed, whenever anything horrid happened, I'd dream of her. Like my subconscious knew how badly I needed her comfort and summoned her to a dream realm, because that's as close as I'll ever get to her.

I flop back on the bed, closing my eyes and wishing I was dead too.

But the sentiment doesn't last long.

Last night, I indulged my grief, sobbing myself to sleep as intense pain laid siege to my body. It's tempting to curl into a ball under the covers and never come up for air. But that would be selfish, because Father also included a list of all my other loved ones, threatening they'd share the same fate if I didn't cooperate.

Everyone I care about is on that list. Even Madam and Liam from ballet, and Robert, my personal trainer.

I don't doubt my father means every word of his threat, and I can't have their deaths on my conscience too.

So, I've got to let this go. To tuck it away in the furthermost place in my mind to properly deal with at a later stage, because today is the day I plot my revenge.

And it can't come fast enough.

Peeling back the covers, I swing my legs out of bed and stand, frothing at the mouth for vengeance.

I'm ready to get even. I don't have it all worked out yet, but I know where to start—by becoming the obedient little girl he wants me to be.

The next three weeks crawl by at a snail's pace, as I painstakingly put my plan into action, but finally, I'm ready to make my first move.

It's six thirty a.m. and daylight has arrived as I stand by the window in my room, staring at the view outside. I have twenty minutes before Wyatt comes to get me for breakfast and five minutes before the supply trucks arrive.

I still have no idea where I am, because nobody will tell me. I've been working on Wyatt, but he's scared shitless of my father, and all I could get him to admit was that I'm still in the US, which wasn't of much help, as I'd already figured that out for myself.

I haven't seen that bastard—I refuse to call him Father anymore even inside my head—since the day he broke my heart. My hands ball into fists as I stare out through the bars that cage me in, and I work hard to quell the rage that is always bubbling under the surface.

I try not to think about it.

Because I'll fall apart if I do, and I must keep my wits about me.

Pressing my face to the bars, I sigh heavily as I skim my gaze over the acres and acres of rolling fields that stretch out in front of this facility. Orange- and yellow-tipped trees break up the bleak monotony, and they're pretty to look at.

I've studied the landscape for clues.

The fields are bordered by fences, and I guess they usually hold livestock or maybe horses, and this is a ranch of some type. But that's not very helpful, because I could be in any number of states.

In the distance is a cluster of buildings, spread out over a vast area with snow-capped mountains in the background. Sometimes, at night, I spot flashing lights and hints of activity at that compound. Occasionally, helicopters land in the dead of night, raising my suspicions.

My father didn't know Atticus and company were planning on gate-crashing my engagement party. His reaction confirmed that. Yet, he could still get me out of the house and to here at short notice, which leads me to the conclusion I'm in Parkhurst.

Or a division of Parkhurst, because this building seems to house the medical wing.

It's the only conclusion that makes sense.

Meaning I'm somewhere in the west.

The rumble of an engine stirs me from my thoughts. Dust clouds mushroom in their wake as the usual supply trucks amble down the wide driveway toward us.

They come every Tuesday and Thursday mornings and on Fridays at seven p.m.

As the men unload supplies from the back, I mentally record the distance from the service side entrance to the truck doors and the scant seconds when the guys unloading the boxes are out of sight. Sneaking on board one of those trucks is the only way I'm getting out of here, but it's risky in the extreme.

It's too bright at this time of day to risk trying it on a Tuesday or Thursday, so I settle on Friday night.

I can't spend another week in this Godforsaken place. I'll be as cuckoo as everyone else if I do.

As the key turns in the lock, I whirl around, plastering a pleasant smile on my face as I move right beside my bedpost.

"Good morning, Miss Manning," Wyatt says, entering my room and casting a lingering glance my way.

"Good morning, Wyatt." I flutter my eyelashes and smile coyly at him. "And please call me Abby. How many times do I have to say it?" I look up at him through hooded eyes, smiling dreamily at him, as I drag my lower lip through my teeth and stare at his mouth.

His eyes glaze over as he walks toward me, his expression betraying everything he's feeling. "I don't want to slip up," he admits, tentatively tucking my long dark hair behind my ear. "The bosses can't know we're...*friends*." He falters on the word, and I know it's because he's hoping we'll be more.

Men are so fucking pathetic.

It's ironic that bastard thinks women are weak because we're ruled by our emotions, when men are definitely the weaker of the two sexes, because they're completely ruled by their dicks.

It's barely taken me any length of time to get Wyatt to fall in lust with me.

If there's anything I can be grateful to that bastard for, it's my ability to entrap men. I know how to work a room like a pro, smiling, flirting, making seemingly subtle touches, and laughing at feeble jokes and even more feeble men. But it was required whenever I attended official functions, and it's a life skill that has served me well.

Wyatt hands me a plastic cup and my daily pill. "You look especially beautiful today."

Barf.

"You say that every day." I grin as I dutifully open my mouth, pop the pill inside, and swallow some water.

The first time he handed it to me, I asked what it was, but he couldn't, or *wouldn't*, say. I guessed it was a sedative, and now that I've witnessed the zombie-like status of most of the residents firsthand, I know I was right.

Flinging my arms around his neck, I say, "And it's the sweetest thing!" I want to gag, but he laps up the cheesy shit like you wouldn't believe. I giggle, and he drops his head on my shoulder as I maneuver the pill out of my mouth with my tongue. Pretending to brush my hair back, I slide the pill from my mouth and stash it in the loose top of the bedpost, along with all the others I've hidden.

"It's the truth." A frown puckers his pale brow as he eases back, and I drop my arms to my sides. "Although I shouldn't be saying stuff like this."

I force my lower lip to wobble. "Don't say that. You like me and I like you. There's nothing wrong with that."

Double barf.

"That's not the way my boss would see it."

"Your boss won't know." I take a step toward him, making a production out of kissing his cheek. "I won't tell."

Conflict flashes in his eyes.

Don't lose your balls now, Wyatt.

He's pivotal to my escape plan, and I don't have the time, or the opportunity, to seduce any other male nurse. I smile sweetly at him, batting my eyelashes again, and the conflict melts off his face.

Sucker.

"C'mon." He takes my elbow. "You can't be late to breakfast."

I memorize the hallways as I walk silently by Wyatt's side, as I've done every morning we take this journey. It's unfortunate they have cameras in the hallway, but it's not surprising given the facility. I'm hoping the staff stairwells are camera-free, because if Wyatt fails to implement that part of the plan, I'll have to take an even bigger risk. I guess I'll find out Friday night.

The heavy doors to the high-level psych ward swing open as we pass by, and a man dressed in a nurse's uniform comes dashing out with a woman huddled into his side. Blood gushes from a deep cut in her cheek, and strands of her hair are plastered to her sweaty brow. The sleeve of her shirt is ripped at the shoulder, exposing a pale, slim arm. Her name badge confirms she's a doctor. "What happened?" Wyatt asks, gripping my arm to halt me.

I keep my eyes trained on the ground, holding my body rigidly still, so they don't suspect I'm lucid. I don't know what's in that pill I'm given each morning, but it's strong enough to have most of the residents walking around like wide-eyed zombies. They can't know I'm not taking mine, so I work hard to copy the other residents' behaviors so they don't suspect. Having sharp observational skills has come in handy around here.

"That bitch in C9 again." Tense silence erupts, and I'd give anything to read their facial expressions, but I keep my head down. "This wasn't a good idea."

"Neither is discussing it in the hallway," the injured woman says. "Let's just go."

I lift my head up at the sound of their retreating footsteps, and Wyatt urges me forward with a hand on my lower back. We move past the security guard's office, and the employee on duty has his feet propped up on the desk while leaning back in his chair as he absently watches the cameras with a cup of juice resting on top of his bulging belly.

While they have all the expected security measures in place, the attitude seems fairly lax. I suspect that's because no one knows about this place, and everyone's too fucked up to escape.

Wyatt opens the door to the cafeteria, guiding me to my usual table, alongside the younger residents. I sit down as a waitress slides a bowl of oatmeal with dried fruit in front of me. Wyatt fetches a glass of orange juice for me before walking to the staff table to join his colleagues.

I take a quick glance at the redheaded girl on my left and the dark-haired boy sitting across from me, but they're as comatose as ever.

Seriously, it's like I've walked onto the set of a horror movie where everyone is pale with these wide eyes and drooping jawlines and the only sounds out of their mouths are these ghostly, ghoulish sounds that give me a mad case of the heebie-jeebies.

I wonder how long I'd have to be here before I'd turn into that.

Or maybe their *supposed* crimes are worse, and that's why my punishment isn't as severe.

Although, if this is an elite facility, I doubt anyone in here has done anything worth punishing.

They probably just outlasted their usefulness.

Most likely, I'm being treated differently because my incarceration has an end date. I wouldn't be much good to that bastard all fucked up in the head, so I'm pretty sure whatever I'm being given isn't as severe as most of these people. Otherwise, there's no way I would've been capable of continuing my studies.

"Eat." The matron chastises me as she passes by, patrolling the aisles as usual.

Without hesitation, I lift my spoon and shovel a mouthful of gloopy oatmeal, ignoring how it clings to the roof of my mouth and makes me want to throw up.

When I've finished eating, Wyatt escorts me to the room where my tutor is waiting. Although there are at least a dozen teenagers here, I appear to be the only one who attends classes, which is another odd anomaly.

Miss Dunbar is an excellent teacher but a lousy subject for manipulation. I tried working on her the first few days, but she didn't bite, and I gave up before she became suspicious. She did, however, let it slip last week that she wouldn't be available for two days as she was traveling home for Thanksgiving.

Which answered the question of how long I've been here.

My fake engagement party to Charlie occurred six days before Halloween, and I know Thanksgiving is late this year, on the twenty-eighth, so that means I've been here five weeks.

That's five weeks of my life I'll never get back.

And five weeks where no one has come for me.

Confirming what I've always known—I'm in this alone.

I'm wearing the standard issue uniform when Wyatt slips into my room, locking the door behind him, on Friday night after his shift is over. I have no clothes or personal possessions, which is unfortunate, because trying to flee in my resident's uniform isn't ideal.

"Did you turn the cameras off?" I ask, sitting down on the bed and patting the space beside me.

He takes off his jacket, flinging it on the back of the chair. "Yes. You were right. John was snoring at the desk, and he didn't even notice me slipping the virus into the system. How did you even know how to do that?" he asks, sitting beside me and sliding his arm around my waist.

I'd given Wyatt a link to a site where I knew he could download a basic virus that would do the job. "One of my best friends is a hacker, and he taught me a few tricks."

If anyone has the power to find me, it's Xavier. The fact he hasn't shown up worries me to no end. Either I'm too well hidden or there's no way of getting me out without detection or something has happened to him. I'm hoping it's number two, but thoughts it could be number three have kept me awake some nights.

"Did you bring the bourbon?" I inquire.

He nods, looking unsure, and I hope he will not back out. I press in close to his side, flicking my hair over my shoulder. "What's wrong, baby?"

Gag.

"I could get fired for this."

Great. Another crisis of conscience. This would be easier if I was wearing a sexy dress and heels and doused in expensive perfume with a full face of makeup and my hair professionally styled.

But I have access to none of those things here, so I'm relying on my natural feminine wiles, praying it's enough. I'd hoped to get through this without having to touch him, but needs must.

I push my bigger bust into his chest, hating how my skin crawls when his eyes darken with lust. Cupping his face, I tilt his head around, pressing my lips to his.

He's not too bad of a kisser, and at least he's not an *oldie* oldie, but kissing him still feels wrong. I pull back when I sense his desire for me rising. "Do you have the whiskey or not? I told you I always need a shot before sex." I trail my tongue across his lower lip, and he slides a bottle of Wyoming Whiskey out from under his top without further argument.

I silently fist pump the air.

I'm in Wyoming!

I wonder if Wyatt did that on purpose or he's just an idiot.

My guess is it's the latter.

My euphoria fades fast though.

That's fucking hours from home, and there's no way I can hitch a ride all the way, like I originally planned, which means I must invoke Plan B. Get into a town, pick up a burner cell, call Xavier to come get me, and hope I can find a decent hiding spot until he arrives.

"I only have plastic cups." I shrug apologetically while taking the bottle from his hands.

Bending down to open the door at the bottom of my bedside table, I purposely stick my butt in the air, swaying my hips and trusting Wyatt is too fixated on my ass to notice me slipping the secret pill concoction into his drink.

Earlier, I ground the pills down using a cup I stole from the cafeteria, dividing the mixture into two lots. I tip half my supply into his drink, swirling it with my finger. I've purposely held half back in case this goes tits up and I need a new plan.

Plus, I don't want to kill the poor sucker.

"Bottoms up!" I hand his drink to him, praying the medication isn't noticeable and that he tastes nothing different. I tilt my head back, tipping the amber-colored alcohol into my mouth, relishing the burn as it glides down my throat. I drain it in one go, indicating for him to do the same, and he doesn't let me down.

Excitement churns in my gut, but I caution myself not to get too carried away. This is only step one.

And this is the tricky part. I don't know how long it'll take to work its way into his bloodstream, and I need to deflect his advances until then.

Kissing I can just about handle.

But making out or any kind of sex is a line I won't cross.

I run my hands up his chest through his cotton uniform top, biting down on my lip because I know he likes that. "You feel so good," I whisper, burying my face into his neck and nibbling on his earlobe. "But I want to feel all of you."

I convince him to remove his clothes until he's standing in front of me in his plain white boxer briefs. He's not in bad shape for an older dude, but there's still *no way* I'd go there. "Lie on your back on the bed," I instruct, and my mind drifts to dangerous, forbidden territory.

One thing I loved most about Cam-slash-Kai was his alpha tendencies in the bedroom. It's the one place I didn't argue, happy to let him take the lead. Commanding Wyatt brings a whole host of memories surging to the forefront of my mind, and a familiar ache stabs me in the chest.

Every memory I have is now tarnished by his betrayal.

And I'd be lying if I said it didn't hurt.

It hurts like a fucking bitch.

"Abby?" Wyatt's concerned voice drags me back into the moment. I push down on his chest, crawling over him and settling on his lap. His hard-on jabs into my ass, and my insides roil in disgust.

I spend a few minutes "worshiping" him. I run my hands all over his naked upper body, looking up at him as I dust kisses across his chest, along his arms, and down toward his stomach. His erection salutes me through his boxer briefs, and nausea swims up my throat as he flexes his hips, silently begging me to suck him off.

I don't know if he's always this timid with women or he's playing nice because of my age, but I'm grateful he's not forcing things. Excitement builds when his eyelids grow heavy a short while later, and it becomes clear he's fighting to stay awake.

"Abby," he slurs, trying to push himself up by his elbows.

I press both hands down on his chest, holding him firmly in place. "Don't fight it, Wyatt. Let it take you under."

"What did you...do?" Those are his last words before he conks out.

Air whooshes out of my mouth, and my shoulders slump in relief. I jump up, springing into action, using the pantyhose I stole from Miss Dunbar to tie his hands and feet to the four posts of the bed.

It won't hold him for long, but I had no rope, so I'm improvising. Besides, I don't expect him to be conscious for at least three or four hours, which should give me enough of a head start.

I briefly consider ripping his boxers off and leaving him naked, but that'd be overkill. They will fire him for sure when he's discovered like this, and I've humiliated him enough. A momentary pang of guilt jumps up and slaps me until I remember he was the one keeping me in a drug-induced haze the first couple of weeks I was here, and all sympathy vanishes.

Grabbing his cell, wallet, and security card from the inside of his jacket pocket, I cast one last glance at him over my shoulder before I creep out of my room.

I tiptoe quietly down the hallways, pleased to see no flashing red lights on the cameras, confirming Wyatt did a stellar job disabling the security system. It was sheer luck that their IT guy is out of town at a party tonight, and it will take him several hours to make it back here to fix it. That should give me enough time to get away undetected.

I check the time on Wyatt's cell, and I have twenty minutes until the supply truck arrives. That should work. I push through the staff door, flying down the stairs, keeping my head down and focused as I descend four flights before reaching the basement level.

Pressing Wyatt's security card against the keypad at the door, I wait with bated breath, relieved when a tiny click resonates and the door unlocks, granting me exit. I poke my head out quickly, conducting a sweep of the place.

It's an underground parking lot, and it's pretty deserted this time of night because all the daytime staff has gone home by now, and most residents don't get visitors. Still, I flatten my back to the wall as I creep toward the exit ramp, my eyes darting in every direction as I watch for signs of life.

I'm almost home free when the sounds of approaching voices send blood thrumming in my ears. I duck down behind the nearest car, praying to every deity known to mankind that they are not heading this way. My pulse pounds in my neck and my heart is beating so fast I fear I'm on the verge of a coronary. The voices halt near me, and I hold my breath, swallowing back bile, as I make all kinds of promises to a God I no longer believe in.

The sound of retreating footsteps is music to my ears, and I slump to the ground, attempting to recalibrate my breathing. When the voices completely fade, I straighten up, scanning the space before I take off jogging toward the exit ramp.

I stop when I reach the top, looking left and right, wondering which way is the fastest route to the service side entrance, when a hand wraps around my mouth from behind, and I'm pulled back against a warm chest.

I lift my leg, ready to inflict some damage when his warm breath skates across my ear. "Don't. It's me, Abby."

CHAPTER THREE

"Charlie?" He lets me go, and I spin around, flinging my arms around his neck and clinging to him. "Oh my God. It's so good to see you!" I admit, momentarily forgetting he's on my shit list, because it *is* so good to see someone familiar.

"Abby." He circles his arms around my waist, hugging me close as he presses kisses to the top of my head. The smell of his cologne wraps around me, and the familiarity is comforting. "What the hell are you doing?" he asks, gripping my arms and scrutinizing my face with troubled eyes.

"What does it look like?" I shuck out of his hold. "Getting the fuck out of this nuthouse."

"You can't." He shakes his head. "You need to go back to your room ASAP."

I narrow my eyes and cross my arms over my chest. "In case you don't know, I'm fucking pissed at you, and I'm done taking orders."

"You're pissed at *me*?" Shock splays across his face, his vibrant green eyes betraying his confusion, before realization dawns. "I'm sorry I haven't visited before. Your asshole father wouldn't let me until now."

That's not what I was referencing. *Doesn't he get that I'm mad at pretty much everyone?* And, if I *am* at Parkhurst, I *will* be plenty pissed that neither he nor Drew came to check on me. And until I know why my father has negotiated a new deal with the Barrons, I can't trust Charlie, as much as it saddens me to admit that. "Were you in on it?" I level him with a penetrating stare. "The night of our engagement, you seemed to know what would happen. How is that?"

He looks behind him briefly before reaching for my hand. I step back away from him. "I can explain but not here," he says. "I'm with your father, and he thinks I came back to get my cell from the car. He didn't spot you, but I did. But if I don't show up soon, he'll suspect something. You need to go back to your room and follow my lead." He reaches for me again, and I take another step back.

A pained look washes over his face. "Please, just trust me, Abby. Everything I've done, I've done for you."

I snort. The number of times the men in my life have said that to me is laughable. I don't trust any of them. Except for Xavier, because he's the only one who hasn't betrayed me or let me down. "Trust you? You let them ambush me twice that night!" I shriek, letting some of my pent-up rage loose. "Once with the engagement and second with the kidnapping."

"I tried to get you to safety!" he shouts. "Oscar was supposed to bring you to Xavier's warehouse, and we would flee to Europe. I had it all set up."

"What?" I splutter.

"Dad was helping. He wants to get you away from your father as much as I do, but everything turned to shit when Atticus Anderson and Wesley Marshall showed up, messing up our plans."

"Why would you do that for me?"

He moves close, cupping my face. "Because we care about you, and we don't want him hurting you any more than he already has."

I blink fast—surprised, overwhelmed, and confused at the news. Then his words properly register, and I press my chest into his, looking up at him with panicked eyes. "Please tell me Oscar's all right?!"

He glances nervously behind him. "I will fill you in on everyone, but you need to get back to your room now. Please, Abby. You're going to ruin everything if you're not there when we arrive."

"What do you mean?" Goose bumps sprout on my arms, and I shiver.

"Dad and I have convinced your father to let you return to Rydeville. We've made a deal so you can live at our house, but if your father finds out you're trying to escape, all deals will be off!" His tone is frantic, and little sweat beads dot his brow. Charlie is usually a very cool customer, which is how I know he's telling me the truth. He's genuinely panicked.

I still don't trust him one hundred percent, but my options are limited now they're here. "Okay." He grabs my hand, and we run back down the ramp into the parking garage, sprinting around the corner. "Oh, shit." I slam to a halt, clasping a hand over my mouth in front of the staff entrance as it dawns on me. "Father can't come to my room!" I blurt.

He frowns. "Why not?"

"Because I drugged a nurse, and he's tied to my bed."

His eyes pop wide, and I can almost see the wheels churning in his mind. "I'll handle it. I'll make some excuse to come to your room first. Just go." He pushes me at the door, and I use Wyatt's card to gain access. "Stay safe," he whispers before rushing off toward the elevator.

I make it back to my room undetected, closing the door and racing to my bed to untie the bindings around Wyatt's hands and feet. I've only gotten one off when there's a knock at the door, and a little whimper flies out of my throat. Adrenaline courses through my veins, and I pray it's Charlie and not my bastard father.

"Abby. It's me. Let me in!" Charlie says, and a relieved breath flees my mouth.

I almost trip over my sneakers in my haste to get to the door, opening it and yanking him inside before anyone sees him. "It's only ever locked from the outside. How much time do we have?"

"Knowing how impatient your father is, I'd say ten minutes. Tops."

"What did you tell him?"

"That I wanted to talk to you first. I told him I'd get you onboard with the plan."

I scowl at him, and he raises his palms. "You want out of here, don't you?"

"Yes, but not if it means selling my soul to the devil."

"We're well past that point," he murmurs, tossing a look over my shoulder. "Fucking hell, Abby."

His lips twitch as he walks toward the bed, taking in the prone body spread-eagled on top of my comforter.

"You untie his other foot while I get his hands," I instruct, conscious of the ticking clock. I pull at the pantyhose around one wrist, ripping it with my bare hands.

"What the fuck did you do to the poor guy?" There's an edge to his voice that he's trying to disguise.

"I seduced him into coming here tonight with some booze. Then I drugged him with the pills I'm supposed to be taking until he passed out and I tied him up."

A muscle clenches in his jaw as he rips the binding from Wyatt's foot. "Did you fuck him?"

"What?" My eyes blink profusely.

"Did he touch you?"

"Who I fuck is none of your business. I don't pry into shit you've done, and if I had to screw him to escape, I wouldn't let you make me feel guilty."

"I don't want to think of you having to do stuff like that."

"Have you forgotten the sick world we live in? You know as well as I do, that we do whatever we have to, to survive."

"I don't want that for you. You deserve better."

This is a pointless argument, and we're wasting time. "Not that I owe you an answer, but I didn't fuck him. So drop it," I say, dragging Wyatt's body down the length of the bed.

He sighs. "Sorry. I... This is a fucked-up situation."

I harrumph. "Tell me something I don't know!" I roll my eyes. "We need to get him into the bathroom."

Charlie nods, lifting Wyatt over his shoulders with a grunt, and I push the bathroom door open for him. He throws him into the tub without ceremony, pulling the shower curtain around him. "Let's hope your father doesn't take a piss."

I scoff. "We need not worry about that. His lordship wouldn't piss in a place like this. He'd rather give himself an infection holding it in."

Charlie chuckles, reeling me into his embrace. "Man, I've missed you."

I wriggle out of his hold, refusing to return the sentiment until I know more. "I need answers, Charlie, and until I have them, you're still on my shit list."

He runs a hand through his jet-black hair, and a few loose strands fall over his forehead. "That's fair. Who else is on that list?"

"Who isn't is an easier question to answer," I drawl, before remembering where we are and what's about to go down. "Shit. He will be here any minute."

A surefire way to piss my father off is to appear unpresentable, and I'm a bit of a mess. I yank my top up, tossing it on the floor as I grab the hand towel, mopping the line of sweat trickling down between my boobs and along my spine. Next, I wet under my aching armpits and wash them quickly with soap. I glance at Charlie, and he's rooted to the spot, his eyes glued to my enlarged chest.

I flick water at him. "Earth to Charlie. Stop ogling my boobs, and grab a new top and pants from my closet. Quickly." I shove at him, pulling him out of whatever trance he was in. He swings into action, running into my bedroom, as I drag a washcloth over my face and tuck stray strands of hair back into my ponytail.

I'm standing in my underwear when Charlie returns with fresh clothes. "So, what are you supposed to be telling me?" I ask while shimmying into my clothes.

He averts his gaze, staring at the floor. "It's like I said before. You're returning to Rydeville, resuming your studies at Rydeville High, living in our place, and, eh, the engagement is back on, and we're getting married three days after graduation."

I figured as much, after what the bastard said, and because there's no other way he would've agreed to it. "But it's only fake, right?" I inquire, pulling the top down over my head. "We're not going through with it."

Charlie's eyes are like laser beams slicing a line through my chest when I poke my head out of the top.

"Seriously?" I shoulder-check him as I push past him into the bedroom. "Can you focus on the important stuff instead of drooling?"

"I'm sorry. I just. Wow. They've like doubled in size and…"

"I hate them," I spit. "So, if you want to piss me off more, keep staring at them."

The door opens that second, and the bastard stalks into the room with a smug grin on his face. He clamps a hand down on Charlie's shoulder. "Liking the new and improved version?" he asks, confirming he was eavesdropping from outside. Thank fuck we were in the bathroom for the rest of our discussion so there's no chance he overheard.

The bastard's eyes drop to my chest, and he licks his lips.

I think I might puke.

Just when I thought I couldn't be any more repulsed by him.

A shiver works its way through me, and despair batters me on all sides as I contemplate how things could get worse.

Charlie reels me into his arms, holding me tight to his chest, instinctively knowing I need it. "I love everything about Abby. There isn't anything that needs improving."

My father laughs, slapping him on the shoulder again. "You should've been an actor, son. You'd clean up on awards night."

Charlie laughs, but it's strained, and I know it's just to appease my father.

"Abigail." I lift my head, fixing my father with a docile stare. "I presume Charlie has informed you of the plans." I nod. "I'm only allowing this because the Barrons have agreed to accept responsibility for you and because the reports from the staff here have been glowing. I'm glad you've come to your senses." His eyes flash darkly. "I had a feeling my letter would help with that."

My reaction is guttural and swift. My body locks up tight. My hands clench at my sides, and my nostrils flare. Rage thunders through me, and my eyes flash with hatred. Charlie tightens his hold on me, and that's the only reason I'm not lunging for my father. "Stick with the plan," he whispers in my ear while pressing a kiss to my temple. "Get yourself under control before he notices."

I count to ten in my head, caging the rage as I eyeball the bastard. "I will do what I'm told," I lie, almost choking on the words.

"Good." The bastard pulls a box from his pocket. "This is yours, and I want you wearing it twenty-four seven."

Charlie takes it, releasing me from his embrace so he can slide the massive diamond on my engagement finger. He tilts my head up, kissing me softly.

A look of amusement dances on the bastard's face when we break apart. "We need to go, Charles. We can't be late."

"I'm ready," I say, desperate to get out of here. The bastard sends me a derogatory glance. "We have business to attend to. Charles will return on Sunday evening to collect you."

"But—"

Charlie places his finger to my lips, halting my words. "I know, baby. I hate to leave you too." His lips pull into an arrogant smile as he addresses my father. "Abby and I never had time to celebrate our engagement." He waggles his brows, and a sour taste floods my mouth as I get what he's insinuating. "I can check into my room later and head straight to the meeting." He checks his watch. "There's enough time." He smirks, and I detest that look on him.

The bastard chuckles, clamping a meaty hand on Charlie's shoulder again. "That's my boy." He grins, and it's downright evil. "Work her over good. She needs a hard fuck to keep her in line. Show her who's boss."

"I fully intend to." Charlie grabs hold of my butt, hauling me into him and squeezing my ass cheeks.

I bite back my retort, but as soon as the bastard is out of the room, I shove Charlie away. "Was that necessary?"

"I'm sorry." He reclaims the distance between us, gently stroking my face. "You know I'd never treat you like that. But this plan only works if your father believes I'm fully committed to doing things the elite way."

"Is this Parkhurst?" I ask.

He nods. "I've never been in this building before. This is where they send family members in need of *medical intervention*." Disgust appears on his face, and I'm glad to glimpse the real Charlie.

"So those other buildings in the distance are the main compound? That's where you've all been going?"

He nods again but gives nothing else away.

"You never answered me before," I say, easing out of his hold and walking to the bed. I flop down on the mattress. All the adrenaline has fled my body, leaving me drained. My arms ache as I roll on my side, fighting a yawn.

He lies down beside me, angling his head so we're facing one another. "I know you need answers, but save them for the ride home because there isn't enough time to explain it all now. I've convinced your father to let me drive you rather than taking the jet, so we can stay a night in a hotel and have some alone time."

I prop up on my elbows, narrowing my eyes suspiciously. "Why are you doing that?"

He tucks my hair behind one ear, peering deep into my eyes. "To give us enough time to talk everything through. There's so much you don't know. So much I couldn't tell you."

"But you're going to now?"

"Yes." He leans in close, and my eyes pop wide as he brings his mouth closer to mine. At the last second, he veers left, planting a soft kiss on my cheek.

"Okay, but I'm holding you to that. I won't be kept in the dark any longer."

"Agreed." He sits up, stalking into the bathroom.

"What are you doing?" I follow him, watching him peer out the window. The bathroom window doesn't have bars on it, but that's because the only way out is via a thirty-foot drop. I'd ruled it out as an escape route early on for that very reason.

"Trying to figure out a way to get this dude out of here before anyone realizes you were escaping." He inspects the bathroom door next, removing the key and curling my hand around it. "Leave the window unlocked, but lock the door from the outside after I'm gone. That way, if he wakes before I get to him, he can't get out."

"But he could make enough noise to draw attention."

Charlie draws the shower curtain back, removing a length of rope from the inside of his jacket pocket. I arch a brow. "I never leave home without it," he quips, and I wonder if his humor is an attempt to deflect the truth of that statement.

He ties Wyatt's hands and feet with the rope and stuffs a handkerchief in his mouth.

"What if he chokes?" I ask, chewing on the inside of my mouth.

"Do you honestly care?" He stands, moving to the sink.

"He's an idiot ruled by his dick, but that doesn't mean he deserves to die," I supply, watching as Charlie clinically washes and dries his hands.

"He can breathe through his nose." He kisses my brow, before hauling me out into the main room. "And he'll be gone before you know it." He holds my face in his palms, looking like he wants to say more. "Get some sleep, and I'll see you Sunday."

He blows me a kiss, before pulling the door shut behind him, and I stand rooted to the spot, wondering what the hell Charlie is up to, because there's zero doubt in my mind that he's playing some game.

And I'm suspecting I may be the prize.

CHAPTER FOUR

"I expect you to behave yourself and do everything Charles says," the bastard tells me, digging his nails into my shoulders as we wait on the front steps for Charlie on Sunday afternoon. He's gone to collect the car he hired for the thirty-hour drive home.

Go fuck yourself.

"Of course, Father." I smile up at him, saying what he needs to hear. "This differs from Trent. I hated him, but I love Charlie. I'm not unhappy about this. At all," I lie.

The bastard nods as he takes a long puff of his cigar. "That pleases me, Abigail. Perhaps there's still hope for you." He flicks the cigar away, digging his nails even farther into my skin in a way I know will leave marks. His eyes narrow to slits as he leans into my face. "But if you're lying. If you're playing me. There will be hell to pay."

"I'm not," I lie. "I didn't want to marry Trent, but I'm looking forward to marrying Charlie." My insides twist painfully as more lies darken my soul.

"And what of Kaiden Anderson?"

This time I don't have to lie. My lips pull into a snarl, and my hands ball into fists as I unleash the anger bottled up inside me. "I hate that manipulative bastard, and I hope he rots in hell."

My response pleases him. He pats me on the head. "Good girl, Abigail."

Patronizing prick.

Charlie chooses that appropriate moment to arrive, pulling up in a top-of-the-line, blacked-out Land Rover. I have no bag, so I skip down the steps and slide into the passenger seat. To keep up appearances, I lean over and kiss him on the mouth. He winds his hand in my hair, drawing me closer and deepening the kiss.

It's not a chore kissing Charlie, but I don't want him getting the wrong idea, so I subtly pinch his thigh, and he breaks the kiss before it turns too intense.

"You two lovebirds have a good trip," the bastard says, sticking his cosmetically altered hideous face in Charlie's window. "And I want you to check in with me the minute you arrive back in Rydeville, son. Mrs. Banks will pack up Abigail's things, and I'll have them delivered to your house."

"Thank you, sir. I'll take good care of her."

"Not too good." The bastard smirks, looking over Charlie's head at me. "You let your fiancé do whatever he wants to your body. He owns it. Not you."

"Like I said, Daddy. This is different." My tone is elevated as I'm losing control of my tenuous emotions.

"We'll see you Tuesday, sir." Charlie floors it the instant the bastard steps away, and the brakes squeal as we hightail it down the driveway at speed.

"I want to kill that fucking bastard for the way he speaks to you and about you," he seethes.

"Get in line," I reply, glancing out the window. "And death would be too easy for him. I want to make him suffer."

"You have a plan?" he asks, slowing down the engine as we reach the entrance gates.

"It's a work in progress."

The gates open, and Charlie pulls the car out onto the road, and I'm free of that hellhole.

"We need to coordinate," he adds, casting a quick glance at me.

"Who's we?"

"Me, Drew, and Xavier."

I pull my knees up to my chest, wishing I had different clothes. Anything but this fucking uniform. "Hold that thought," I say, looking into the back seat, eyeing up Charlie's bag. "Do you have anything I can change into?"

"I've a couple of T-shirts and some sweats."

I climb into the back, rummaging in his duffel bag and removing a Ramones' tee. "I didn't know you were into the Ramones?" I say, stripping out of the uniform.

Charlie's gaze meets mine momentarily through the mirror. "It was a present from Lil."

"I didn't know your sister was into punk rock, and isn't she a little young?"

"She's fourteen and going through a phase." He turns right onto the highway. "Or at least I hope it's a phase."

I climb back into the front wearing the shirt. It's long enough to pass as a shirt dress. Charlie's eyes lower to my thighs for a fleeting second. "Why do you keep looking at me like that?" I ask, eyeballing him.

"Like what?" He feigns innocence.

"This isn't real." I point between us. "You know that, right?"

Silence engulfs us for a few beats before he clears his throat. "You know we'll probably have to get married. It's the safest way to keep your father off your back."

"We have six months to figure out a solution. No offense, but I don't want to marry you."

A muscle clenches in his jaw, and awkward tension fills the air.

"I thought you had questions," he says, after a while, and I latch onto the lifeline with both hands.

"What happened to Oscar?" I whisper, my lip wobbling as I force bile back down my throat. I remember hearing the gunshot the night we were fleeing. And now that I know it was Louis who took me, I'm terrified for the bodyguard who is more like my father than my father.

Charlie grips the steering wheel tight. "Maybe we should wait for questions and answers until we've stopped someplace."

A sob bursts free of my chest. "Please don't say he's dead!" Tears roll freely down my cheeks. "Please don't say I got him killed too!"

He reaches out, rubbing my bare thigh, clearly conflicted. He sighs, glancing at a signpost up ahead. "He's not dead, babe. But he is in a coma." He watches my reaction carefully.

"Is he going to make it?"

"I don't know, but he's got the best of care. He's in good hands, and all we can do is pray he comes through."

"What about his family?"

"Drew is taking care of it," he says, removing his hand from my thigh and returning it to the wheel.

"Why didn't my brother come to see me?"

Charlie puts the car into cruise control and looks at me. "At first, it was because of his injuries, and we didn't know where you were, although we suspected he'd sent you to Parkhurst."

"My father hurt Drew?" I guess.

He bobs his head. "Your father beat the crap out of him after Atticus revealed his involvement in the safe heist. Drew fought back initially so your father had his goons strip him naked and tie him to a chair, and he let them all go at him." He sighs. "It's a miracle he didn't kill him."

Nausea churns in my gut. I haven't forgotten the beating I endured at my father's hands, and it was probably much worse for Drew. That bastard would want to kill him for his so-called betrayal, but he would never let it get that far, because he needs him. "How did Drew wrangle his way back into my father's good books?"

"Drew convinced him he was double-crossing the new elite, and it was his way of protecting the contents of the safe, until they went rogue."

My brows climb to my hairline. "And my father believes that?"

"Drew told him he recorded the theft on his cell and he was waiting until he uncovered where they stashed the paperwork before handing it and the video over to the authorities."

"*Does* Drew have a recording?" I ask, because it wouldn't surprise me. It's the usual M.O. with the elite.

"He did, but his cell got smashed up during the shootout, and he didn't have a backup."

"I bet that made Father suspicious."

Charlie shrugs, keeping one eye on the road. "The jury's still out, but he's giving Drew the benefit of the doubt."

"Because he's his heir."

"There's more to it." Charlie white-knuckles the steering wheel again. "I know you think your life has been shit, and that your father has treated you like crap, but it's nothing compared to what Drew's endured."

My spine turns rigid with tension. "What exactly does that mean?"

"We've seen more violence and depravity than you could ever imagine," he admits.

"At Parkhurst," I surmise.

"Partly."

"And you're still not going to tell me, are you?"

He slants pleading eyes on me. "Abby. We *can't* tell you, and it's better you don't know. It would change how you feel about all of us."

That may well be the case, but I'm sick of all this protective bullshit. "I'm sick of all the lies and secrets, Charlie!" I roar, throwing my hands up. "All it does is blindside me! I can't defend myself if I don't know the full truth."

He glances sideways at me as he takes the next exit. "You don't need to defend yourself. We'll keep you safe. Nothing like this is ever going to happen to you again."

"Are you fucking kidding me?" I explode, yelling at him. "None of you have kept me safe! The only one looking out for me is me." I pound my fists on the dash out of sheer frustration and rage.

"That isn't true." He stretches his hand across the console, settling it on my thigh.

I slap his hand away. "Don't placate me, Charlie. Don't insult my intelligence."

His jaw locks up tight, and tension filters into the air again.

I'm so sick of this shit.

Of living this life.

And my previous determination to escape has strengthened in recent months.

I need to get away from Rydeville. To start over somewhere else.

"We *will* keep you safe," he grits out after a few tense minutes.

Resting my head back, I close my eyes, knowing there's no point continuing this fight. He will not tell me anything. "You can't promise me that," I say, opening my eyes a couple minutes later. "None of you can. Not while that bastard is still in control. Not while he's still breathing."

"He won't be in control for much longer."

"How?" I sit upright again.

"Drew is doing what he needs to, to win back your father's trust, and now that Jane's gone, there are no limitations to what he can do to ensure that happens. And—"

I swivel in my seat. "Back up there! Jane's *gone?*" My eyes splay wide. "Gone where? And why?" I splutter.

Charlie slows the car down, taking the turn for a place named Loth's End. "Drew will tell you more, but he went to her father after the shootout and told him to take the family far away from Rydeville. They left the next day."

My mouth hangs open. "But we know where she is, right? I can still get in contact with her?"

Charlie shakes his head, drawing to a halt alongside a curb. "That would defeat the purpose. Drew did what he had to do to keep Jane safe."

"But he loves her! They are so much in love." I can't believe this.

"I know, and it's killing him. He's—" He sighs, scrubbing a hand across his smooth jawline. "He's not in a good way, Abby. Losing you and Jane is bad enough, but the things he has to do to keep your father and Trent from guessing his true allegiance are destroying his spirit. We both know Trent won't let this go. You humiliated him, and he's a fucking psycho, so Drew's sticking close to him to ensure he doesn't get to you." He pins troubled eyes on me. "But I'm worried about him. About his ability to pull this off and not lose himself."

"Now you're scaring me." Drew is still on my shit list because he stood by and did nothing while they assaulted me but he played no part in the crap that went down at the engagement party, and if he pushed Jane away, then I know there is tons he hasn't told me.

Charlie takes my hand in his. "He needs you. I know he failed you, which is something he won't ever stop beating himself up over, but he's been trying to protect you behind the scenes for a long time, and intervening would've jeopardized everything."

"Maybe if he'd told me what he's doing I would understand, but everyone thinks they need to keep me in the dark for *my protection*," I hiss.

Charlie grips my head, drilling me with somber eyes. "It *is* for your protection, Abby, and one day we'll admit everything, but for now, just believe that we are all working to keep you safe."

"That's a big ask. Especially when I know you've all lied to me and betrayed me in some shape or form. How am I supposed to trust anyone after that?"

"You have known me your entire life, and your brother would take a bullet for you. I don't know Xavier all that well, but he genuinely seems to care about you too. You can trust us."

"And what about the new elite?" I croak, summoning the courage to ask about them. "Where are they? And do you trust them?"

"They're gone, and no," he says through gritted teeth. "I don't trust any of those fuckers."

"Gone where?" I ask, hating how my heart thumps painfully at the news.

He shrugs. "Into hiding. Your father and Christian Montgomery have filed legal and criminal complaints, and the cops are looking for them. Seven men lost their lives during the shootout, and the authorities are looking for someone to blame. There are warrants out for their arrest."

I shake my head. "That figures." I rub a tense spot between my brows. "How are we ever going to get justice when that bastard has everyone in his back pocket?"

"There are ways," he cryptically says, pulling out his cell while looking behind me.

"What are you doing?" I inquire, swiveling in my seat and inspecting the clothing store we've pulled up in front of.

"Calling the store owners to see if a little cash incentive will get them to open up for you. I'd have brought you stuff from home, but everything happened at the last minute and there wasn't time."

An hour later and I'm browsing the aisles in the store alone, while Charlie makes some calls from the car. Cash incentives work—especially in small towns where there is little passing trade. I select some jeans, a shirt, sweater, socks, pajamas, and underwear in my size, dumping them on the counter for the clerk to ring up, and then I head to the cosmetics section and grab what I need.

While I'm paying for everything with Charlie's card, I try to bribe the cashier into loaning me her cell on the sly, so I can call Xavier, but she adamantly refuses.

I don't know what Charlie said or did to make her comply, but I give up trying to persuade her when it's obvious she won't be swayed.

So much for hos before bros.

The bitch won't even tell me where the nearest payphone is.

I use the bathroom to change into my new outfit and freshen up before leaving the store. Charlie is lounging against the wall with a smile on his face. He takes my hand. "You look beautiful."

"I'm only wearing jeans." I arch a brow.

"It doesn't matter what you're wearing. Your beauty shines from within."

I'm about to make a gagging sound when I notice the sincerity in his eyes, and I clamp my mouth shut. Shit. *Does Charlie have feelings for me?* Because if he does, we've got a major problem.

I've always adored Charlie, and even though I'm wary of him now—because he's still holding out on me—he rescued me from that hellhole, and I know he's genuinely doing what he believes is in my best interests.

I love him but not like that.

Even if he is an amazing kisser and there is some shared chemistry.

"Thanks," I murmur, keeping my thoughts to myself because I'm not ready to get into that conversation. Not with a long-ass trip ahead of us. But it *is* something we must discuss sooner than later.

"Are you hungry?" he asks, swinging our hands together as we walk in the opposite direction of the car. "I found a nice little restaurant a couple blocks down, and they're holding a table for us."

"I could eat. Weeks of enduring that shit they call food has left me dying for something tasty."

"How is Xavier?" I ask when we are seated at a cozy table in the corner of the Italian restaurant. "I thought he would've found me."

"We all knew where you were, Abby, but we couldn't just storm in and rescue you. Not without consequences."

A massive grin graces his mouth. "Although, we had to chain Xavier up for a while until he got that message."

My jaw hangs open. "Please tell me that's a joke?"

He shakes his head. "Drew and I took turns babysitting him. He kept promising he wouldn't go after you, but as soon as we'd let him go, he'd take off." He chuckles. "Drew went apeshit on his ass, and we had to go hardcore to get him to cooperate, but he finally understood." His humor dies.

My heart soars for the first time in ages. "I knew there had to be a reason he hadn't come for me."

He threads his fingers through mine. "We all wanted to rescue you, but we couldn't."

"I get that now, but you try spending five weeks as a prisoner, surrounded by people so effed up they might as well have been zombies, having no one for company, and dealing with—" My lip wobbles and tears well in my eyes.

"I know, Abby, and I'm so sorry." Charlie's face softens, and his tone is gentle as he draws circles on the back of my hand with his thumb.

I squeeze my eyes shut to ward off the pain. "I don't want to talk about it," I whisper.

"It's okay." He lifts me out of my chair, situating me in his lap. His arms wrap around me, and I bury my face in his neck, needing his comfort. I'm starved of human affection, and it's been a lonely few weeks.

"He will pay, Abby," he whispers in my ear, smoothing a hand down my hair. "We're not letting him get away with it."

"I just need to pull in for gas," Charlie says, when I question why we're pulling off the highway again.

My appetite vanished after my mind drifted into forbidden territory, but I still forced a few mouthfuls of pasta down. Then we hit the road, and we've been driving for four hours.

It's dark now, and we've agreed to drive for another couple of hours and then pull in someplace for the night. Charlie entered a town on the GPS that looks suitable, and I'm busy researching motels on his cell.

Charlie pulls into a gas station on the outskirts of town, glancing anxiously around as he kills the engine. I expect him to get out, but he grips the steering wheel tight, looking like he has the weight of the world on his shoulders.

"What is it?" I ask, unbuckling my belt and leaning forward, touching his elbow.

My eyes startle when he turns to me with fierce determination etched upon his face. "I know you love him, Abby. Even after all he's done," he says, and I don't need to be a mind reader to know he's talking about Kaiden. "But he doesn't deserve you! And you have options."

I squirm uncomfortably on my seat, wondering why he's chosen this exact moment to tell me all this. I drop my hand from his elbow, and he reaches across the console, circling one hand around the nape of my neck. "The night of our engagement," he says, peering deep into my eyes as he runs the tip of his finger across the diamond ring I'm wearing. "I meant every word I said." His pulse is throbbing in his neck, and he's shielding nothing from me now.

I gulp over the panic building at the base of my throat.

"I love you, Abby. I always have and I always will, and I want to marry you for real."

Before I can voice any response, he smashes his lips against mine, kissing me passionately.

He keeps a hold of my neck when he eventually breaks the kiss, imploring me with his eyes. "Don't say no until you've considered it. I know your head is all over the place, but I promise you everything I've done, everything I'm *doing*, I'm doing because I love you and I want you in my life. Forever."

"Charlie. I—"

He kisses me again, and my head spins. "Promise me you'll think about it. He's not your only option."

I want to tell him Kaiden isn't *any* option, but I can't lie to myself. I hate Kaiden.

As much as I hated him when he first showed up to school.

Probably more.

But there's a fine line between love and hate, and I fucking hate that I still love him too.

"Okay." I place my hand on his hard chest. "I'll think about it."

He rests his forehead against mine before kissing me once again, only this time it's a fleeting brush of his lips against mine. "I love you. Don't forget," he says, climbing out of the car.

My brows knit together as I watch him fill the car with gas, my sixth sense on high alert.

Charlie is acting weird.

He blows me a kiss as he walks toward the store, and unease slithers inside my veins.

He has just reached the door when it flies open, and a guy wearing a black ski mask shoves him to the ground, swinging a bat to the side of his head.

Terror has a vise grip on my heart, and I'm scrambling out of the car before my brain has processed it, racing toward him when I'm yanked back by my shirt. Muscular arms wrap around me from behind, and someone pulls a covering down over my head.

"No fucking way," I shriek, lifting my legs up into my chest and rocking forward with all the strength I can muster. The guy holding me loses his balance, and I tip forward again until his arms drop and I'm free.

Yanking the covering off my head, I spin around, thrusting my clenched fist out, glancing the side of my attacker's face as he's straightening up. He's wearing a ski mask too, so I've no clue who's trying to take me this time.

But I'm fucked if I'm getting taken against my will again.

I kick him in the balls, shoving my foot into his crotch with all my might. "I am not." I swing at his chest this time, landing a decent punch because he's too distracted cradling his junk to deflect my throw. He staggers back, cupping his crotch, while cussing and moaning. "Getting fucking kidnapped again."

I kick him in the chest, pushing him to the ground and jumping on top of him. I swipe the ski mask off his head, blinking to ensure my eyes aren't deceiving me.

"What the actual fuck?" I stare at a face I was recently reacquainted with.

"Way to go, dipshit," a familiar voice says at my rear. "*You* can explain this one."

CHAPTER FIVE

"What the fuck do you think you're doing?" I snap, pouring venom into my words as I glare at Maverick—aka Rick—Anderson. I'd have known it was him by his voice if he hadn't already whipped off his ski mask after lifting me off his younger brother.

"I'll explain on the way," he says, reaching for my arm. "We've got to go before someone shows up."

I jerk back, narrowing my eyes again. "I'm not going anywhere with you." I glance over at the door, my heart thumping wildly against my rib cage at the sight of Charlie sprawled unconscious on the ground. "And if you've hurt my fiancé, I will end every single one of you." I send daggers at the guy who tried to take me as he awkwardly climbs to his feet. He's still cupping his crotch, and I can't get a good look at his face to see if it's Joaquin or Harley. Until the engagement party, I hadn't seen either of those boys since they were little kids, so I'm not sure if I could even tell them apart now. There's only a year between them, and all the Anderson boys look so alike.

"Your fiancé?" Rick inquires, arching a brow and pinning his warm brown eyes on me.

"You heard me." I thrust my hand forward, showing off my

sparkling diamond. "So, whatever feeble effort this is on Kaiden's part, he's too late. *You're* too late. I don't need your help. And I don't need *him*."

"Rick!" The other brother pokes his head out the window of an SUV parked at the side of the station. "Get a fucking move on."

"You're coming with us." Rick grabs hold of my arm. "Whether or not you like it."

"No. I'm not." I yank my arm back, ready to swing for him, when my wrists are pulled back behind me, and a sweaty palm clamps down on my mouth.

"Don't make us hurt you," the brother holding my arms says.

I lift my leg to knee him in the balls with the heel of my foot when he bites down hard on my shoulder, and I lose my focus, crying out as my leg drops to the ground.

"What the hell?" Rick shouts, glaring over my shoulder.

"I'm improvising," the guy holding me supplies. "Kai said she was feisty, but I'd no idea she was this bad."

"Kai will chop your fucking cock off if you hurt her. She's pregnant, for fuck's sake."

Everything locks up inside me, and pain consumes me to the point I don't put up any resistance when Rick slings his arm around my shoulders, walking me toward their car.

Kai sent them to fetch me, and I *want* to see him. Because I need answers, and I want to inflict suffering. Charlie said they'd gone into hiding, so this is probably my only opportunity.

A new plan forms in my mind, and I go willingly with Rick, not mouthing any further protest.

"I'll go with you," I say, tugging on his arm to stop him. "But I need to check on Charlie first."

"Charlie will be fine," he insists, tugging me forward.

"He's not fine!" I shout, pointing at him. "He isn't moving!"

"That's because I gave him a sedative," he admits, and I launch myself at him, roaring as I drag my nails down his face, drawing blood, before the other Anderson pulls me away. I don't have the long, shapely nails I usually sport, but my shorter nails are jagged thanks to the lack of manicures in Parkhurst, and they work effectively.

"Can't we give *her* a sedative?" the guy struggling to hold me says. "Because this journey will be hell on Earth if she's going to swing for us every chance she gets."

"Abby." Rick's gaze is thunderous as he dabs at his bleeding face. Strands of dark hair falls across his brow, and he jerks his head, tossing them out of his eyes. "Unless you want me to give Charlie a lethal shot, you will get in the fucking car and behave."

I want to spit in his face, but I won't lower myself. "I hate you as much as I hate your asshole of a brother."

"I don't expect any less," he says, sighing as his features soften a little. "Just get in the car before we're all arrested." He wipes his face with a tissue.

"You can't leave Charlie there like that."

"The staff will take care of him."

"What if they don't? I'm not leaving until I know they've taken care of him."

"Don't get your panties in a bunch. As soon as we're back on the highway, I'll call it in. I promise." I plant my hands on my hips, narrowing my eyes. "The faster we get out of here, the quicker he gets help," he argues.

I send one last look at Charlie, feeling like a treacherous bitch, as I climb in the back seat alongside the other brother. Rick slides behind the wheel, and the asshole who tried to grab me takes shotgun.

Rick peels it out of here, pointedly locking all the doors and pinning me with a warning look through the mirror. "Message Sawyer Hunt," he tells the brother sitting beside him, and he nods.

"How did you know where to find me?"

"We were watching the elite, and when Charlie made plans to travel with your father alone, we had a hunch it was to do with you. We staked out Parkhurst until we saw you leaving with him, and then we followed you."

"Hey." The guy sitting beside me leans forward, smiling tentatively. I narrow my eyes to slits but say nothing. His hair is as dark as his brother's, and his eyes are the same shade of brown, but his features are more babyish even if his body is honed to perfection. All four Andersons are hot as hell, and they clearly enjoy working out because this guy is as ripped as his older brother.

"We're not your enemy, Abby," Rick says, keeping his eyes glued to the road as we head toward the interstate.

"If this is your attempt at being friends, I pity your enemies," I retort, ignoring the guy at my side and staring at the landscape as it flashes by through the tinted window.

"It might have started out like that, but things changed once Kai got to know you," Rick says.

I snort, shaking my head. "Don't bullshit me. Everything was a lie. Everything was a manipulation to get to my father." I force my hands to my stomach. "You even used an innocent child as a pawn." Anger bleeds from my eyes as I stare at him through the mirror. "What kind of sick bastard deliberately sleeps with someone with the sole purpose of getting them knocked up?"

"That's no—"

"Save it, Rick," I bark. "I don't want to hear it."

At least not from him.

I want to look Kaiden in the eye and ask him if he was the one who messed with my birth control. I have no proof that's how they did it, but I suspect I'm right, because Kai had no concerns fucking me without condoms. If he wanted to get me pregnant, that was the perfect solution.

Except I've had lots of time to think about how it all went down in the ballroom, and I remember the look of horrified shock on his face just before his father revealed the baby news.

My eyes flit to Rick's through the mirror. I remember him whispering in Kai's ear just before the baby bomb was dropped, and it's not a stretch to think it involved Rick.

Someone was in my room that first night in Jackson's house. The night after I was sexually assaulted. That could've been Rick. He has the medical knowledge and obvious contacts to switch out my pill. Or he could've put something into the drip.

I'm convinced it went down one of those ways.

But I'm still undecided whether Kai was involved or not.

Which is why I'm waiting until I'm face to face with him to have this conversation.

"Call an ambulance for Charlie," Rick says, turning to his brother in the passenger seat. He immediately calls it in, and a few of the knots in my stomach unravel.

"Kai loves you," the guy sitting beside me says. "And he's going crazy worrying about you and the baby."

"Sure, he is." I snort. "That's why it's taken him weeks to come looking for me."

"Harley's right," Rick says. "And it's only taken weeks because we had to wait for an opportunity to get to you. Parkhurst is like Fort fucking Knox, and it was too risky to attempt a rescue."

"If he loved me, he'd have found a way." That's another way I know he's full of shit. He told me just before everything went down that what we shared was real, but if that was true, he'd have done absolutely everything to get me out of there.

But he did nothing.

"It's not that simple," Rick supplies, as we speed ahead on the highway.

"It doesn't matter, anyway. I hate him."

"We had to lock him up to stop him from going after you," Harley says, staring at me with earnest eyes. "He seriously wants to kill us for blocking him."

"Har." Rick cautions him with a warning look. "She needs to hear it from Kai."

"Right." Joaquin snorts, leveling his older brother with a suspicious side eye. "If you think that gets you off the hook, you—"

"Shut up." Rick glares at him. "We're not discussing this now."

Joaquin flips him the bird. "She's gonna go postal on both your asses, and this time, I'm not holding her back."

"You've changed your tune," Rick says, blowing the horn at a car who cuts across the lane in front of us, letting a string of expletives loose.

"If you want to remain inconspicuous, rein in the road rage. Unless you want my father to catch us."

"Hunt has us covered," Joaquin confirms, looking over his shoulder at me. "We're good." He wets his lips, dragging a hand nervously through his dark hair. "And, eh, sorry for biting you back there."

"You *bit* her?" Harley shouts, shock splaying across his face.

I look at the raised, angry mark on my shoulder. "You broke my skin, but I've endured worse." I shrug.

Harley throws back his head, laughing hysterically as he points at Joaquin. "Oh, my fucking God. This is priceless!" He snickers. "He will go apeshit on your ass."

Joaquin stiffens a little before puffing out his chest and flexing his considerable biceps. "I can take him."

Harley cracks up laughing again. "Didn't you see what he did to Rick?" He holds his stomach, convulsing with laughter. "Sucks to be you, dude!"

"What did he do to you?" I ask, fixing my eyes on Rick through the mirror.

"He beat the fucking shit out of him," Harley says, his laughter disappearing. "And he deserved it too."

My eyes meet Rick's in the mirror, and his face conveys so much emotion. I grind my teeth to the molars, not asking the obvious question, because the answer is written all over his face.

Rick is the reason I got pregnant.

Now, all that's left to discover is if Kai was in on the plan.

CHAPTER SIX

"**M**ake yourself comfortable, Abby," Rick says, ushering me into the motel room. We've stopped here for the night because it's almost ten p.m., and it's pitch black outside with little visibility on this remote stretch of road. Rick seemed keen to keep going, but Joaquin demanded it, insisting on sleeping in a proper bed. "The boys can take the other room and I'll stay in here with you," he adds, as Joaquin and Harley disappear into the interconnecting room to dump their bags.

"I have nothing to sleep in," I say, because they left all my stuff in the rental.

"I'll grab you some stuff." He hands me his cell. "Jot down what you need, and I'll get it. I need to go out for food, supplies, and run a few errands."

What errands can he be making at this hour of the night? I think it, but I don't verbalize it, because it suits me if Rick disappears for a while. I kick off my sneakers and sit down on one of the single beds. Resting my back against the headrest, I pull my knees into my chest as I type out a few items. "How long will we be on the road?"

"We should reach our destination Tuesday evening."

"Why won't you tell me where we're headed?" I asked this

question on more than one occasion in the car, but all three remained tight-lipped.

"It's safer if you don't know."

I sigh, staring at the ceiling, praying for patience I know I don't possess after hearing the usual reply. "Do you all spout shit from the same Elite 101 manual? Because I swear to fucking God, if I hear that or *everything we're doing is to protect you* one more fucking time, I will lose my shit!"

He chuckles. "I can see why my brother's crazy about you."

My nostrils flare as I jab my finger at him. "That's also on the list of statements I never want to hear repeated."

"It's the truth."

I curl into a ball on my side. "I don't want to hear it."

The bed dips as he sits down beside me. "Give him a chance to explain, Abby."

"Why should I?" I bark, rolling onto my side so I'm facing him. "He betrayed me in the worst way."

"Things are never as they seem."

I glare at him.

"That's on your list too?"

"What do you think?"

He chuckles. "For what it's worth, I'm sorry for everything you've gone through. You were innocent in all this, and you should never have been hurt."

"I'm used to being hurt. It's part of normal life for me." My voice is devoid of all emotion. At this stage, I'm numb to it all.

"That's horrible, and Kai doesn't want that for you. It's why he sent us to get you."

I raise a palm. "It's been a long day, Rick. And it will be a long few days if you keep this up. The only person I want to hear an explanation from is Kai, so please. Just. Stop."

He nods, glancing over his shoulder and I notice his younger brothers standing by the door, quietly listening.

"Joaquin will come with me," Rick says, leveling me with a serious expression. "Can I trust you not to try anything if I leave you here with Harley?"

"What the hell am I going to do? We're in some hick town in the middle of Nebraska, and I've no car, no cash, no cell, and no clothes besides the ones on my back. It's not like I have any options," I lie.

He inspects my face like a drill instructor inspecting a line of new recruits. I hide my true intentions behind a familiar mask, and he nods. "Okay." He stands, hovering over me like a giant although he's not as tall as Joaquin who is the tallest of all the Anderson brothers. He's like a beanpole on steroids with his long, lean frame, wide shoulders, and bulging biceps. "Do *not* make me regret this," Rick says.

I flip him off, and Harley chuckles.

"Behave." Rick pins warning eyes on Harley.

"Relax, big bro. We're just going to watch TV and maybe grab some snacks." Harley looks to me for approval, and I nod.

"Sounds like a plan." I slant a genuine smile in Harley's direction, because he's the only Anderson who hasn't hurt me.

"We should be back in a couple hours," Rick says, grabbing Joaquin into a headlock as he hauls ass out of the door. The door slams shut behind them, and silence engulfs the room.

"So, um, what movies do you like?" Harley asks, shuffling nervously on his feet.

"I'm in the mood for something violent and bloody. Mafia or action adventure. I don't mind. Just something that'll give me ideas for my reunion with your brother." I flash him an evil grin, and he laughs uncertainly as he scrolls through the movie options on the TV.

I get up and walk toward him, thrusting my hand out. "I'll grab some snacks from that store in reception. You got cash?"

His brows knit together, and he purses his lips for a moment. "I'll get the snacks, and you can pick the movie."

I yank my sweater up over my head, letting my shirt ride halfway up my stomach. Then I make a show of stretching my arms up over my head, ensuring my shirt pulls tight across my ample chest. "I could use the walk and the fresh air after hours being cooped up in a car." I slide my hands across my stomach. "I need to exercise to stay fit and healthy for the baby." I flutter my eyelashes at him, and his cheeks redden.

This will be too easy.

He rubs a hand along the back of his neck, piercing me with his beautiful brown eyes, looking utterly torn. His eyes aren't as dark as Kai's, but they have the same little amber flecks. "You won't run away, will you? Rick would blow a gasket, and Kai will literally kill me if we return without you."

"Hey." I rub my thumbs across his brow, smoothing out the little lines denting his skin. "I meant what I said to Rick. I've nowhere to go, and I wouldn't do that to you," I lie, imagining my black, black soul bursting into flames. "How old are you, Harley?" I've been trying to figure out a few things on the ride here.

"I'm fifteen."

"And Joaquin is, what, sixteen?"

He nods.

"You got a girl?" I ask, trailing my fingers down his face. His cheeks flush again as he shakes his head, and he's adorably cute. He may look all man, but he's still so innocent.

This will be like taking candy from a baby.

A pang of guilt washes over me, but I shove it away. This is no time to grow a conscience.

"Why is that?" I ask. "You're hot and sweet and easy to talk to."

Harley kept the conversation going in the car, and it's clear he's the peacemaker or the catalyst for keeping the peace.

He shrugs, and his cheeks are on fire. I drop my hands, figuring I've tortured him enough for now. "Kai says I've to concentrate on school and there'll be plenty of time for girls later."

My face contorts unpleasantly. "What a fucking hypocrite!" During one of our bedtime conversations, Kai admitted he'd lost his virginity to a high school senior when he was fourteen. And, thanks to the gossip doing the rounds at school, I know he's no angel with women. He's the screw them and leave them type. Perhaps I should've paid more attention to the rumors and not started anything with him. "And he's not your father. He doesn't get to tell you what to do."

Harley shrugs, pulling his wallet from the back pocket of his jeans. "He kinda was growing up, and he's only looking out for me. He doesn't want me making the same mistakes he did."

Now, that's interesting.

"By the way, what happened to your dad? Did my father kill him that night?" Can't say I'd lose any sleep if Atticus Anderson was ten feet under. But he's the only surviving parent the guys have, and I wouldn't wish that on any of them. Besides, if Atticus is alive, he'll continue his vendetta against my asshole father, and I'm all for that, provided Atticus is finished using me as a pawn.

Harley pales. "He would have if it wasn't for the Kevlar vest he was wearing." He rubs a hand across his chest. "He has a few broken ribs, and he's bruised all over his chest, but he's okay."

"I hope he's still going after my father."

"He's more determined than ever," Harley confirms, extracting a fifty and handing it to me. "Get me Doritos, M&Ms, Hershey's, Skittles, and Twizzlers."

I look him up and down. "If I ate all that crap, I'd have a belly to rival Homer Simpson's." I pat his rock-solid abs. "Where do you put it all?"

His Adam's apple bobs in his throat as he attempts a casual shrug. "I work out a lot."

I trail my hands up his defined chest, licking my lips provocatively, and look at him through hooded lashes. "I can tell."

His chest is heaving, and the bulge in his pants is growing more pronounced as I continue caressing his upper body. "I think I'll need more cash."

"More than fifty? We're only buying snacks." His brows knit together.

"I'm starving," I lie, smiling seductively at him. "And I'm eating for two." Reaching around, I remove his wallet from his back pocket, giving his ass a cheeky squeeze for good measure, hoping it will distract him from his suspicion. He looks frozen on the spot, unsure of how to handle this situation, and I almost feel bad.

Almost.

Harley is sweet, and I don't want to trick him, but this may be my only chance to contact Xavier, and I'm not passing up the opportunity because I feel guilty for seducing Kai's younger brother.

If these were different times, they'd probably burn me at the stake for this.

I pull back abruptly, removing another fifty as I smile at him. I repocket his wallet, patting his ass this time, and his cheeks are so red I reckon I could warm my hands off them.

Kai should have taught his little brother better.

It's not my fault he's so clueless with the opposite sex.

"Pick a movie. I'll be back soon." I press my lips to his warm cheek and take my time walking to the door, swaying my hips, knowing full and well his eyes are glued to my retreating form. The second I'm outside, I race along the path toward the reception area, scanning over the vehicles in the parking lot until I spot what I'm after.

The bell jingles as I walk into the dingy lobby. "Hey." I greet the girl with dreadlocks behind the counter. "Is the store still open?"

"Have at it," she says, not even lifting her head up from whatever she's engrossed in behind the counter.

I push the door to the small store open, quickly locating the snacks Harley wants. I add a bottle of tequila and frantically search the limited shelves for cell phones, but I'm shit out of luck. It was always a long shot. Guess it's time to invoke Plan B.

"I'll take these," I say, plonking my items down on the counter at reception.

She calculates the cost on a small calculator while keeping one eye on the movie on her cell phone. "You know any place in town that sells cell phones at this hour?" I ask.

"The mini-mart across from the park is open twenty-four hours, and they sell disposables."

I silently fist pump the air while she shoves our snacks in a bag. Her fingers curl around the tequila bottle, and she finally lifts her head, eyeing me with big brown eyes. "How old are you?"

"Twenty-one," I lie, not expecting it to work, because I could pass for nineteen, maybe twenty, at a push, but there's no way I can pull off twenty-one without a full face of makeup.

"That works." She smirks at me before totaling everything up, and I hand over the cash.

"One other thing. Do you know who owns that Honda out front?" I inquire.

Her eyes narrow in suspicion. "Why you asking?"

"I was hoping to borrow it to ride to the mini-mart."

She looks me up and down, and a muscle ticks in her jaw. "It'll cost you." She folds her arms, gauging my reaction.

I unbuckle my watch, placing it down on the counter. It's the only item of value I have on me. I'd happily trade my diamond ring, but my bastard father will string me up if I return home without it. "They can have that. It's Gucci. Retails at two thousand."

Her eyes go out on stalks as she examines it. "This the real deal?"

"It is."

Her gaze flits to the massive diamond on my finger, and that's all it takes to convince her. She slips the watch on her wrist, removing a set of keys from a drawer. "The ride's mine. You can take it, but you put a scratch on her, and I'll gut your pretty body from head to toe." Her eyes penetrate mine. "We clear?"

"Crystal." You'd swear it was a vintage Harley the way she's talking about it, not a cheap Honda. But I keep my mouth shut, taking the keys from her outstretched hand. "I'll have her back by midnight."

"Hey, girl," she calls out after me. "You know how to ride?"

I grin, and images of riding my Kawasaki Ninja 300 float through my mind. "I'm good."

She smiles. "Sweet."

I race back to the room, stuffing the keys down the front of my jeans so Harley doesn't notice.

"I got tequila!" I sing, bursting through the door and waving the bottle at him.

He frowns. "I don't drink."

"Oh, come on." I sit on the edge of the bed beside him, nudging him in the ribs. "Live a little. We're on a road trip. Tequila is basically an essential." I press my mouth close to his ear. "And it's a rite of passage. One you can't pass up."

"Rick will freak out."

What the fuck did these guys do to their brother? They might as well wrap him in cotton wool and be done with it.

"You're not afraid of your brother, are you?" I quirk a brow, sending him a challenging stare.

He puffs out his chest. "Course not."

"Good." I grab two glasses from the bedside table, pouring a generous measure in Harley's while I heavily dilute mine with water. "You find a movie?"

"*The Godfather* okay?"

"Hells yeah." I hand him his drink. "The last time I watched it, after this stupid party your brother dragged me to, I visualized Kaiden in place of every victim. Imagining his face getting blown to bits never got old."

Harley looks at me like I've grown ten heads, and I realize I just fucked up. He's fiercely protective of Kai and thinks the sun shines out of his backstabbing ass.

I mess up his hair, giggling. "I'm kidding!" I drop beside him again. "Drink that and tell me it doesn't feel good." I clink my glass against his. "Cheers!" I drain mine in one go, and not to be outdone, Harley knocks his back too.

His face pulls into a grimace and he sticks his tongue out. I can't help laughing, but it's genuine this time. "It'd be better with salt and lime, but beggars can't be choosers." I grab his glass and refill it. "Another couple and you'll be begging for it."

He looks warily at me, so I sit closer, pushing my body right up beside his, and lick up the side of his neck. "You smell gorgeous," I murmur. "I'm glad Rick left you here and not Joaquin. He's too grumpy and no fun at all."

My words do the trick, and soon, we're barely paying any attention to the movie as I ply poor, innocent Harley with shot after shot while I basically drink water.

"I don't feel so hot," he slurs after a while, and thank fuck, because I'm running out of time. I have forty, maybe fifty, minutes, tops, before the others arrive.

"Why don't you lie down." I push him down flat on his back. "I'll get you some water."

"Need to sleep," he mumbles, curling on his side and shutting his eyes. Two minutes later, he's snoring softly, and I creep out of the room.

I sprint to the bike, pulling the helmet on and flooring it out of there. Thankfully, there's a big sign for the mini-mart, and I find it easily. I have just enough cash left to pay for the disposable cell and some credit, and I call Xavier once I'm outside the store.

"Abby?" he asks before I've said a word.

"How'd you know it was me?"

"Thank fuck." Air whistles down the line. "I've been praying you'd call."

"This is the first opportunity I've had, and I don't have long."

"Are you okay? Are you hurt? I'll tear those new elite fuckers from limb to limb after I've gouged out their eyeballs with pitchforks, pissed on them, and set them on fire."

"Wow. That's very specific."

"I've had nothing but time to plan their deaths. I have lots of creative ideas."

I smile even though he can't see it. "I miss you."

"Miss you too, but stop fucking around. Where are you?"

"I'm in a town someplace in central Nebraska. I have a plan. Listen carefully."

"Shoot."

"You have this number now, and you can track me, right?"

"Affirmative, Double oh-seven."

I roll my eyes, grinning. "The Anderson brothers are taking me to Kaiden. They won't tell me where, only that it will be Tuesday evening before we arrive. I need to speak to him. I want answers, but then I want you to come and get me the hell away from him."

"Gladly, darling. Just turn your cell on once you arrive. I'll track you and ride to the rescue."

"Thanks, dude. I don't want to waste a second longer in that asshole's company than I have to."

"I second that."

"Is Charlie okay?" I ask, kick starting the engine.

"He's fine. He flew home a few hours ago. He's pissed they got the better of him, and he's got a goose egg the size of a football on the side of his head, but he'll survive."

"Good. Look, I've got to go. I'll text you Tuesday night."

"Stay safe, babe, and if you run into trouble, switch that cell on, and I'll find you."

"I will. See you soon." I hang up before he can reply, hightailing it back to the motel.

I'm about a mile away when I spot Rick's SUV behind me in the distance. "Fuck. Shit. Crap." I curse under the helmet, pushing my foot to the metal until I reach the motel. I park the motorcycle in record time and race into reception, tossing the keys across the lobby to dreadlocks. "Thank you! And not a scratch!" I holler over my shoulder before racing out of there.

Thankfully, Harley is still out for the count when I reach the bedroom, but there's no time to get him out of my bed and into his own room, so I make a rapid decision. I strip down to my undies, throwing my clothes across the floor, and climb under the covers. Keeping one eye on the door, I get Harley out of his shirt and jeans, and I fling them across the floor too.

The sounds of hushed conversation and the *thump, thump* of booted feet tickles my eardrums as I mess up my hair, scoot in under his arm, and rest my head on top of his warm chest. I place his other arm around me and close my eyes, literally two seconds before the door to the room opens.

"What the actual fuck?" Rick shouts, and I fight a smile.

CHAPTER SEVEN

Rick is shaking my shoulders, and I can tell it's difficult for him to be gentle.

Because he most likely wants to strangle me.

"Abby!" he hisses, and I blink repeatedly, pretending to be half asleep.

"Wha?" I rub at my eyes as I sit up, letting the sheet pool at my waist.

Rick curses under his breath. "Cover yourself up, for fuck's sake."

"Wha?" I feign confusion, enjoying his discomfort way too much to make it easy on him.

He cusses again. "Stop staring," he snaps. At Joaquin, I guess. "It's bad enough we've found them like this. We don't want to give Kai any more ammunition to go postal."

"What's going on?" I murmur, pushing strands of hair out of my eyes and staring at him.

"You tell me." He folds his arms across his chest, pointedly looking from me to a still unconscious Harley. "And what the fuck is this?" He holds up the half-empty bottle of tequila.

"It's tequila," I deadpan, stretching my arms up over my head and standing.

"What the ever-loving fuck are you doing now?" He averts his eyes to avoid staring at my semi-naked body.

"Going to the bathroom to pee." I glare at him. "That okay with you?"

He pulls something out of a bag. "Put that on before Joaquin creams his pants."

I smirk, making a meal out of slipping the oversized T-shirt down over my head.

"You will give me gray hairs," Rick mutters, staring at the ceiling as if looking for divine inspiration.

"Hey, Joaquin." I smile flirtatiously at him as I walk past, sashaying my hips on purpose. His brown eyes are heated as they latch onto my body, and he's doing fuck all to hide the fact he's shamelessly ogling my tits. I think it's fair to say Rick and Kai's interventions have had less success with their other brother.

I listen to Rick berating Joaquin from behind the closed bathroom door, chuckling to myself.

I can have lots of fun with this.

Payback is a bitch, Kaiden Anderson.

"How much of this did he drink?" Rick asks when I return to the bedroom. Joaquin isn't around, so Rick must have sent him to his room with his tail between his legs.

I flop down on the edge of the bed, stretching my bare legs out. "Pretty much all of it."

"Fucking hell." He rubs the back of his neck repeatedly.

"I could hardly drink it now, could I?" I arch a brow.

"That's what I thought, but there were two glasses."

"I had to pretend to drink it or he'd never have tried it."

Rick sends daggers at me. "You deliberately seduced him under false pretenses?" I shrug, not confirming or denying it. "Why would you drag him into this?" He claws a hand through his hair, looking like he wants to throttle me again.

"Oh, chill out. It was only a bit of fun. Harley needs to let loose now and then. You two might think you're protecting him, but he's got to live his life."

"That is not your decision to make," Rick says through gritted teeth. "Harley's only fifteen, and he's a good kid with great grades and a bright future. Kai and I have spared him the shit we had to put up with, and I'm sure as fuck not going to let you use him to get back at Kai, if that's what you're up to."

Guilt threatens to breach the surface, but I swallow back my discomfort. It's not like I did anything. Sure, he'll probably have the hangover from hell tomorrow, and it will piss Kai off, but I didn't touch him, even if that's what I want them to believe. "It just happened, okay? You need to relax. Or get laid."

"Let me guess?" He smirks. "You're offering?" He shamelessly skims my body, and that rubs me up the wrong way.

"I'm not a slut, and I resent the insinuation! Until I met your asshole of a brother, I was a virgin, and he's the only guy I've had sex with."

"Now you're saying you didn't fuck Harley?"

I sit up on my knees, my eyes blazing with indignation. "I never said I did. You're the one jumping to conclusions."

"Because you got my little brother drunk and climbed into bed with him."

"We fooled around a bit before he passed out," I lie, because I want Kai to hear about this, "but that's not the same as fucking him."

"Sucks to be you, little bro," Joaquin whispers to his sleeping brother, quietly chuckling. I hadn't heard him return. "Thanks for taking the heat off me, Abby. I owe you."

Rick and I both scowl at him, but I don't dignify his comment with a response.

Frowning at the mattress strewn across the floor at Joaquin's feet, I ask, "What's going on?"

"I'll sleep there," Rick says. "You." He points at the empty bed he's supposed to be sleeping in. "Get your annoying ass in there."

I can't resist winding him up a little more. "You shouldn't have to sleep on the floor. You can stay in here to babysit Harley, and I'll sleep in the other room with Joaquin." I give him my best "butter wouldn't melt in my mouth" expression.

"I'm down with that plan," Joaquin says, shooting me a naughty wink.

Rick growls, shaking his head. "This will be a long-ass couple days."

Things are tense in the car the following day, and Harley can't even look me in the eye. I feel shitty, but I can't back out now. And it's not just because I want to piss Kai off. I need to hide the truth, or it's all for nothing. If Rick discovers Harley passed out, he'll quiz me about what I was up to, and I can't have anyone finding the cell and ruining my chance at escape. I don't know what Kai plans to do with me once we reach our destination, but I plan on spending minimal time in his presence.

We find another motel Monday night, and this time, Rick secures separate rooms, keeping me well away from his little brothers, and he doesn't let me out of his sight.

We set out early Tuesday morning, and by six p.m., we cross the state border into Connecticut.

A half hour later, Rick takes the exit for Mistbury, a small town with a population of three thousand one hundred and six, according to the sign we pass. I keep my eyes peeled, checking for landmarks and mentally mapping the route in case Xavier needs details.

We drive through the small town, out past the main residential area, into a more remote part. It's so pretty out here. The narrow roads are edged by thick shrubbery and dense woodland, and the few properties we pass are extravagant and well-maintained. Majestic trees, sporting amber-colored leaves, sway in the breeze, and I can almost hear them whispering in greeting as we glide past.

Rick maneuvers the SUV up a bumpy dirt track, and I grip the handrail on the side of the door as I'm jostled from side to side. I press my nose to the glass as we drive for miles, with no land or people in sight. Rick slows at large double gates, tapping in a code on the keypad. I can't decipher the numbers he's inputting, but I'm on high alert, surreptitiously scanning the surroundings for anything that might help Xavier. I strain my neck as far as it will go, but I can't see much over the large wooden gates and the massive, high wall that stretches on either side, securely enclosing the property. Barbed wire runs the length of the wall on top with mounted cameras at regular intervals.

"What is this place?" I ask, growing uneasy.

"It belongs to a friend of mine from college," Rick says, as the gates open and he moves the car forward.

"They're big on security, huh?"

"They have reason to be," he cryptically replies, as I whip my head around, drinking in the massive landscaped grounds which seem to go on forever. The gates automatically close behind us as we drive up a wider, smoother driveway lined by a row of tall trees.

"I can't believe you're hiding out in Connecticut. Isn't it a little risky to stay this close to home?"

"That's the beauty of it," Rick says. "They won't expect us to hide right under their noses."

I nod, because it makes sense. It's sneaky, and I love it.

When we round the next bend, a few buildings come into view in the near distance. I lean forward in my seat, poking my head through the gap in the front seats, as I lock eyes on the beautiful wooden cabin. "Wow. It's beautiful."

The house is gigantic. Out front, the façade is a mix of wood and decorative cream stone with a triangular-peaked roof. A similar structure looms over it at the rear with two large windows built into the alcoves, but the roof on either side is rectangular. An elevated, railed deck spans the width on both sides. The right-hand part of the house has small windows, but the left-hand side has floor-to-ceiling windows that I imagine let in plenty of light.

"Wait until you see the inside." Rick veers right just before we come to the cabin, heading toward the cluster of smaller buildings. "My friend's mom is an interior designer, and she designed everything. It's spectacular."

"I wish it was summer," Joaquin says, "so we got to use the lake."

As Rick pulls the car into one of the side buildings—which is actually a six-car garage—I can just about make out the large lake in the background, the water glistening eerily under the cover of nightfall. I can visualize how incredible it'd be hanging out here in the summer, and whoever owns this has found a little piece of heaven on Earth.

Rick parks the car, and we climb out. Butterflies scatter in my chest, and bile floods my mouth at the thought of my imminent reunion with Kai. The guys grab their bags from the trunk and start walking toward the open doors.

"Hang on! I left my bag in the back seat." I yank the door open, bending over the seat so they can't see as I remove the cell and switch it on. Then I stuff it back in the pocket of my jeans, pull my sweater down over it, and grab the plastic bag containing my measly possessions.

I wipe my sweaty palms down the front of my jeans as we walk, barely feeling the bitterly cold wind swirling around me.

"Here." Rick removes his jacket, draping it around my shoulders as we walk the short distance from the garage to the cabin. "I'll take you shopping tomorrow, and you can get everything you need."

I arch a brow. "How long are we staying here?"

"Indefinitely."

That surprises me. "What about school?"

"You're worried about school?" He shoves his hands deep into his pockets, as he pins me with an inquisitive look.

I shrug. "You can't keep me prisoner here indefinitely," I say, watching with my mouth in my throat as the door to the cabin opens.

"You're not a prisoner, Abby. Kai wants to keep you both safe."

"And if I want to leave, he'll let me?" My heart is pounding behind my rib cage as a familiar tall, dark-haired form steps out onto the front porch.

"You'll need to discuss that with him," Rick says, a smirk spreading across his mouth as he spots his brother.

My feet slam to a halt of their own accord at the bottom of the steps, and I lift my eyes, instantly meeting his. Pain slams into me, almost knocking all the air out of my lungs.

It's been five weeks since I last saw him, and the time apart hasn't eliminated the connection between us. I feel it in the prickles on the back of my neck. In the rampant throbbing of my pulse. In the instant ache between my thighs. My entire body tingles as every molecule recognizes his presence, and the craving is almost like a high, urging me to run into his arms and never let go.

His gorgeous dark eyes drill into me, invading all my senses as he peruses my body from head to toe. Danger seeps from his pores, mingling with relief, frustration, anger, and something darker and more intense. His eyes are on fire. Part lust. Part residual hate. And it shouldn't turn me on.

But it does.

I wet my dry lips, ungluing my tongue from the roof of my mouth as I steel my spine in readiness.

My body is screaming at my head as a violent inner battle starts up.

The attraction between us has always been off the charts, making it difficult to stay away from him even when he was tormenting me. But anger is a storm that's mushroomed into a tornado over the weeks of our separation, and the need for vengeance is stronger.

He will pay for all the lies, the secrets, and the ultimate betrayal.

Rick, Harley, and Joaquin greet their brother, and he hugs them one by one, but his eyes remain locked on mine the entire time, as we battle it out with silent deadly looks. Rick whispers something in his ear, and he nods curtly, never taking his eyes off me.

I force my legs to move, and blood thrums in my veins with each step I take that brings me closer to him.

Rick glances at me briefly before following Joaquin and Harley into the house, leaving us alone.

I plant my sneakered feet on the porch, sidestepping Kai so he's forced to turn around.

We face off, and tension bleeds into the air.

The woodsy, citrusy sent of his cologne wafts around me, testing my self-control, but I stand firm, narrowing my eyes as I glare at him, purposely ignoring how fuckable he looks in the dark jeans hugging his slim hips and muscular thighs and the tight-fitting gray Henley that clings to his biceps and chiseled abs. The top is unbuttoned, offering a glimpse of the chest tattoo I've admired at close quarters. The growth on his chin and cheeks is thicker than usual, but his hair looks recently cut, the sides shorn close enough to highlight the skull tattoo I adore.

Kai is devastatingly gorgeous.

There's no doubt about it.

And the dark glimmer of hate still lingering in his eyes only adds to the appeal. My body strains toward him, pleading with me to touch him. And the craving is almost uncontrollable.

My heart aches because there was a time I allowed myself to hope. To think I might have someone worth fighting for.

I allowed myself to fall, and despite what he's done, those feelings are still there, bottled up inside me.

But I fucking hate him too, and I make sure he reads that in my eyes.

I'm vaguely aware of our audience, whispering in hushed voices at the back of the hallway as his brothers watch our silent face-off.

Kai's eyes drift lower, latching onto my enlarged chest before wandering lower to my flat stomach.

Pain slams into me again, and I hope I have the strength to do this. Subconsciously, I flatten my palm over my stomach, and his eyes burn with undisguised rage as he's dazzled by the giant diamond on my ring finger.

I momentarily gloat, thinking of all the ways I can use Charlie against him.

His head jerks up, and he takes a step closer.

I stand my ground, tilting my chin up defiantly and piercing him with a venomous stare.

He closes the gap between us, pressing his body against mine as he glares at my mouth. Adrenaline courses through my veins, and my heart is hammering against my rib cage. Our eyes enter a battle again, and his nostrils flare as he trails his fingers up my arm, along my collarbone, and over my neck before gripping my chin.

I keep the same hateful expression on my face as he tips my chin up, staring at me with a mixture of desire and frustration. "I can't decide if I want to kiss you or kill you," he admits, his voice bordering on a growl, sending shivers tiptoeing up my spine.

"That's not a dilemma I'd struggle with," I coolly reply.

"And why is that?" he replies in an equally cool tone, but the way his body is locked up tight gives the game away. His hand continues to grip my chin, but I don't struggle.

I flash him a malicious smile. "Because I know my mind, and killing you trumps kissing you every time."

CHAPTER EIGHT

"It's cute how you lie to yourself, but I know the truth," Kai says, and I pull away, fighting the urge to wipe that smug smile off his face. "Your body betrays you every single time." He sweeps his heated gaze over me again, before settling on my lips. "You're begging to be kissed." He presses his hot, arrogant mouth to my ear. "Screaming to be fucked."

Conceited asshole. So much for his supposed concern for me.

"You're full of shit, because I *loathe* you." I roll the word around my tongue, piercing him with a scathing look. "You've fed me a pack of lies, and I'll never forgive you for it!"

Something close to remorse briefly flashes across his face. "You haven't exactly been wholly truthful now either, have you?" He crosses his arms, daring me to challenge him.

My jaw hangs open for a moment. "Are you fucking kidding me?" I roar, shoving at his immovable chest.

"You're every bit as deceitful as me. What else do you think this thing is between us?" He smirks as he points between us, and it enrages me. I lash out without thought, slapping him viciously across the face.

His cheek reddens, and he grits his teeth, looking like he wants to bash my head against the wall. Or maybe choke all the air from my lungs.

"Kai." Rick steps in between us. "Abby needs to eat and rest up, or have you forgotten she's pregnant with your baby?"

Kai steps back, forcibly calming himself down. "I've hardly forgotten, Rick." He drills a pointed look at his brother. "And butt out. This is between me and *her*."

"I'm glad to see you haven't changed one bit. You're still a raging, fucking asshole."

"You're no saint yourself."

"What the fuck have I done?"

"You concealed the pregnancy and your engagement," he hisses. "And you fucking ran!"

I step up to him, poking my finger in his chest. "I ran because you hid the documents stolen from the safe and you wouldn't tell me why! And I didn't know about the engagement! I told you my father had kidnapped me and locked me in my room. I was completely in the dark when you grabbed me into the bathroom before the party."

"And the baby? How long had you kept that a secret from me?"

"I only discovered it the day after I left you. I'd gone to the doctors to renew the prescription for my pill. She always runs regular tests, including a blood draw, a urine sample, a Pap smear, and a pelvic exam before writing a new script." My chest heaves. "The urine sample confirmed my pregnancy, and I was so shocked I stumbled out of her office barely paying attention to my surroundings, and that's how my father's men could sneak up on me."

I snap out of my melancholy, prodding my finger repeatedly in his chest. "So, I didn't lie. Not like you," I snarl, brushing past him.

"It doesn't mean you're fucking innocent. You've done things you're not proud of too."

I slam to a halt and spin around. "God, you really are an asshole.

You can't just apologize. You have to throw shade and try to downplay your despicable actions."

"I've never hidden my asshole side. You know that more than anyone."

His flippant attitude annoys me, but I'm done with this convo. "Please don't change on my account, because it helps me hold on to my anger." I step back toward the door as I speak. "And if you think you're keeping me here, you've another think coming, because once I get answers, I'm going back home. To. My. *Fiancé*." I waggle the fingers on my left hand.

"Over my dead fucking body," he growls, moving into my personal space again. "You're *mine*," he snarls. "I *own* you."

"Like hell you do."

He fixes dark eyes on me. "You're not marrying Charlie fucking Barron."

I smile sweetly at him. "You don't get a say."

"That baby you're carrying says differently."

"You can have visitation rights, but this baby will live with Charlie and me. You can't force me to stay with you."

"So, you'd marry that motherfucker, and give up your shares in Manning Motors, just to spite Kai?" Rick says, his voice dripping in disbelief.

There was a time I'd gladly have exchanged my shares for my freedom. But not anymore.

Now I know how badly my father wants them, there is no way I'm relinquishing them to him. Not after the things he's done. Getting my revenge is more important, so I'll let him believe I'm on board with this new engagement, and toe the line, but he is going down. And I'll be the one to do it.

"I'd do it to spite your father, because he's every bit as bad as my asshole sperm donor, and there's no way I'm letting him steal my shares." I flick my hair over my shoulder. "But that's not the reason. I want to marry Charlie," I lie. "He loves me, and he'll protect me. He hasn't bullied me, lied to me, or purposely slept with me to fuel a sick agenda!"

"Your naivety is showing again, sweetheart," Kai taunts. "You have no clue who Charlie Barron is." He yanks me into him, cementing his arms around my waist and nudging his hips against mine. "And he doesn't turn you on like I do." His eyes blaze with a different heat. "I'm the only one who can fuck you hard, exactly the way you like it." One hand moves down between our bodies, and he cups my pussy. "This pussy is mine, and you know it."

"Jesus, Kai." Rick exhales, jerking his gaze to the hallway. "Tone it fucking down."

"I'm not a baby, Rick," Harley says, walking forward. "And I'm sick of both of you treating me like a little kid."

A wide smile crosses my mouth as I pull back from Kai, stumbling a little and falling into Harley. I reach up, cupping his face. "You tell him, baby."

Silence descends, and Harley trembles behind me, but he's too much of a gentleman to push me away.

Kai shoots a cutting look in Rick's direction while Joaquin attempts to hide his laughter with a cough. "What the fuck?" Kai says, his eyes searching behind me.

"It's been a long trip. Let's all freshen up, and we'll talk after." Rick slaps Kai on the shoulder, drilling a look at him until he relents. With more gentleness than I'd expect, Rick pulls me away from Harley. "C'mon. I'll show you to your room."

I don't look back as I let Rick lead me away, and I'm barely noticing the beautiful cabin because I'm too strung out at our unexpected reunion. I stupidly thought Kai would try to scoop me up into his arms and protect me.

But he's an even bigger asshole.

He doesn't get to be mad at me.

I'm the only one who has an entitlement to anger.

We walk up the stairs, entering a large master suite. "Make yourself at home," Rick says, opening his arms. "There are towels in the bathroom if you want to grab a shower or a bath, and just come down to the kitchen when you're ready."

I nod, sinking onto the soft velvety gray couch, kicking off my sneakers and curling my feet underneath me as I look around.

It's a massive space, divided between this room—which is a private living room of sorts with two couches, a coffee table, and an open fire with a wall-mounted TV hanging overhead—and a separate bedroom. The walls and floors are polished wood, and the vaulted ceiling has exposed beams. I stand, walking to the roaring fire, holding up my hands and allowing the heat to warm my chilled body.

This reminds me of the night I first met Kai. Of standing in front of the fire in his little cabin by the beach, feeling lost and alone and unsure of my path in the world.

I turn around, walking to the wooden railing and peering down into a huge open living space below. No one is around, so the others must have gone to their rooms, or they're in the kitchen.

I walk through the side door into a stunning bedroom. A giant four-poster bed, the frame painted in black, occupies prime real estate in the room. It's dressed in white, pink, and gray linens with a bunch of fluffy cushions thrown over it. A soft patterned rug lines the floor, and retractable blinds cover the large open window at the back. I press the button and open them, leaning into the window as I admire the outside space.

Although it's dark out, the place is all lit up. The gardens at the rear are landscaped with neat flower beds and boxes housing shrubbery. The area at the front is a cream-colored stone patio arranged around a long pool with a walkway leading down to the lake in the near distance.

If I owned a place like this, I would never want to leave.

It's breathtaking.

Woodland rims the lake on all sides, and there isn't a house or a sinner in sight.

It's remote and private, making it the perfect little hideaway.

I stare out the window, lost in thought, for a while. Eventually, I drag myself away, drawing the blinds closed as I inspect the rest of the room. Matching bedside tables and dressers finish out the room which leads into a huge walk-in closet on one side and an en suite bathroom on the other.

I take my plastic bag and cell with me into the bathroom, closing and locking the door. While the tub fills, I sit on the toilet seat and tap out a quick text to Xavier.

I spend ages in the bath, using some feminine products to wash myself, hoping whomever owns them doesn't mind. There were men's and women's clothing hanging up in the closet, so it's obvious Rick's friend has a regular girlfriend. Whoever they are, they have money and good taste.

When my skin puckers like a prune and the water turns lukewarm, I get out, draining the tub as I wrap a towel around my head. I wipe the condensation from the mirror, examining my body in the full-length mirror properly for the first time since all the shit went down. I cup my heavier breasts, and an automatic grimace spreads across my mouth. I don't think I'll ever get used to them. I liked my smaller boobs despite popular opinion. I move my hand lower, smoothing my palm over my stomach, fighting a wave of tears.

Suddenly, I can't bear to look at myself any longer, and I spin around with my heart lodged in my throat. Pulling a large bath towel off the heated radiator, I tuck it firmly around my body. I brush my teeth, pee, and pat my hair to remove the excess moisture before combing it. Checking my cell before exiting the bathroom, I frown when I see the undelivered text. I attempt to resend it, waiting a minute to ensure it's delivered this time, but it pings back undelivered again, and I've a bad feeling about this.

I step into the bedroom and shriek at the hulking form spread-eagled across the bed. Discreetly, I slip the cell into the plastic bag, depositing it on the bedside table as I glare at my ex. "Get the fuck out of my bedroom."

"Actually, it's *our* bedroom," he confirms. "I demanded the master suite so you're comfortable."

"Hell will freeze before I share a room with you again," I promise.

He slides off the bed, unfurling his long limbs as he stands. His eyes drink me in, latching onto the little water droplets still clinging to my shoulders, and I feel naked. "Can we have a do-over?" he asks, softening his voice.

I snort, pointing at my stomach. "I don't see how that's possible unless you have a time machine in your possession?"

"I meant a do-over for earlier." He walks confidently toward me. Placing his hands on my shoulders, he moves me over to the bed, forcing me to sit. My body tingles in every place he touches me, and a dull ache starts between my thighs. I hate the way he affects me so potently, and I wish my body would accept the memo.

Kai's deplorable, through and through.

And there's zero chance of redemption.

He threads his fingers through mine, but I wrest my hand back, tucking both hands under my arms and away from him. Not to be deterred, Kai forcibly removes one hand, lacing his fingers in mine again.

I roll my eyes but give up fighting the inevitable, because there are bigger battles to pick.

"Why do you want a do-over?" I ask, staring straight ahead rather than looking at him.

"Because I didn't want our reunion to go down like that." He cups one side of my face, forcing my gaze to his. "Are you okay? Did they hurt you?" His mask is down, and concern shows on his face.

I gulp, taking a moment to compose myself before I lie. "They didn't hurt me. I'm fine."

"And the baby?"

The vulnerable look in his eyes almost undoes me, and I can only nod.

"I didn't know, Abby." His eyes penetrate mine, beseeching me to believe him. "I didn't know they did that to you." He drops his hand from my face, and his Adam's apple jumps in his throat, as his chest heaves. The truth is transparent, and some knots in my chest unravel. It doesn't alter the fact he still betrayed me, but it helps take away the sting.

"Why did you always have sex with me without condoms?"

"Because I fucking loved being inside you with no barrier. I was clean, and you were on the pill. Or so I thought." A murderous look washes over his face.

"Was it Rick?" I choke out, and he bobs his head.

"Why?"

"Because we've been conditioned to hate you most of our lives, and when our father said he needed me to do it, I didn't stop to question it like I should have," Rick answers, stepping into the bedroom uninvited. Kai narrows his eyes at his brother. "I can't let you take all the blame," Rick says, crossing the room.

"And he did all that shit to me because he blames me for losing the love of his life, *my mother*, and ruining their escape plans?" My voice drips with condescension because it sounds no more believable than the first time I heard it.

"Dad's fucked in the head," Kai admits, and I snort.

"That's an understatement." My jaw clenches. "He's the reason they sexually assaulted me." I grind my teeth to the molars.

"Something else I didn't know until the ballroom," Kai says.

"Something neither of us knew, and the extent of his relationship with your mother," Rick adds.

"I'm assuming he knew I gave my virginity to you, but how did he find out?" My jaw is tense as I question Kai.

"He didn't find out from me," Kai says, and a muscle pops in his jaw. "I didn't tell anyone about our night on the beach." His eyes plead with me to believe him. "You saw Hunt, Lauder, and Rick's reactions when you let that slip."

I did, and I know he's telling the truth.

"It doesn't alter what happened. Your father knows the elite. He had to have known what'd happen if that truth came out, yet he still did it. All for the sake of revenge. He's as bad as the others, and there's nothing you can tell me that'll ever justify him using me to further his aims."

"There isn't anything to justify it. It was wrong. *He* was wrong, and *I* was wrong, but you don't understand what it's been like these past ten years." Rick props his butt against the edge of the dresser. "Kai can give you more of the background, but Dad turned to alcohol when we left Rydeville, and he was a drunk until about two years ago when he got sober. He spent years trapped in an alcohol-induced haze, and his sole focus was getting revenge on your family. Your father took everything from him, and in his eyes, you were the trigger that fired the gun that left him penniless and broken."

"I was seven years old. I didn't know any better."

"We know that now," Kai quietly says. "But when you've had something drummed into your brain every second of every day, for years, you believe it, even if your rational mind knows it's not fair or true."

I still think it's a bullshit excuse, but I don't probe further, because there are other more pressing questions I need answers to.

"Did you switch out my birth control or put something into the drip?" I ask Rick.

"I switched out your pill," he admits, and at least he has the decency to look ashamed. "Our uncle Wes owns Femerst. It's a pharmaceutical company which produces medication solely for fertility-related conditions. They have this award-winning medication that's used to stimulate ovulation, and we swapped your pills out with it. It was easy for Wes to replicate the packaging and shape the pills so they looked exactly like your prescription."

I jump up and slap him across the face, relishing the resounding thud that echoes around the room, and the way his head whips back from my powerful strike. "I will never forgive you for violating me like that."

To think I used to have a crush on this guy.

Unfortunately, my taste isn't any better now I'm all grown up.

"I wouldn't expect you to." Rick rubs at his cheek, but he doesn't criticize me for lashing out, accepting it like Kai did at the door. "I nearly didn't go through with it when you admitted you gave Kai your virginity." He looks at his brother. "He hadn't told me, and everything clicked then."

"What do you mean?" I cock my head to the side.

"Kai, Hunt, and Lauder were supposed to manipulate and intimidate you into cooperating so we could get at your father's safe," Rick admits.

"But you were too fucking stubborn for your own good," Kai butts in, and I flip him the bird as I sit back down on the bed, leaving a decent gap between us this time.

"So, Father invoked Plan B," Rick confirms.

"Which was what?" I have an idea, but I want to hear him say it.

"I was to seduce you and then manipulate you into helping," Kai says, looking sheepish.

Nausea churns in my gut, and I hate how gullible I was. How easy it was for him to get me into his bed. Self-loathing consumes me, as it has many times in the past few weeks.

"Dad came to me," Rick continues, "because he was worried Kai was falling for you and losing control." I snort at the ludicrous nature of that statement, and Kai pins me with a deadly look that might have scared me one time, but I'm not scared of him anymore.

He's the one who should fear *me*.

"Dad needed to get into that safe," Rick continues, "because he believed the proof your mother had collected was in there. Proof that confirmed your asshole father killed our mother, and he could use that to put him away."

Tension descends for a few beats. "Hang on." My brow puckers, as I recall the words spoken the night of the engagement party. "I thought you already had the proof. Your dad said my aunt gave it to him." My gaze bounces between them.

Kai shakes his head. "He was pretending to draw your father out."

"Wasn't it in the safe?" I ask.

"We hoped so, but it wasn't among the contents we retrieved," Kai confirms.

"Fuck." I rub a tense spot between my brows. Now that I know Atticus is still alive, I'm banking on him nailing my father's ass to the wall. If he doesn't have proof, my father committed murder, it doesn't leave us with much to go on.

"Dad knew there was a chance it wouldn't be there. Your father has always outwitted him, at every turn, so this time, he was determined to gain the upper hand," Rick says. "Dad knew your shares would automatically transfer to your husband upon marriage, so he decided not to outwardly intervene in your relationship. He thought it best to let nature take its course. He figured you guys would fall in love and a wedding would be inevitable."

"But the bastard took it a step too far," Kai says, fuming, and I'm surprised at the poison infusing his words. He stands, pacing the floor, wringing his hands in front of him. I eye him curiously.

"It's like Dad said," Rick supplies, going on, regardless of his brother frantically pacing the room on the verge of a blowout. "He wanted insurance. He wanted to ensure you had to marry Kai. So, he asked me to switch out your pills, and he made me promise not to tell my brother."

"I get why you'd have no loyalty to me," I say, "but how could you do that to your brother?" Rick is no better than Drew.

"I was a stupid fuckhead for agreeing, but I thought I was doing the right thing. Avenging our mom's death is something both of us want." He eyeballs Kai. "I figured if Dad was right about Kai falling for you, then it was up to me to see the plan through to fruition." He exhales heavily. "And I thought having a baby together might not be such a big deal if you were into one another."

I want to inflict pain on Maverick Anderson so badly, and I sit on my hands to avoid lashing out.

Rick scrubs a hand along his stubbly jawline. "When you told me Kai was the one you gave your virginity to, I was astounded, because he hadn't told us. I realized then that he was protecting you, and I had second thoughts about interfering."

He leans forward, resting his elbows on his thighs. "I almost didn't do it, but there was too much at stake. And I saw the way you looked at one another." He smiles knowingly at me, and I purse my lips. "You both tried to deny it then, like you're trying to deny it now, but I know what I see."

I flip him off, and Kai growls.

"You love each other, and that sealed the decision."

"You're delusional. We've always hated one another," I say even if it's only half a truth.

"I should give you another black eye," Kai threatens, stalking toward his brother with clenched fists.

"This time, I'll fight back," Rick promises, rising and stepping up to his brother as my mind whirls to process all this new intel. "I deserved the beating you gave me, but I won't be your perpetual punchbag. I'm sorry, and you've got to forgive me."

Kai growls again, but I jump in before this goes south, not wanting to lose the opportunity to learn more seeing as they're in a sharing and caring mood.

"Does that mean you didn't know about the real will?"

"No one knew about that," Rick says. "Dad may have reconsidered tampering with your birth control if he'd known you'd forfeit your shares to your father if you got pregnant and didn't marry the baby daddy, because it was an uncalculated risk."

"I didn't know about any of this," Kai says, eyeballing me. "Or the fact Dad was planning on taking you that night and holding us both hostage until the baby was born and we got married."

That doesn't surprise me. I only wish Atticus had succeeded where Louis did. "Except my father got the better of him again, and he got to me first," I say.

Kai sinks to his knees in front of me. "I was fucking terrified of what he'd do to you." He anxiously scans my face. "And I was ready to burn down his fucking house, to put a bullet through his skull, if he didn't tell me where he was keeping you, but he outwitted us all again."

"Because he blamed your family for the shootout and paid off his buddies to issue warrants for your arrests."

Kai shakes his head. "Our contacts have already made that go away."

"They have?" I frown, because I don't recall Charlie telling me that. "So why are you hiding out here then?"

Kai casts a glance at Rick over his shoulder. "You didn't tell her?"

"Thought it was best she heard it from you."

"Heard what? What don't I know?" My gaze bounces between them.

"Your father wants to protect his interests. To ensure I'm not around to marry you."

"I don't understand." All the tiny hairs lift on the back of my neck, and my sixth sense already knows I will not like this.

"Your father has put a hit out on me, Abby. If he finds me, I'm dead."

CHAPTER NINE

My brain hurts. I don't understand, and it makes little sense. But that's because I'm trying to apply logic, and logic won't work because my father is a psychopath.

I don't just throw that out there in jest.

I've Googled it, and he meets the definition, and some.

According to stats I read, over thirty percent of executives in senior level positions in business display psychopathic tendencies.

Go figure.

Michael Hearst definitely falls into that categorization, and, in his psychotic brain, Atticus is the devil incarnate who needs taking down on multiple levels. There's no doubt in my mind that's why he did it. And it's why he wants Kai dead.

My hatred for Atticus Anderson intensifies. His meddling has hurt me on several fronts, and I will never forgive him or his older sons for how they've fucked up my already fucked-up life.

Kai stares at me, watching my brain fail to compute everything. My emotions are veering all over the place. I hate him as much as I love him, but I don't want him to die. I don't want *anyone* to die, because then justice hasn't prevailed.

"Well, that sucks," I admit, once I've gotten my wayward

emotions under control. His face contorts in annoyance. "What? Did you think your little dramatic statement would have me declaring undying love?" I cross my arms over my chest, and the motion reminds me I'm still in a towel. "Because, news flash." I poke his solid chest with the end of one finger. "I still fucking hate your guts."

"He didn't know, Abby," Rick says, coming to his brother's defense.

"I'm adding that to my list too!" I glower at Rick. Kai's brow creases in confusion, and conflicting emotions briefly flash on his face. I lean in close. "You may not have known about the plan to get me pregnant, but you still lied to me. For months! You fucked me knowing I had no clue who you were! You held me in your arms at night all the while you were betraying me."

I rise, stepping around him, adopting a cold, harsh glare. "I found it in my heart to forgive you for the callous way you treated me at the start, but I can't forgive you for this." I put my face all up in his again. "I *won't* forgive you for this. You're already dead to me."

Before he can respond, another hulking form enters the room claiming our attention. Sawyer is wearing black jeans and a tight-fitting black button-down shirt with his hair styled back in his usual fashion, looking perfectly poised and presentable, as he strides across the room to me. He thrusts his arm out, flipping his palm up. "Hand it over."

Kai rises, watching the interaction between me and his friend with sharp eyes.

"Hello to you too," I deadpan, tipping my head to the side.

A charming smile graces his lips, and he leans down, kissing my cheek, lingering a fraction too long. A predictable low growl rumbles from Kai's chest, and Sawyer smirks. "It's good to see you," he says, his eyes roaming my towel-covered body, and fury rolls off Kai in waves.

It's good to know he's still as possessive as ever. I can work that to my advantage.

"And I'm glad you're safe," Sawyer adds, straightening up and thrusting his palm out again. "But you still need to hand it over."

"I don't know what you're talking about," I protest, knowing full and well he's somehow detected my cell phone.

His gaze lands on the pathetic plastic bag on the bedside table, and he reaches it in three long strides, not asking for permission as he rummages through it, finding the evidence immediately.

I sigh in resignation, rolling my eyes to the ceiling.

"What the fuck?" Rick says, shock splaying across his face when he spots the cell in Sawyer's hand. "I searched her when we first picked her up, and she didn't have that on her. I swear."

"Who knows where you are?" Kai questions, pinning me with his "no bullshit" lens.

"No one knows where I am," I truthfully reply.

"Don't fucking start with me, Abby!" he barks. "It's too dangerous."

My nostrils flare. "Listen up, asshole, because you seem hard of hearing." I step right into his space. "No one knows where I am because the text I sent Xavier went undelivered."

"She called him," Sawyer confirms, not looking up as he scrolls through the call log on the phone.

Kai exhales heavily, stabbing me with a venomous expression. "You knew you were coming here, so there was zero reason to involve his annoying punk ass."

"You kidnapped me against my will. That was all the reason I needed. That, and he's the only other person besides Charlie I trust."

His eyes glaze over, and if looks could kill, me, Charlie, and Xavier would be ten feet under by now. I flip him the bird, loving how easy it is to push his buttons.

I think Kai might be losing his touch. Imagine that.

"You're testing my every last nerve." He's struggling to rein in his temper as he grabs my elbow harshly. "What the fuck did you tell him?"

"Fuck. You." I rip my arm away, nearly losing my towel.

Kai looks like he's ten seconds away from personal nuclear detonation when he throws me over his shoulder and stalks into the closet.

"Let me down, jerk face!" I pummel my fists on his back.

He places my feet on the ground in the middle of the mammoth closet with more tenderness than I expect. Especially with how he's glaring at me like I'm Damian from *The Omen*. "Put something on," he demands, waving his hands at the rows of female clothing.

"They're not my clothes."

"Faye won't mind."

I arch a brow. "Faye?"

"She and her husband own this place."

"And, what, they're letting you stay here indefinitely?"

"They're letting us stay here for as long as we need to." He takes a step toward me. "Now, stop deflecting, and pick something to wear. You're not going back out there in a towel."

I smirk, planting my hands on my hips. "Then I guess we're staying put."

A cool breeze wafts over my skin as he whips the towel off me in one lightning-fast move, leaving me standing buck-ass naked in front of him. Indignation and fury charge to the surface, and I'm tempted to lunge at him and beat him with my fists, only I know from previous experience how quickly he can restrain me.

His eyes zoom in on my chest, and a familiar lust-drenched haze burns in his eyes. "Fuck. Me," he rasps, biting down on his lower lip in a way that always turned me on.

"In your dreams, asshole." I hold my head up high as I brush past him, deliberately shoulder-checking him. I browse through the clothes hangers.

His strong arms wrap around me from behind, and I'm hauled back against his warm chest. "I don't think so, baby," he whispers. He runs his nose along the column of my neck as one hand moves up to cup my left boob. He kneads my flesh roughly, and a strangled cry escapes my mouth at the pleasure-pain sensation his touch invokes. While my breasts aren't quite as sensitive as they were a few weeks ago, they are still tender. Pressing his growing erection into my ass, he licks my neck and nips my earlobe, and liquid warmth floods to my core. "You'll be on your knees begging me to fuck you before the week is out."

"Still delusional, I see," I retort, attempting to remove his hand from my breast.

"Keep denying it, but I don't believe you." He moves his hand down lower, pausing momentarily on my belly, and I squeeze my eyes shut at the rapid onslaught of emotion. His hand is on the move again, and I whimper when he slides one finger inside me, thrusting his solid hard-on into my ass and grinding his hips. "Liar," he whispers, pumping his finger slowly in and out of me.

That one word brings reality crashing down upon me, and it's all I need to come to my senses. Jerking my elbow back into his gut, I free myself and spin around with rage rampaging across my face. I poke my finger in his chest, as fire incinerates me on the inside. "There's only one liar in here, and it isn't me!" I screech. "You have some nerve"—I prod his chest with my finger again—"calling me deceitful and a liar when every word out of your despicable mouth has been a deliberate manipulation of me!" I slam my palms into his chest, shoving him forcefully as weeks of pent-up frustration run free. "I fucking hate you!" I scream. "And I hate this Godawful chemistry between us! But I will fight it. Like I'll fight you." I pound my fists into his chest while he stands mute as a statue, letting me hit him, examining me like I'm some weird alien creature. "Every. Fucking. Step. Of. The. Way!"

"Ahem." A throat clearing pulls my gaze away from Kai.

"What?!!" I snap at Sawyer, halting my attack.

"Quit fucking around, and get out here. We need to talk." His eyes drop down my body, and I remember I'm stark naked.

Freaking awesome.

"You might want to put clothes on first." Sawyer licks his lips as he fixates on my breasts. "Although it seems a shame to cover those beauties." He waggles his brows, and Kai comes out of his semi-comatose state, whipping me behind him and shielding my body from sight.

"Get the fuck out before I knock you into next week."

"Losing your touch, Anderson," Sawyer taunts, backing out with a smirk on his face.

Silence descends, and we stare at one another for a few beats. But I've said what I wanted to say, and I need to stop sharing air space with him, so I focus on the closet, inspecting the clothes as I try to find something to wear. I choose a short black cotton jersey dress with long sleeves, because all the jeans and pants look way too long. Kai watches me silently, and I ignore him, giving him my back as I pull the dress over my head.

"Underwear and bra," he barks.

"I'm not putting some other woman's underwear on even if it is clean." I fold my arms across my chest.

"I can see your fucking nipples," he hisses.

"Tough." I move to go past him, but he stops me.

"Stay. Here. And don't test me. You might be pregnant, but that doesn't mean I can't put you over my knee and spank the shit out of you."

Liquid lust floods my body at his words, and he smirks. "Told you." He presses his mouth to my ear. "Liar." He slides his hand up under the dress, brushing the tips of his fingers along my slit. "And if the others weren't outside, I'd drop to my knees and prove it."

My knees wobble, threatening to go out from under me, and I inwardly curse my stupid, weak hormones. He kisses the top of my head while winding an arm around my lower back to steady me. "It's okay, baby. I missed you too." I don't need to look at him to see the gloating smirk, because it's all too obvious in his tone.

I flip him off, pouting and glaring at his retreating form, wondering how he's maneuvered into pole position.

It won't last long though, and I'll never stop battling him.

Even if my body refuses to cooperate with my mind.

He returns a minute later, dropping a pair of plain cotton panties and my bra on the bench before whipping the dress up over my head, exposing my body to him again. I scowl. "I'm well able to dress myself."

He smirks, grabbing the panties and dropping to his knees. "Lift," he commands, tapping my foot.

I ignore him, keeping my feet firmly planted on the ground, and I can keep this up all day.

I gasp, stumbling back and gripping onto the side of the closet as his hot tongue swipes along my folds. "What the hell are you doing?" I pant, hating how needy I sound. It's been weeks since I've known any action, and my body has grown accustomed to regular daily workouts.

I've missed sex with him.

Not that he'll ever hear those words leave these lips.

I won't give him any more opportunity to gloat.

"Every time you disobey an order, I'm sticking my tongue inside you. It's not a chore. But you might not like an audience. And if we're not out there in two minutes, the others will move the meeting in here."

Pushing his face away from my groin, I lift my foot, admitting defeat. He pulls my panties up my legs, fixing them in place, not missing the chance to brush his fingers against my pussy. I narrow my eyes, and he grins, flashing me a blinding smile that disarms me, momentarily stunning me into silence.

When he smiles at me like that, it's like I'm basking in the most heavenly sunshine. It's like a luminous light that shines only for me. My heart pumps faster, my breathing stops and starts, and my resolve weakens. His face draws me in, like it has on countless other occasions, and I'm leaning toward him before I've even registered the movement.

"Baby." Standing, he cups my face. "I've waited five long weeks for this." He lowers his mouth, and his lips are mere millimeters away from mine when I wake up.

I duck down at the last second, slipping out of his embrace as he kisses air.

Holy shit.

I've seriously got to keep my distance from him.

Because his sexual allure is like a spell. One I'm powerless to resist.

And I'm determined to be stronger this time. He doesn't get to betray me and have me again.

This time we're playing by my rules.

And he'll learn that lesson the hard way.

CHAPTER TEN

"**S**top getting your panties in a bunch," I tell Sawyer. "I called Xavier on Sunday night when we were in the middle of nowhere in Nebraska. I had no clue where we were heading because the guys refused to tell me. Xavier doesn't know where we are," I huff out. "Unfortunately."

"For his sake, I hope he doesn't," Sawyer replies.

"Are you threatening him?" I lower my voice, stepping up close. "Because I'll fucking *end you* if you harm one purple hair on his head."

"There's the sass I've missed so much," Jackson says, finally making an appearance. He saunters toward me with that infamous shit-eating grin of his, his messy blond hair tousled all over his face and those mischievous blue eyes raking me in from head to toe.

I fling my arms around his neck, stretching up to nuzzle my mouth into his neck. "I missed you too. So, so much." I cling to him, pressing my body flush against his, feeling imaginary daggers embedding into my back the more I hold onto him.

It takes Jackson all of point five seconds to notice the obvious change to my silhouette. "Holy fucking shit, beautiful." He holds me at arm's length, his eyes almost bugging out of his head as he ogles my boobs. "Your tits are fucking fantastic."

"I had a feeling you might like," I tease, gripping onto his waist as I shamelessly flirt with him.

"Can I feel?" he asks, making a cupping motion with his hands as he waggles his brows.

"If you want to eat shit for the rest of your life," Kai replies, injecting himself into our conversation.

"You can feel," I blurt, wanting to take back control. Before Kai can protest, I grab Jackson's hands, planting them firmly on my chest. His heated gaze meets mine for a split second, and then he's gone.

In the blink of an eye, he's thrown to the floor, landing unceremoniously on his butt. He curls into a ball, clutching his stomach and cracking up laughing.

"You'll pay for that," Kai says, pulling me back, and he's practically dripping in rage.

"Bite me."

"I'll do more than that," he says, and my body hums with expectation.

"Oh, God." Sawyer emits a frustrated sigh. "I can't believe we're back to this." He shakes his head.

"She's a fucking handful," Rick agrees, and I swing for him. This time, he's ready, and he holds my fist in his hand, halting my punch before it makes contact.

"It's his fault too!" I protest.

"And now, you sound like a whiny three-year-old."

I stick my tongue out at him. "Don't forget you're on my Anderson shit list too."

"And let me guess. The only one not to make the list is Harley."

"Harley's sweet and hot as fuck," I say, purely to get a rise out of Kai. Plus, I know I'm about to lose that angle, so I want to piss him off first.

Kai tugs at his ear, like he can't believe what he just heard. "Come again?"

"Now, it adds up," Rick says, grinning. "You didn't hook up with Harley. That was an excuse so—"

He's cut off when a meaty hand wraps around his throat, restricting his air supply. Kai is puce in the face as he slams his older brother into the wall. "You have two seconds to explain before I dig a pit outside and bury every fucking one of you!" he yells, his gaze bouncing between the three guys in the room.

"What the actual fuck…" Joaquin says, rushing into the room, his words dying out when he spots Rick smashed against the wall with Kai's hand around his neck, "is going on?"

Harley races in behind him, sending panicked eyes in my direction, and guilt churns in my gut.

"That's what I'd like to know." Kai bores a hole in the side of Harley's head, and his cheeks darken. "Over here now," he commands, slapping Rick's cheek before releasing him. Rick punches him in the gut, but it's lacking power because Kai doesn't even flinch. He just smirks. That horrible smug smirky thing he does that makes me want to claw my nails down his face.

"Asshole," Rick spits, rubbing at his neck.

Kai ignores him, slinging his arm around his younger brother's shoulder in a threatening manner. "Spill. And hold nothing back, or I'll know."

"I'm sorry, Kai!" Harley says, his voice quaking. "I shouldn't have drunk the tequila because I got wasted, and I don't remember any of it, but I didn't mean to do it. I know she's your girl, and I'd never have touched her if I wasn't so trashed." The confession spews from his mouth like projectile vomit.

"What did you do?" Kai locks eyes with me as he asks his brother the question.

"I don't know," Harley wails, and his lower lip wobbles. "All I know is they found us in our underwear in bed." He pins sorrowful eyes on his brother. "I'm sorry, Kai. And I promise it won't happen again. Please don't hate me."

Fuck this shit. I've got to end this before poor Harley cries. "Nothing happened," I admit, because I can't stand to see the anguish in Harley's eyes. "I just made it look like that." Harley's head whips around to mine, his eyes splayed wide. "I'm sorry. It was a shitty thing to do, but I had to cover my tracks and there wasn't time for anything else."

"Because you snuck out and bought the cell phone," Rick says, joining the dots. I nod. "How? You had no cash."

"I sweet-talked Harley into giving me cash for snacks, made a deal with the girl in reception so I could borrow her ride, and then got him drunk superfast so he passed out and I could leave."

Jackson chuckles. "Resourceful as ever, beautiful, and my offer still stands." He palms his crotch, giving it a quick stroke. "Whenever you ditch the caveman, I'll be right here waiting."

"As will my fists," Kai cuts in. "I'm fucking warning you, Lauder. You're on thin ice with me, so quit that shit. She's carrying my baby, and I'm fucked if I'll sit by and let you drool all over her. That goes for all of you." His gaze bounces between his brothers and his friends. He lets Harley go. "You too, Har."

His voice and his expression gentles, and it's fascinating watching him handle someone with kid gloves. "It's okay. I don't blame you." His eyes settle on mine momentarily. "It's hard to deny her when she lays on the charm." He messes up Harley's hair, and I smother a smile when Harley scowls, swatting his hand away. "Don't go anywhere alone with her because I don't trust her not to try something again."

I roll my eyes. "Oh, puh-lease. There's no need to make out like I'm Mata Hari."

"Who's Mati Hara?" Harley asks, scratching the side of his head.

"*Mata Hari* was a Dutch dancer who used seduction tactics to spy for the Germans during World War One," Sawyer explains.

"Xavier told me about her one time," I say. "One of his many random but interesting facts." I tap a finger off my chin, fighting the laughter bubbling up my throat. "Now that I think about it, you two are *so alike*. You're virtually a match made in heaven. I know Xavier thinks you're hot. Do you think he's hot?" I ask Sawyer, waggling my brows. "If you let him come here, I'll sign up to play matchmaker."

"Does anyone have a muzzle?" Sawyer replies, pursing his lips and narrowing his eyes.

"I'm only trying to inject some energy into your love life. No need to be mean."

"I'm perfectly capable of finding a willing partner to share my bed with no interference from you." He crosses his feet at the ankles as he leans back against the dresser. "And we all know that's a smokescreen. You're just trying to get your buddy here."

"Do you blame me?" My brows climb to my hairline. "You could at least give me one ally."

"*We're* your allies," Jackson says, anxiously swiping his hands up and down the front of his jeans.

"And it's safer for Xavier if he doesn't know where we are," Sawyer says, and I believe it when it comes from his mouth.

"He told me to turn the cell on when I got here and he'd be able to trace it," I admit.

"When did you turn it on?" Sawyer inquires.

"When we reached this property."

His shoulders relax. "It's fine then. He can't trace you in this town."

"Why not?" I'm naturally curious when it comes to tech stuff.

"There are a few places in the US that are satellite black spots, and this is one of them," Sawyer says.

"What exactly does it mean?" I ask, although I can guess.

"Think of it like a black cloud over this town masking everything from sight. So, even though your father is deploying high-tech strategies using satellites and software image recognition to search for us, it hides us under the cloud."

"How do you connect to the net then?"

"I have a USB dongle connected to a private hidden network owned by my father."

"And why wouldn't my cell work here?"

"Because I installed a blocker. We use ours with a code which bypasses the security, so don't even think of trying to steal ours. The code has to be input with every action, and you won't be able to use the phone without it."

"And Rick's friends just happened to have a cabin in *this* town?" I'm skeptical in the extreme.

"They chose this spot for the privacy it offered them."

"So, they're, like, famous or something?"

"Or something," Rick cryptically replies. "The most important thing is we're hidden here, and we need to keep it that way."

A loud yawn escapes my mouth that second, and a blanket of tiredness swathes me. My eyes close for a nanosecond, and I sway a little on my feet. An arm encircles my waist from behind, and I'd know his touch anywhere.

"Get out," Kai says, and my eyes pop open. "Abby's tired."

"You want something to eat, beautiful?" Jackson asks, as the others dutifully shuffle toward the door.

"I got it covered," Kai barks, his tone warning Jackson to back off.

I shuck out of his hold. "You can leave too."

He smirks. "Nice try. I'm going nowhere."

I snatch my measly plastic bag up. "Then I'm taking another room."

His smirk extends and I want to smack him in his gorgeous mouth. "There are only five bedrooms here and they're all occupied. You're stuck with me. Deal with it."

"I'll sleep on the couch," I say, walking toward the door where Sawyer and Jackson are lounging, watching this play out.

"You're not sleeping on the couch." Kai fists a hand in my dress, yanking me back.

"Stop manhandling me! I'm not your property." I wriggle out of his hold.

"Stop pissing me off, Abigail." His eyes burn with uncaged frustration. "You're pregnant with my kid, so that means I get a say. And I'm saying get your cranky ass in that bed asap!" He turns me around by the shoulders, frog marching me toward the bed.

"Get your hands off me."

"Not happening, baby." He pats my ass and a red haze creeps over my retinas. I spin around, my hand raised, ready to slap him again, but his reflexes are fast, and he grabs both my wrists as he pushes me back into the wall. Keeping my arms above my head, he presses his body along the length of mine, and I pray for self-control.

He let you believe he was Camden Marshall for months, and he was an obnoxious, cruel asshole.

He put his cock in you when you had no idea he was Kaiden Anderson.

He deserves nothing but your wrath.

I repeat those statements on a mantra in a loop in my mind, hoping they sink in.

Honestly, it's embarrassing how much power he has over my body, and I need to win back control.

"Stop fighting me, because you know what it does to me, or do you need a reminder?" He swivels his hips, drilling his point home.

"Get your motherfucking lying cock away from me," I hiss, and Jackson chuckles.

"Do you mind?" Kai says, whipping his head around to glare at his friends.

"Not at all," Jackson says, idly tapping his fingers off his jean-clad thigh. "Don't worry about us. We're enjoying the show."

"I'll grab the popcorn," Sawyer jokes, grinning.

"I'm glad someone's amused," Kai drawls, "because I'm two seconds away from putting her stubborn ass over my lap and teaching her a lesson she won't forget."

"Don't hold back on our account," Jackson says, winking.

"I thought you were on my side!" I holler.

"I'm always on your side, beautiful, but that doesn't mean I'm against punishing you."

"Lauder." Kai's growl is back, and he's riled up. I feel a smug sense of satisfaction knowing that I've wound him up nice and good from the minute I arrived here.

"Do everyone a favor and fuck off to the couch," I say. "Because it's you go or I do."

"I'm not sleeping on the fucking couch!" he roars.

"Jackson." I calmly call out, avoiding eye contact with Kai.

"Yes, beautiful."

"Can I sleep in your room with you?"

"Sure thing." He walks forward with a spring in his step. "Grab your shit and let's go."

A strangled sound rips from Kai's chest, and he looks like he's about to implode. Dropping my hands, he steps back and starts pacing, scrubbing a hand back and forth across his stubbly jawline, as if he's trying to talk himself off a ledge. "You're lucky you're pregnant," he says, pointing at me. "Because that's the only reason

I'm not angry-fucking that disobedience out of you."

"It wouldn't be happening whether I'm pregnant or not," I argue. "You and me are done. Finito. Sayonara. Arrivederci. And however you say finished or goodbye in a hundred different languages."

He grabs fistfuls of his hair, and his mouth opens and closes as he wages some form of inner battle. I know he wants to punish me, but the pregnancy card is already paying dividends. He sends a scathing look at me before storming out of the room, violently shoving past Jackson and Sawyer on his way.

I share a grin with Jackson. "Oops. Was it something I said?"

CHAPTER ELEVEN

The battle of wills with Kai drains me, and I crawl into bed, not remembering how or when I fall asleep. Only that I wake up, in the middle of the night, crying out as the usual nightmares torment me. I bolt upright in the unfamiliar bed, the cotton dress stuck to my back like glue.

"What's wrong?" a gruff voice asks, and I shriek as a blurry form moves at the side of my bed. "Shush, babe. It's just me." Kai sits upright in the chair, rubbing his sleepy eyes.

"Are you trying to give me a heart attack?" I slam a hand across my chest, willing my thumping heart to calm down.

"Of course not."

"Then what are you doing in here?" I lean back against the headrest. "I thought I made myself perfectly clear."

"Don't." He leans forward, and shadows cast strange shapes across his handsome face. "I don't want to fight with you."

"You can't keep forcing yourself into my life when I don't want you in it."

He releases a tired sigh. "We both know that's bullshit, but whatever."

My tummy grumbles loudly, reminding me I haven't eaten in hours.

Kai stands. "I'll get you something to eat."

"You don't have to do that." I don't want to be beholden to him, and him doing nice shit for me weakens my resolve.

"I'm offering. Doesn't happen often, and I suggest you accept."

I can't see his face properly in this light, but I know he's glaring at me, and challenging me to argue. I should decline, but I'm too exhausted, and way too tired to fight this fight, so I give in. "Okay, thanks."

He pads quietly out of the room, and I use the opportunity to pee, brush my teeth, and strip the sweaty dress off my gross body. I take a thirty-second shower to freshen up, taking care not to get my hair wet, and then I find a light nightdress belonging to Faye and change into it before slipping back under the covers. I switch on the lamp by the bed, noticing the bottle of water and a box of vitamins on top of the table.

I pick the box up, reading the label with a lump in my throat. Out of the corner of my eye, I notice Kai returning with a cup and a plate. I put the box down and sit up straighter in the bed.

Wordlessly, he hands me the steaming mug, and a freshly made sandwich.

"Thank you."

I wolf the sandwich down, enjoying a little internal laugh when I think of how disgusted the bastard would be if he could see me now. Perhaps that's why I cuss a lot more these days. I'm subconsciously rebelling against everything my father asked of me. He's got to be pissed I'm missing, and I'm thinking being isolated here could be for the best.

My eyes meander to the box of vitamins as I set my empty plate down.

"I, uh, picked them up in the pharmacy in town," Kai explains. "Rick told me to get folic acid, but the pharmacist recommended those multivitamins. She said it's what everyone is taking during pregnancy nowadays."

I eye him over the lid of my mug as I sip my hot chocolate. He's such an enigma, but I don't trust he's not up to something. "What game are you playing now?" I narrow my eyes. "What's in those pills?"

He leans forward, resting his elbows on the edge of the bed. "I'm not playing any game, Abby. Not anymore." His earnest expression crashes into me. "And it's just vitamins. I swear. Why can't you believe I just want to take care of both of you?" His voice turns soft, and the sandwich threatens to make a reappearance.

"I'm tired." I put my half-empty mug down on the table, sliding back under the covers. Rolling onto my side, I face the wall, fighting the imminent onslaught of tears.

"Abby," he whispers, and the bed dips as he sits down. "I want to hold you."

"Don't, Kai." My voice cracks and I'm losing control of my emotions. "Just don't."

The bed jerks as he gets up, dropping into the chair again with a loud, frustrated sigh. "Just so you know, I'm not giving up," he whispers. "You can push me away. Bait me. Lash out at me. Do your worst. And I'll take it. Because I deserve it. But I'm going nowhere, Abby. I'll be your perpetual shadow, because no one or nothing is taking you from me again." The chair squeaks as he gets comfortable. "And that includes you."

I'm the first one up the following morning, and I'm glad, because I'm jittery and on edge and I need some alone time to formulate a new plan. Baking has always soothed me, and the house is fully stocked, so I spend a couple of blissful hours baking pancakes, muffins, and cupcakes, leaving them on the counter to cool while I grab my coffee and a blanket and head out onto the deck which faces the rear of the property.

Kai already has my heart and my head in a tailspin, and I wish I knew how to cut the ties that bind us, because I'm sick of being a slave to my hormones and my emotions. Except for my anger. I cling to that, because it's the only barrier, the only weapon, I have against him.

I'm tucked up under the blanket, enjoying the fresh brisk air slapping my cheeks, when the door slides open and Jackson sticks his head out. "What the fuck are you doing out here?" he inquires, shivering. "It's cold enough to freeze my balls off."

"It's not cold under the blanket." I tilt my head to the side. "Grab a coffee and come join me."

He returns a couple minutes later wrapped up in a puffy jacket and scarf with a beanie pulled down over his head. "You're such a wimp." I open one side of the blanket. "Come on. I'll let you siphon some of my body heat."

"Tempting as that is, beautiful, I still value breathing. And Kai already wants to murder me in cold blood and feed me, in little pieces, to the sharks at the Rydeville Aquarium."

"This caveman act is getting real old," I admit, warming my hands around the fresh cup of coffee he hands me.

"Get used to it. You're his baby momma. It will only get worse."

I stare out at the lake, wishing I could dunk my entire body into the water until I can't feel anything anymore.

"He was so worried about you," Jackson says, slurping from his mug. "We all were."

"Maybe if you'd told me what was going on, things would've turned out differently that night."

"Truth." He leans back, sliding his arm along the seat behind me.

"But you'd run off to Jane's, and that asshole Atticus brought his plan forward. There wasn't any way of warning you."

I turn sideways to look at him. "You don't like him either, huh?"

"He's a twisted old fuck, and he basically checked out for years, leaving Kai and Rick to run things when they were only kids themselves."

"If that's the case, why does he have such a strong hold over them?"

Jackson shrugs. "I used to joke it was like Stockholm Syndrome, and now I'm not so sure I wasn't right."

"He's their only surviving parent," Sawyer says, startling both of us as he steps out onto the deck. "And even if he's a shitty one, he's all they have." He walks toward us, taking the space on the other side of me. I open up the blanket, and he tucks it up under his chin, smiling at me.

"They want to please him," I surmise.

Sawyer nods. "And they were kind of brainwashed into believing all Mannings were the scourge of the Earth."

"Gee, thanks." I roll my eyes.

"Apart from you, it's not far off the mark," Jackson says.

"Drew isn't like that," I quietly say, feeling the need to defend my brother, even if I'm torn over his loyalty. Jackson and Sawyer exchange a loaded look, and I glare at them. "No more fucking secrets. If you've something to say, just say it."

"Drew's…acting a little strange," Sawyer says. "And no one knows what the fuck he's up to."

"You've spoken to him?" Because the last I remember the old elite and new elite weren't on speaking terms.

"Not directly, but we have people watching stuff for us back in Rydeville," he confirms.

"Word on the street is your twin is your father's newest bitch,"

Jackson adds with a bite to his tone, his knee tapping up and down.

"If that's the case then he's playing some angle."

"You really believe that or you're trying to convince yourself," Sawyer asks.

"My whole life Drew has been there for me. I don't understand what he's up to now, and I'm still pissed at him for not protecting me in the office that day, and for keeping shit from me, but I've had time to think about it, and I think it's part of some bigger plan."

"For your sake, I hope that's true," Jackson says.

"Stop." I clamp my hand down on his knee. "Why are you so jittery? You were like that last night too."

"Because going cold turkey sucks."

Shock splays across my face. "You're giving up your stoner ways?"

"Don't get too excited," he says. "It's only temporary until Harley and Joaquin go back to school."

"Ah, I get it. Kai and Rick don't want you setting a bad example." He nods. "Wow. They really are protective of them."

"You've no idea," Sawyer says. "They would take a bullet for their brothers, and they've done everything to keep them shielded from this world."

"But it's more than that," Jackson says.

"Lauder." Sawyer silences him with a warning tone.

"What else don't I know?"

"Tons, beautiful. There's tons of stuff you don't know."

Sawyer rolls his eyes. "I think I preferred you when you were a non-interfering stoner."

"Can't say I enjoy having a clear head, but it's brought some perspective," Jackson admits.

"Like what?" Kai drawls, emerging on the deck in a black puffy jacket similar to the one Jackson's got on. His long legs are encased in dark jeans and he's wearing scuffed black boots on his feet.

Jackson glances over his shoulder. "Like Abby shouldn't be kept in the dark any longer. She deserves to know the full truth."

"Says you and whose army?" he asks, standing in front of us with his usual disapproving scowl.

"Look at what all the secrets and lies have done to our families," I say. "Do we want to continue that tradition?"

Kai props his butt against the railing, a muscle tensing in his jaw as he eyes me huddled in between his two best friends. "No, but what Lauder fails to understand is that sharing certain truths places you in grave danger, and I will not do that."

"You'd rather keep lying to me." My mouth pulls tight.

"I will tell you when it is safe to do so."

"That's fucking bullshit! Keeping me in the dark puts me in more danger because I can't see the trap until I've fallen in. At least if I knew what to look out for, I could avoid it!"

"I'll tell you what you need to know, and the rest of the time I'll be the one watching your back. I'll ensure you don't fall into any traps."

I snort, tossing the blanket off and rising. "Don't do me any favors, Cam!" I snap, and he flinches. "What?"

"You called him Cam," Jackson says.

"Because it's all I knew for months." I rein my anger in, curiosity getting the better of me. "How did your cousin die, anyway?" I ask, softening my tone. "All your father said was he'd died when he was two. What happened?"

"He had a rare heart defect," he says. "My aunt put him to bed one night, and the next morning, she found him dead in his crib. They've never recovered from it, and they were too afraid to risk having any more kids."

"I'm sorry. That's so sad."

"Taking his identity never felt right to me." He comes closer, and his chest brushes against mine. "And it never felt right hiding who I was with you, either. But there were good reasons for it. I know you're pissed. But I meant what I said to you that night, Abby. You mean *everything*." He palms my face, peering deep into my eyes. "And I won't apologize for doing what I believe is right to protect you and our unborn child. You just need to trust me."

I remove his hands from my face and take a step back. "How can I after everything you've hidden from me? And now you stand here, blatantly confirming you're continuing to conceal things and you expect me to *just trust you*?" I shake my head. "Trust must be earned, *Kaiden*, and all you've done is earn my wrath." I walk toward the sliding doors, turning at the last second. "And I don't know if there is any way to return from that."

CHAPTER TWELVE

"Please let me call him." I send doe eyes at Sawyer. "I know you have a way of communicating that's safe. Xavier will go crazy because he hasn't heard from me."

Kai walks into the living room with a box in his hand.

"And I need to make sure Charlie is okay. I'm worried about my fiancé." I *am* worried for my friend, because I'm sure the bastard blames him for losing me, but I tagged that on the end purely for Kai's benefit.

Predictably, Kai slams the box down on the coffee table, sending daggers in my direction. "For the last time, you are not marrying that asshole." His eyes flit to the glistening diamond on my hand. "And take that fucking ring off before I pry it from your finger."

I've been wearing it to piss him off, and I love that it's working. "You're not involved in this decision." I curl my feet up under me, smiling sweetly at him as I prepare to deliver the blow. "I love him, and I *will* marry him." I shrug, as if it's no biggie. "And we've already consummated our relationship anyway."

Tension bleeds into the air, and Kai's eyes flash with a dark warning. "That better be a lie."

"It is," Rick says, glancing up from the book he's immersed in.

"We tailed her all the way from Parkhurst, and she wasn't out of our sight."

I smirk. "It happened Friday night when he showed up at my room with my father."

"You're lying." Kai's jaw is taut as he glares at me.

"I'm not." I stare him straight in the eye and blatantly lie. "You've been gone for years. You've no idea what we mean to one another."

"Enlighten me," he says, cracking his knuckles.

"He was my first kiss," I truthfully admit, "and I've spent years wishing my father had chosen him for me instead of Trent."

Another fact.

"And I'd always secretly hoped the reason Charlie never fucked around at Rydeville High or had a steady girlfriend was because he shared my feelings."

Now, that part is most definitely a lie.

Well, the part about me hoping that was the reason. After Charlie's declaration, there's a part of me that now believes it might be true.

Whether it's the truth doesn't matter though. Because it's a plausible statement, and Kai is buying it.

Planting his large palms on either side of me, he leans down, caging me in and fixing me with a menacing look. "Charlie is a dead man walking if he has laid a finger on you."

"I guess now isn't a good time to mention he kissed her. Repeatedly," Rick supplies.

Kai jerks his head up, shooting an exasperated look at his brother. "And you were going to tell me this when?"

"It's obvious she's not into him, so I didn't think it mattered."

"I'm into him," I blurt. "I'm *really* into him. He's the only one I want."

Kai thumps the arm of the couch, and a vein pops in his neck. "*You are mine*, and we both know it."

"I'm *his* now. And I've never been happier."

Kai rolls his neck from side to side, pounds his fist into the couch, and grits his teeth in a way that looks painful as he contemplates my words. His dark eyes stab me in warning, and I've never seen him so enraged. "That motherfucking, double-crossing, two—"

"We don't have time to waste on Charlie Barron," Sawyer says, cutting across whatever Kai was about to say. He levels him with one of those intense looks I've seen all three of them share.

"What is that?" I ask. "What are you silently communicating?"

"Nothing." Sawyer dismisses it with a wave of his hand, and my blood boils.

"God, you're infuriating."

Kai barks out a laugh, straightening up. "You're kidding, right?"

"Suck dick." I flip him the bird and get up, jabbing him in the ribs as I push past.

"Where the fuck do you think you're going?" He yanks me back by my shirt.

"To my room."

"You mean *my* room?" His look is suggestive in the extreme. "I can get behind that plan."

My lips tug up. "Actually, I've changed my mind. I'll hang out in Jackson's room." I shrug. "Maybe watch some pornos or play strip poker."

"Get your annoying ass in the car," he snaps, grabbing my elbow.

"Eat shit and die."

"That muzzle suggestion is sounding more and more appealing," Kai says to Sawyer. "Can you order one online and have it delivered?"

"I'm on it." Sawyer smirks, and I flip him off too.

Kai slaps the keys in my hand. "Go wait for me."

"I don't take orders from you." He slaps my butt, and I yelp, rubbing my sore ass as I glare at him. "I still don't take orders from you." I fold my arms across my body, daring him to slap me again.

He does.

Even harder this time.

I swing my fist, aiming for his face, but he takes hold of my wrist, stalling me. "You don't want to push me, baby. Do what you're told, or I'll redden your ass and make it so you can't sit down for a week."

"I hate you."

"Right now, the feeling is mutual. *Get* in the car."

I stomp out of the room, mumbling obscenities under my breath the entire time. I'm halfway across the path between the house and the garage when I spy Jackson up ahead. He's in his running gear, and he's jogging straight toward me. "Sup, beautiful?" he pants, yanking the buds from his ears when he reaches me.

"You went running without me?"

He swipes his arm along his sweat-slickened brow. "Didn't think you'd be up for it in your condition."

I snort. "I'm pregnant, not incapacitated. And keeping fit is important."

"Cool." He shoves damp strands of hair back off his brow. "I go running every morning, and you're welcome to join me. There are tons of good routes to run on the grounds."

"It's a date."

"What is?" An angry voice barks at my back.

"Your misguided possessiveness is pathetic." My lips curl into a sneer. "And you'll give yourself an ulcer if you keep this up."

"The only thing giving me an ulcer is you," he retorts, grabbing my elbow and dragging me away from Jackson.

"You're hurting her," Jackson says, pinning angry eyes on his buddy as he takes a step forward.

"No, I'm not. And even if I was, it's none of your business. I won't tell you again, Lauder. Butt the fuck out."

"Someone needs to remind you to remove your head from your ass," Jackson says. "Before you fuck everything up."

"Pot, kettle, black, dude." Kai keeps a tight hold on me as he manhandles me toward the garage.

"Why are you pissed at him?" I ask, glancing over my shoulder. Jackson hasn't moved from his spot, and he's watching us as he sips from a bottle of water with steam practically billowing from his ears. Kai's last retort got to him.

Kai ignores me at first, hauling me to a large Land Rover with blacked-out windows. He opens the passenger door, grips my hips, and sets me down in the seat, before strapping me in as if I'm a little kid and incapable of buckling a seatbelt.

He slides in behind the wheel, slamming his door shut with more force than necessary. His knuckles blanch white as he grips the wheel tightly, making no move to start the car. "Why aren't *you* is a more interesting question."

"Jackson hasn't betrayed me."

"Hasn't he?" He swivels in his seat, facing me. "Hunt and Lauder were part of the plan too. They both kept stuff from you, but I'm the only one you're mad at."

"They weren't concealing their true identities!! And they weren't sleeping in my bed at night and holding me in their arms like it meant something."

"Of course, it meant something." He starts the engine. "And you fucking know it."

I won't dignify that with a response, so I stay quiet, pouting and sulking and plotting ways to hurt him.

Sawyer steps in front of the car, just as Kai is about to drive forward. He comes around to my window, gesturing at me to lower it. Kai presses the button from his side, lowering my window all the way. "What?" I snap.

"Wow. Someone's in a good mood."

I cross my arms and glare at him. "Did you want something?"

"Don't call Xavier from town. Your father is most likely tracking him, and he can trace the call to here. I know you're mad at Anderson, but don't put his life in danger."

"I would never put his life in danger," I truthfully admit. "No matter how mad I am at him. Contrary to what you seem to think of me, I don't condone violence or murder."

He places his hand on my forearm. "I know that, but a friendly reminder of all that's at stake can't hurt."

I offer him a curt nod. "I won't call Xavier. I promise." And I mean it.

I expect Kai to offer some commentary on that discussion as we drive away from the house, but he's stubbornly silent. We don't speak *at all*, even though I'm dying to know where we're going. But it can't be far, and I won't give him the satisfaction of asking.

We emerge from the long driveaway onto the bumpy narrow road, and I pull my legs into my chest, wrapping my arms around them. He glances at me strangely.

"What?" He ignores me. "Why did you look at me like that?" I demand.

"No reason," he coolly replies, and I scowl at him. His lips pull into a smile. "You hate not knowing, don't you?"

"Doesn't everyone?"

His good humor fades, and he tightens his grip on the wheel. "I know you're winding me up about Barron, but I want to make myself absolutely clear. No other man is raising that kid but me."

I snort. "Because you're *so* qualified."

His nostrils flare. "I basically raised my brothers, and they've turned out okay."

"You're hardly a worthy role model," I scoff, pulling my mouth into a sneer.

The car lurches to the side of the road and slams to a halt. I bounce in my seat with the motion. "What the fuck does that mean?" he spits out.

"You're not capable of raising a kid. You're an abusive, bullying asshole who lies like it's second nature. That's hardly a sound moral compass to teach an impressionable child. God only knows how many ways you've fucked up your brothers. I feel sorry for them."

Steam is practically billowing out of his ears, and his fingers twitch as his gaze drops to my throat. "You want to wrap your hands around my throat. Don't you?" I taunt as I unbuckle my belt and climb across the console. "*Do it.*" I arch my neck, thrusting my face all up in his. "I already know the truth of who you are. Do it. You hate me because I'd rather kiss, fuck, *and* marry Charlie Barron than raise a kid with you." I lick his cheek. "You want to hurt me," I whisper against his ear. "I see it in your face." I lick his other cheek, and he's grasping the wheel so tight now I doubt any blood is flowing to his fingers. "I see it in the way your muscles are straining against your shirt." I drop my hand to his lap, rubbing my palm against the growing bulge in his pants. "I feel it in your growing erection." I nip at his earlobe. "You want to hurt me, so do it."

I'm off his lap, and back in my seat, before I've even blinked. He radiates anger. Like, I can almost see it dripping off him in thick, gloopy lumps. "You don't know what you're saying." His voice is guttural and low. "Heed this warning, Abby." He grips my chin, tipping my head back. "This is the last time you'll mention taking that baby from me." He tightens his grip, and it hurts. His jaw clenches, and his chest is heaving, and I've definitely struck a nerve. "I want to fuck you up so bad for this," he admits. The menacing look on his face and deathly quality to his voice work this time.

Now, I'm afraid.

But I'm not apologizing.

I'll say sorry when he does.

He lets go of my chin, and I resist the urge to rub at it. "I'm not losing that baby." His determined eyes drill into mine, and a shiver works its way through me. My heart races around my rib cage, and I've stopped breathing. "No one is taking him or her away from me." His eyes glaze over, his entire body shakes with unrestrained anger, and he looks seconds away from losing it.

"Don't move!" he barks before climbing out of the car and stalking across the road. He disappears into the forest, and I let out the breath I was holding.

Adrenaline still flows through my veins, and nausea churns in my gut, but my skin tingles all over, and a deep ache pulses between my thighs.

I wonder if Kai felt like that all the times he was pushing me. It's a weird blend of arousal and sheer terror that is both exciting and shameful.

Closing my eyes, I lean my head back as I wait for him to return. I doze off until I'm woken by the loud slamming of the door. I jerk my eyes open, regarding him carefully. His mask is back in place as he kick-starts the engine and maneuvers the car back out onto the road. He refuses to look at me, or speak to me, and that suits me perfectly.

My gaze flits to his shredded, bloodied knuckles, and I turn my head toward the window so he doesn't see my smile.

I'm getting to him.

And it feels good.

Fuck feeling guilty.

This is no time to grow a conscience.

After all the shit he's pulled on me, I'm entitled to some payback.

CHAPTER THIRTEEN

Kai pulls the car into a parking lot of a small shopping mall and parks the car. He gets out, without uttering a word, rounds the front of the car, and opens my door. "Out."

"Is that anyway to speak to your baby momma?" I chastise.

"You have ten seconds to get your ass out of that seat or I'm turning around and going back. It's no skin off my nose if you want to continue borrowing Faye's shit."

I scramble out of the car, trailing behind him as we approach the row of storefronts. It's bitterly cold today, and a harsh wind swirls around me, causing me to shiver uncontrollably. He comes to a halt in front of me, turning around as he unzips his jacket.

"I don't—"

He places his hand over my mouth as he slips off his jacket. "Don't test me."

I say nothing as he puts the jacket on me, zipping it up to my chin, and I fight the delicious tremors running riot throughout my body as his hands brush against me. Taking my hand, he walks with purpose toward the store at the far end on the right-hand side.

"I'll wait outside. Let me know when you're done," he says, without looking at me, when we reach our destination. Flattening his back against the window of the women's clothing store, he settles in to wait, stretching out his long legs and crossing his ankles at the feet.

I move to enter the store when he clamps a hand down on my arm. "Grab a warm jacket. Weather forecast isn't great for the next couple weeks. There's even talk of snow."

I bob my head before pushing through the double doors into the store. I grab a cart and start loading up on essentials. They don't have a huge selection, and it's hardly haute couture, but what they have is stylish and good quality, and it should last me until I can figure out a way to get the hell away from here. I toss some makeup and toiletries in the cart too, bringing them to the girl at the counter to ring up. Her eyes are out on stalks as she surveys my stash, and I'm guessing they get little business around here.

I poke my head out the door. "I need cash."

Removing his wallet from the back pocket of his jeans, he pulls out a wad of bills, thrusting it in my fist. "If you need more, let me know."

I pay the pretty cashier, and as I'm reaching for the bags, the door swings open, and I sense him invading my airspace. The cashier's eyes light up in interest, and she unbuttons a couple buttons on top of her shirt and leans forward on the counter as Kai approaches, ensuring he's got a perfect view of her cleavage.

If I wasn't so pissed, it might impress me. Girl's got game. And balls as big as any guy because it's clear he's here for me, yet that doesn't stop her flirting her ass off. "Hi there." She flashes him a blinding smile. "Is there something I can help you with today?"

"I don't know," he says, shooting her a blinding smile in return. "What are you offering?"

"Whatever you like," she purrs in response, and she's just short of jumping over the counter and throwing herself at him.

I might as well be invisible, and my claws come out. "Sorry, I didn't get your name," I say, turning around and inspecting her name badge. "Candy." I shove the bags into Kai's chest and plant my hands on my hips. "Someone should have a word with your parents. That's way too sweet of a name for a dirty ho."

Her face transforms, a look of heated indignation appearing on her features. She straightens up, attempting to look down her nose at me. "Excuse me?"

"I wonder what your boss would think about you flirting so obviously—and pathetically, I might add—with the customers' boyfriends."

Her shoulders stiffen. "He was flirting with *me*," she says, all smug and superior. "And is it any wonder if he's stuck with a bitch like you?"

I'm opening my mouth to retaliate when Kai drops the bags, reels me back, and leans forward, putting his face all up in hers. "That's my baby momma you're disrespecting, so I'd tread carefully if I was you." His voice reeks of danger, and I just know he's giving her one of his lethal stares. The kind to dampen your panties and scare the shit out of you at the same time.

She's all flustered, and her mouth is opening and shutting like a fish out of water.

"Are we done?" I ask, inspecting my nails and sounding bored on purpose.

"We're done, babe." Kai pushes off the counter, grabbing my face and planting a quick hard kiss on my lips. My head is spinning when he slings his arm around my shoulders and steers me out of the store.

"You two nutjobs deserve one another," she screams after us, and I burst out laughing.

"Truer words have never been spoken," Kai deadpans, winking at me as we walk toward the car. "And I needed to prove a point," he adds.

"Okay. I'll bite."

"You were jealous even though you knew I was provoking you." He tightens his arm around my shoulder.

"I guess I deserve that." Because I've made him jealous since I arrived.

He helps me up into the car, buckling me into my seat, purposely brushing his fingers against my body, and I want to wipe the smug smile off his face.

He climbs in beside me, securing his seatbelt, but he doesn't start the car immediately. "It's not for the reasons you think," he says, peering deep into my eyes.

"Why then?"

"I wanted you to see that you already consider yourself mine." He kick-starts the engine with another smug grin on his face. "You can deny it all you want, Abby. But we both know the truth. You just confirmed it back there."

"What are we doing now?" I ask as Kai pulls up in front of the quaint diner on the main street in town.

He kills the engine, spearing me with a look. "What does it look like we're doing?" He rolls his eyes.

"Do not roll your eyes at me." He does it again, and I flip him off.

"You're getting far too fond of that, and it's beneath you." He dares me to argue, snatching my hand before I can shove my middle finger up again, planting a kiss on my knuckles before I can raise an objection. "And we'll both need to rein shit in when the baby comes."

My heart does that twisty thing again, and I wrest my hand away. "Stop touching me."

"You like my hands on you," he says, climbing out of the car. Like before, he walks around to the passenger side, opens the door, grips my hips, and lifts me down.

"No. I don't." I pout.

"Every time you deny it, you just prove my point." He laces his fingers through mine, pulling me up onto the curb. "So, continue lying, but you're no better than me."

"It is not the same thing, and you know it."

He spins around, dropping his hands to my lower back and drawing me into his body. "Everyone tells lies, Abby. Especially in our world. But it's the motivation behind the deceit that matters."

"That's the biggest load of bull crap I've ever heard and a convenient excuse to hide behind."

"I'm protecting what's mine, and I'll never apologize for that."

"You can't keep lying to me, Kai, irrespective of the motive."

He leans down to kiss me, and I turn my head to the side. His lips brush against my cheek, and I smirk, but my victory is short-lived. Cupping my face firmly, he holds my head in place as his mouth descends, and this time, I'm powerless to stop it. I clamp my lips together, refusing to kiss him back, and he chuckles against my mouth. "You're driving me fucking insane, babe," he says, thrusting his hips into my pelvis. "But it turns me on like you wouldn't believe." His tongue prods the seam of my lips, demanding entry, and my resolve is wavering.

"You're sick in the head," I retort, realizing my mistake the second the words leave my mouth. He seizes the opportunity, pushing his tongue into my mouth while angling his head and deepening the kiss.

And I'm a goner.

His kisses suck me in and claim every part of me.

I feel the seductive caress of his lips in every molecule of my being.

Filling me up.

Heating me on contact.

Confirming his truth, and making me a liar, but I can't stop.

My body melts against him, and my hands have a mind of their own as they creep up his broad chest and circle his neck. Our kissing turns frantic, and I can't get enough. I claw at him, pulling him closer, needing this connection as badly as I need air to breathe.

And we're devouring one another.

On the sidewalk.

In broad daylight.

In front of everyone.

I know all this. But I can't stop.

No one has ever kissed me the way Kai kisses me.

His mouth can worship and punish me at the same time, and he ignites an inferno in my body with every sweep of his hot lips.

I'm grinding against him as intense need floods my core, and I'm considering jumping his bones when a loud chuckle breaks through the lust-fueled haze in my brain, clearing my thoughts.

I rip my mouth from his, disgusted with myself.

"Young love." A portly man with a mop of gray hair and a thick bushy mustache smiles warmly at both of us. "I remember it well." His happy smile fades a little. "Enjoy it, young'uns, because the years fly by, and before you know it, your loved one is gone, and all you're left with are the memories of her kiss."

"I'm so sorry for your loss," I say, feeling an overwhelming need to comfort him.

"You've got a good one there, son," he says to Kai. "Make sure you hold on to her."

"I'm trying, sir." Kai's response startles me. "But she isn't making it easy."

The man chuckles again, his melancholy forgotten. "Then she's definitely worth fighting for," he says, before adding, "Now, you two, have a good day." He tips his hat and walks off, leaving us staring after him, both in a bit of a daze.

"Can we call a truce?" Kai asks when we're seated in the diner a few minutes later, having just given our orders to the waitress.

"Why would I do that?"

"Because all this arguing can't be good for the baby."

"What do you know about what *is* and *isn't* good for the baby?" I sip on my soda.

"I've had plenty of time on my hands lately, and I've been reading some pregnancy books."

My jaw drops to the floor, and he smiles.

"I'm sure I'm as close to an expert as you can get. Lucky for you." He waggles his brows before lifting his glass and drinking. I love the way his Adam's apple bobs in his throat when he swallows—it's sexy as fuck.

He smirks, and I lower my eyes, inwardly cussing. I can't drop the ball although maybe it's time for a slightly different strategy.

He's called me out on the deliberate flirting, so perhaps a more subtle approach will work.

"It probably is lucky," I admit, pinning him with puppy dog eyes. "Because I know next to nothing. I had no access to the net or books while I was at Parkhurst and no one to talk to about it."

He frowns a little. "They didn't check you out?"

"They did," I blurt, furiously backtracking. "But they wouldn't answer any of my questions."

"We need to book a doctor's appointment," he muses.

"There's no need. I'm only eight weeks pregnant, and they rarely conduct ultrasounds until week sixteen, so there's plenty of time."

"I thought you knew nothing?" he queries, leaning back in his seat as the waitress slides our plates in front of us.

I wait for her to leave, using the opportunity to calm down and keep a cool head. "The doctor in Rydeville told me that. She said she'd set up an appointment."

"I'll get Rick to organize something," he says.

"I'll be back in Rydeville in time to attend my appointment." I hold my chin up defiantly.

He stops with his burger midway to his mouth, setting it back down on his plate. "You can't go back to Rydeville. It's not safe."

"It's safer than being on the run," I retort.

"Not where your father is concerned." He takes a massive bite of his burger. I stab a fry with my fork and pop it in my mouth, chewing slowly. "And we can't be separated. I don't want to miss a second of your pregnancy. I want to be with you every step of the way."

Emotion clogs my throat, and I put my silverware down, unable to eat in case I choke. "Why?" I whisper.

"Why?" he asks, as if I'm crazy. "You're carrying my child. It's my responsibility."

A different kind of pain slices across my chest. The type that maims and sucks all the oxygen out of your lungs. I'm in agony on the inside, and it's too much pain to disguise.

He reaches across the table, clasping my hand. "Stop it, Abby."

"Stop what?" I yank my hand back.

"Whatever that crazy hormonal brain of yours is telling you right now."

"My crazy brain isn't telling me anything. You're the one that said it's your *responsibility*." I pierce him with a loaded look. "Don't do me any favors, Kai."

He grabs my hand more firmly this time. "That didn't come out right. Yes, it's my responsibility, but it's much more than that." He leans across the table. "Surely you see how much I care. I've never felt this way about any woman before. *Ever*." His eyes are like laser beams burning me with intense heat. "From the moment I met you, you've consumed my thoughts. You are my world, Abby. I want this baby."

His jaw tightens, and his eyes blaze with determination. "And I want you."

"That's—" My ears prick up, and I whip my head around, my eyes almost bugging out of my head when my gaze lands on the TV. "Oh, fuck," I whisper, staring in horror at my image on the screen. I read the headline with a mounting sense of trepidation.

MISSING MANNING HEIRESS IN GRAVE DANGER. SIZABLE REWARD FOR INFORMATION LEADING TO HER WHEREABOUTS.

CHAPTER FOURTEEN

Kai follows my gaze, shock splaying across his face. He throws a few bills down on the table. "We need to get out of here. Now." His face flashes on the screen, and my stomach churns sourly as I lock eyes with the waitress. All the blood has drained from her face as she recognizes us.

Kai takes my hand as he walks with urgency toward the exit, but I tug on his arm, holding him back.

"Abby," he hisses, as I step toward the waitress. "Don't."

"She could turn us in!" Fear bubbles to the surface as I look at him. "I need to try."

He thinks about it for a few beats, nodding curtly. I walk to the counter as she eyes me warily. "Please," I say, in a low voice, hiding my face behind my hair because the other diners don't appear to have noticed us or made the connection. "Please don't turn us in." I level her with earnest eyes. "My father is a monster who has abused me for years." I put my ring hand on the counter on purpose. "I ran off because I told him I was pregnant and engaged to the man I love. He's someone he doesn't approve of, so he's concocted this fake story to find us." I pray for forgiveness as I slide my hand across my tummy. "I'm begging you, on my unborn child's life, not to report this."

Kai slides his arms around me from behind, resting his chin on top of my head. I place my hands over his, on top of my stomach, pleading with my eyes. Slowly, she nods, and I slump against Kai in relief.

"I saw you outside," she admits. "And I could tell you were very much in love." She looks over my shoulder at Kai. "But I still need you to look me in the eye and tell me you mean her no harm."

"I promise I won't hurt her. I just want to keep them both safe. If her father finds us, there's a chance none of us will come out of this alive." I can't see his face, but his tone is even and sincere.

"I believe you," she says, glancing anxiously around. "You should go now before someone else recognizes you."

"Thank you."

"Good luck to you both."

We race out the door without looking back.

"Fuck." Rick slams his hand against the wall in the living room. "This is a nightmare. Where the hell are we going to go?"

"*We're* not going anywhere," Kai says. "We'll stay here, but you need to bring Harley and Joaquin back home, and you return to Harvard."

"What about Dad?" Rick asks.

"What about him?" Kai snarls. "You three tell him nothing. If he doesn't know where I am, he can't get to me."

"You know that won't cut it with him."

"Then tell him he's dead to me! And leaving me alone is in his best interests, because if I get my hands on him, who knows what I'm liable to do." Pure liquid venom spills from Kai's mouth, and I'm shocked to see it directed at his dad.

"What if the waitress changes her mind and reports it?" Rick asks, changing tack.

"She won't." I perch on the edge of the couch. "I'm good at reading people, and she won't say anything."

"I agree," Kai says.

"Wow." Jackson grins, his gaze dancing between us. "This is progress."

I poke my tongue out at him, and he chuckles.

"You did good, Abby," Sawyer says, lifting his head from his laptop.

"She did more than good," Kai supplies, and I detect a hint of pride in his voice. "She could've turned us in, turned *me* in, but she didn't." His eyes bore a hole in my skull as he stares at me, and a fissure of electricity crackles in the space between us.

"You have proof you can trust me," I say, holding his gaze. "The ball's in your court now."

Sawyer nods respectfully at me. "Staying here is *our* best option," he says, glancing at Rick. "Manning has eyes and ears everywhere, and this is bait. He wants us to run so he can find and kill Kai and take Abby back to Rydeville."

Pain stabs me in the heart, like a hundred tiny knives pricking me all at once. Kai can't die. It's as simple as that. "That is totally his M.O., and we can't leave. But you guys can't either, because if he locates you, then he'll locate us."

"I have it covered," Rick says.

"How?" I ask.

"The guy who owns this place has access to a private jet. They can pick us up here and drop us directly home."

I shake my head. "That won't work. The pilot has to lodge a flight plan, and they can trace it back here."

Rick smiles. "The pilot is his dad, and his brother is an FBI agent with mad IT skills that make Sawyer's skills look like chopped liver." His phone pings in his pocket. "And, speak of the devil." He grins, walking backward. "I've got to take this. I'll make arrangements." He swipes his finger across the screen, turning around and walking toward the door. "Hey, man. I was just talking about you."

"He sounds like a handy friend to have," I say.

"Chopped liver, my ass," Sawyer grumbles, stabbing his keypad as if it's done him an injury.

Kai and Jackson exchange grins. "Don't worry, dude," Jackson says, slapping Sawyer on the back. "You're still our number one."

"Fuck off," Sawyer snaps, and my mouth forms an O. Sawyer is one cool cucumber, and it's not like him to lose it. I file that little tidbit away for future.

"You're not speaking to your father?" I ask Kai, kicking off my sneakers and swinging my legs up onto the couch.

He drops on the end of the couch, lifting my legs and placing my feet in his lap. "That asshole is dead to me." I arch a brow. "Don't look at me like that!" he snaps.

"Why?"

"Why do you fucking think?" He drags a hand through his hair.

"I don't know. That's why I'm asking." He's said that to me before, and I've always loved throwing his words back at him.

"Because he's manipulated me for the last time. I'm done with his shit." His eyes penetrate mine. "Done making excuses for all the crap he's pulled." He squeezes his eyes shut for a couple seconds. "What he did to you, what he did to us, is unforgivable. That was it for me."

Silence engulfs the room, and the weight of what hasn't been said adds tension to the air.

"Kai."

His eyes flit to mine.

"Where are your baby brothers?" Jackson hinted at something the other day, and it got me thinking.

I was only seven when I attended Kai's mom's funeral, and I

remember his baby brothers. They were only one and two, respectively. But I kinda got confused then, because when we were hanging out as kids, it was always the Anderson four. Rick, Kai, Joaquin, and Harley. It got muddled in my head, and I forgot about the other two because the only time I'd ever seen them was at the funeral. Emma had given birth to them after she fell out with my mother, so I never knew the two youngest. All this time, I've been thinking Kai had three brothers, but he has *five*.

Yet no one has mentioned them.

Not even once.

And that's weird.

Sawyer and Jackson lock eyes on Kai. "Tell her, man," Jackson says as Sawyer closes his laptop and stands. Together, they walk out of the room, leaving us alone.

Kai's chest heaves up and down, and the urge to comfort him is riding me hard, but I resist.

"My father gave them up for adoption," he admits after a few beats.

My jaw slackens. "What?!"

He rubs his hands up and down my legs as he stares off into space, looking deep in thought. "Dad was a mess after your mom died." He looks over at me. "Rick and I thought it was a delayed reaction to our mom's death, but as we got older, and we listened to his drunken ramblings, we realized Dad was mourning another woman." His eyes bore into mine. "Your mother." He shakes his head, averting his eyes again. "Anyway, Dad checked out, leaving Rick and me to look after our younger brothers, but we didn't have a fucking clue how to look after babies, and Rogan and Spencer were always crying. Dad would shout at us to shut them up, and we tried, but—"

"But you were only kids yourselves, and it was unfair of him to burden you like that."

He shrugs. "We came home one day from school, and they were gone. Just like that." He lowers his head, and his chest shakes.

I crawl toward him, wrapping my arms around him in a temporary cease-fire. "I can't believe he just gave up two of his kids. What kind of asshole does that?"

"The elite kind." Kai hauls me into his lap, circling his arms around me and resting his chin atop my head. "I know you've had a shitty childhood too. Our fathers are made of the same stuff. They're both narcissistic, arrogant, assholes who use their kids to further their aims." His breath oozes out in spurts. "But my eyes were closed to it for too long. I allowed him to manipulate me. To buy into the notion you were partly to blame." He tips my chin up. "It sounds ludicrous now, but years of living with someone spouting the same shit all the time starts to sound sane after a while."

"And it wasn't just that," Rick says, sauntering into the room, and I wonder how long he's been listening. "He was drunk all the fucking time, and he was obsessed. He talked about your mom incessantly. And he poured all his rage and frustration into hating on a little girl. He blamed you for her death, but we didn't realize they had made plans to run away together until he admitted that in the ballroom." His eyes are remorseful as he stares at me. "I hate that we bought into it for so long, but it's hard to describe what we lived through, to explain how it became something we latched on to, to stay close to our father. A man who didn't deserve our support or our loyalty."

"Your father left us penniless," Kai continues explaining. "We literally had nothing."

"Uncle Wes gave us his apartment in New York, but that is all the help we got," Rick says. "Because, until recent years, Wes blamed our father for his sister's death. He knew about his affair with Olivia, and he always believed our mother was second best. He thought she committed suicide because she knew he was still in love with her best friend and she was unhappy. Dad was adamant that Hearst had murdered her, but Wes refused to believe it."

"Until your aunt came forward and told them what she knew, and then things changed," Kai adds.

"Dad got sober, and they patched up their differences and started plotting revenge," Rick supplies.

"And the rest you know," Kai murmurs.

I store it all away to process later. "Where are Rogan and Spencer now?"

Rick's eyes well up. "We don't know. We didn't have money to find them, and we were only kids."

"Uncle Wes was furious with Dad when he discovered he'd given them up. I know if Dad had asked him, he would've taken them in, but Dad's a stubborn, proud old fucker, and once Wes cut him off, he refused to reach out to him," Kai says.

"Wes is on the case now, and Hunt's father is helping, but the adoption is sealed, and records aren't public, and because parental neglect was a factor in the adoption decision, they won't release any information to Dad," Rick confirms. "So, we basically have no idea where they are."

"We don't even know if they are still going by the same first names," Kai says, and I hug him closer.

"I didn't think it was possible to detest your father anymore, but I do. How could he give up two of his kids?" I cry out.

"Because he's a heartless bastard," Kai says through gritted teeth.

"Why didn't you hate him for this?" I ask, genuinely puzzled how they could support this man with anything.

"Because it felt like our fault," Kai says, strain evident in his voice. "We've always believed we failed, because we didn't look after them properly and they took them away."

I cup his beautiful face. "Did you draw that conclusion, or was it put in your head?"

"He'd blame us when he was shitfaced," Kai admits.

"And yet you both still supported him with his plan to take my father down. To take *me* down." I'm trying to understand it, but I genuinely don't get it.

"Because we're royally fucked up, Abby," Kai says, abruptly lifting me off his lap and placing me down on the couch. He looms over me, and the pained look etched upon his face points to years of inner turmoil. "And you're right to keep your distance from me, because I'm no good for you."

With those parting words ringing in my ears, he strides out of the room, looking like he has the weight of the world on his shoulders.

CHAPTER FIFTEEN

Kai disappears for the rest of the night, and although I want to comfort him, I don't seek him out. My head and my heart hurt, and for the first time since coming here, I'm second-guessing what I'm doing.

The sound of female laughter tickles my eardrums as I make my way downstairs the following morning. I turn the corner into the beautiful living room and stop dead in my tracks.

Kai is cozied up to a gorgeous brunette on the couch, and she's laughing at something he's said. He's smiling at her, in a way he usually reserves for me, and that raises my hackles. He says something else to her, too quiet for me to hear, and she cracks up laughing, placing her hand on his elbow, and I see red, especially when I notice he's still wearing the same clothes he had on yesterday.

Did he go out and pick up some floozy for the night? And he has the nerve to bring her back here and flaunt her in front of me?

I charge across the room, my sneakers squelching off the polished hardwood floor as anger races through my limbs. The woman jerks her head in my direction as I round the couch, drawing to a halt in front of them.

I was wrong before.

She's not just gorgeous.

She's breathtakingly stunning, and I don't say that lightly. With her full mouth, big eyes, thick, lustrous hair, and knockout figure, she is "stop the lights" beautiful. She also looks somewhat familiar, but I don't know why. I'm not into chicks. But I'd consider turning gay or bi for her. The thought lands like sour milk in my stomach as hurt batters me on all sides. Dismissing my errant thoughts, I fixate my gaze on Kai, sending him a poisonous look. "What the fuck do you think you're doing?"

He leans back, stretching his arm around the back of the couch behind her, and my hands ball up at my side. "Talking. What's it to you?" He smirks, and I want to ram my fist into his smug face.

"I knew you were full of shit." I glance at her briefly, and her brows pull together in confusion. "And I'm done playing your games. I'm leaving, and I don't give a rat's ass if my father discovers your location. He can nuke your cheating ass for all I care!" I shoot her a venomous look before I stomp off.

I almost make it to the door before I'm scooped up and flung over his shoulder.

"Let me down, you motherfucking good-for-nothing slimeball!" I pound my fists against his back, wriggling and struggling as he walks toward the couch. "Ow!" I cry out as he swats my ass hard.

"Stop fucking wriggling, or I'll smack you again."

"You wouldn't dare."

He swats my ass a second time, and I lose it, kicking and screaming and slapping his back.

"Wow. That's an interesting dynamic," a deep voice I don't recognize says as Kai flops down on the couch, wrangling me onto his lap.

I raise my hands to slap him, but he restrains my wrists, holding them between our bodies as he attempts to calm me down. "Stop fucking fighting!"

"Screw off, jerk face." I blow strands of messy hair out of my face.

"This is their version of foreplay," Rick explains, and I lift my head in his direction, my mouth dropping open when I spot the guy standing by his side, looking at me with bemusement on his face.

Holy fucking shit.

I instantly recognize him.

And this dude is seriously hot.

The online pics I've seen haven't done him justice at all. His pale blue eyes twinkle with mirth, and his lush mouth parts slightly, offering a glimpse of perfectly white, perfectly straight teeth. A layer of fine stubble covers his jawline, and his hair is styled similarly to Kai's. He's wearing a black blazer over a white shirt with dark jeans and black boots, and he looks good enough to eat.

"Oh my God," I blurt. "You're Kyler Kennedy."

"In the flesh," he says, grinning.

"I'm a massive fan of your mom," I say.

Along with you and your brothers.

That is some crazy hot gene pool. I think it, but I don't say it even though I want to because it would piss Kaiden off. But I've just figured out who the brunette is, and I don't want to disrespect Kyler's wife.

"She redesigned our pool house last year," I say, "and I got such a kick out of it. My mom adored Kennedy Apparel, and she hero-worshipped Alex, and I wish she'd still been alive to see the awesome job your mom did with the place," I gush. "It's seriously my favorite place to hang out in my house," I continue, without pausing for a breath, "and you've got to tell her I said hi, and—"

Kai covers my mouth with his hand, muffling the rest of my sentence, and I shoot daggers at him. "That was the worst example of word vomit I've ever had the misfortune to hear," he says. "The muzzle hasn't arrived yet, so someone had to shut you up."

I'd flip him the bird if I had use of my hands, but he's still securing them with his other hand. I bite down hard on the palm covering my mouth, and he wrenches his hand back, narrowing his eyes at me.

"You dare to bite me?" His tone is deathly quiet, but it promises a world of pain.

"I couldn't fucking breathe, asshole." I wriggle on his lap again, attempting to get free.

"Keep doing that if you want to get fucked six ways from Sunday." He smirks, while I wish the ground would swallow me whole.

"And you have the nerve to call *me* embarrassing!"

Kyler coughs to disguise his snort of laughter, and, of their own volition, my lips turn up at the corners. I glance at him, and he waggles his brows, grinning mischievously, and my heart is in a puddle somewhere on the floor.

"This is rich," Kai growls. "You throw shade at me for talking with Faye, and now you're mooning over Kyler like a prepubescent girl on her period."

"I am not." I smile apologetically at Faye, feeling like an ass for jumping to the wrong conclusion about her and hoping she's not pissed I have a crush on her man.

"Don't lie, babe." He tweaks my nose. "Because I always know."

"You're insufferable."

"And you're hot when you're angry."

"Okay. Enough." Rick rolls his eyes. "It's like herding kittens."

"You're hurting my wrists. Let me go."

"Ask me nicely."

"Screw off, Kaiden."

"Remind you of anyone?" Faye says, grinning up at her husband.

"Wow. You have the most gorgeous accent," I blurt, because it seems I can't control my fangirl gushing.

"Thank you, Abigail, but I still don't get how every American I meet is fascinated with Irish accents."

Kai releases my wrists, repositioning me on his lap so it's more socially acceptable. I attempt to maneuver onto the couch, but his arms wrap around me, caging me in, and I give up fighting. "It's Abby," I say. "And I apologize if I was rude earlier."

"There's no *if* about it," Kai drawls.

"No one asked you, asshat." I huff. "And you wrote the manual on bad manners."

Kyler chuckles. "I don't think we were that bad," he says, pinning his wife with a sultry look.

She folds her arms and narrows her eyes. "Remember the night I injured my foot and you crept up on me in the kitchen?"

"There was no creeping involved. You were as loud as a herd of elephants," he replies.

She sighs, rolling her eyes and winking conspiratorially at me. "I rest my case."

"Men." I shake my head, and she smiles.

A dashing older man enters the room, blowing on his hands. "Christ, it's cold out there. How are we fixed, folks?"

"I'll grab my brothers, and we're good to go then," Rick says, shaking hands with the man. "Thanks for doing this, James. We appreciate it."

I squeal as his name clicks with me. "Oh, my—"

Kai's hand is over my mouth again. "Excuse my girlfriend. She has a bad case of foot-in-mouth disease." Rick is smirking as he exits the room, heading to find Harley and Joaquin, no doubt.

I'm momentarily blindsided as Kai's words reverberate inside my brain. His use of the word *girlfriend* has me all hot and bothered, and I hate that I like how it sounded rolling off his tongue.

Time to regain some control.

I ram my elbow into Kai's rib cage, and he winces, his hands instinctively dropping away. I jump up, straightening the front of my dress as I walk toward Kyler's father. I thrust my hand out. "I'm Abigail Manning. It's a pleasure to meet you, Mr. Kennedy." He shakes my hand, smiling warmly at me. "I apologize for the caveman over there." I cast a sharp glance over my shoulder at Kai. "I just wanted to say that Alex designed our pool house and she did an amazing job. I'm a big fan of her work."

"I'll pass on your compliments, Abigail. She'll be thrilled to hear that." I'm not sure of the current status of their marriage, but Alex and James Kennedy are still close despite being separated for years. Having met them both, I can see where their sons get their good looks and charisma from.

The Kennedy men are infamous around Boston, and tales of their escapades are widely reported. They've had their fair share of family drama, and there were plenty of skeletons in their closets, so I'm guessing that's why they're comfortable helping us out with our predicament.

"We're all packed," Rick supplies, appearing in the doorway with his younger brothers in tow.

"Great. Let's get cracking then." James tips his head at Kaiden. "Stay safe, young man." He smiles at me. "And look after this young lady."

Kai stands, nodding before he walks to where his brothers congregate. James leaves to get the plane ready, and I stand beside Faye and Kyler, a little awestruck, if I'm honest.

Kyler pulls his wife into his side, pressing a kiss to her temple. "I know the circumstances are less than ideal, but I hope you're enjoying your stay here," Kyler says.

"I am. Thank you for letting us stay." I skim my eyes around the room. "You have a beautiful home. And now that I know who owns the property, I can see Alex's touch everywhere. I don't know why I didn't pick up on that before."

"She did an incredible job," Faye says in a soft lyrical tone. "And she has a wonderful eye. This is one of our favorite places on the planet."

"I'll bet. You're both at Harvard too, right? That's how you know Rick?" They nod. "It must be nice having a place to escape to on weekends and during school breaks."

"It is, and that's exactly why we purchased this place," Kyler agrees. "It's been a Godsend."

Now I understand the high-tech security and choice of location for their vacation home. I thought living under a spotlight in Rydeville was bad, but it's nothing compared to the attention the Kennedys garner. It must grate on their nerves.

Kai appears with Sawyer and Jackson, and I make my goodbyes to the Kennedys, walking toward Joaquin, Rick, and Harley. "Stay safe, guys." I hug Joaquin and Harley, holding in a smile as Harley's cheeks stain red.

"You too." Rick lifts his duffel bag. "Go easy on him." He jerks his head in Kai's direction. "He feels things deeply, Abby, even if he doesn't show it." I don't acknowledge his statement because I'm making no promises.

I walk to the kitchen to grab some breakfast, and I'm sitting at the stool in front of the island unit, munching on some toast, when Faye walks in. "Hey. Do you have a couple minutes to talk?" she asks, moving to the Keurig and pouring herself a mug.

I finish chewing and set my toast down. "Sure."

She slides onto the stool beside me. "I just want to check you're okay." She peeks over her shoulder, but we're alone. "It's my first time meeting Kaiden, and while he seems like a good guy, I couldn't leave here today without checking you're here because you want to be here." She peers into my eyes. "Things seem intense, and I have some experience of dealing with hot-headed arseholes." Her wide grin is warm and meant to relax me.

"Kyler was like that?" I can't keep the incredulity from my voice because that isn't the image I have of him. If the media reports are true, he's always surprising Faye with romantic gestures, and he got shot trying to protect her a few years ago. He's swoon-worthy in the extreme.

She grins. "He was a total pig when I first met him, and he did some stuff that really hurt me." Her face contorts unpleasantly. "All because he thought he was protecting me." She rolls her eyes, and I snort.

"Yep. I have one of those too."

She nods sagely. "I recognized that." Propping her elbows up on the counter, she rests her chin in her hands. "But the thing I've learned is guys like Kyler and Kaiden might appear abrasive, and they might drive you to distraction, but there is no guy more loyal or more protective, and when they open their hearts?" A dreamy expression appears on her face. "There is nothing more intense than being loved by a guy like that."

"He doesn't love me." I shake my head. "And I don't need or want the complication of loving a guy like that." It's cold, and not entirely true, but I say what I need to.

"You sure about that?" Her face showcases her surprise.

"Kaiden's not capable of romantic love. He's too closed off. Whatever love he has in his heart he reserves for his family and his friends. Not for me."

She eyes me for a long time, opening and closing her mouth in quick succession as her gaze flits from my face to my ring and back again. I doubt she knows much of my background, so I guess she's assuming I'm engaged to Kaiden. Perhaps she was going to ask me but thinks better of it. "I'm not sure that's true, but you know him better than I do." She casts a glance at her phone. "Shoot. I need to go before James sends out a search party." She drains the last of her coffee. "And you're sure you want to stay?"

"I'm good, but thank you for asking."

"Okay then." She stands, pulling me into a quick hug. "I wish we had more time to chat. I have a feeling you and I'd get on like a house on fire."

"Me too." My warm smile is genuine.

She slips a card into my hand. "That's my contact info. Call or email me anytime. I mean it. If you need anything or you're in trouble, get in touch."

"Thank you so much. You've no idea what that means to me." That this stranger would make such an offer reminds me there are good, generous, kind people in this world.

I haven't encountered many of them.

It also reminds me of Jane, and I wonder where she is and if she's doing okay. I can't imagine she's coping well without Drew, and I wish I was there to help her deal with her broken heart.

"Take care of yourself." She gives me one final hug before leaving, and I turn to the sink, rinsing out my mug in slow motion, waiting for him to announce his presence.

I dry and put my mug away when he steps forward.

He wears a mask I haven't seen in a while, but it's one I'm well accustomed to. Disgust clings to his eyes, and his emotions are on lockdown as he stalks toward me. I knew he was listening, and I knew my comments would hurt him—but not this much. A pang of remorse hits me in my chest, and it's getting harder to hold on to my anger.

Kai is getting to me, and my head is a mess as I now question *everything* I'm doing to get back at him.

But I stand my ground, refusing to be intimidated or take it back.

He deserves to hurt.

To grovel.

To fight to prove his feelings for me are genuine.

I demand no less.

I deserve no less.

He steps up close, his chest brushing against mine as he glares at me. "You don't know what I'm capable of." His tone screams death and destruction, and a shiver works its way up my spine, but I hold firm, maintaining a cool composure. "But keep pushing me, and you might just find out."

CHAPTER SIXTEEN

The house is much quieter without the Anderson brothers, and I'm rapidly going out of my mind as boredom sets in. Sawyer is locked in his office for most of the day while Jackson has returned to his stoner ways, and it's not as much fun now I can't partake. Kaiden is avoiding me, and he spends a lot of his time in the impressive gym housed in one of the outbuildings. The rest of the time he's holed up with Sawyer, but every time I suggest I can help, the door is literally closed in my face.

"Here." Kai strides into the bedroom, thrusting a small package at me. Now the others have gone, there are two spare bedrooms, and he moved into one without me even asking. My comments to Faye about his ability to love seems to have struck a nerve. He's maintaining distance between us, and I'm woman enough to admit I can't stand it even if I'm the one who orchestrated it.

However, I know he still sneaks in here at night, because I'm attuned to his presence, and I always feel him in the room. He doesn't know I'm aware, and I'd rather keep it that way. My feelings are an epic clusterfuck of disastrous proportions, and the more my anger fades, the more I crave him.

I don't know how much longer I can keep hiding the truth.

"What is it?" I ask, accepting the package and ignoring the way my skin heats when his fingers brush mine.

"Something to stop your bitching and whining." He walks off, and it's natural to shove my middle finger up at his retreating form. "I felt that," he says, and I flip him off another few times for good measure.

When he's gone, I open the box, and my heart soars when I remove a Kindle Oasis e-reader. It's linked to his account, and he's set up a Kindle Unlimited subscription for me. A couple of pregnancy books are already loaded to the device, and my heart feels like it might beat a path out of my chest. I set it down and go after him, heading to his bedroom first.

I rap on the door, and it eases open. Sounds from the bathroom confirm he's in the shower, and I'm backing out of his room when I spy the open sketchpad on the bed. I'm a nosy bitch, especially with Kai's artistic talent, and I feel only a little twinge of guilt as I stride toward the bed. I sit down and snatch it up, turning it over onto his current drawing.

Pressure sits on my chest as I take in every exquisite detail of the sketch. A dog-eared photo is paperclipped to the top of the page, and Kai's replica is almost a mirror image. He is just that good.

It's Emma Anderson, Kai's mother, and she's cradling two babies in her arms. The one hooked in her left arm is tiny, and clearly a newborn, and the other baby is older, sitting upright on her lap, reaching his chubby fingers out toward his new brother.

Tears prick my eyes as I brush my fingers over the broad pencil strokes, quickly turning the page before my tears destroy the picture. This next drawing is of me. I'm asleep in the master bedroom, but Kai has used his imagination to include a baby in my arms. I'm curled into a ball with our sleeping child cradled against my body.

Sobs rip free of my soul, and I drop the pad, racing from his room back to my own.

The pain in my chest is so intense I'm struggling to breathe. I sink to my knees in my bedroom, wrapping my arms around myself as I rock back and forth with tears streaking my face. I crawl on my hands and knees to the bed, bury myself underneath the covers, and cry myself to sleep.

When I wake, it's pitch-black in the room and outside. My throat is as dry as the Sahara Desert, and a heavy ache castrates my heart, reminding me of earlier.

"Abby."

I scream at the unexpected sound of his voice, and he reaches out, taking my hand. "Calm down before you give yourself a coronary."

"You know better than to creep me out like that!"

"And you know I like to sit here and watch you sleep."

"Don't bother being nice if you hate me again."

"I don't hate you, Abby. I never really did," he admits, dragging his hand through his hair. "It's what you represented, but I'm man enough to admit I was wrong."

Nausea churns in my gut, and guilt threatens to consume me.

"I cooked pasta," he says, not waiting for a reply.

Which is good.

Because I've no idea how to respond to him right now.

"And I set some aside for you because you missed dinner. Let me heat it up for you."

"Why are you being nice to me again?"

He threads his fingers through my hair. "You're not my enemy, babe, and I'm not yours. We have enough of them without turning on one another." I nod, because he's right. "I know what you're doing, but it won't work. It might piss me off temporarily, but I meant what I said. I'm going nowhere." He presses a kiss to my hair, and I fight a new wave of tears.

I need to tell him.

But I don't know how.

And once he knows what I've done, he'll hate me for real this time.

I have fucked everything up.

My lower lip wobbles, and he notices. He cups the back of my head. "Shush. It's okay, baby. Just let me take care of you."

My eyes convey everything I'm feeling, and he bends down, kissing me softly. When he lifts his gaze, I see uncertainty there, which surprises me, until he bends down again, this time to plant a gentle kiss on my tummy over my shirt.

The tender gesture slays me on the inside, and I chew on the inside of my cheek and dig my nails into my sides to hold myself together. "I'll be back," he whispers, kissing me again, and I watch him exiting the room, hating what I've done, knowing there's a chance he'll never forgive me.

"Is there some imaginary monster chasing our asses, because why else are you running like your life depends on it?" Jackson queries, in a breathless tone of voice, as we race around the path in the wooded area at the side of the lake, the following morning.

"Everyone has monsters they're trying to outrun," I say, panting as I wipe sweat from my brow.

I love running in this kind of weather. As Jackson is fond of saying, it's cold enough to freeze his balls. It's difficult to warm up at first when my limbs threaten to crack and splinter, thanks to the bitter cold, but once we pick up our pace, my legs loosen, and I welcome the crisp bite of the air stinging my cheeks as we run.

"So true," he says, in a much quieter voice, and I slow my pace to check on him.

"You want to walk the rest of the way back?" I ask.

"You saying I'm unfit?"

"You *are* unfit. You can thank your weed addiction for that." I nudge him in the ribs. "Although, I give you ten out of ten for effort."

"High praise indeed," he says, stopping and bracing his hands on his bent knees. I swipe my water bottle from my backpack and guzzle it down. When I'm done, he's regained control of his breathing, and we pick up a leisurely stroll.

"It's Christmas in a couple weeks, right?" He nods. "So, are you guys going home or what?"

"We can't go home. It isn't safe."

"Will your mom be pissed?"

"Yup. I'm dreading making the call."

"Maybe you could ask James Kennedy to fly you under the radar."

"We can't risk it. Your bastard father will expect one of us to show our heads over the holiday season."

"I'm sorry."

"It's not your fault, beautiful." He slings his arm around my shoulders, pressing a kiss to my temple. "We'll do our own Christmas here, and I already have a few ideas how to make it special."

"Let me guess." I tip one finger off my chin. "Hash cakes for breakfast, lunch, and dinner, and the evening's entertainment is watching *Hot Cop Nails Naughty Mrs. Claus Under the Christmas Tree.*"

He throws back his head, laughing. "This is why you're one of my favorite people."

I shoulder-check him, grinning. "You're one of my favorite people too."

He lifts his little finger. "Pinkie swear?"

I laugh, shaking my head as I wrap my pinkie around his. "Pinkie promise."

"What is this?" Sawyer questions a couple hours later when I usher all three guys into the living room. I've pushed the couches to one side, so there's room for the flip chart.

"We're strategizing." I point at all three of them. "Sit your butts down."

Sawyer frowns. "Is that my flip chart?"

"It is," I confirm, pushing him down onto the couch.

"How did you get into my office?"

"I picked the lock."

He looks at Kai. "Forget the muzzle. We need to handcuff her to the bed."

"I'm down with that plan," Jackson says, predictably rubbing a hand along his crotch.

"Don't start that shit again," Sawyer says. "We finally have peace. Let's try not to ruin it."

"Enough shit talk," I instruct. "We have fathers to defeat, and we're making a concrete plan."

"What the hell do you think Kai and I have been doing since you got here?" Sawyer asks, crossing one leg over his knee.

"Shutting me out of your planning, and that stops now. This impacts me, and if you won't include me, then I'll go rogue." Kai smirks, and my hackles raise. "Got something to add, caveman?"

"I'm just wondering what took you so long, firecracker." I poke my tongue at him, and he smiles. "Let's hear it, babe."

I flip back the cover, revealing the sheet I already prepped. "I've listed our main enemies in order of priority. *One.* Michael Hearst. *Two.* Atticus Anderson." I level Kai with a pointed look, expecting him to argue, but he merely nods. "*Three.* Christian Montgomery. *Four.* Trent Montgomery."

I wait for one of them to interject, but I have their complete attention, so I continue. I pace the room as I talk. "Taking my father down is tricky, because he covers his bases and he has tons of law enforcement in his back pocket, but there's got to be some jurisdictions his influence doesn't extend to."

"The issue with that," Kai says, "is we have to lodge criminal charges in the state where they committed the offense."

"There has got to be one judge, somewhere in the state of MA, who isn't corrupt?"

"I wouldn't bank on it," Sawyer says.

"But your fathers are influential as hell, and they want to see my father brought to justice. Surely, there is something they can do?"

"Dad has already lodged charges against your father for the fraudulent theft of his company," Kai says, telling me something I wasn't aware of. "But, it's like your father and dickhead Montgomery said in the ballroom. They are already burying him in red tape, and at this rate, it'll take years to come to court, if it even sees the light of day."

I scratch the side of my head. "So, we're back to the murder charges. We have to find evidence to pin either my mother's or your mother's murder on him."

A muscle pops in Kai's jaw. "Except we have no clue where to find the evidence your mother stole proving he murdered my mom. We were so sure it'd be in your father's safe."

"And my aunt didn't know where she'd stashed it?"

He shakes his head. "Your mom wouldn't tell her because she said it wasn't safe."

"Maybe he found it and destroyed it," Jackson says. "I know that's what I'd do."

"But you're not a psycho."

"That's debatable," Sawyer deadpans, and Jackson flips him off.

"My father would hoard the evidence like a trophy, because it was the first nail in your father's coffin," I say to Kai. "This vendetta they have against one another has consumed them. My father would gloat over the evidence and take it out whenever he wanted a reminder he's King Big Dick."

Jackson chuckles, inhaling a long drag from his joint.

"If that's the case, then your father has more than just the evidence of my mom's murder," Kai says, sitting upright.

"He has evidence of all his crimes," I murmur, getting excited. Of course, he does! *Why have I never considered this before?*

"Where would he store that?" Sawyer asks. "Think carefully, Abby."

"I've already thought about it," I admit, "and there are any number of places in that creepy mansion he could hide it." I prop my butt on the edge of the couch. "But I don't think it's there." Three sets of eyes lock on mine. "I think it's at Parkhurst."

Sawyer and Kai stare at one another.

"What?" I ask, my tone laced with suspicion.

"We've considered the same thing," Sawyer admits.

"But that place is a fucking fortress," Kai says. "There's no way we'd get in and out of there undetected, and that's if we even knew where to look."

"*We* don't," I say, leaning forward. "But my brother might."

CHAPTER SEVENTEEN

"We need to mend bridges with Drew and Charlie. We need to resume working as a team again. Xavier included," I say, because it's the only logical choice.

"It's too risky," Kai says, shifting on the couch and avoiding eye contact.

"They can't be trusted," Sawyer agrees, casting a surreptitious glance at Kai that doesn't escape my notice.

Why are they being so cagey? We all worked together before. Until they screwed us over. But we still have a common enemy and reconciling is not insurmountable.

"I don't see that we've other options," I argue. "Hiding out here indefinitely is not a good idea, because nothing is moving forward. It's only a matter of time before my father finds us. It's best to tackle it head-on. Let me contact Drew. See if he can make a deal with my father in exchange for him calling off the hitman on Kai."

"Absolutely not." Kai jumps up, stalking toward me. His hands automatically move to my stomach. "It's not safe for you or the baby." His features soften as they always do when he's talking about our child.

It was even easier than I thought.

My stomach flips, and I quickly switch the subject. "My father isn't the only one looking for us. There's also your father and the Montgomerys. We're like sitting ducks just waiting here."

"Dad's obsessed with regaining his land and his business," Kai says, "and he knows I'm pissed. He won't come near us for a while."

I don't believe that for one second, and I doubt he does either. "C'mon, Kai. Stop trying to shelter me. Your father orchestrated my pregnancy to use it as leverage. He won't stop until we're back under his control." I take his hands in mine. "It's only a matter of time before Harley caves and tells him where we are. Your father will take advantage of his good nature and manipulate him into it somehow."

"Abby is right," Jackson says, crossing his feet at the ankles. "We're on borrowed time."

We all trade worried looks. And while no one confirms it, we all know our days here are numbered.

I've been in bed for hours, but I can't sleep. I told the guys I was tired and headed to bed early, but it was a lie. I couldn't stomach looking at Kai knowing what I've done and what I need to do. It's weighing on my mind, and the more I think about it, the more I'm feeling all the emotions I denied myself. I'm close to breaking, and I'm scared. I was hurt when I decided to play him at his own game. I wanted to make him pay for his betrayal, but I fear all I've done is hurt myself.

I'm going to lose him, and I'll deserve it.

Because it was a despicable thing to do. And now I'm thinking more clearly, I wish I hadn't sunk so low.

I don't want to lose Kai.

Because I love him.

I love him so much, and I wish things were different.

I wish I didn't have to break his heart.

The door opens quietly, and my breath hitches in my throat. Kai pads across the floor toward the bed, and I don't disguise the fact I'm awake. He sits on the side of the bed, brushing hair back off my face. "What's wrong?"

"Everything," I whisper.

"Hey." He sweeps his thumbs under my eyes, catching the moisture pooling there. "It'll be okay. I'm not letting anything happen to you."

I scoot sideways, folding back the covers. "Can you hold me?" This might be my last chance to feel his arms around me.

Wordlessly, he climbs in beside me, and I roll over onto my other side, unable to look at him with my treacherous eyes. He hauls me against him, until my back is pressed solidly against his front, and I close my eyes, savoring the feel of his arms as they go around my waist, and the comforting warmth emanating from his body. "I'll hold you every night if you let me," he whispers against my ear, sending shivers cascading over me. He tightens his grip, in a wholly protective manner, and tears spill out of my eyes.

Why did I deny myself this? Why did I cling to the hatred and the betrayal instead of forgiving him when it became clear he was being honest with me?

I could blame my hormones.

Or my fucked-up upbringing that causes me to do whatever is necessary to survive.

But concealing this was low. Cruel. Deliberately hurtful.

And it seems so pointless now.

"Don't cry, baby. I know you're scared, but we'll figure out a solution."

He thinks he knows the reason for these tears, but he's clueless.

"It's why we've been locked away in Hunt's office," he continues. "I know you think I was cutting you out, but I wasn't." His hands slide lower, palming my stomach. "You shouldn't have to worry about any of this shit. Your sole priority is nurturing our little one." His hand rubs across my belly, burning me through my sheer nightdress. He presses feather-soft kisses to my neck, and my chest is heaving with unimaginable pain. "And I want to start planning." His hand is scorching hot on my belly now, as if my skin is on fire, and I can't handle it. "I've kept a note of some names I like, and I have an idea about where we can go after the baby is born, to keep him or her away from our fathers, and I—"

"Stop!" I cry out, wriggling out of his hold. Wracking sobs rip from my soul as I bolt upright in the bed. I face him with tears streaming down my face. "Don't say another word. I can't hear it."

Concern shimmers in his eyes as he sits up, opening his arms and attempting to draw me back into his body. "What's wrong, baby?"

I wet my lips and swipe at the hot tears coursing down my face. "I... I... I have something I need to tell you."

"Okay." He scoots closer, and I jump up, unable to bear his touch. His eyes examine my face, and his chest heaves. "Just spit it out." His tone is even, but his face betrays his burgeoning fear.

"I should've told you this when I first arrived, but I wanted to make you pay."

He eyeballs me, imploring me to continue.

"You lied to me, Kai! You tricked me into thinking you were someone else, and for weeks, while they imprisoned me at Parkhurst, I wondered if *everything* was a lie. If you were in on the pregnancy plan too."

"I told you I wasn't. I would never do that to you."

"I know," I whisper, pacing in front of the bed. "I know that now."

"What are you saying, Abby?" He climbs out of bed, but keeps his distance, staring at me cautiously.

"I was still so angry. I wanted you to feel what it felt like to be deceived. To believe you had something, but it was all a lie."

"What are you lying about?" He steps toward me, and I instinctively take a step back. "What have you done?"

"I'm sorry," I blurt, and wracking sobs fill the silent space around us.

The bars around my heart shatter, and it all comes out.

Weeks of unacknowledged grief.

Unbearable loss.

Intense heartbreak.

It culminates in a barrage of internal pain and self-loathing.

I scream, and it's birthed straight from my blackened soul. I can scarcely see him through the river of tears blurring my eyes. "I wanted to hurt you, and this will kill you, but it's killed me too!"

His face portrays his own inner battle, and I sense he's torn between wanting to comfort me and fearing the unknown. "Tell me, Abby."

"I…" My voice chokes as more tears clogs my throat. My stomach churns as I cry, and the transparent terror on his face sends me over the edge. "I'm sorry." I back toward the door. "I can't."

I race out of the bedroom, down the stairs, and out through the front door, running across the front field, directionless and with no plan except to flee the anguished look on his face.

I can't say the words out loud.

Because then it's real.

I hardly feel the light snowdrops landing on my body as I run or the icy chill underfoot as I race barefoot along the grass. The snow isn't sticking because it was raining earlier, but the terrain underfoot is soft, and my feet sink into the ground, splashing mud against my calves.

"Abby! Stop!" Kai calls out, giving chase.

I keep running even though I know it's futile.

"Stop." He appears in front of me, spinning around and holding my shoulders to halt my forward trajectory. "Just stop."

"You'll hate me," I sob. "I know it, because I hate myself." I drop to my knees, burying my head in my hands, sobbing my heart out. There isn't a single cell in my body that isn't in agony as pain batters me from all sides.

He sinks to the muddy ground in front of me. "I need to know the truth, Abby. If this is about the baby—"

"There is no baby!" I sob, lifting my head to look at him. He deserves to hear this face to face. "The bastard took them!" I can barely speak over the heavy weight pressing down on my chest. A numbed shock splays across his face. "It was twins," I whisper.

My sobs mix with his heavy breathing, sounding loud in the otherwise still night air.

"Tell me everything." His voice is monotone, and if it wasn't for the tortured expression on his face, I'd think he was devoid of feeling.

"I spent the first couple weeks at Parkhurst confined to bed in a constant drugged state, so I didn't properly understand," I explain in a shaky voice. "Until my father gave me an envelope. Inside was a medical report confirming the successful abortion of twin fetuses." More tears leak out of my eyes, but I force myself to continue because I owe this to him. "He also included a list of everyone I love with a promise that if I didn't conform to his plan, he would start killing them one by one." I eyeball him. "You were top of the list."

"Twins?" he croaks. "It was twins?"

I nod. I thought it was hereditary, but now, I'm guessing it was the fertility drugs.

"Why would he do that?" Kai asks. "Keeping you and the baby—babies..." He corrects himself, and tears shimmer in his eyes, destroying me anew. "Keeping them alive was his best leverage. All he had to do was keep you from marrying me, and then the shares were his."

"I have some theories," I admit, sniffling. "I think this is bigger than Manning Motors. That's only one part of several moving pieces, and me not being pregnant out of wedlock was more important." Acid crawls up my throat. "It removes any impediment to marrying Charlie," I add, and I expect his dark scowl. "But mainly, I think he did it to spite your father. To take away his insurance plan. To ensure he didn't share a grandchild with him. And…" Air whooshes out of my mouth. "He did it to break me. To show me he owns me body and soul, and there's nothing I can do about it."

I cup my bigger bust as a sour taste floods my mouth. "For years, he wanted me to have breast augmentation surgery, and I always refused."

Kai's jaw hardens. "He did that to you while you were knocked out?"

I nod. "At first, when I noticed, it gave me hope because I thought it meant I was still pregnant, but after he confirmed he'd forced an abortion on me, I knew what he'd done." My heart hardens, and my tears dry up. "I couldn't figure it out because there are no scars on my boobs, but he gave me this literature on the surgical options once, and I remembered there's a less common procedure where they go in through your armpit, so I'm guessing that's how it was done."

I glance down at them. "I hate them. I never wanted bigger boobs. I was happy with the ones I had." Tears prick the backs of my eyes again. "But mostly, it's because every time I look at them, I'm reminded of what he's done."

My chest heaves, and another onslaught of tears arrives. I wrap my arms around my waist, rocking back and forth as I cry. This is what I get for locking all my feelings up and denying my grief an outlet. "He took our babies, Kai!" I cry out. "He murdered them with no guilt or remorse."

My piercing screams penetrate the air, spurring Kai into action. He takes me into his arms, and I cling to him, needing his comfort, as I scream and scream, finally letting it all out

When my screams die out, I rest my head on his shoulder, circling my arms more tightly around his neck. His woodsy, citrusy scent wraps around me like a comfort blanket. "If he can do that, he'll do anything," I say, sniffling. "I've always known he was a monster, a psycho, but this proves there's literally nothing he won't do to achieve his aims." I shiver, but I don't know if it's the snow covering me in a light, wet layer or the reality of our situation. "He doesn't care, Kai." I bury my face in his neck. "And I think he might have succeeded."

I peer deep into his eyes. "He's destroyed me, and I'll never recover from this."

CHAPTER EIGHTEEN

Kaiden

I hover over her bed, watching her sleep, wanting to soothe her and kill her at the same time. She cried herself to sleep in my arms, and I reined in my emotions, but they need an outlet. Or I'm liable to hurt her.

And though I'm beyond enraged, I don't want to hurt her, because she's already in her own personal hell.

The circle must end.

But first I need to deal with my fucked-up emotions.

I tiptoe out of the room, quietly closing the door behind me. I walk with purpose toward the kitchen where I know Hunt and Lauder are waiting for me. Her screaming and crying in the bedroom must have woken them up, and they fled outside after me. I appreciated that they hung back, but I knew they would want to know.

"Is she okay?" Lauder asks, worry evident on his face.

My fists shake with violent urges, and I'd happily take my aggression out on his face. He's crossing a line with her, and he knows it. "She's asleep, but she's not okay."

"What is it?" Hunt asks, handing me a bottle of bourbon.

I uncap the bottle and knock back a few mouthfuls. The burn coasting down my throat is welcome, but it doesn't come close to matching the burn inside my veins. "Her father aborted the babies while she was unconscious."

Lauder drops his mug, and it shatters into smithereens on the floor. "Babies?" he queries, his face ashen.

I nod. "She was carrying twins." I take another glug of whiskey.

"She deceived you." Hunt's penetrating gaze locks on mine. "Why?"

"Payback." I swipe another mouthful of whiskey, before setting the bottle down on the island. While getting drunk is tempting, that's not what I need.

"I can't say I blame her," Lauder admits as he picks up pieces of broken porcelain off the floor.

"And I can't say I'm surprised you'd pick her side," I snap.

"I understand it to a point," Hunt says. "Because she didn't know if you'd deliberately gotten her pregnant, but she should've fessed up once she knew the truth." He shakes his head. "I'm disappointed in her."

"I lied to her about who I was, and we've all seen evidence of her anger." I flatten my palms on the counter as fury builds momentum inside me. I'm trying to hold on to that thought, because I know I've hurt her and lied to her and I know this is how Abby copes. She doesn't take things lying down. Her fighting spirit and her survival instincts are some of the things I love most about her.

But I'm so fucking mad she tricked me.

All week, she's let me believe she was pregnant.

All week, I've been harboring notions of us as a family, and I've been actively making plans.

All week, I've been living a charade because none of it was real.

"That doesn't excuse it," Sawyer says. "She's gone out of her way to piss you off since you arrived, and now this?" He arches a brow, and an overwhelming urge to defend her sweeps over me.

"She was hurting, Hunt." I rub the dull ache spreading across my chest. "Look at everything she's been through. She wanted to hurt me back and regain some control, and I can't hold that against her. Not after all the shit I've done to her." The words imprint on my heart and my soul, making me realize my anger is misplaced. He slowly nods, getting it.

Yes, I'm pissed she did it. And I'm hurting over our loss.

But it's not her I'm angry with.

The murderous rage I feel toward Michael Hearst is unlike anything I've ever felt. I've spent the best part of my life hating him, and his assault on Abby only compounded it.

But this.

This is…

A shuddering breath leaves my body, and I have no way of articulating the venom I possess for that man.

He will suffer. Even if I die ensuring vengeance.

"That bastard needs to pay," Lauder says, as if he has a direct line to my thoughts.

"I should've persevered the night I broke into their place and gone after him instead of stopping to tackle Louis."

"Louis deserved to die." Hunt grips my shoulder. "And we all knew it was a long shot. Hearst is well protected. You stood no real chance of getting to him."

"I need to get out of here." I eyeball Hunt. "There's a fight club in Nexton, a couple towns over."

"It's too risky, Kai."

I crack my knuckles. "I don't have a choice." I let him see the darkness clawing at my insides. "I need to beat someone to a bloody pulp, or I'll take it out on her."

"She's been hurt enough." Lauder's response is predictable, and it grates on my nerves.

"Stop fucking interfering." I hiss. "She's mine to worry about, and I know she's hurting. This has devastated her." I grip the side of the island. "Why the fuck do you think I'm risking discovery? I need to fight, or I'll do something I regret. I don't *want* to take it out on her."

And while a part of me knows she needs to be punished so she knows not to fucking keep shit from me again, I can find more creative ways of making her suffer.

Hunt has been watching me. "Okay." He straightens up. "But we'll need to make contingency plans to leave sooner than later."

"Agreed." I level a look at Hunt. "Start the car, and I'll follow you out."

He leaves, and I face Lauder. "Can I trust you to watch over her and not touch her?"

He faces off with me, anger splaying across his features. The enforced weed ban when we first arrived here made me realize it's been so long since I've seen genuine expression on his face. Even now, I'd take his anger over his casual, stoner face any day.

"I haven't laid a finger on her," he says through gritted teeth.

"But you want to," I challenge.

"Doesn't mean I would."

"See that you don't." I glare at him. "She's *mine*."

"She could've been mine," he bravely retorts, straightening his shoulders.

"We both know that," I agree. "But she chose me." I back down, sighing. "I don't want to fight you. And as pissed as I am, I don't want to take it out on her either."

"You won't. And I would never cross that line, bro. She's your girl, and I'll keep her safe." He clamps a hand on my shoulder. "Go."

I nod and exit the kitchen, grabbing my jacket before leaving the house.

"This place is a shithole," Hunt exclaims, as we step into the grungy bar on the outskirts of town. Lighting is dim, but it doesn't disguise the shabby décor. Paint peels off the walls, and the scuffed hardwood floors have seen better days. The mismatched tables and chairs only add to the whole look and feel of the place. Several heads turn in our direction as we walk in, eyes narrowing suspiciously.

"It's a typical biker's hangout. What'd you expect?" I say as we walk toward the bar.

"It's a far cry from New York," Hunt says, maintaining his usual unruffled manner.

"It's more real than any of those bars we used to go to," I say, leaning over the counter to capture the blonde bartender's attention.

"Hey there, handsome." She blatantly eye-fucks me as her eyes roam my body, but she does nothing for me. There is zero action happening in my pants. I wouldn't mind a fuck because it's been weeks, but the only woman I want underneath me is the current source of my pain. "What can I get you?"

"I'm looking for Mike."

She eyes me with even more interest as she crooks her finger at me, motioning me closer. I prop my elbows on the counter and lean in. Her breath falters a little, and her eyes glaze over, but I'm not here to fuck some random chick.

I'm here to pound some random fucker's face until he's barely breathing.

That's the only way I'll get my rage under control.

"Mike!" I snap my fingers in her face.

"Impatient much?" She smirks, not intimidated, and I must be losing my touch.

"Always," I growl. "Now where can I find him?"

"Head back out the door, take the alleyway, and knock on the brown door at the rear of the building."

I stalk off without thanking her, and Hunt follows behind me.

"You sure you want to do this?" Hunt asks, scanning the room once we're inside. It's a much smaller venue than the usual warehouses I fight in, but I'll take what I can get.

A ring is the focal point in the space, and two burly guys are beating the shit out of one another, watched by boisterous, drunk dudes. There isn't much standing room, and the crowd thrusts and sways, shouting obscenities and encouragement.

The betting is laughable compared to the circuits I'm familiar with, but I don't care.

It's not about the money for me anymore, and even when I was fighting for my brothers, to ensure we had enough cash to look after them, it was always more about the high.

I know I'm a sick fuck.

But I'm the product of my upbringing.

Still, it could be worse.

After what I've heard about Parkhurst, I think I drew the long straw.

There's no telling how fucked up I'd be if we'd stayed in Rydeville and they had forced me into that depraved world.

I glare at Hunt, and he laughs. "Try not to kill him," he says, as the previous fight ends with one guy hauled unconscious from the ring.

"I'm making no promises," I say, ripping my shirt off my back and handing it to him.

The MC ushers me into the ring a few minutes later, and I assess my opponent with my mask firmly in place. Fighting is as much about mental intimidation as it is brute force or skill with my fists.

The guy I'm fighting has at least thirty pounds and fifteen years on me. His hard life is etched in every coarse line on his face. His full beard is in direct contrast to his bald head, and ink covers his entire upper body. He's solid, bulky, and he has some muscle definition, but there's no way he spends hours in the gym daily like me. Still, he's a formidable opponent, and judging by his conceited stare, he thinks victory is a sure thing.

Normal dudes would be afraid.

But I've never claimed to be normal.

This arrogant asshole is the perfect vessel for me to unleash my aggression.

The introductions are made, and I ignore the chorus of boos and hisses leveled my direction. They'll be singing a different tune when the fight is over.

The bell chimes, and we're off.

I dance around the ring, letting him lunge at me, easily evading contact because I'm light on my feet. I gather necessary intel. Watching his tells and learning his moves. Once the crowd boos, vocally demanding bloodshed, I swing my fist, landing a strong uppercut to his left cheek.

We go at one another, and he's a worthy competitor. Every thrust of my fist to his face and his torso fuels the adrenaline coursing through my veins. I hardly feel his hits as I release the monster locked up inside me, pouring all my frustration and rage into the fight. Sweat drips down my back and over my brow into my eyes, but it doesn't stop me. I throw punches, over and over, barely drawing a breath.

His face fades out, and I'm attacking Michael Hearst, laying into him with every ounce of pain and loathing in my body.

The dude tires before me, and when I spot the weakness in his eyes, I pounce. I charge at him, pummeling his body and his face repeatedly as he struggles to push me away. His breathing is labored, his will to end this alive more powerful than his arrogant need to win.

When he falls to the ground, I jump on him, relinquishing my anger with every punch.

My fists pound into him.

Bone crunches.

Blood splatters.

Sweat flies.

And still I don't stop. Fueled by naked fear and raw rage, the like I've never felt before.

When I'm eventually dragged off him, and announced as the winner, it feels good. My knuckles ache and my body radiates pain, but I've released some of my inner demons.

"Better?" Hunt asks, handing me my shirt.

I use it to wipe the blood and sweat off my chest and face as I climb out of the ring.

"Yeah." We hustle through the room, with hostile vibes openly directed at us.

Most bettors bet on their local legend, and they've just lost their shirts, so I'm public enemy number one.

As much as the thought of a group fight excites me, I'd prefer to walk out of here than leave on a stretcher or in a body bag, so I keep my head down and ignore the taunts thrown at me.

We push out into the alleyway, and the frigid air is like a balm to my hot skin.

"I want to bury that bastard Hearst," I say, when we're back in the car and Hunt is driving us home. I grind my teeth to the molars and flex my damaged knuckles, feeling the truth of those words resonate in every nook and cranny of my being. "I'll enjoy taking him down." I crick my head from side to side. "He'll regret the day he stole from me."

"Did you know?" I bark down the phone the minute he answers.

He sighs. "Yes."

"Thanks for the heads-up," I snap.

"It wasn't my place to tell you. You know that."

"That's why that fucker agreed to let her come to me, isn't it? He wanted her to break me."

"I'm not so sure what his motivations are," he admits, sighing. "We're barely talking, and I'm not involving him in shit anymore. But it doesn't matter, because you two needed to heal together."

I crank out a bitter laugh. "How the fuck is she expected to heal from that?"

"Are you saying you won't take care of her?" His tone turns icy cold.

"I'll take care of her. But it's not like slapping a Band-Aid on a wound!"

"Just love her, Kaiden. Show her there's a different way." I don't respond, and after a minute of silence, he adds, "Don't make me regret my decision."

"I won't," I admit, sighing as I drag a hand through my hair. "She's still my everything. Even if I want to throttle her for using this against me."

He chuckles. "Can't say I'm surprised."

I don't share his humor, and I want this to be done. "We need to change the plan."

"Why?"

"Because I've probably just compromised us."

His grunt of frustration trickles down the line. "Do you have something in mind?"

"I do." And I fill him in.

CHAPTER NINETEEN

Abby

My eyes open, and they're heavy and sore thanks to last night's crying-slash-breakdown-session. But I feel a little lighter too. Or maybe lighter is the wrong word. Because my loss, *our* loss, is a scar on my heart that will never heal. But...there is something freeing about telling the truth and releasing some emotional torment.

Movement in the room startles me, and I jerk my head sideways.

Light is trickling into the room through tiny gaps in the blinds, highlighting his silhouette. Although he's slouched in the chair, Kai is fully alert. My heart pounds in anticipation as I sit up, rubbing my eyes and squinting at him. "Do you hate me?" I blurt, because terror is doing a number on me. I hate how vulnerable I sound, but I'm wide-open after my revelation, and I couldn't disguise my emotions even if I tried.

He put my needs first last night. Holding me. Getting in the shower with me to wash off all the mud. Soothing me while he blow-dried my hair. Cradling me in his arms until I fell asleep.

But I'm not naïve. He comforted me because I was in agony, and he was in pain too.

But he's had time to think about it now.

Time for anger at my deceit to seep into his brain.

"I don't hate you, Abby. I've told you that. And I understand why you did what you did."

I slump against the headrest in relief even if I still don't know where we stand. "Why are you all bloodied and bruised?" I ask, frowning as I take in the torn skin on his knuckles and discoloration on his chin and cheeks.

I'm guessing the injuries extend beyond his face, and it's obvious he's been fighting.

He ignores me, standing and moving to the end of the bed. In one lightning-fast move, he throws the covers off and grabs my ankle, tugging me down the bed. Panic alternates with excitement as he hovers over me, his eyes glimmering with dark menace and sultry promise. "What are you doing?" I stammer as he pulls my legs down over the edge of the bed, nudging my knees apart.

"Punishing you," he confirms through gritted teeth as his callused palms start a slow, seductive trail up my legs.

My core throbs as liquid heat rushes to my lower regions. "You're not leaving me?" My eyes pierce his as I question what's going on.

Crawling over my body, he holds himself upright by his palms, and dangerous vibes roll off him in waves. "You can't get rid of me that easily." Lowering his head, he licks the side of my neck, and a whimper flies out of my mouth.

"But I lied to you."

Rolling onto his side, he presses his body flush to mine as he glares at me. Yanking the straps of my nightie down, he pinches my nipple.

Hard.

And it fucking hurts.

But I prefer rough treatment over a tender touch because I hate these new boobs and everything they represent, so, if he must touch them, I'd prefer he treat them like this. "Do it again and I won't hold back." His words send shivers tiptoeing up and down my spine, and I arch my back, pressing my boob into his hand. I writhe in need, beseeching him with my eyes. "Promise me." He tugs on my other nipple so hard my eyes water.

"I won't keep stuff from you again."

He lowers his head to my chest, sucking one taut nipple into his hot mouth, and a loud moan slips out of my mouth.

I'd wondered if I'd lose sensitivity in my breasts after the augmentation, and now, I have my answer. Kai has a wicked mouth made to deliver intense pleasure, and I doubt there's a single part of my body he could touch that wouldn't be highly sensitive to his caress.

He roughly kneads my other tit while he continues to bite and suck my nipple, and my panties are soaked with need and longing. "You are mine, Abigail." He rolls my nipple between his teeth, and I cry out at the pleasure-pain sensation.

"Are you mine?" I pant.

He stops what he's doing, lifting his head and glowering at me. "You don't deserve the answer."

"Then you don't deserve to fuck me," I snap, shoving at his shoulders.

"You think you have a choice?" He arches a brow as he sits back on his heels, yanking the hem of my nightie up. He tears my panties off and plunges two fingers inside me. "Your body has already decided."

I snarl at him, hating that he's right.

Removing his fingers from my pussy, he pushes my legs up to my chest, stretching them out to the side as wide as they will go. Then he slides down the bed, lying flat on his stomach and parting my folds. "You need to be punished for your sins. Starting now."

My pussy floods with warmth at his words, and I prop up on my elbows watching him smirk as he licks a line up and down my slit. A guttural moan filters through the air as I give in to my carnal desires. There is no point arguing because I want this as much as he does. He can call it punishment if he likes. We both know what this is.

"Are you sore?" he asks, softening his voice a little.

"No." I gasp as his tongue plunges into my channel and he devours me while rubbing at my clit with two of his fingers. My hips buck up, and I'm thrusting my pussy into his face, urging him to go faster as my climax builds.

Abruptly, he stops, ripping his delectable mouth and tongue from me seconds before my orgasm peaks, and I fist the covers in frustration. "You only come when I let you." His eyes challenge me to disagree, and I bite down hard on my lip to stop my protests from escaping my mouth.

He stands, tugging at his clothes, and I shamelessly ogle his ripped body as he undresses. "Does it hurt?" I ask, sitting up and lightly tracing my fingers along the bruising on his ribs.

"I like the pain." He shoves me down onto the bed, dragging me a little closer to the edge, before he strokes his hard cock with one hand and plays with my clit with his other one. "Grab a condom from that drawer," he commands, jerking his head at the bedside table.

"I thought you liked fucking me bare?"

"I do, but I'm guessing you're not taking birth control, and after everything we've been through, I think it's safer to use them."

His thoughtfulness almost undoes me, so I make no remark as I remove one and hand it to him, watching as he expertly rolls it on and lines himself up at my entrance. "This won't be gentle."

I consent with a nod, and he slams into me in one fast thrust causing me to scream out. Placing my legs up over his shoulders, he rams into me hard, and my breasts jiggle and shake with the movement. With one hand, he grips my hip, and his other hand tweaks my breast, pinching and digging his nails into my soft flesh.

Kai is fond of angry sex, but this is on a whole other level.

A thrill rushes through my veins. If this is what punished feels like, then I'll gladly let him punish me daily.

He rams his cock so far inside me I swear it hits off my cervix, and then he pulls out slowly, only to thrust back inside in an aggressive move, pivoting his hips as he pounds into me, over and over. His hand continues to knead my breasts, alternating between them, as he pulls and tugs painfully on my nipples.

My body is jostled with his movements, and every nerve ending is on fire.

I couldn't describe this as lovemaking, and he's avoiding kissing me, but I can't deny I'm loving every second. I'm writhing on the bed as pressure mounts in my body again, and my need to come is almost unbearable. My fingers move of their own accord, sliding down my body to frantically rub at my clit. "No." He slaps my hand away, replacing my fingers with his own as he toys with me, pushing down hard and then withdrawing, driving me fucking crazy with need.

My climax is lingering in the background, ready to burst forth and send me to heady heights, but every time I get close, he pulls back, either removing his fingers or his cock until I'm thrashing about underneath him in frustration and begging to come.

He flips me over, keeping a firm hand on my neck as he shoves my face into the comforter. His cock jams inside me and he resumes his relentless pounding. I push my hips back, gripping his cock with my pussy as I rock back and forth on his erection, desperately seeking my release.

"Who do you belong to?" he growls, swiveling his hips in a way that curls his cock inside me, and a whimper flies out of my mouth.

"You," I gasp. "Always you."

"Good girl." He leans down over me, slowing his thrusts as he fucks me while covering my back with his hot body. One hand slips underneath me, and he cups my breast. "I should refuse to let you come," he whispers, while nipping at my earlobe, "but I'm feeling generous." He straightens up, clasping my hips again as he ruts into me like a wild animal, grunting and moaning as his climax builds. He furiously rubs my clit while pounding into me so hard I see stars. The instant he shoves his pinkie into my ass, my orgasm rips through me like a tornado, and I scream so loud there's no doubt Jackson and Sawyer haven't heard. Kai roars as his climax hits, continuing to pivot his hips and grind into me as we both ride the waves together.

We collapse in a sweaty, tired heap on the bed, both struggling to bring our breathing back to normal.

I drag him into the shower a few minutes later, because we're both coated in his blood now and we need to get clean. After, he helps me change the bed linen before we crawl under the covers, exhausted. He pulls me into his body, spooning me from behind, and I latch onto his strong arms, closing my eyes.

A wave of contentment washes over me as we remain locked in our embrace. And it speaks volumes.

Because things are still unresolved between us.

I'm still destined for an arranged marriage to a man I don't love.

And there's still a hit out on Kai.

But for this one precious moment, it's just him and me.

And it's everything.

"Abby." He brushes my damp hair aside, pressing a lingering kiss on my neck.

I turn my head slightly. "Yeah."

"I'm yours." He sucks harder on my neck. "I always have been."

His words are music to my ears, and the biggest smile spreads over my mouth as my eyelids grow heavy, and I drift off to sleep.

"Get the fuck up!" Sawyer yells as I slowly come to.

Kai holds me against his chest, pulling the covers up over us to shield my naked body. But Sawyer is too busy racing around the room to notice. He grabs my bag and starts shoving stuff into it.

I have never seen Sawyer anything but cool and collected, and this panicked version terrifies me. "What's happened?" Kai asks, already climbing out of bed.

"We've been compromised. We need to leave. Now!"

I'm already sliding out of the bed, hugging the sheet around me. "Go. I'll grab the rest of my stuff."

Sawyer nods, and a few strands of dark hair fall across his brow. "Be downstairs in five. There's no time to waste."

Kai grabs my face and kisses me hard on the lips. "Hurry, babe."

I yank on jeans and a sweater before shoving my feet into sneakers. I'm just zipping up my bag when Kai comes back with a gray duffel bag slung over his shoulders. "Ready?"

I nod, and he grabs my bag as we run from the room.

Two blacked-out Land Rovers are parked at the entrance to the house when we step outside. Sawyer thrusts keys, a cell, and a gun into Kai's hands. "It's best to split up. Take the rear entrance, and we'll head out the main one and hopefully draw them away from you."

"Did you notify the Kennedys?" Kai asks.

Sawyer nods. "I sent the emergency code through the system Keven Kennedy set up, and I sent a message to Kyler directly. They have personnel on the way to secure the property."

Kai nods, dragging a hand through his hair. "Good."

"Drive as far as you can without stopping," Sawyer suggests, "and once you're sure you're not being tailed, stop somewhere and call Drew on that line. It's secure."

"Wait. What?" I ask, my puzzled gaze bouncing between them.

"I'll explain later," Kai says, giving me a nudge. "Get in."

Sawyer grabs me into a hug. "Stay safe." He looks over my shoulder at both of us. "No heroics, Kai. There is still a hit on your head. Call Drew, and he'll organize to get you out of the country safely."

"I know what to do," Kai shoots back.

I slip out of Sawyer's embrace as the driver side door on the other Land Rover opens and closes, and Jackson appears, carrying a gun. He offers it to me. "I hope you won't need this, but take it."

I check the safety is on and slip it into the back waistband of my jeans. "Thanks. Be safe." I fling my arms around his neck. "I don't want anything to happen to either of you."

"We'll be fine. Just get our boy to safety and lie low."

I move to extricate myself, but he pulls me in closer. He presses his mouth to my ear and whispers, "I'm so sorry about the babies."

A messy ball of emotion lodges in my throat, and my stomach flips over as I nod. I can't think about that now.

"We need to leave." Kai pulls me back, steering me toward the car, and I hop in as I watch him hugging his friends. I slip the gun in the glove box, wiping my clammy hands down the front of my jeans, and praying like I've never prayed before.

If we've been compromised, it can only mean the bastard has located us and is on his way to kill my lover and drag me home. I don't want to return to Rydeville, and I can't lose Kai, so I hope we can pull off whatever plan he has in mind.

Tires squeal, sending plumes of dust and gravel in our wake as both cars head off in different directions. Kai drives across the field on the right-hand side of the property, and I grip the handrail as I'm bounced all over the place. But I don't complain, and I don't ask questions even though I'm full of them.

My eyes skim our surroundings in a continual loop, and I keep a close eye on the area behind us through the mirror as Kai maneuvers the car over uneven terrain. We drive across fields, the ground becoming bumpier the farther we go, until we come to a narrow dirt track. The brakes screech as Kai makes a sharp turn, and my stomach lurches to my toes. I grip the handrail tighter. Kai grasps my free hand, squeezing it briefly, and our eyes meet for a fleeting second. I squeeze his hand back, letting him know I'm okay.

We drive for a few miles until we arrive at a set of double gates. They are smaller than the main gates at the entrance to the property but made of the same sturdy wood, and there's a keypad on this exit too. Kai punches in a code, easing the car out through the gates very carefully. We both strain forward, looking up and down the road, but there isn't a sinner in sight.

Kai turns right, flooring it as we speed away from Kyler and Faye's house.

It's killing me not to ask about Drew, but Kai needs to keep his eyes on the road, and his wits about him. I won't do anything to jeopardize our escape, so I save my questions for a later time.

We drive for hours, along back roads and side streets, avoiding the highways as much as possible, and I doze on and off.

I wake when the car jerks to a halt, squinting at the motel sign in the dim evening light. "Where are we?"

"Maine." Kai unbuckles his belt and rubs the back of his neck. "Are you okay?"

"I'm fine." I twist around, glancing out the rear window. "We weren't followed?"

He shakes his head. "I didn't spot anyone. The guys met a couple vehicles entering Mistbury as they were leaving, and they purposely snagged their attention."

My heart rate speeds up, and my breath falters in my throat. "Are they—"

"They're fine," he rushes to reassure me, threading his fingers through mine. "Jackson has mad skills, and he got away from them. They're safe." He presses a kiss to my brow. "Check us in while I make a call."

My eyes meet his. "I want to talk to my brother."

He contemplates it for a minute before nodding. Removing his wallet, he hands me a wad of cash. "Register us in false names, and don't give up any personal information."

I glare at him. "I am *not* an idiot. I know what to do."

He presses a bruising kiss to my lips. "I know, babe. I just love winding you up."

I stick my tongue out at him, and the ghost of a smile appears on his face. Removing his hoodie, he hands it to me. "Put that on and keep the hood up and your head down. Maintain a low profile. If you think anyone has spotted you, leave immediately."

I do as I'm told, and adrenaline spikes at the inherent danger of the situation. He slaps my ass as I toddle off to the reception area, and I give him the finger.

I'm chuckling when I return to the car five minutes later with our room key. Kai is impatiently drumming his fingers off the steering wheel when I open his door. "What?"

"I'm waiting for Drew to call me back. Why are you smiling?" he inquires, slipping out of the car.

I follow him around to the trunk. "This will mean fuck all to you, but I registered us as Cole Reynolds and Austin Lowes."

He shoots me some serious side eye while retrieving our bags from the trunk.

"They are characters from a book called *I Dare You,*" I explain. "It's one of my all-time favorite books. Cole is the ultimate super-hot asshole bad boy, and Austin is this fierce leading lady who takes no shit from anyone, especially her boyfriend."

"Huh." He locks the car, slinging both bags over one shoulder, before taking my hand, and pinning me with a sarcastic grin. "Sounds like us. Good call, babe."

The room is basic, but it's clean and fresh smelling, and that ticks the main boxes. I flop down on the bed as Kai dumps our bags on the floor, stifling a yawn. I wonder if the reason I'm tired way more than usual is the aftermath of the procedures my bastard father forced on me. Pain penetrates my heart, and I close my eyes to ward off an incoming bout of emotion.

The bed dips beside me. "Talk to me."

My eyes flash open, and I'm not fast enough to hide my pain. He lies down beside me, pulling me into the comforting embrace of his arms. "I'm so sorry, Abby," he whispers, smoothing a hand up and down my back.

"For what?" I ask, surprised, because Kai isn't one to apologize usually.

"For the things you've had to endure. For saying I wanted to fuck you up. For letting my anger get the best of me. For not being there to protect you and our babies."

I rest my head on his chest, wrapping my arms around his waist. "It shocked me when I first discovered I was pregnant, but the love I felt was instant," I admit with a lump in my throat. I rub my hand across his chest. "I wanted to have your babies. And I hate that bastard for taking that from us."

"I do too. I know we're young, and we live in a shitty world, but I wasn't unhappy about it. And I already loved them too." He presses a kiss to the top of my head, and my heart melts at his words. "I'm sorry I failed you," he adds, his voice choking. I look up into his beautiful brown eyes, spotting the pain there. "If I'd told you everything the night of the safe heist, you wouldn't have left the house, and I could've kept you safe."

I cup his face. "You didn't do this, Kai. It's *not* your fault."

He opens his mouth to speak, but the vibration of his phone ringing ends whatever he was about to say. He removes his cell from his pocket, and I thrust my palm out, sending him a look that dares him to deny me.

He hands it over without protest, and I hit the accept button.

"Anderson." My brother's deep voice oozes down the line.

"It's me," I say in a level tone of voice. "We need to talk."

CHAPTER TWENTY

"Are you okay? Is he keeping you safe?" Drew asks with worry threading through his words.

"I'm fine, and yes." I glance at Kai. "What's going on, Drew?"

"We're working together to keep you safe and to take Dad down."

I'm glad he didn't lie or attempt to fudge his answer because I would've gone postal on his ass. On both their asses. Because Kai's back on my shit list for concealing this.

"How long?"

"It happened after the shootout." Air exhales down the line. "Look, I know you have tons of questions. Anderson should be able to answer them, but I need to talk to him now. Although this line is secure, I don't like taking chances. I need to apprise him of the plan."

"You know I hate being kept in the dark like I'm some feeble princess who can't look after herself."

"No one thinks that of you. There is a much bigger picture here, Abby. You've seen Parkhurst. Maybe now you have a sense of how completely fucked everything is."

"This is about Parkhurst?"

"Parkhurst and Dad. I'll fill you in when I see you. I promise. I need to talk to Kaiden."

"When will I see you?"

"I don't know, but hopefully soon."

"Okay."

"Abby."

"What?"

"I trust Kaiden to keep you safe. You can trust him too."

"I know."

"Good. Talk to you soon. I love you."

"Love you too," I say, reluctantly passing the cell to Kai.

I listen to their conversation, but it's mainly one-sided and I glean little. I try to summon patience as Kai scribbles illegible shit down on a notepad, but I give up and take a shower instead.

When I emerge from the bathroom, he's propped up against the headrest, wearing only jeans. I try not to ogle his impressive chest, but it's a challenge I don't meet. I crawl up the bed in my towel with my damp hair clinging to my back. He rakes his gaze over me, smiling. "You look beautiful."

"Thank you. But flattery will not get you out of this Q and A."

He tweaks my nose. "I wasn't trying to deflect. I was just speaking my mind." He kisses me softly before climbing off the bed. "I need to grab a shower, but when I'm done, I'll answer all your questions."

"Kai." I call out, and he stops in the bathroom's doorway. "We'll be okay, won't we?"

He walks back to me, palming my face. "You can count on it." This time his kiss is long and deep, and with every sweep of his lips and every thrust of his tongue, he's reassuring me. "Okay?" He rubs his thumb along my swollen lower lip.

"Okay." I sit up on my knees, curling my hands around his neck and pulling him down for another kiss. When we break apart, he rests his forehead against mine, and the words linger on my tongue. I want to tell him I love him. That he makes me feel safe. And I feel protected when I'm with him. But something is holding me back.

He saunters toward the bathroom, and I ogle his toned back, marveling at the way his muscles flex and roll as he walks, my libido well and truly reawakened since our hot sex session this morning.

I pull on clean jeans, a top, and Kai's hoodie and wander to reception where I pick up some drinks, chips, and sandwiches. Kai is sitting on the bed in only his boxers when I return, and I lick my lips as my eyes trail the length of his body, remembering how his powerful thighs shook as he fucked me senseless a few hours ago and how little beads of sweat had glistened on his tattooed chest.

"Keep eye-fucking me and I'll have you impaled on my dick, all questions forgotten, in less time than it takes to blink."

"Maybe wear some clothes," I suggest, waggling my brows as I remove some of my purchases, handing them to him. "If I'm hungry, you must be starving."

"Ravenous," he says with hunger in his eyes, but he's not looking at the food.

I shouldn't tease him, but it's not in my nature to take the moral high ground, so I strip out of my clothes in front of him, standing in only my panties as I pull on sleep shorts and a top.

"If you're trying to torture me, it's working," he admits, stroking his hard-on through his boxers.

I scramble onto the bed beside him, grinning smugly. "Eat, because you'll need sustenance for my interrogation," I say before leaning in close to his ear. "And if you're a good boy and you answer all my questions, I'll let you eat me after."

I cross my legs, fighting the throbbing ache building between the apex of my thighs.

"Sounds like a fair deal with one alteration," he says, sending me a wolfish grin as he toys with the hem of my flimsy top. "It's got to be a naked interrogation."

I roll my eyes. "If I interrogate you naked, we won't be doing much talking."

He plants his hand on my bare thigh, heating me on contact. "That doesn't sound like such a bad idea." He licks his lips, and my pussy rejoices.

I remove his hand, because I know it'll distract me. "How did you end up working with my brother again? And are Charlie and Xavier involved too?"

"When you went missing, I broke into your house intending to murder your father."

I almost choke mid-chew. "I know my father. Security must've been crazy after the gunfight, so how the hell did you get in?"

"We used your tunnel."

My mouth drops open, and I blink excessively. "How did you know about that?"

"Drew told us."

Jaw to the floor again.

"How did he know about it?"

Kai shrugs, swallowing a few mouthfuls of water, and I avoid looking at his sexy swallow so I keep focused. "You'll have to ask Drew. All I know is the night before the heist, he told us about it in case we needed an escape route."

I know Drew couldn't have built the tunnel because it's been there longer than our seventeen and a half years on this Earth, but was he the one responsible for the upgraded works to the tunnel and the rear exit? And if he was, why did he do it? My brother and I are long overdue a talk, and I file those questions away with the others I need to ask him.

"What happened?"

"Well, we didn't get near your father for two reasons." His jaw hardens, and his entire body tenses. "The first was that asshole, Louis."

My stomach does a twisty motion, and a sour taste fills my mouth. "What did he do?"

"Nothing, because I put a bullet through his skull before he could move a muscle."

I stare at him, abandoning my sandwich and crawling into his lap. I smack a kiss on his lips. "Thank you, baby. You're my hero."

"Your response should disturb me, but I guess I'm as fucked up as you, because all it does is turn me on." He jerks his hips up, and I feel the growing bulge against my ass.

"As much as I'm down to ride your cock," I admit, grinding against him. "I need answers more. Continue." I climb off his lap, picking my sandwich up again as he eyes me with amusement.

"I wish he hadn't died so painlessly," he continues. "I was on top of his dead body pounding my fists into his skull before I even realized it. Lauder and Hunt were trying to pull me off, but I was lost in a fit of rage, and if Drew hadn't come along, we most likely would've been captured by your father's men."

"Drew helped you."

He nods. "Drew got rid of the body, and Xavier wiped the camera feed. Then we held a meeting, the six of us, and thrashed everything out."

"What did you discuss?" I ask, because that's not a satisfactory answer.

"We fessed up to why we'd hidden the documents from the safe although they'd already pieced the facts together from the night of the shootout." He puts his sandwich and drink aside, turning to face me. "I told him I'd no idea my father had sabotaged your birth control and that I wasn't a part of the plan to get you pregnant. He could see I was genuine, especially when I begged him to tell me where you were."

"And did he?"

"He didn't know where you were although Charlie and Drew guessed he had taken you to Parkhurst. They were as anxious as we were to rescue you, so we agreed to work together."

Certain things slid into place. "That's how Xavier knew you guys had taken me. And Charlie knew your brothers would kidnap me. That's why he said it," I muse.

"Said what?" Kai asks, instantly alert.

"Uh, nothing." I attempt to dismiss it, but he's having none of it.

"This truth thing works both ways." He points between us. "Our relationship won't work if we don't trust one another implicitly. That includes sharing everything. So, spit it out."

"We're in a relationship?" I blurt.

He winds his hand around the nape of my neck. "You're my girl, and I'm your guy. What else would you call it?"

I climb back onto his lap. "I can't believe you forgave me so easy."

He grips my ass cheeks, squeezing. "What makes you think you're forgiven?" He slaps my ass hard. "This morning was only the start of your punishment. You'll suffer for deceiving me, but I'm done punishing myself." He drags my head down, kissing me with possessive intensity. "You're mine, and I'm not letting you go again."

"There's just one tiny problem," I reluctantly admit. "I'm technically engaged to Charlie." I wet my dry lips. "And just before he got out of the car that day, he told me he loved me and that he genuinely wanted to marry me. He implored me to keep my options open, saying you weren't the only choice."

His eyes darken to almost black, and a muscle pops in his jaw. "I fucking knew it! I could tell every time he looked at you." He grabs both sides of my face forcefully. "I'll only ask you this once. Do you love him?"

I shake my head. "I don't love him like that." His eyes narrow, and I glare at him. "Don't do that. He's one of my best friends, and I love him the same way I love Jane and Xavier. In a purely platonic way."

I want to add that the only one I love is him, but I'm fucked if I'm going to make myself that vulnerable.

He can say it first, and then I'll return the sentiment.

His face contorts, and a myriad of conflicting emotions glints in his eyes. His features soften as he loosens his hold on my face, caressing my cheek with his fingers. "There's something I need to tell you about Charlie. This'll make me sound like a jealous asshole, but it's more than that. I've wanted to tell you all week, but it means exposing you to something risky."

He bites down on his lip, pausing.

"Don't second-guess yourself. We agreed no more secrets. Just tell me." I lean down and kiss him.

"Charlie is the reason you—"

The door to the hotel room crashes inward with a resounding thud, cutting off Kai's statement. I jump off his lap, lunging for the gun on top of the bedside table, when a familiar figure storms into the room, flanked by two armed goons.

"I've found them," Charlie says into his cell, frowning as he skims his eyes over my semi-dressed body, his gaze lingering on my braless chest. "I'll have your daughter back in Rydeville before midnight."

CHAPTER TWENTY-ONE

"What have you done?" I'm horrified as I stare at Charlie, wondering if I've ever known him at all. I inch toward the bedside table as Kai slowly climbs off the bed, keeping his gaze locked on Charlie the entire time.

Charlie gestures with his eyes toward Maurio and Benjamin. I understand it's a warning to be careful what I say in front of my father's bodyguards. "Your father has your best interests at heart," Charlie says. "As do I. Which is why you *will* return to Rydeville with me."

"Over my dead body," Kai growls, stalking toward Charlie with murderous intent.

I grab my gun at the same moment Maurio and Benjamin withdraw their weapons, pointing them at Kai. I race in front of my boyfriend, shielding him with my body as I hold the gun out in front of me. "Back down or I'll shoot." I level the gun at Benjamin's chest, gritting my teeth and steadying my hand. I don't want to shoot him. But I'll do it to protect Kai if it comes down to it.

"Wait outside," Charlie commands them in an authoritative voice.

"Our instructions are to remain by your side at all times," Maurio calmly replies.

"I don't care what your instructions are," Charlie says, eyeballing him. "I'm in charge. Leave. Now." His cold tone matches the threatening look on his face.

Maurio considers it for a moment, glancing briefly at me, and I spot the flash of indecision before he concedes. Lowering his gun, he slips it back into his gun strap. "You have five minutes." The two of them leave, and a layer of stress lifts from my shoulders.

Charlie locks the door behind them and comes to stand in front of me. "You can put the gun down now, Abby."

I take a step closer, pressing the muzzle into his chest, right in the spot where his heart is. "Can I?"

Kai circles his arm around my waist from behind, holding me tight as I keep the weapon pressed to Charlie's chest. "I won't hurt you, and I'm not on your father's side," he adds in a hushed tone. "I've only ever been on yours."

Kai snorts. "Bullshit."

Charlie's eyes darken as he glares at Kai over my shoulder. "I'm already resenting saving your ass, so don't push it."

"What does that mean?" I ask.

"It means there's no longer a hit out on him." He glances over my shoulder, pursing his lips. "You're welcome." Sarcasm drips from his tone.

I lower my arm while maintaining a hold of the gun. "And the price is I return to Rydeville and marry you?" I surmise. He nods. "My father isn't trustworthy. How do we know he's called off the hit?"

"He won't jeopardize our marriage, because it's too important."

"Why?"

"It's elite business. I'm not at liberty to disclose it."

"Can't or don't want to?" Kai asks, moving us back a few steps and creating some space between us and him.

"It's Parkhurst rules. Abigail understands that." His eyes rake me up and down. "Get dressed and grab your things. We need to hit the road before your father changes his mind."

"She's not leaving with you." Kai's tone is territorial in the extreme.

I place the gun down on the bed and turn around in his arms. "Babe."

"No." He shoots me down before I've said anything else. "No one is taking you from me again." He pulls me in closer, flattening his palms on my back. "Especially not that asshole." I can't tell if he means my father or Charlie or both of them.

"He will kill you if we stay together." My heart thumps painfully at the thought of separation, but it doesn't seem like we have much choice. If I'm not in that car in the next few minutes, I've no doubt Maurio and Benjamin are under strict instructions to murder Kai and take me by force.

"I'll take my chances." His jaw sets in a stubborn line.

"I won't let you. Your life means more."

Anger flares in his eyes. "My life means jack shit without you in it."

"Now he gets all romantic." I roll my eyes, trying to lighten the horrid tense atmosphere, even though my heart is singing at his declaration.

"Abby." That one word is a warning.

"Trust me," I mouth. "You know it has to be like this," I say out loud for Charlie's benefit.

He slams his mouth down on mine without warning, devouring me with his lips and his tongue, conveying everything he can't verbalize. I want to do this about as much as he wants me to do it. But we both know it's the only way.

Charlie clears his throat. "We need to go now, Abby," he says in a clipped tone, disapproval hovering in the air.

Reluctantly, I pull away from Kai, ignoring the panicked fluttering in my chest and pain in my heart. The torment in his eyes reflects how I'm feeling, and I'm sick to my stomach as I grab some clothes and run into the bathroom to change. I emerge two minutes later to discover the guys in a tense standoff.

"Keep your grabby hands to yourself," Kai warns.

"She's my fiancée," Charlie says, doing little to disguise his smug smile. "And her father expects to see displays of affection. It's a dirty job, but someone's got to do it."

Kai rams his fist into Charlie's face, landing a firm blow to his nose, and blood spurts from the wound. Charlie swings his fist, glancing the side of Kai's jaw and they go at it, throwing vicious punches at one another in quick succession.

"Stop!" I snap out of my mini daze, forcing myself in between them. "This isn't helping."

"You're not doing it," Kai snarls, pulling me into his side while wiping blood off his upper lip. "I don't trust him."

"You don't have a say," Charlie replies, dabbing at his bloody nose. "If we aren't on the road in the next few minutes, they will put a bullet in your skull. Is that what you want for Abby? To have that on her conscience?"

Kai pulls me back into his chest, wrapping his arms around me again. "I know what you're doing, and I'll be watching," he threatens Charlie.

"Oh, I forgot to mention one important element of the deal," Charlie adds, fighting a lip twitch. "Stay away from her, or it's forfeit."

I'm not shocked. I expect no less of my father. I twist around in his arms. "You need to let me go," I whisper while my eyes articulate a different sentiment. "We always knew it would come to this."

Taking his hand, I plant it over my heart. "You're the only one who owns my heart. Forever."

He rests his forehead against mine, bundling me into his arms. "I love you," he whispers over my mouth, his warm breath fanning my face, and it's amazing how those three little words cause my heart to soar and deflate at the same time.

"I love you too," I say, much louder, wanting Charlie to hear.

We pull apart, silently agreeing to the plan with our eyes. Kai pulls on his jeans, watching me with a tortured expression as I shove my toiletries and pajamas into my bag. I remove the box with my engagement ring from my bag, stuffing it in my pocket. Charlie slings my bag over his shoulder before taking my hand and leading me to the door.

I cast a glance over my shoulder at Kai.

"Stay safe," he mouths, working hard to rein in his anger and frustration.

"You too."

Charlie pulls me forward, ignoring Kai as he closes the door behind us, ushering me toward the car.

I ignore Charlie the entire four-hour ride back to Rydeville, much to his obvious dismay. Kai's words linger in my mind. He was going to tell me something about Charlie, but Charlie interrupted us before he got the chance. What's abundantly clear is Charlie is up to something, and I can't trust him. I don't think he'd hurt me, but his profession of love has clouded his judgment, and that scares me. More than that, it hurts. Because Charlie was one of the few people I genuinely thought I could count on, but I realize I don't know the real Charlie at all.

I sit upright in my seat as we round the corner toward my house.

"Why are we here?" I ask, instantly suspicious. "I thought you said I'd be staying at your place?"

"Your father wants to talk to you, and you need to box up the rest of your stuff. Mrs. Banks has already moved most of your clothes to my house, but I insisted she left your personal possessions for you to sort through."

"If you're expecting my gratitude, you'll be waiting a while." Bile churns in my gut as we drive up the driveway toward the mausoleum that has never felt like a home. I remove the engagement ring from the box with a heavy heart, pretending I don't see Charlie's happy smile as I slide it on my finger.

He parks in front of the house as the security car trailing us continues on to the large garage. Charlie kills the engine and turns to face me. "You're pissed. I get it. But this was the only way to keep him alive."

"Don't do that," I hiss. "Don't pretend like you've done this for him."

"I'm not pretending," he deadpans. "I've done this for you."

"Why?"

"Because I love you, and, for reasons I don't fully understand, he's important to you." He shrugs, appearing indifferent, but his muscles are corded into knots and his jaw clenches. "For now."

"Didn't you hear what I said back there?"

"I heard you, but people change. Feelings change. And I know you have feelings for me."

"Not the feelings you're suggesting." I level him with an earnest look. "I don't love you, Charlie. I love Kaiden. Being kept away from him won't change that."

"Well, I guess you must fake it then," he barks. "Because *your* life and *his* life depend on your father buying into our engagement." He sighs, dragging a hand through his dark hair. "Look, I'm not stupid.

I know you love one another. But there is no scenario where your father will ever permit it." He takes my hand, rubbing circles on my skin with his thumb. "He approves of me, and I can take care of you. I'll give you a good life, and I'll treat you the way you deserve. In time, you'll learn to love me."

He is fucking delusional, but I won't continue arguing the point. Because a lot of what he has said is true. Kai's survival means I must be with Charlie. At least until we figure out a way out of this mess. If Charlie wants me to buy into his fantasy, and it's the best way of safeguarding Kai's life, then I'll do it.

"Fine."

He arches a brow. "Fine?"

"But I'm only doing this for Kai," I say before getting out of the car.

He comes up behind me, placing his hand on my lower back. I shuck out of his reach, stabbing him with a cautionary look. "I will do what I have to in public, but no touching unless it's absolutely necessary."

He raises his palms in a conciliatory gesture. "Whatever you say." His tone is affable, but I don't miss the glimmer of determination shining in his eyes.

I inwardly curse as I step foot into my house for the first time in weeks.

Because I've just realized I'm in the middle of another battle.

One for my heart.

CHAPTER TWENTY-TWO

"I trust you've come to your senses, Abigail?" the bastard says as we enter the formal living room over on the west wing of the house.

Charlie slides his arm around my waist, and I lean into him as we walk across the patterned rug toward the blazing fire. On the outside, Charlie is the epitome of cool, calm, and collected, but his body is wired tight, every muscle straining in anticipation, and danger radiates from him with every step we take toward my father.

I've sensed this about him before—this lethal calm that hides the feral beast caged within.

Provided it's used in my favor, I've zero issue with him unleashing it. However, I'm not some naïve little princess. I know his idea of acting in my best interests isn't the same interpretation I'd apply. Charlie has the potential to be a formidable enemy, and if I don't play the game the right way, that's exactly what he'll end up being.

"You say that like I wanted to get kidnapped?" I coolly reply while taking a seat beside Charlie on the hard leather couch across from my father.

He's sitting comfortably, one leg crossed over the other, with the prerequisite whiskey in hand. "Don't be facetious." He sips his drink, eyeing me over the rim of the glass. "We both know you loved being back with that delinquent."

"If he's a delinquent, it's your fault for ripping his life apart," I snap, letting anger get the better of me. Charlie squeezes my side, but I ignore him. "You know, by murdering his mother, stealing everything from his father, and leaving them to rot in poverty planning their vengeance."

The glass smashes to the ground, shattering into tiny shards as he storms toward me, grabbing my chin and stretching my neck up painfully. "You seem to have forgotten your place, daughter, and it's time I reminded you." He fists a hand in my sweater, yanking me to my feet. His eyes roam over me in disgust. "You look like a common peasant."

"Mr. Hearst." Charlie stands.

"Be very careful with the words you say next, Charles," the bastard warns.

I daren't look at Charlie, so I can't tell what expression is on his face when he says, "She's my fiancée. I'll be the one to discipline her."

What the actual fuck? I thought he'd try to stop him, but no, he's going along with it. A red layer coats my eyes, and anger burns the back of my throat, but I say nothing, show nothing, keeping a neutral expression on my face even though I want to murder both men.

Charlie's statement calms him down, somewhat. "Trouble?" he asks, momentarily distracted by Charlie's swollen nose.

"Nothing I couldn't handle," he coolly replies.

Father shoves me at my fiancé, straightening his shirt and tie, before a familiar sneer creeps across his ugly mouth. Panic bubbles up my throat. "Let's see if I've made the right choice." He levels Charles with a menacing look.

I work hard to keep my face neutral because I refuse to show any fear in front of him. Instead, I cling to my hatred, using it to bolster my determination to take him down, no matter the cost.

He tore my babies from my body without permission. Inserted these hideous breast implants knowing I didn't want them. And now he's blackmailing me into another arranged marriage.

He doesn't get to keep doing this shit to me.

He *will* pay.

I repeat that mantra over and over in my mind, using it to anesthetize me from what's about to happen.

"Twenty slaps on her bare ass. Right here. Right now."

I seethe underneath my skin as Charlie turns me in his arms and demands, "Jeans off now." His face is a mask of cold indifference, and I can't tell if it's an act or not.

Embracing my anger and my hatred, I remove my jeans, carefully setting them aside and standing with my chin up, daring him to do his worst. Charlie sits back down on the couch, patting his lap.

"Panties off," my father instructs, and I know he gets off on this sick shit.

I hook my thumbs in the top of my panties, ready to remove them, when Charlie grabs my hips, pulling me across his lap, facedown. When I'm stretched out, with my face pressed into the arm of the couch and my ass slightly tilted, he removes my panties, pushing them down my legs to my ankles.

An involuntary cry rips from my mouth as stinging pain lances across my ass with the first slap. I bite down hard on my lip as Charlie wastes no time doling out my punishment, slapping my ass in quick succession. I want to believe he's doing this fast, to get it over and done with, rather than he's doing this deliberately, because it hurts more when there's no time to recover in between, but honestly, the jury is out.

Squeezing my eyes shut, I ignore the pain and the humiliation, focusing on my anger and my rage and cementing my determination to bring him down.

"Nice job," the bastard says. "I'm partial to that shade of red on my women."

I swallow my disgust, relieved when I feel Charlie drawing my panties back up my legs.

"No." Charlie stops for a second at my father's command. "Let her stand and put them back on herself."

My lip trembles at his undisguised desire to see my naked pussy, and intense fear overtakes me.

My father has never looked at me in a sexual way or put a hand on me in that regard, but I've always known he's capable of it. I don't know what goes on in his sex dungeon, but I doubt it's legal or in any way pleasurable for the women.

"No." Charlie's voice is resolute as he defies my father, pulling my panties back up into place. "No one gets to see her pussy but me." My stomach sours, and I cringe as I brush against the bulge in his pants. Knowing doing that to me turned him on doesn't sit well with me.

What angle is Charlie playing, and am I the ultimate prize, or is he playing for bigger stakes?

My father chuckles, clearly amused, which is a shock. Any time Drew stands his ground, he's met with vicious fists.

Charlie grips my hips and places me on my feet. Snatching my jeans, he hands them to me while maintaining eye contact with my father as he rises.

"How do you expect to achieve that after you're married with your newly elevated status within the order?" the bastard asks.

I lean a hand on the couch to keep my balance as I shimmy my jeans up my legs, feigning indifference when I'm avidly listening to their conversation.

"I'm not sharing her." Charlie stubbornly crosses his arms.

"I probably shouldn't mention I've had my hands all over her tits." My father smirks, baiting Charlie, while I struggle to hold on to my stomach contents.

"That better be a joke," I hiss.

A cruel glint glimmers in his eye, and his lips curl up at the corners. "It's important after breast augmentation to massage the tits daily so they don't turn hard or settle in the wrong position. You were unconscious during the recovery period, so Wyatt and I took care of it for you." He smirks, lowering his gaze to my chest. "You're welcome."

I feel violated all over again.

I've no clue what Charlie did with Wyatt, but in this moment, I hope he put a bullet through his sleazy skull. A retaliation is resting on my tongue when Charlie pulls me into his arms, pressing a kiss to the top of my head. "The only man touching her from now on is me."

A belly laugh rumbles from my father. "You rarely have an issue sharing women." He cocks a brow, and that sick feeling is back in my tummy. I purposely avoid looking at Charlie because Father wants to rattle me, and I won't give him the satisfaction.

"Whores are different," Charlie deadpans, and I'm at risk of losing what little food is in my stomach. "She'll be my wife, and I intend to respect her."

The bastard slaps him on the shoulder. "Such noble, misguided goals."

I risk a sneaky glance at Charlie. He looks composed, but the vein throbbing in his neck says otherwise. He's primed to explode, which is interesting. He isn't enjoying this, which means it's all part of the act. "My father avoids it with my mother."

My father's amused grin disappears. "And that's one reason he'll never advance, but you, my boy." He clamps down hard on his shoulder. "You're destined for greater things. We both know it."

"I won't share her," Charlie repeats, and I'm surprised he's challenging my father and still breathing.

The bastard's stare is calculating as he assesses Charlie. "This conversation is a little premature, don't you think? You're not even married yet. You might change your mind." He leers at me, and nausea travels up my throat. Charlie tucks me possessively under his arm, and I shiver uncontrollably as potent fear breaks free. Father glances at his Rolex. "I made plans, so let's conclude our business."

Charlie resettles me on the couch beside him, draping his arm across my shoulder and keeping me close. I chew on the inside of my mouth to avoid wincing as my sore ass hits the hard leather. Summoning restraint from some deep hidden place, I dig my nails into my sides to avoid lunging at Charlie before I earn further punishment.

"You will tell no one you were pregnant," my father says, piercing me with a warning look. "And, as far as anyone knows, you are still a virgin and you will remain a virgin until your wedding night."

I want to know why it's so important, but there's no point asking a question I'll get no response to.

"How do you expect to keep that hidden when there were others privy to the discussion the night of the engagement party," I say.

"That is being dealt with. All you need to concern yourself with is presenting as the dutiful, virgin bride to be."

"I'll do it," I say. "On one condition." I straighten my spine. "You will not touch, maim, or kill Kaiden Anderson, any of his brothers, or any of the people on that list, either by your own hand or via a paid hit."

My father smirks. "It's amusing you think you have any negotiating power."

"It's amusing how you disregard me so flippantly." I lean forward. "If anything happens to me or Kai, or anyone else I love, a statement will be sent to every reporter and law enforcement office in the US confirming everything you've done to me and others."

His smirk widens. "I own most of those people. I can make it go away like that." He clicks his fingers.

"You don't own everyone, and it will be enough to cast suspicion."

"You think the delusional musings of a teenage girl will garner any real interest?"

"I think the people you're trying to fool would sit up and take notice." I'm bluffing, because I have set none of this up yet although I plan to. While I don't know if my instincts are correct, Drew claims this is bigger than Manning Motors, and I know this is connected to Parkhurst, and considering the bastard is so focused on appearances, there has got to be someone he is trying to impress or deceive. "And you reported me as a missing person, splashing my face all over the news, in case you'd forgotten."

"That's a non-issue. We have informed the media of my delight at your return," he deadpans.

"You brought a spotlight on my head, Father. It's enough for the media to pay attention if I come forth with a statement."

The door opens, and Mrs. Banks pops her head in. "Your guest has arrived, sir."

"Bring her to me," he says without looking up at our housekeeper.

"She will test your patience at every turn," he says, looking at Charlie. "Are you sure you can handle her?"

"I'm right here," I protest.

"Shut your face, Abigail." His fists clench at his sides, and I know I've struck a nerve. I add it to my mental notepad to analyze later.

I open my mouth to offer some snarky retort, but Charlie pinches my arm in warning, and I clamp my mouth shut again. "She will submit, and I will keep her under control."

"See that you do." He stands, and we climb to our feet.

"I give you my word that nothing will happen to that delinquent," he agrees, eyeballing me. "But if you cross me, all deals are off, and he's the first one I'll go after. Do you understand?

"I understand."

"Good."

The door opens again, and a tall, skinny blonde with big lips and even bigger tits enters the room. She's wearing a minuscule white minidress and sky-high stilettos. Diamonds drip from her neck and slender arms. "Darling." She drapes herself around my father, and I'm not fast enough to disguise the look of disgust from my face. She looks like she's only a few years older than me, and it's just so wrong.

Grabbing her by the wrists, he pulls her around in front of him, licking his lips as he eye-fucks her. "Strip and get on your knees."

He ignores her as she lifts the hem of her dress without argument, focusing on me. "You will stay the night here. Your brother has missed you."

He's not asking. But I want to see Drew anyway, so I nod.

"And I expect you both here for dinner every Sunday."

"We'll be here," Charlie says, averting his eyes as the woman pulls her bra off, standing before us in only her panties and high heels.

"Aren't you going to introduce us?" I mock.

"She's no one," he says, opening the buckle on his belt, his lips twitching as my mouth pulls into a grimace. "Stay if you want to watch," he adds, challenging me with a knowing look. His loud laughter follows me as I race out the door with Charlie hot on my heels.

Once the door is closed, I spin around, shoving Charlie in the chest. "You can leave." I stab him with a venomous look, my ass still stinging from his hand.

"I had no choice."

"There are always choices," I say, and I'm reminded of Sawyer saying the same thing to me one time. "And you had no issue standing up to him on the sharing thing." A shiver works its way through me at the thought of all that entails.

"I know how to handle your father."

"Because you understand how his mind works?" I query, wondering if Charlie shares similar psychopathic traits, because he's a bit all over the place, and I can't get an accurate reading on him or his agenda.

His eyes drift upward, toward the spot where one of the hidden cameras is mounted to the wall. "Not here. Let's talk in your bedroom."

He moves to take my hand, and I shove my elbow into his ribcage. "Don't fucking touch me."

He grabs my elbow, dragging me along the hallway. Pressing his mouth to my ear, he whispers, "We need to perform for the cameras, or do you want your boyfriend to be killed?"

That sobers me up, and I stop fighting, letting him hold my hand, but the second we're behind closed doors in my room, I push him away. "Start talking."

"I'm sorry that had to happen, but it won't be the last unpleasant thing I'm forced to do if you continue to berate him." He steps toward me.

I hold up a palm. "Don't come any closer unless you want a black eye. I am fucking pissed."

"I couldn't tell."

"Do not joke with me either."

"Jeez, tough crowd."

"Charlie," I growl, grabbing fistfuls of my long hair in frustration.

He walks to my bed and sits down, patting the space beside him. "Please, sit."

"Did you not hear what I just said?"

"I'll take my chances." He pats the bed again.

I sit my butt down as far away from him as possible, and his face drops. "I'm on your side, Abby. And I'm doing everything I can to help you. Why the hell else would I broker a deal with your father to save Kai's life if it wasn't about helping you? It's not as if I like the asshole. He's stolen you out from under me before I had a chance to show you how good we could be."

"Don't do that." I can't handle emotional blackmail right now.

He scoots a little closer. "It's the truth." His hands twitch at his sides and I can tell he wants to touch me, but he's holding back. "I love you, and I want to spend my life with you, but if he's your choice, I will let you go."

I examine his face for evidence of the truth. "I thought you wanted to marry me and give me a good life."

"That is still on the table. And we can do that in Rydeville or far away from here. We can get married and disappear, if that's what you want."

"You'd leave your family to run away with me?" Skepticism laces through my words.

"Yes." He doesn't hesitate to respond. "It's what I was planning to do the night of the shootout."

"You said Oscar was meant to take me to Xavier's warehouse that night and we would flee to Europe, but how did you know to plan that in advance?"

"I knew it wouldn't take you long to figure it out." He runs his hand through his black hair as worry lines form on his brow.

"If you want me to trust you, Charlie, you need to be honest with me."

"Telling you this places you in greater danger, but I don't see there's any way of sheltering you from it now." He moves closer until there's only a small gap between us. His emerald green eyes penetrate mine. "Most everything that's going on is connected to changes happening within the order, and at Parkhurst."

"What is the order?"

"It's the hierarchy within the US elite structure. Drew can fill you in on it, but changes are coming, and my father wants out before it happens. A couple years ago, a faction within the elite contacted him, concerned about your father's agenda and the level of support he was garnering. They asked for his help, and in exchange, they promised to grant him freedom. To let him leave the elite. Leave Rydeville. And put it all behind him."

"Why does your father want that?"

"Because he's never wanted any part of it. He inherited it. It was his legacy, but it's never been what he's wanted for his family. He's gone to extreme lengths to shield Mom from the worst excesses of the order, and, occasionally, he's flouted the archaic rules, even though it was risky."

He crosses his ankles. "When your father and Christian Montgomery orchestrated Atticus Anderson's demise, Dad realized he was stuck. That there was no way out, and he tried to toe the line. But your father is power hungry, and the more he gains, the worse he becomes. When the offer came from enemy quarters, it didn't take him long to decide to help them."

A light bulb goes off in my head, and my eyes pop wide. "Holy shit. Your father's been working with Atticus Anderson, hasn't he?"

Charlie nods.

"And that means—"

"That I've been working with the new elite from the beginning."

CHAPTER TWENTY-THREE

That must've been what Kai was about to tell me back at the hotel. I dig my nails into the comforter. "You're all motherfucking lying bastards." Every muscle in my body tenses. "Was Drew in on it too?"

"No. Drew knew nothing until they took you to Parkhurst, and then I confided in him. It's one reason he's pissed with me. Why I'm on the outside now."

"You knew there would be a face-off that night at the party."

"I did, and I knew it would get messy, so I'd pulled Oscar aside earlier that day and explained. He agreed to stash his car near the old rear entrance and to get you to safety until I could come for you."

"Why didn't you tell me?"

"I couldn't tell you without admitting the full truth, and it's always been safer if you didn't know."

And here we go with the broken record again. "I swear the next person who says that is gonna get a bullet in the brain." I'm seething as I glare at him. "And how the fuck was it safer keeping me in the dark?" I hiss, standing and pacing. "You enabled them to bully and humiliate me!" I lunge at him, and a loud crack echoes around the room as my palm impacts his cheek. "You facilitated everything by working with them behind my back."

"I deserve that," he calmly replies, giving nothing away.

Something else occurs to me, and I narrow my eyes. "Did you know about the pregnancy plan?"

He vehemently shakes his head. "I didn't even know you were pregnant. Neither did my father. Turns out, Atticus wasn't as forthcoming as we'd been."

"That's how the guys knew their way around my house. How they knew there were cameras in the main living areas. How they knew about the safe." I climb back onto the bed, resting my back against the headrest and pulling my knees up to my chest. "Your father told them everything."

That fucking son of a bitch. I inwardly seethe. I knew his compassion was too good to be true. That he wasn't doing it out of the goodness of his heart. I'll add him to the list of cruel, ruthless, self-obsessed bastards, alongside my father and the Montgomerys.

"He did, but Atticus abused his trust by hiding the true nature of his plans." He twists around so he's facing me. "My father loves you like a daughter. I hope you know that. And he's always known how deep my feelings ran. He'd never have agreed to partner with Atticus, Wes, and their associates if he'd known they would use you as a pawn."

"But you knew what the new elite were up to."

"It was planned so they'd arrive when we were away in Parkhurst. They were supposed to manipulate you to earn your trust so they could gain access to the house without suspicion. I was furious when I found out what they were doing to you. Sawyer had promised you'd be treated with respect, but he's a fucking liar because he did nothing to stop his friends from abusing you."

My head is on overload, and I'm trying to decipher the myriad of threads floating through my mind. I recall Sawyer's obvious disgust the day Kai made me kneel at his feet in the cafeteria. His annoyance when he came into my living room to find Kai and Jackson groping me. His frustration with them the night they used me to help them break into my father's office.

"He tried," I admit. "But no one tells Kaiden Anderson what to do."

"And yet you still love him." He grinds his teeth, and his jaw flexes. "Maybe I should bully you and treat you like shit. Perhaps you'd fall for me then."

"He doesn't treat me like shit, and there's so much more to him than that."

"He's continually lied to you, Abby." Frustration thunders through his tone.

"So have you. So has pretty much everyone. I should hightail it out of Rydeville and let my father kill all of you. I don't know why I'm loyal when it's not shown to me in return."

"But it is," a familiar voice says, and I jerk my head to the doorway, jumping up when I spot Drew. "All the guys in your life would take a bullet for you. They would die before letting anything happen to you."

I race across the room, throwing myself into his arms, way too happy to see him to be mad. He pulls me into his warm embrace, and we hug it out for ages. I rest my head on his chest, and he presses a kiss into my hair. "Missed you, A."

"Missed you, too, D."

When he tilts my chin up, forcing my gaze to his, I smother my shocked gasp as I take in the state of him.

His usually coiffed hair has grown out, curling around his ears and down the nape of his neck, and it's messy on top, in a similar fashion to Jackson's hair. A thick layer of stubble covers his chin and cheeks, and bruising shadows linger in the curves under his bloodshot eyes. "You look like shit." My gaze drifts to the jagged scar over his lip, and there's another similar one just over his eyebrow.

"Feel like shit too," he says, surprising me. I expected a snappy retort.

"We have lots to catch up on." I take his hand, dragging him over to the couch.

"I should go," Charlie says, standing and rounding the end of the bed.

"You should." Drew's cold tone matches his critical expression.

"I'll collect you in the morning for school," he tells me. "And we can swing by here after to pick up the rest of your stuff."

"Okay."

He leaves, and Drew walks to the door, checking the hallway before closing and locking it. "I don't trust him. We've frozen him out, and I expected him to push back, but he hasn't, and I'm suspicious."

"I don't trust anyone, and I'm suspicious of everyone."

"That's fair."

"I'm glad you agree." I purse my lips.

"Abby." Compassion splays across his face. "I'm so sorry for what that fucking bastard did to you, and if I hadn't been almost comatose in the hospital for two weeks, I'd have gone after you. It probably wouldn't have made much difference, but I would've tried."

I want to believe him, but...

"Are *you* okay?" I run the tip of my finger over the scar across his lip. "He did this?"

Drew bobs his head. "I thought he would kill me this time. I fought back, but he pulled in four of his guys, and five against one are never good odds."

"We need to get rid of him, Drew. I can't live my life like this. I *won't* live my life like this."

"I'm with you, A. I have been for a long time."

"You have a plan." It's more of a statement than a question. He nods. "You'll share it?" He nods again.

"I hope you mean that, because I don't want to be on opposing teams, Drew. We won't succeed unless we work together, and that means you have to stop shielding me."

"I know."

The truth radiates from his every pore, and I think we might be able to get somewhere. "You won't get another chance, D. You get that, right? If you let me down again, there is no coming back from it."

"I won't fail you again." His eyes flash with steely determination, and I sincerely hope he means that, and that he'll stick to it.

"How did you get back in his good graces?"

"I told him I was double-crossing the new elite. That I recorded the theft, and I intended to use it to put them behind bars. That they were meant to bring the documentation to me, and I'd safeguard it. I told him I wanted to prove I could handle things without running to him. Thank fuck, my cell was smashed beyond repair during the shootout so he couldn't confirm or deny it."

"And you think he bought that?" I'm skeptical in the extreme.

"He's on the fence, but I'm his only male heir and the timing is sensitive, so he's no choice but to give me the benefit of the doubt." His face turns pale, his mouth contorting into a grimace. "I'm working my ass off to prove my loyalty, but I'm still on probation. One false move. One hint that I'm playing this game, and it won't be pleasant."

Fear for my brother turns the blood in my veins to ice. If the bastard finds out what he's up to, he will kill him.

A pregnant pause ensues, and there are so many things I want to say to my brother I don't even know where to start. I want to ask him what he's doing to prove his loyalty, but I sense I'm better off not knowing. "Where is Jane?" I ask instead.

His face contorts in pain. "I don't know."

"How can you not know?" I wail. "She was the love of your life!"

"*Is*. She *is* the love of my life, and it's because I love her so fucking much that I sent her away. I've tried to protect both of you, but all I've done is continually put you in harm's way." His shoulders slump in defeat.

"What did you say to her father to get them to leave?"

He drops onto the couch, burying his head in his hands, and I sit down beside him, snaking my arm around his back. He rests his head on my shoulder. "I told him some truths about Parkhurst, the order, what Father is planning, and the kind of life Jane would have if she married into it. I told him to run. To never look back and never come back." His voice cracks. "They were gone less than twenty-four hours later."

"I'm proud of you, Drew."

"Don't." He lifts his head. "Don't be proud of me unless I've done something genuinely worthy of it. And I haven't." He shakes his head, and the look of sheer agony on his face destroys me.

"What if Father goes after them? They were part of the elite, and they shouldn't have run."

"He's juggling too many balls, and they're not important in the scheme of things."

"He won't forget."

"No." He scrubs a hand across his stubbly chin. "He won't. But I have contingencies in place." Fire blazes in his eyes. "He won't get near her."

"Agreed."

He sighs, offering me a tentative smile. "It's good to have you back."

"I'd like to say it's good to be home, but it's really not." I skim my eyes around my bedroom, feeling like a stranger in my own space. "And I won't even be living here."

"That might work to our advantage."

I peer into his eyes. "How?"

He stands, pulling me up with him. "I'll tell you when we get there."

"Get where?"

"To Xavier's warehouse. The others are meeting us there in an hour, and we'll fill you in on the rest."

I kill the engine on the Kawasaki just as we reach Xavier's warehouse. Riding the open roads again for the first time in months is exhilarating, and it's lifted my spirits.

Drew hops off first, holding the bike as I disembark. "I'm capable of doing that."

"I know you are, but I'm trying to be a gentleman."

"You're trying to butter me up." I prod him in the chest. "Because you know I'm about to go apeshit on your ass."

"There is that." He grins, and it's good to see him smile.

I stand under the camera at the corrugated iron doors, poking my tongue out. The doors click open a millisecond later and I dash into the warehouse, letting Drew wheel the bike in behind me.

Xavier is zig-zagging across the room, heading in my direction, his face awash with emotion, and my heart does a twisty jump. I run toward my remaining bestie, jumping up and wrapping my legs around his waist a little too enthusiastically when we eventually collide. He loses his balance, falling to the ground with me straddling him.

"Oomph." He squeezes his eyes shut for a minute, and I know

that landing hurt like a bitch, but he doesn't whine. "I missed you. You crazy bitch," he says, yanking my head down and smacking a kiss against my lips.

"Missed you too. You deceitful bastard," I retort, tugging on his brow ring.

"Ow." He rubs his fingers over his brow, pouting.

I sit back on his lap with my knees on either side of his hips. "You're lucky I didn't yank on your cock ring."

"You have a cock ring?" Sawyer splutters, entering the room at an opportune moment.

"It's a Prince Albert *piercing*," Xavier confirms, winking at him upside down.

"Why is it called that?" I inquire.

"It's named after Prince Albert who was reputed to have had the piercing done shortly before his marriage to Queen Victoria in 1825."

"I love how you know the most random, odd facts," I admit. "And I love your new red hair," I add, tugging on the spiked Mohawk. "You look fierce."

"I'd love to know how you knew about his cock piercing," Drew adds, sounding unhappy.

"I'd love to know that too," a familiar deep voice says from behind me. "And why you think it's acceptable to straddle some other dude when you're *mine*." Kai lifts me off Xavier in one fell swoop.

"Way to make an entrance, beautiful," Jackson says, blowing me a kiss as he leans against a crate.

Kai spins me around in his arms, and I forget how to breathe. We've only been separated about seven hours, but it feels like forever since I've seen him. He's wearing a familiar pout, one that promises I'll pay for sitting in Xavier's lap, and my body combusts internally. I trail my fingers along his gorgeous face, melting under his heated gaze.

He's sexy as fuck with his dark hair, dark eyes, neat stubble, full lips, and ripped body, and I can't believe he's all mine. The memory of our declarations back at the hotel are still fresh, and I fling my arms around his neck, pressing my mouth to his, uncaring we have an audience.

He angles his head, directing the kiss as his tongue invades my mouth, licking me all over. Fireworks detonate inside me, and I forget where we are and that I'm pissed at him again. He yanks my body in flush to his, placing his palms on my ass, as a possessive growl emits from the back of his throat.

"Unless you want me to kick your ass six ways from Sunday, you'll remove your tongue from my sister's mouth and your hands from her butt."

Kai smirks as he pulls his lips from mine, keeping his palms on my ass on purpose.

"Payback is a bitch," I reply, teasing my brother before I remember Jane is gone. Drew's face turns to stone. "Shit, sorry, D."

"Get used to it," Kai says, looking at me like he wants to eat me alive.

I smile sweetly at him as I lift my knee and ram it into his balls. He doubles over, cupping his crotch, as his face twists in agony. "What the fuck?" he rasps.

"That's for not telling me about Charlie."

"I was just about to when he burst into the room!" he protests in between panting.

"Not good enough." I turn my stink eye on Jackson and Sawyer too. "And that goes for you two as well."

"They deserve a knee in the junk too," Xavier says, draping his arms around my shoulders. "We can tag team them. I claim Hunt."

Jackson smirks. "Took you long enough."

Sawyer elbows Jackson. "Go smoke a joint or jump off the roof or something."

"Touchy subject, dude?" Jackson slaps him on the back.

"Is anyone serious about taking my father down or we're just here to joke around?" Drew says, impatience bleeding into the air.

"No need to get your panties in a bunch." Xavier drops his arms, taking my hand in his.

"He needs to get laid," Jackson, unhelpfully, supplies. It's his standard response when someone is grouchy, but my brother does *not* appreciate it.

If looks could kill, Drew would have him buried alive right now.

He storms off toward Xavier's office, and I glare at Jackson. "That was mean."

"Never pretended to be nice," Jackson says, shrugging.

My arm almost wrenches out of its socket as Kai yanks me away from Xavier. "I should put you over my lap and redden your ass for that stunt."

"You'd be too late," Drew says, shouting over his shoulder. I pin him with a "shut the fuck up" glare. "Charlie already beat you to it."

Deathly silence greets his statement, and I sigh. "How'd you even know about that?"

Drew shoots me an apologetic look. "I was watching the camera feed. But I turned it off before he delivered your punishment."

"Jeez, that makes me feel so much better."

Kai grabs my shoulders and we slam to a halt. "What happened?" I give him the cliff notes version. "That's it. He's fucking dead, and he's mine."

When the time comes, he'll have a fight on his hands.

"Shit," Drew says, approaching me and looking as pale as a ghost. "Dad perved on you?" I nod. "You need to stay away from the house, and from him, A. I mean it. You have no clue how fucked in the head he truly is."

"And you do?"

He squeezes his eyes shut momentarily. "Just avoid him, Abby. Promise me."

"That's an easy promise. You know how much I despise him."

"What happened after that?" Kai asks, threading his fingers in mine as he struggles to contain his anger and frustration.

"Let's head into my office," Xavier says. "It's secure, and I'd feel more comfortable there."

We all traipse in after him, taking seats at the round table while Xavier locks the door, securing us in his impenetrable lair. The row of high-tech monitors and screens on the front wall are powered off, except for the screens hooked up to the security system. They broadcast different images of the exterior of the warehouse on a rotational loop.

"Okay, let's hear it. And hold nothing back," Kai says, leaning his elbows on the table and warning me with his eyes.

"First, you're all complete fucktards for working with Charlie and his dad and not telling me." Sawyer opens his mouth to speak, but I raise my palm to halt him. "I'm not interested in hearing more lies or the usual bullshit excuses. You're still on my shit list," I say, glancing from one to the other, "but I'm choosing to forget about this, because the more we dwell on stuff that's happened, stuff we can't change, the less we are discussing what to do about my father, and I don't want to lose focus."

They all bob their heads.

"And all the secrecy ends here." I level them with a deadly look. "No more secrets. No more lies. No more shielding me from the truth. We're in this together, and I'm on an equal footing or you're all dead to me." I let my gaze dance between them, pausing on Kai's face. "I'm not joking. I'll take off, and none of you will ever find me."

Kai's face hosts a multitude of competing emotions. He likes I'm standing up for myself, hates that I still don't fully trust him, and he's afraid I'll carry out my threat.

"We're a team," Kai says, eyeballing me. "And no one is keeping anything from you again. I give you my word."

I stare at him, before dragging my attention away and looking at each one of them to ensure I see the same commitment staring back at me.

"Good." Some of my stress lifts, but there's still a long way to go. They've all betrayed me, and they need to win back my trust. But, for now, I'm satisfied we're on the same page.

"What exactly did Charlie say?" Sawyer asks, helping to redirect the conversation where it needs to go.

I repeat it verbatim, noticing how Kai's hands grip the armrests when I relay how he told me he loves me.

"And he said he'd let you go if Kai was your choice?" Drew asks, his brows climbing to his hairline.

"He did."

"I'm not buying it," Jackson says. "It's obvious he's hot for you, and no guy just gives up like that."

Kai drills him with a freakishly scary look, and they face off for a few seconds.

"I'm not buying it either," Drew supplies, cutting in to avoid another confrontation. "And I don't trust him anymore. He is planning something."

"Agreed," Sawyer says. "But I don't think he's giving up. I think this is all part of his strategy."

"At least this way, Abby can keep a close eye on him and try to determine what he's up to," Drew says.

"I don't like you being there with him." Kai peers deep into my eyes. "Who knows what he might do to you?"

"He won't hurt me."

"I wouldn't be too sure of that." Kai grips the edge of the table as a muscle pops in his jaw.

"Kaiden." Drew pierces Kai with a knowing look, conveying some hidden message.

"No." Kai's voice is so sharp it could cut glass. "Fuck this shit. She deserves to know, and I'm done keeping secrets." He laces his fingers in mine. "Abby can handle herself."

"I know she can, but this will make her task more difficult," Drew argues.

"Or easier," Xavier interjects.

"Just tell me." I sigh, screaming inside.

I get to a point where I think there are no more secrets and lies only to discover I've scarcely begun peeling back the layers.

"Babe." Kai squeezes my hand tighter, tilting my face with his finger and keeping my gaze fixed on his. "Charlie was the one who let it slip about your virginity. He's the reason they assaulted you."

CHAPTER TWENTY-FOUR

I'm gobsmacked. Pissed. Hurt. Confused. Shocked. And about a hundred other different emotions. "How? Why?" I ask through gritted teeth.

"It wasn't deliberate," Drew explains.

"That you know of," Kai retorts.

"I've known him my whole life."

"No one knows who he is. You've just admitted that!" Kai argues back.

Drew's nostrils flare. "I know he's loved Abby forever, and he'd never have orchestrated that on purpose."

"How did it go down?" I ask.

"Charlie overhead us talking about it, and he relayed the intel to his father," Sawyer says.

"And *Charlie's* asshole father told *his* asshole father," Xavier says, jabbing his finger at Kai.

"Why would Charles Barron do that to me?" Out of all the elite, he has been the most kind and compassionate toward me. *But it was all a lie.* Achieving his own goals was all that mattered. I bet even his attempt to intervene was only half-hearted. Most likely done for Charlie's benefit. Not for mine.

"Because he knew Plan B was for Kai to seduce you, and he thought it interesting that Kai hadn't told his father the truth," Jackson says.

"But he didn't realize how far Atticus would take it," Drew explains. "He didn't know about the pregnancy either."

Silence engulfs us, and Kai pulls me into his side, pressing a fierce kiss to my temple. Tears sting the back of my eyes as I look at the naked pain on his face. He rests his forehead against mine, and I allow him to comfort me.

The others are quiet as we have our moment, and when we break apart, I'm shocked to find tears rolling down Xavier's face. He rounds the table, crouching down in front of me and taking my hands. "I'm so sorry, sweetheart." He looks over my shoulder at Kai. "Sorry for both your loss. He had no right to do that. *They* had no right to do any of it."

Pain lodges in my throat, and I swallow harshly. "Thank you," I whisper. Kai drapes his arm around my shoulder, kissing my cheek.

"We didn't get to talk to you either, beautiful," Jackson says, his eyes shining with sympathy.

"We hate what he's done to you, and he's going down," Sawyer promises.

I'm fighting to control my emotions, and I don't know if I can deal with this now.

"Enough," Kai grits out, his voice choked. "We appreciate it, but…"

He doesn't need to say anything else.

Everyone gets it.

Xavier returns to his seat, and I clear my throat. "I presume you know this from talking to Charlie," I throw out to the room.

"Yeah," Drew confirms. "Although he only fessed up after they had taken you. He'd been hiding the part he played since that day in the office."

"Which is why we can't say for sure it went down like that," Kai says. "And why I don't like my girl spending time with him, let alone living with him."

"His parents and his sister live there too."

"His place is a fucking mansion. They might as well be invisible," Kai hisses, and I run my thumb across the top of his hand in a soothing motion.

"Give me a cell and a gun, and I can take care of myself."

"And you'll see her at school," Jackson reminds him.

"About that." Drew leans forward in his chair. "Do *not* shoot the messenger." His eyes fasten on Kai's. "Charlie will be all over Abby at school, but you can't intervene, and you can't talk to her or even look at her."

Steam practically billows out of Kai's ears, and he looks like he wants to tear Drew apart, limb by limb. "Hey." I cup his face, forcing him to look at me. "You're the only one I want, but Drew is right. The bastard has promised to stay away from all of you if I go along with this virgin bride bullshit, provided no one finds out about my pregnancy. I've got a part to play, but that's all it is, Kai." I caress his cheek. "It's a *role*. An *act*. And it's more than just convincing the public. I need to convince him too."

"No!" Kai jumps up, grabbing fistfuls of his hair. "No fucking way."

"Yes, way. There is too much at stake to mess this up. None of it will be real."

Placing his palms on the sides of my chair, he shoves his angry face all up in mine. "You expect me to sit there and *do* nothing, *say* nothing, when he's groping and kissing you?"

"I had to put up with that for weeks when you had that slut bag Rochelle grinding on your lap every day! And you put your dick in her mouth!"

"It isn't the same!" he retorts.

I shove at his chest. "You're right. It isn't! Because you did that purely to fuck with my head. And I'm doing this to protect your life!" I scream, losing the tenuous hold on my emotions.

"Back the fuck down," Drew calmly says, appearing behind me. "I mean it, dude. You will not speak to my sister like that."

"Fuck off, Drew."

Drew grabs him into a headlock in a lightning-fast move none of us see coming. "Quit bitching and moaning. You still have your woman, and she's prepared to do whatever it takes to keep you safe and ensure you get to be together. You have *nothing* to complain about."

Kai rams his elbow back into Drew's gut, extracting himself from the chokehold. "Don't pretend you know what I'm feeling because you know jack shit."

I stand. "Kai." I circle my arms around his neck, and when he tries to push me off, I cling on harder, pinning him with a vicious look. "I will not let him touch me intimately or fuck me." Kai looks like he wants to explode. "I kept Trent out of my bed for two years, so I can handle this with Charlie." I grip his neck more firmly, pressing my body against his. "And when he's kissing me, it'll be your lips I'm imagining."

Someone makes a gagging sound.

"Pass that puke bucket in this direction when you're finished," Xavier says, grinning at Jackson. "I just threw up in my mouth."

"I know I'm a hypocrite," Kai says, blocking the others out and concentrating on me. "But the thought of any man putting his hands on you makes me want to commit murder."

"Save those sentiments for my father, and yours, and Charles Barron because they are the real enemy." I peck his lips. "And we can do this if it means we get to be together permanently when it's all over."

Slowly, he nods, and a resigned sigh slips from his mouth. "I fucking hate this, but you were right earlier. We can't lose focus."

"Thank fuck for that," Drew says.

We reclaim our seats, and I look my brother square in the eye. "Charlie mentioned something about changes within the order, and he implied everything is tangled up with that. We need to know what's going down."

Drew nods, glancing at his watch briefly. "Let me give you some background. I know you guys know some of the shit that goes down at Parkhurst," he says, eyeing Sawyer, Jackson, and Kai, "but that's only the tip of the iceberg." He reaches across the table, snagging a bottle of water from the pile stacked in the center.

"There are elite, and towns like Rydeville, in every state in the US. There are the same tiers of authority—founding families who reign supreme and other families who come from legacy wealth who form the inner circle. Parkhurst is the governing body of *all* the elite. But only the founding fathers and their successors are members; however, all the elite have access to the facilities."

He looks at me as he pops the cap on his bottle. "You were in the medical facility, and they have several others. Educational. Sporting. Legal. Defense. They provide support services to the elite across the country, and in return, the elite abide by the rules handed down from the council, offer preferential rates for key services and products via their companies, and other stuff I'd rather not get in to."

"You can't hold shit back," I snap. "You just promised."

"If I was to explain everything that goes on in that place, we'd be old and gray by the time we left here. I will tell you what is pertinent for you to know and no more."

I don't bother arguing with him, because I'll work on him in the coming weeks. For now, I want to hear the parts he's willing to share. "Go on." My voice is clipped, and he looks surprised.

"There is an order within Parkhurst, depending on your status. Heirs who have yet to assume control, and fulfil their legacy, like me, Trent, and Charlie, are at the bottom of the food chain."

"Father commented earlier that Charlie had 'newly elevated status.' You would've missed overhearing that part. What does that mean?"

Shock splays across Drew's face. "Are you sure?"

"Positive. I was listening carefully to everything they said."

"It means Father has promised him something. And he's done something to warrant the promotion."

Blood leaches from my face at the thought of what he might've done. "Do you think it's something to do with me?"

Drew shrugs. "Probably, but it could be anything."

"It just reinforces how dangerous Charlie is," Kai says. "And how careful you need to be."

I turn my head to face him. "I know."

"I'll see if I can find out anything," Drew says, "But let's move this forward." He sits up straighter in his chair. "As I was saying, there's an order. Heirs who have assumed no control yet are at the bottom. At the other end of the scale, we have the council. They are the most senior, high-ranking elite members within the order and within the country. The council is made up of a president, vice president, a chairman, and five executive officers. They rule with an iron fist, and what they say goes. They hold supreme power over all the elite, and they hold considerable power and influence within the political system in the US. The current council president is retiring because of ill health, and it's the first time in twenty years the position is up for election."

"Father thinks he has a shot at the role," I surmise.

Drew takes a few mouthfuls of water. "Unfortunately, he has more than a shot at it. He has been campaigning behind the scenes for *years* which leads some to believe he is behind the current president's sudden ill health." Drew shrugs. "I wouldn't put that past him. But whether he was involved doesn't matter. He has enough votes on his side to win this thing, and that is something none of us want to see. If they elect him president of the council, he is *un-fucking-touchable*, and our lives will be a living hell."

"That's what this is all about? It's never been about Manning Motors and the auto-drive program?"

"It's all connected. Father must tick a lot of boxes. Being a successful businessman at the top of his game is only one part of it. He must have the right contacts. His children must marry well. And, above all, we must obey the rules. You already know it's frowned upon for females to have sex before marriage. It's unheard of for the daughter of a president to not be a virgin on her wedding day."

"Holy shit," Xavier exclaims, fiddling with his lip ring. "I couldn't make this shit up if I tried."

"It's the most archaic rule of all," Drew agrees.

"Don't any of these people realize it's the twenty-first century and women have equal rights to men?"

"You have heard Father spout that 'women are weak' line forever. Except it's not just a line he throws out there to get a laugh. He genuinely believes that. As do most of the high-ranking men within the elite. They get off on the power they exert over their wives and their daughters. They force their women to do shit no normal husband or father would ever do to their loved one."

My stomach twists into knots at his inference. I don't need an overactive imagination to guess some of the stuff he's implying.

"Is your father aware of this?" Sawyer asks, directing his question to Kai.

"I don't know, but if I had to guess, I'd say yes." He taps his fingers off the table, staring off into space. "He was part of that world before they expelled him when Hearst stole everything from him. The guy who originally contacted my father is a member of the elite. Someone he was close to in the past. Another founding father from a different state. But that's as much as I know, because Dad has painstakingly hidden his identity." Kai glances at Drew. "All I know is, he has a vested interest in seeing Hearst being taken down. Is it possible this faction lobbying against your father behind the scenes—the group who reached out to my father and Wes—is trying to stop him from assuming the presidential role?"

"They are," I say. "Charlie pretty much confirmed it to me earlier. He said that's why his father agreed to help."

"Now, it's making more sense," Sawyer muses.

"I've heard rumblings of discontent, but as an heir, I'm not privy to a lot of what goes on," Drew says. "But the political machinations work in the usual way, and there will always be dissenters despite how popular Father is within the hierarchy."

"Why is he popular?" I inquire. "Doesn't anyone see what a psycho he is?"

"Darling, half those assholes are psychos," Xavier says. "I don't need to visit Parkhurst to know that."

"Xavier is right," Drew says. "They feed on the bullshit he's selling and lap it up. You've got to remember these people are some of the richest, most arrogant bastards in the world, and they thrive on power and control over others. They have no morals and zero remorse. They will do as they please and not feel an ounce of regret. They rule on fear and violence, and most elite in the order are trapped with no way out. I don't know who makes up this dissenting group, but they're brave bastards, because if Father finds out, he will annihilate them to make an example."

"If they are so anal about the rules and traditions, how is it that Father is in the running for this position? He's only an elite by marriage. Surely, they'd prefer a pure blue blood for the role?"

"They would, but there's nothing in the rules that says he can't apply for the position because he is still part of the elite and he is the successor of a founding father by virtue of marriage."

"Because Mom and Genevieve are no longer alive or because they were women?" I ask, even though I can guess the answer.

"Because they were female." I shake my head in frustration as Drew shoots me a sympathetic look, while drumming his fingers off the table. "What *is* unusual is the fact he's garnered the bulk of the support, but there is little the outgoing president or existing council members can do about it. Majority poll will elect the new president, and Father is the front-runner as it stands."

"We need to find out who this group is," I say. "The ones hiding behind Atticus, Wes, and Charlie."

"No fucking way, Abby." Drew slams his fists down on the table. "You will stay a million miles away from order members."

"Fuck off telling me what to do."

"You know how pissed you were over what went down in the office that day?" he bites back. I grind my teeth to the molars. "Well, that is fucking nothing to these men! It's not even a blip compared to the things they do to women. I'm sure I don't have to spell it out, but if you go sniffing around these guys, none of us can protect you. And, trust me, if they get their hands on you, you will *never* recover from it. They will ruin you for life."

A chair slams as Jackson jumps up, racing from the room. Kai shares a loaded look with Sawyer before Sawyer stands and follows him outside. "What's up with that?" Xavier mouths to me, and I shrug.

"I'll be careful," I suggest. "Like, I can use the opportunity with the Barrons to find out more. That's not so risky."

"I'm in agreement with your brother on this," Kai says, cupping my face. "You are not to involve yourself in that. Don't even ask Charlie any questions, because we can't trust he won't relay them to his father." I'm opening my mouth to protest when he cuts me off. "If I can set my feelings aside over your fake engagement, then you will do this."

"*I'll* see what I can find out," Drew says, "but you're leaving it alone."

We'll see.

"Then we're back to our initial plan," I concede. "Trying to dig up dirt on Dad we can use, and I have an idea."

"Okay." Drew drains the last of his water, tossing the empty bottle over the table and into the trash can. "What is it?"

"So much of this is tied up with the elite, and rules, and the past, and there's got to be something there we can use against him. Atticus gave us lots of valuable intel at the ballroom, but certain things about both of their relationships with Mom don't add up. I have questions, and there's only one person who might answer them."

"Trent's mom," Drew says, catching on fast. Sylvia Montgomery was best friends with Emma Anderson and our mom from the time they were toddlers, and she's the only person who knows what really went down.

"No fucking way," Kai interjects, and Xavier laughs.

I roll my eyes to the ceiling. "Enough with the caveman routine, or we'll just continue going around in circles."

"You're not going near that asshole."

"Agreed." I smile sweetly at him. "Sylvia attends a shrink in town every Tuesday at five p.m. I'll wait outside and force her into talking to me."

"I thought she never left the house," Xavier says, remembering stuff I told him previously.

"She rarely does, but anyone unfortunate enough to live with those two bastards would need psychiatric help."

"Okay, fine," Drew says, looking at his watch and standing. "That sounds like a good place to start." He shoots me an apologetic look. "We've got to go."

"We're not finished talking." I've got a bunch of other questions.

"I have something I must do, and I can't be late," Drew cryptically says.

"Do you think the evidence Mom uncovered proving Dad murdered Kai's mom is at Parkhurst?" I ask, blatantly ignoring his last statement.

Drew shakes his head. "My belief is Dad never found it. I think it's still hidden wherever Mom put it."

"Any ideas on where that could be?"

He shrugs. "Your guess is as good as mine."

"We have to find it."

"And fast," Kai says. "Because if they elect your father council president, then it's useless."

"Let's put our thinking caps on," Drew agrees, removing his jacket from the back of his chair. "And then join heads and see if we can come up with some options."

"Wait," I call out, as he strides toward the door. "There's one more thing I need to know." I stand, needing to be upright for this. Kai rises, watching me closely. "How long have you two been working together?" I ask, my gaze dancing between Xavier and Drew.

Xavier's alarm is clear for everyone to see, and air whooshes out of Drew's mouth, confirming my suspicions. You'd think I'd be numb to betrayal by now, but I'm feeling their treachery in every part of my being.

Every single person in my world has betrayed me, and I'm feeling more alone and vulnerable than ever. Even Jane has let me down although I'm not so emotional that I don't understand it wasn't by choice.

The only person I can truly count on is myself.

The others must earn back my trust before I'll fully believe in any of them again. Saying they'd die for me proves nothing, because it's just words. Their actions in the weeks ahead will prove whether they are sincere

Until then, my survival is in my own hands.

And I'll be making decisions that benefit me.

Escaping is tempting, and I'm not altogether convinced that I won't just run off.

For now, I'll stick with the plan, but if they let me down again, I'm getting out of here.

Kai wraps his arms around me from behind, and I lean against him, letting the warmth from his body drive out the bitter cold spreading throughout every part of me. "Was any of it real?" I ask Xavier, my voice projecting my anguish.

"The stuff that mattered was." He approaches me, pleading with his eyes. "I love you, Abby. You're my best friend, and I'd catch a grenade for ya," he says, quoting one of his favorite Bruno Mars songs. "All of that is true."

"How and why?" I ask that question of my brother.

"You came back from Aunt Genevieve's funeral changed. I could tell the difference." He glances at Kai. "I didn't know what'd happened, but I knew you were planning something, and it terrified me." He steps closer. "I'd already lost Mom," he whispers. "I couldn't lose you too."

"What did you do?" My voice is devoid of emotion.

"I hired Xavier to hack you, knowing how you'd respond, and I've been paying him to work with you ever since."

CHAPTER TWENTY-FIVE

My jaw slackens, and my heart leaks blood by the bucketful. "I can't believe you'd do that to me."

Drew steps forward, ignoring Kai's warning hiss. "I won't apologize for helping you in the only way I could. I had to be sneaky in case Father found out because then everything I'm working on would be in vain. I'd studied the plans of the house, and I discovered the tunnel. I cleared it out, reinforced the electrical wiring, and fixed the rear gate. I was trying to figure out a plausible way of telling you about it when you stumbled across it yourself."

I'm so conflicted right now. I can't deny it warms my heart to know my twin went to such extremes to help me. To know I wasn't wrong about his intentions or his love for me. To understand it's part of a bigger plan he's working. But the way he went about it kills me. Betrayal was on every corner, and I was blind to it. "How could you lie to me like that? We used to tell each other *everything!*"

"This was the best way I could help you escape and ensure you were safe. Mom died because she wasn't cunning enough. *You are.* I know that, Abby. But I wanted to ensure you had as much support as I could give, even if I knew I was helping you to leave me." He takes my hand in his. "I want the best life for you, and I know that's not here. Not married to Barron."

He eyeballs Kai. "I always suspected you two would end up together, and I trust you with her. But mark my words, if you do anything to hurt her again, I will hunt you down, rip out your insides with my teeth, and feed them to you one disgusting morsel at a time."

"You don't get to threaten him. You've hurt me too." I cross my arms. "You all have."

"I'm holding myself accountable in the same way," Drew replies.

"I got the memo," Kai deadpans. "And you've nothing to fear from me. We both want the same thing."

Drew nods. "I know you have lots of questions, and I know you're hurting, Abby, but it'll have to wait. We must go." His face and voice brokers no argument.

"Abs." Xavier calls to me.

I stare at him, spotting the remorse and fear on his face, but I just can't deal right now. "I need time."

"You're my girl," he adds. "That won't ever change."

I don't reply, letting Kai walk me out.

Drew wheels the bike outside while Kai pulls me over to the wall, caging me in with his muscular arms. Sawyer and Jackson have vanished. "I'll miss you," he says, sweeping my hair off my shoulders.

"I'll miss you too."

He rubs at my lower lip. "You hanging in there?"

"Barely," I honestly admit. "I keep thinking I've reached the end of the line. That I know everything there is to know, but there's always more."

"It's a fucking mess," he agrees, kissing the tip of my nose. "But I'm here for you."

"Except you're not really."

He removes something from his back pocket, handing it to me. "Got you a new burner cell." He loops his fingers in the back of my jeans, reeling me into his hot body. "Call me every night before you go asleep. And if anything happens, I'm your first call." He tips my chin up. "Right?"

"Right." I wrap my arms around him, resting my head on his chest, listening to the comforting beat of his heart. "Tell me we can do this and win," I implore, peering up at him, because I desperately need reassurance.

"Losing isn't an option. We have too much at stake," he says before his lips descend. His kiss is tender and loving and wholly at odds with how he usually kisses me, because he instinctively knows this is what I need. I melt against him, and it's a physical and emotional wrench to pull away when Drew impatiently calls my name.

"I don't want to say goodbye." I smile sadly at him.

"Then don't." He presses a hard, desperate kiss to my lips. "Message me when you're in bed, and I'll see you tomorrow even if it's from across the cafeteria."

I crush myself to him, slamming my lips against his as footsteps approach.

"Guys," Drew says. "I'm sorry. But we need to go."

Kai breaks our kiss, caressing my face before letting me go. "Later, firecracker."

He swats my ass, and I spin around, blowing him a kiss as I walk backward. "Later, caveman."

Drew's lips twitch as he wordlessly hands me my helmet, and we climb onto my bike. Then I kick-start the engine and floor it out of there.

"A." Drew calls to me as I'm walking down the hallway toward my bedroom.

I turn around, leaning against the wall as he walks toward me. Silently, I stare at him.

"I know it's a lot to take in. And I know you're pissed, but I had the best of intentions."

"I know," I admit, sighing, because I genuinely do. And I instinctively know there's more Drew is doing, so my issue isn't his motivation. "But it's the sneaking around and the lying that gets to me. That and the fact I thought I had a true friend in Xavier."

"You do, Abby. That guy cares about you a hell of a lot. I hope you can find it in your heart to forgive him because he's one of the good guys." He levels me with a sober look. "And there are so few of them around."

After he walks away, I realize he never asked for forgiveness for himself.

I've only just gotten into bed when my stomach rumbles, reminding me I haven't eaten in hours and I missed dinner. I could ring down for something, but it's late, and I don't want to act like a pampered bitch, so I get up. Wrapping my silk robe around my body, I slip on my pink fluffy slippers and exit my bedroom.

I'm yawning as I walk down the stairs when movement up ahead captures my attention. I'm about to call out after Drew when I notice his attire. I frown as my eyes take in the sharp black suit, crisp white shirt, and snazzy red tie. I step off the stairs and creep into the shadows as he turns around, watching the hint of a frown appear on his brow as he glances up at the staircase.

He's clean shaven, and he's used gel to smooth his hair back from his face, and I can smell his cologne from here.

What the hell is he up to, and where is he going this time at night?

It's almost midnight.

On a school night.

And my spidey senses are tingling.

I tiptoe after him, maintaining a reasonable distance and keeping my back flattened to the wall, in case he should turn around and spot me. But he doesn't. Distracted and on edge, he walks through the house, over to the very far west side of the property.

I clamp a hand over my mouth to stifle my shocked gasp as he punches in a code on the secret door and enters the forbidden dungeon.

Acid churns in my stomach, and my pulse is throbbing wildly in my neck. I make a split-second decision, hoping I don't regret it, darting forward and catching the door just before it locks.

I slip inside, waiting at the top of the dark, narrow stairs to ensure Drew has descended, and the door locks behind me, before I make a move. Strip lighting on either side of the stairs is the only illumination in the otherwise dark space, and my pulse is spiking to record highs as I put one foot in front of the other. When I reach the bottom step, I turn around the corner, facing another dark passageway with the same strip lighting on either side. Butterflies scatter in my chest and my stomach is lodged in my throat as I walk forward, scanning the dark hallway for signs of cameras, but I see none.

I've purposely avoided investigating what goes on in my father's dungeon for a variety of reasons, but I know this is not the public entrance. There is another, restricted entrance off to the left-hand side of our driveway, secured by high, black wrought-iron gates and accessible by a code that alternates on a monthly basis, where invited guests go. I have that intel courtesy of Oscar, but he refused to answer any more questions about what goes on, making me promise I would never venture down here.

Thoughts of Oscar bring him to the forefront of my mind, and I make a vow to find out where he is and to visit him at my earliest convenience. I feel like a piece of shit that I didn't ask Drew about him. All I know, from what Charlie told me, is he's in a coma and that he's being looked after.

But given what I know now about Charlie, I can't even trust it's the truth.

I force my thoughts of Oscar to one side when I reach the end of the hallway and come to a dead end in front of a single black door. Rhythmic beats tickle my eardrums from behind the closed door, and goose bumps sprout along my arms.

With sweaty palms, and a heart that's trying to beat a path out of my chest, I turn the handle, praying it doesn't bring me slap bang into the middle of a clusterfuck. I step onto soft, black carpet, walking toward the billowy black curtain softly swaying in front of me. The music is much louder in here, but the sultry beats seem more like background music. Drawing a brave breath, I peek through the curtain, my eyes widening in shock.

A rope hangs horizontally in front of the curtain, with a "restricted" sign hanging from the top, confirming it's a cordoned-off area. But that offers little comfort as my eyes drink in the scene.

It's what I imagine a high-class sex club or strip joint in Vegas might look like. It's a massive room, as big as the ballroom in the house, if not bigger, decorated opulently in shades of red, gold, and black. A few strategically placed chandeliers hang overhead, interspersed sparingly around the room.

A circular rotating bar occupies prime position in the center of the space with a line of stools positioned in front of the counter. Most of the stools are occupied by older men in formal attire. At the back of the room is a large stage with a cluster of tables and chairs situated around it. A heavily made-up girl is gyrating around a pole, naked, watched by a crowd of older men, many of them with their hands stuck down the fronts of their pants.

Ignoring the sick feeling in the pit of my stomach, I look around the rest of the space.

On the left-hand side is a rectangular elevated section with eight ornate gold-encrusted chairs. A group of men is standing around the dais, chatting and drinking. My father sits on one of the gold chairs, talking to a gray-haired man sitting beside him. Two naked women are on their knees, one in front of each man, sucking their dicks, as the men chat casually, like it's commonplace to have a blowjob while discussing business.

I'm guessing, down here, it probably is.

I'm turning away in utter disgust when I spot Drew talking to a group of four men. Two of them look around our age, and the other two are older. Drew has a tumbler in hand, and he's throwing his head back, laughing, looking for all intents and purposes like he belongs here. But the taut pull of his shoulders, his rigid posture, and the slight tick in his jaw reveal a different picture.

It helps.

But only a little.

Turning my attention to the right-hand side of the room, I clamp a hand over my mouth to stifle my horrified gasp as I struggle to comprehend the scene accosting me. Overhead lighting is dim, but large lamps illuminate the multitude of open stalls, exposing the sordid acts in full swing.

In the first stall, an older lady with flowing blonde locks is sobbing as a man ruts into her ass from behind. He has one hand wrapped firmly around her neck, and her face is turning a distinct shade of blue. Another man watches from a recliner chair, laughing and joking with the man hurting her, while he pumps his bare cock. He reaches forward, gripping the woman's chin before licking her face like she's a dog.

In the second stall, a girl with long, dark, wavy hair flowing down her back is bouncing on top of an older guy, dutifully riding his cock, while another man fucks her ass from behind and a third guy fucks her mouth. The guy behind her yanks her head back by the hair, giving me a full view of her face and upper body.

A tear rolls down my cheek at the glazed, indifferent look in her eyes that confirms she's on something.

But she is so young, and my heart is breaking.

She can only be fourteen or fifteen at the very most.

Pain spears me through the chest as I cut my gaze to the next stall.

It's another young girl this time, wearing a similar zoned-out expression, but she's tied to some contraption, and she has a collar around her neck and cuffs on both ankles. They have her arms stretched up over her head with her legs spread wide, exposing her fully to the group of men standing around her. Some of them are naked, stroking their cocks, while others are still in dress suits, drinking and joking as they watch men paw at her and take turns in her pussy.

I avert my eyes, but at the last second, I spot a familiar face, and my stomach dips to my toes. I watch, disgusted beyond words, as Trent tugs at his cock, smirking at something the guy beside him says as they wait their turn with the girl. Trent is kneading one of her tits and tweaking her nipple in a way I know hurts, because he used to do the same thing to me.

The stalls extend to the far end of the room, but I've seen enough. I can't watch anymore.

I need to get out of here.

Before I throw up all over the place.

And before Trent spots me.

That thought propels me into motion, and I spin around, ready to flee this horrible, horrible place when I slam into a warm, solid chest.

Panic races through my veins as large hands grip my arms and squeeze.

CHAPTER TWENTY-SIX

"What the hell are you doing here?" Charlie demands, digging his nails into my arms as he grips me painfully.

"I could ask you the same thing," I hiss.

Charlie is a master of discretion, and it's usually hard to read him. But not now.

Fury and fear are etched upon his face in equal measure, and his body trembles with raw anger as he drags me out of the room, back along the dimly lit corridor, and up the steps. He punches in the code on the wall-mounted keypad and the door clicks open, revealing the empty hallway in my house.

He doesn't utter a word as he drags me along the corridor, through the house, over to the other wing, and down the corridor where the security camera room is. Waves of hostility and anger roll off him, raising all the tiny hairs on the back of my neck. He lets me go to pick the lock, swinging the door open and pulling me inside. "Wipe the feed," he demands.

I'm tempted to tell him to screw off, but the intensity of his emotions are scaring me a little, and the last thing I need is the bastard discovering I know his twisted secret, so I log into the system, my fingers flying over the keyboard as I wipe the footage and doctor the evidence so it's not obvious.

"It's done," I confirm, standing.

He grabs my elbow, pulling me out of the room, checking it's properly locked before hauling me toward the stairs. "Let go of me." I attempt to wriggle out of his grasp, but he tightens his hold. He has never been this rough with me, and this version of Charlie is freaking me out. "Stop manhandling me! You're hurting me."

"Don't. Push. Me." A muscle clenches in his taut jaw as he forces me up the stairs.

I obey for once, waiting until we're in the safe confines of my bedroom to shove him off me. My victory is fleeting though, because I've only just wrenched my arm away when he pushes me back against the wall, caging me in with his muscular arms and his powerful, angry body. My chest heaves as I watch him struggle to control himself. "Do you have any idea of the danger you were just in?" he growls, and I can tell it's an effort not to shout.

"I wanted to know."

"And do you feel better for knowing? Safer? Less afraid?" His eyes burn with a host of different emotions.

I bite down on my lip, squeezing my eyes shut before shaking my head.

"What would you have done if I didn't show up?" His green eyes penetrate mine in a challenging stare.

"I was leaving."

He slams his fist into the wall over my head unexpectedly, and I jump. "Unless you had the code, there's no way you could've gotten out of there."

He's right. But I didn't know that when I followed Drew. I presumed the door opened from the inside like a normal door, but I should've known better. I'm smarter than this, and my reckless decision could've landed me in a lot of trouble.

Of course, I'm not admitting that to him.

"Drew had to return at some point. He would've let me out."

"And what if it'd been your father returning first?" He grips my chin, tipping my face up. "What then, Abby? How would you have explained it?"

"From my vantage point, it didn't look like Father would leave anytime soon."

"Your father is anything but predictable. You, of all people, know that." He rubs his thumb along my lower lip, and his gaze darkens in a way I'm familiar with. A visible shudder passes over him. "If they'd gotten their hands on you." He squeezes his eyes closed for a moment.

"I must remain a virgin," I say. "He wouldn't have let them fuck me."

He snorts. "There are a lot of other creative ways they can hurt you, Abby. Fuck it." He thumps the wall again. "You're too smart to pull careless shit like this." He rests his forehead against mine. My instinct is to push him away, but I remember I've a role to play.

"I wasn't thinking, but I'm okay. No one saw me, and we covered our tracks."

"I need you to promise me you won't go near there again."

A sour taste floods my mouth. "Trust me, I've no desire to revisit." I cup his face, forcing his head up. "Why were you there?"

His mask comes down. "It was elite business."

I snort, pushing him away this time, only noticing the custom-fit suit he's wearing now. "This is comical." I shake my head. "All that bullshit you spouted about loving me, and protecting me, and you were going there to have sex with underage girls?"

He closes the gap between us, pressing his body against the length of mine, flattening my spine to the wall again. "I was not going there to have sex." He slams his mouth down on mine before I've had time to guess his move. I keep my lips sealed, refusing to kiss him back. Not because I don't want to betray Kai, although I *don't* want to, but because it's natural in this scenario.

I shove at his shoulders, and his nostrils flare as he's forced to break the one-sided kiss.

"How dumb do you think I am?" I hiss. "I saw what they were doing down there. And you expect me to believe you were just going to drink and talk shit with those assholes?" I plant my hands on my hips. "This is just like my engagement to Trent all over again." I narrow my eyes. "You have no intention of being faithful to me, do you? And if you can't keep it in your pants while we're engaged, then you certainly have no intention of staying loyal after we're married."

"Don't fucking compare me to him. I am nothing like Trent!" he roars, and I'm kind of proud that I've gotten the elusive Charlie to crack a little.

"A likely story." I step away from him. "You disgust me." Images of those poor girls materialize behind my retinas, and my stomach drops to my toes as nausea travels up my throat. "I can't believe you'd do something like that. How could you have sex with someone so young? Especially when they've clearly been drugged into cooperating?"

He moves back into my personal space. His previous frustration is gone, replaced with a half-smug look.

Is he pleased at my reaction?

"The only person I desire is *you*. The only woman I want to have sex with is *you*." Spoken like a true politician. Evading the question and expecting it to suffice.

"You can't touch me until our wedding night."

He runs the tip of his finger up and down my arm, making my skin crawl. "We both know that's not true. Your father already believes we're fucking."

258

"It's not gonna happen." I glare at him, and he backs down, stepping away and creating some distance between us. He looks contrite, but I don't know if it's genuine or not.

"I apologize for kissing you without your permission, and you know I'd never force you or make you do anything you don't want."

"I know nothing, Charlie," I truthfully reply, sauntering toward the couch and flopping down. I kick off my fuzzy slippers, pulling my legs up into my chest. I rest my head on my knees, looking sideways at him as he sits beside me. "I don't trust you. Don't trust anyone except myself."

"Has something else happened?" He angles his body toward me, arching a brow.

"Just that I've found out everyone has lied to me and that no one can be trusted."

"I know I've got to earn your trust again, but I'll show you I'm sincere."

I lift my head, examining his handsome face for clues. "If you mean that, you can start by telling me what the fuck is going on downstairs."

"Do you really want to know?"

I nod. "I can't un-see it now, and—" I close my eyes, hating the images that burn through my retinas. I blink, rage resurfacing. "It's disgusting, and so wrong, and I feel ill at the thought that's been going on in the basement of my house for years while I slept up here, ignorant of the depravity taking place under this very roof."

"This is the world we exist in," he replies, displaying little emotion. "And I've seen far worse."

"What do you mean?"

"What do you think we've been doing at Parkhurst all these years, Abby?" Slipping off his dress shoes, he pulls his feet up onto the couch, bending his knees and leaning back against the arm, so he's facing me.

"Training? Learning how to take over the family businesses?" I hear how naïve that sounds now. Truth is, for years, that's what I thought they were doing every year they went there.

I know better now.

"We *were* training, but it involves a lot more than just physical defense or learning how to manage a business."

"Like what?"

"Like how to kill a man. How to fuck a woman. How to control and exert power over those who are less than us."

"Have you killed someone?" I know he's skilled with a gun. We all are. And after the shootout in the ballroom, I know how experienced all the guys are.

He nods.

"Did you lose your virginity at Parkhurst?" I ask, because it seems the next logical question.

He nods again.

"How old were you?"

"Thirteen."

My jaw drops. "But you were only a kid."

"Within the order, you're a man at thirteen. Losing your virginity at that age is a rite of passage, and one of the initiation tasks."

"Initiation tasks?" I feel like I've wandered into the pages of a dark romance book.

"We must complete several stages and tasks before turning eighteen. Only after successful completion, and graduating high school, can we climb the ranks of the order and become fully fledged members of Parkhurst."

"What would happen if you didn't do it?"

"They would kill me."

My eyes blink rapidly. I want to call bullshit on it, but this is the elite we are discussing, and none of their traditions or rules have ever made much sense to me. "Couldn't you fake it?"

He shakes his head. "There's a public ceremony."

I swing my legs around, adopting the same position as him on my side of the couch. "Are you saying you lost your virginity at a ceremony where people were watching?" I say in a high-pitched tone of voice.

"Yep." He looks vaguely amused.

"I'm glad to see it hasn't affected you." I scowl, feeling sick all over again.

"I'd been in training for it for months," he confirms as my horror grows.

They forced that on them when they were *twelve?*

"My hormones were running wild, and I'd become slightly addicted. I wasn't keen on everyone watching, especially my father, but it wasn't a chore."

"What did training involve?" I ask although I'm unsure if I want to know.

His lips kick up at the corner. "Upon your twelfth birthday, you're assigned a woman as your sexual mentor. Imelda was mine. She was twenty-two and hot as fuck. Her job was to educate me on all things sex related. She taught me everything I know."

My mouth gapes open. *What the actual fuck?* I'm grossed out all over again. Not just because it's morally wrong, and it amounts to child abuse, but because the way Charlie is speaking about it, bragging almost, is wrong on so many levels. *What have they done to the guys to make this acceptable?*

"But you said you didn't lose your virginity until you were thirteen. I don't understand," I say, because his statement is contradictory.

"Penetrative sex was off limits until the ceremony, but she showed me how to give and take oral, and I fucked her pussy and her ass with my fingers and vibrators. We watched pornos, experimented with toys, and I was in the room when she had sex with other guys so I could take notes."

"That is…disturbingly gross and sick." Acid coats the insides of my mouth. "How on earth does someone get a job as a sexual mentor, anyway?" I'd like to know where they get these sick bitches from.

"All the women who perform roles within Parkhurst are either carefully vetted or from an elite family."

"Why would any of the elite pass their daughters over as sexual mentors?"

"It's a great honor."

I throw up a little in my mouth, and I can't keep the shock off my face as I listen to the nonchalant way he discusses being abused as a child. Because, make no mistake, that's exactly what this is.

"Some men offer their wives up too," Charlie adds. "Trent's mentor was thirty-five, and Drew and I loved teasing him about it."

I don't speak for several minutes, too horrified to form words.

"Oh my God," I say after a few beats of silence, as realization dawns. "Trent's mentor must've liked it rough, and there's no way in hell I want to hear anything about my brother's mentor." Nausea swirls in my gut. "Can we move off this subject before I hurl my guts up?"

He scoots forward, pressing his mouth to my ear. "I know it's distasteful to you, but I'm a skillful lover. When I get you in my bed, you will scream my name all night long."

That just might be the sickest statement of all. *How can he be proud of his skills knowing it came from being sexually abused and publicly debased as a child?*

Approaching footsteps are the only thing that saves Charlie from a knee in the junk. "Fuck," he hisses, glancing at his watch. "Don't fight me on this, just go with it." His eyes convey silent warning.

I don't have time to respond before he slides me down underneath him and presses his body over mine. His lips descend again, and I kiss him back this time, ignoring the protests screaming in my head when he frantically unknots my robe, shoving it off my shoulders, and slipping his hand up under my top. With his other hand, he pulls my leg up, wrapping it around his waist, before grinding his hips into mine just as the door to my bedroom flies open.

A deep chuckle reverberates around the room, and I'm not faking the freezing. Charlie removes his hand from under my top and pulls away from me. Sitting upright, he straightens his suit, smirking as he levels a knowing look at my father.

"I thought I might find you here," the bastard says.

"Massage duty," Charlie quips, curling his hands in a cupping motion, and I want to smother him in his sleep. "Someone's got to do it." He slips his feet into his shoes and ties the laces.

I pull my top down and fix my robe around myself, sitting up and plastering a fake smile on my face. "Funny," I deadpan, leaning over to kiss him, hating every second of this. "Thanks for dropping by. I'll see you in the morning."

He stands, reeling me into his arms, and dipping me down low as he kisses me deeply, like he did that night on the stage. Except, this time, I don't see any stars through the red haze of anger coating the backs of my eyes.

CHAPTER TWENTY-SEVEN

School the following day is a strange experience without Jane by my side. All day, suck-ups approach me, telling me how happy they are that I'm back. My engagement to Charlie is all over the school, and I garner envious looks from several of the girls when they spot the massive diamond on my ring finger.

Charlie is waiting outside my class to escort me to the cafeteria. My nerves are shot to hell at the prospect of seeing Kai and not being able to talk to him. Jackson was in one of my morning classes, and it took mammoth effort to ignore him. The elite have spies all over the school, so I can't risk even the slightest look for fear it'll get back to Charlie.

Or Trent.

Because he wants payback, and landing me in it with my new fiancé and my father would be right up his alley.

Charlie takes my bag and slings his arm around my shoulder as we walk through the crowded hallway toward the cafeteria. The masses part to let us through, and I force a smug smile on my face, while inwardly calculating how many days we have left until Christmas break.

I contain my surprise as Charlie leads us toward our old table.

The one where Trent is sitting with Shandra Farrell by his side. Drew looks up as we approach with a genuine smile on his face. He pulls out the chair beside him for me, and I round the table, ignoring my ex and his new plaything.

Although, I have to say I'm surprised at Shandra.

She's one of the inner circle, from a respectable, well-liked family, and she's super smart and very career-orientated. She's not the type to hang off any guy, especially a douche like Trent.

"I'll get your lunch," Charlie says as I sit down beside my twin.

"Thanks, babe." He pecks my lips briefly before walking off toward the counter.

"Look what the cat dragged in," Trent says, propping his elbows on the table and glaring at me.

"Aw, did you miss me, small dick?" Mention of his dick resurrects last night in my mind, and all good humor fades. "Or were you too busy forcing yourself on innocent girls to notice?"

Drew pinches my thigh under the table, but I ignore him.

Trent smirks. "I don't have to force myself on anyone." He grabs his crotch. "They're lining up to ride my cock."

"Thanks for that," Shandra says drily, stabbing a piece of lettuce like she wishes it was his head.

Trent grabs hold of her hips and slides her over onto his lap. "They want me, but they can't have me," he tells her. "I told you we were exclusive, and I meant it."

I cough. "Bullshit."

"You say something, whore?" Trent snaps just as Charlie returns.

Charlie places a tray down on the table before coolly turning to Trent. "You want to say that again to my face?"

All the tiny hairs lift on my arms and the back of my neck, and the atmosphere in the room alters. But it's not because Charlie and Trent are squaring off to one another.

It's because the new elite have just entered the cafeteria, sucking up all the oxygen and claiming all the attention in the room. I don't look at the door, because I'm not sure I'm strong enough to resist Kaiden's lure. And I don't need visual confirmation to know he's here because I can sense his presence the instant he sets foot in any room. Maybe it's our potent connection, or his intense aura, or it's the audible gasp that rings out around the room, or the subtle shift in the air, but whatever it is, I could walk into a hundred rooms and immediately know he's there.

Drew grips my hand in warning, and I shoot him a frustrated look, telling him to back off, that I know what to do.

Things have progressed while my mind has wandered, and Charlie has yanked Trent up out of his chair, and he's fisting his shirt and snarling in his face. "You *will* apologize or I'll put your face through the nearest wall," he says in a clipped tone.

"I'll apologize when she does. She started it by trying to embarrass me in front of my fiancée," Trent retorts.

My head whips to Shandra's hand, and I don't know how I missed the whopper pink diamond on her hand. "You're engaged?" I screech, asking the obvious.

"Jealous much?" Trent asks, smirking.

I ignore him, fixing Shandra with a genuine sympathetic look. "Commiserations."

"Fucking bitch," Trent snaps, and Charlie shoves him across the floor, slamming him up against the wall.

You could hear a pin drop in the room.

"Listen up carefully, Montgomery. You don't speak to my fiancée like that *ever*. You don't disrespect her, or even fucking look at her, or you'll have me to deal with."

Trent pushes Charlie away. "I'm quaking in my boots." He shoots him a derogatory look as he shoves past him. "And you needn't worry about your precious fiancée. I'm through with the slut."

"Need I remind you of the conversation we had last week with our fathers," Drew calmly says as Trent reclaims his seat beside Shandra.

Trent grinds his teeth and his knuckles blanch white. "I don't need a reminder."

"Good." Drew leans back casually in his chair. "Because I'd hate to inform my father you're already breaching the terms."

Charlie sends Trent a smug grin as he drops into the seat on the other side of me and drapes his arm around my shoulder.

Shandra clears her throat, and her eyes twinkle with mischief. "I hear commiserations are in order for you too," she teases, eyeballing me.

"Charlie is the catch of the century." I smile adoringly at him. "I've zero complaints."

I send her a pointed look to say, "unlike you, you poor bitch."

Charlie grins, delighted with my fake sentiment, pressing his lips to mine, and I don't know if he believes it or he's just playing along.

A scuffle breaks out in the background, and I pull away from Charlie, grabbing some items off the tray, pretending like I'm not aware of what's happening.

"Get the fuck off me." Kai's angry tone is like a dagger straight through my heart, because I know he just witnessed that. I want to look up so badly, but I remind myself of why we're doing this and stick to my resolve.

Trent grins, and the menacing glint in his eye spells trouble. "Guess Anderson didn't get the memo." He pops a piece of pasta into his mouth, chewing slowly while I mentally compile a list of ways to kill him. "Was murdering his bastards too subtle for him?" he adds when he's finished, and I explode.

Jumping up onto the table, I throw myself on top of Trent, and we crash to the ground in a tangle of limbs. I don't even feel the impact as the chair breaks underneath our combined weight, and we hit solid ground. Grabbing hold of his head, I bounce it off the floor, slamming it up and down before he flips me off.

Strong hands reach around me from behind, attempting to lift me up, but my reflexes are fast. I lunge at Trent, scraping my nails down his cheeks, enormously satisfied when he roars in pain. Arms reach for me again, and I rip my stiletto heel off one foot and smash it into the side of Trent's head, getting two good hits in there before Charlie throws me over his shoulder.

Blood gushes from Trent's temple and trickles from his injured cheek, but it's not enough. I want to slice his cock off and feed it to him before I chop him into itty-bitty pieces and pin his severed head to the wall. *How dare he say that to me!!* I pummel my fists into Charlie's back. "Let me down! I want to fucking kill him!" I yell.

"You're going down for this," Trent threatens, pressing a paper towel to the wound on his temple.

"You snitch and it'll be the last thing you do," Drew says, standing and walking around the table. He glares at Trent. "You deserved that. And if you ever repeat that comment or make any of those remarks to my sister again, I will fucking end you myself." Drew puts his face all up in Trent's. "This is your last warning." Drew walks over to us. "Get Abby out of here."

Charlie nods, striding toward the exit with me still strewn over his shoulder. In my peripheral vision, I spot Jackson and Sawyer physically restraining a fuming Kai. Our eyes meet across the room, and I want to go to him so badly. Especially after Trent's cruel words because the only arms I want comforting me are his.

But I won't be selfish.

We silently communicate, and his pain, anguish, and longing are mine too, but we can't fall at the first hurdle. We are stronger than this. I subtly shake my head just before Charlie exits the cafeteria, leaving chaos in our midst.

"I'm not saying he didn't have it coming to him," Charlie says, when we're outside in his car a few minutes later. "But you can't go around attacking people. Your father would go apeshit on my ass because I'm officially responsible for you."

"Trent won't say anything because he'll land himself in hot water if he does."

"Agreed, but you need to stop and think before you react, Abby."

"Why are we even *at* that table?" I question, wincing as a dart of pain shoots through my hip. I'm a little achy in parts, but Trent cushioned most of our fall, so I'll live. I'm betting his back will be black and blue by tomorrow, and it couldn't happen to a more worthy recipient.

"Your father has patched things up with the Montgomerys, and we were given strict instructions that things were to return to normal."

I add a note to my mental checklist to ask Drew how the bastard has made amends with Trent's father.

"It hasn't escaped my notice that the new elite have returned," he adds, and my spine turns rigid.

"So?"

"So I told Kaiden it was a part of the deal."

"You told Kai to stay away from me," I correct him. "You said nothing about him not being permitted to return to school."

He examines my face carefully. "Stay away from him, Abby." A muscle ticks in his jaw. "You're my fiancée now, and I won't be made a fool of."

I'm walking toward my last class of the day when I'm yanked sideways into a room, and Kai's hot mouth is on mine before I've had time to scream. His tongue plunders my mouth like an invading Viking, taking what he wants with brutality and violence. A metallic taste trickles into my mouth as he bites down hard on my lip, drawing blood. I push him away. "What are you doing?" I hiss. Charlie's threat is still too fresh in my mind, and this is risky as fuck.

He shoots me a shit-eating grin Jackson would be proud of as he locks the door and stalks toward me. "What the fuck does it look like?"

"Like you're crazy as shit and have a death wish," I say, backing away from him.

His eyes are thick with lust, his body cloaked in anger, and he wears it proudly like body armor.

I scramble around desks as I avoid capture. All the while he advances. Like this menacing form hell-bent on punishing me.

Liquid lust races through me, and my core pulses with a desperate need.

I love it when he's like this.

Looking at me like he wants to fuck me so hard I'll bleed.

My body purrs in anticipation as my back slams against a solid obstacle.

I know I'm sick and twisted, but I think that's why we're so well matched.

He wants to punish me, and I want to be punished.

He grips my hips, reeling me into his body, grinding his pelvis against mine. His boner juts into my lower stomach, drenching my panties. "You need a reminder that you're mine."

"Yes," I pant in agreement even though I'm fully his, and we both know it.

His lips collide with mine again, and we devour one another as if we'll never get to kiss again. My hands are greedy motherfuckers as they roam up and down his back and squeeze his hard ass cheeks, pulling him closer as I spread my legs wider to accommodate his hot body. I grind against him as he tweaks my breasts through my shirt.

Without warning, he flips me over, swiping the contents off the desk with a clean sweep of his hand, and bends me down over it. Tugging my skirt up to my waist, he pushes my panties to one side and slides three fingers inside me.

A string of expletives leaves my mouth, and he chuckles.

"Your filthy mouth turns me on."

"Your filthy cock does it for me," I rasp.

He rams his fingers inside me, stroking me in frantic movements that are borderline painful. Yet when he pulls out, I cry out at the loss. The telltale sound of the slide of his zipper, followed by the tearing of paper as he rolls a condom on, has me moaning in anticipation.

"Hold on, baby."

That's his only warning before he slams into me in one fast thrust, and a scream rips from my mouth before I can stop it. His hand covers my mouth, while he holds my hip with his free hand, helping to direct his movements as he flexes his hips and solidly pumps into me.

He fucks me hard and fast over the teacher's desk, grunting and cursing as he works me over good. His hand moves from my hip to my clit, and he rubs my swollen nub with firm strokes until my orgasm creeps up on me out of nowhere. I'm pushing my ass back and gripping his cock as my inner walls spasm uncontrollably. He bites my shoulder, muffling his own cries as he comes, pumping into the condom inside of me, covering my back with his warm body as I come back down to Earth.

Wordlessly, he helps clean me up with some tissues from his jacket pocket. Then he tucks his cock away and zips his pants up. Leaning down, he crushes his lips to mine in one final kiss. "Be safe, babe."

"Always."

"Wait one minute, and then follow me out," he instructs before striding across the room and leaving without a backward glance.

I use the time to fix my makeup and brush my hair, and then I leave, checking the hallway both ways to ensure no one is around, smiling to myself as I slip into class late, making up an excuse.

CHAPTER TWENTY-EIGHT

The next few days pass by without incident, and we settle into a familiar routine. Living with the Barrons' is okay. I have my own gorgeous room, which Elizabeth, Charlie's mom, had professionally remodeled especially for me.

She's super excited about the wedding, already planning a lavish reception, and it's all she wants to talk about at the dinner table each night. I usually walk away with a pain in my face from all the forced smiling and fake gushing. Charlie is pleased I'm indulging her, but I feel mean because I'm lying to her. I don't have the heart to explain it's all for nothing, because I've got to maintain this charade.

Charlie drives me to and from school and he is attentive and considerate—the picture-perfect boyfriend—at all times. We still sit at the elite table at school, but Trent is ignoring us so it's not as much of a headache. Chad has been filling me in on the gossip I missed, and Drew spends most lunchtimes silent and introspective.

I'm worried about him, but every time I inquire, he tells me he's fine. I want to go over to the house to talk to him, but I'm eager to steer clear of the place too. "Can you drive me to ballet after school?" I whisper to Drew at lunchtime. "I need to speak to you."

"Sure. Maybe we can grab something to eat beforehand."

"Perfect." I kiss his cheek. "I'll wait for you at your car."

"I don't see why I can't come," Charlie pouts when school ends and I break the news that I'm riding with my brother.

"I want time alone with my twin, and you can't shadow me everywhere," I say, closing my locker and stuffing my books in my bag.

"Your father only relented on the bodyguard and the driver because I assured him I'd keep you safe," he says, taking my hand as we walk toward the exit.

I roll my eyes. "My brother is hardly a threat."

Charlie opens the door, and I step outside, pulling the collar of my coat up to ward off the icy-cold wind. We escaped the snow in Connecticut, but it looks like it's followed us here. The forecast for the weekend predicts snow, and I'm preparing for a cold one.

"I don't enjoy being away from you," he says, reeling me into his arms at the top of the steps.

Electricity crackles in the air, and my body has a mind of its own as I whip my head around, looking down at the two guys watching us from the curb.

Kai locks eyes with me, holding my gaze captive, and I suck in a sharp breath. I swear he gets hotter every time I see him. My fingers twitch with a craving to touch him, longing to run my fingers through his silky-soft hair, to examine every inch of his inked skin. The fiery depths of his eyes confirm a similar hunger, but there's a dark promise in his gaze too.

I shiver as I recall how he fucked me possessively against the wall in the janitor's closet just before lunch. Every day, he finds some opportunity to steal me away, and our pairing is always wild and frantic. Sneaking around is so risky, and we shouldn't be doing it, but I'd be lying if I said I wasn't getting off on the forbidden nature of our relationship.

But Charlie has been growing more brazen. Hauling me into his lap and kissing me any chance he gets. I know he's doing it to test Kaiden, and I hate it, but we've got to stick to the plan.

I'm staring at Kai, and I know I shouldn't be, but it hurts to wrench my gaze away. Sawyer gives me a subtle cautionary nod as Charlie jerks my face back to his. His eyes blaze with indignation. "You are *my fiancée*," he hisses. "And you just eye-fucked him for everyone to see."

"I'm sorry," I murmur, stretching up and pulling his mouth down to mine, hoping Kai can forgive me. "I'm trying."

"Well, try harder," he barks, ripping his mouth from mine. "Unless you want him to wind up dead."

"I don't know how long I can do this," I admit to Drew, as we pick at our food in the diner a half hour later. "I feel like a cheating slut every time I let Charlie kiss me. And I know he's kissing me in public to piss Kai off, and it's working."

"Kai needs to get over himself," Drew says in a monotone voice.

"Would you feel that way if I was Jane and you had to watch another guy mauling me?"

He pushes his plate away. "That was a low blow."

"I know, but I've noticed how harsh you've been to Kai. Is that because of me or some other reason?"

He sighs, leaning back in the booth and staring at the ceiling. "I'm still pissed that he concealed his identity from me."

"Hey." I prod him in the chest. "I was the one sleeping with him. If I can forgive him, you can too."

Drew lowers his eyes to mine. "He was my best friend for years, and I'd often wondered where he was. What he was up to."

"You should patch things up with him. He's going to be in my life, which means he'll be in yours."

"I know," he says, slurping his drink through his straw. "But I think I'll make him sweat a little more."

I almost choke on my burger, but I'm glad to see some animation back on my brother's face. I soften my voice and my expression. "How are you really doing, Drew? You've been so quiet. I'm worried."

"Don't waste your energy worrying about me."

"That's a virtual impossibility, and you know it." I reach for his hand. "Talk to me. You can't bottle it all up."

"I miss her," he whispers. "I miss her so fucking much."

"I know. I miss her too."

"It's like I've lost half of myself, and I don't know who I am without her." He props his elbows on the table, resting his face in his hands. "More than that," he adds, piercing me with a serious look. "I'm scared of who I might become without her."

"You're still you." I squeeze his hand. "And you're one of the best people I know."

An agonized expression washes over his face, and he yanks his hand from mine. "You wouldn't say that if you knew the things I'd done."

I remember Charlie's explanation regarding their virginity, and I wonder what other things they've had to do. I don't think I want to know. "If they've forced you to do things to survive, I would never hold that against you."

"At what point do you have to stop and accept responsibility— even if it's something that's been technically forced upon you? If you're the person who took the action, you are still to blame."

"I don't know, D. I've done things I'm not proud of, but we're in a fight-or-die world, and I'll always fight. In my heart, I know I'm a good person." I pause for a beat. "A good person forced to make difficult choices. Forced to do bad things. But I never doubt what's in my heart."

"I never used to. Not until I lost half of mine."

I'm still mulling over his words later as I leave the ballet studio after rehearsal.

Drew is drowning, and I don't know how to save him.

A black Land Rover with dark windows pulls up to the curb, and the window lowers as I walk toward it. "Come on, slowpoke," Drew says, shooting me a tender smile. "Hop in the back," he adds, winking.

My brow puckers as I approach the car, wondering what he's up to. When I open the back door and slide inside, the biggest grin spreads across my face when I discover Kai waiting for me.

I move toward him the same moment he reaches out for me, and I melt into his arms as our mouths meet. He holds my face in his large palms as he kisses the shit out of me, and I could happily die in this moment.

"Buckle up, lovebirds," Drew says, revving the engine impatiently.

"What's going on?" I ask, reluctantly moving away from Kai to put my seat belt on. He straps himself in, wrapping his arms around me and holding me close. "And why are you here?" I ask, stretching my head back to look at him.

"Aren't you happy to see me, baby?"

I cup his cheek. "Of course, I'm happy to see you, but I recall my brother warning you to keep your distance." I eyeball Drew through the mirror. "What's changed?"

"Nothing," Drew replies, glancing briefly at me as he glides the car out into the traffic. "But we need to do something, and I figured it was safe to bring Kai. I know what it's like to crave the person you love. I can't do anything about Jane, but I could do this for you."

I unbuckle my belt and lean forward, poking my head through

the gap in the front seats, and kiss my brother on the cheek. "Thank you. I love you."

"Love you too, sis."

"Sit your fine ass back down," Kai says, fisting a hand in my sweater and yanking me back. "And put your belt on."

"Happy?" I arch a brow as I secure my belt and nestle into the crook of his arm.

"With you in my arms, always."

Drew makes a gagging motion.

"Shut. Up. I'm guessing you were ten million times worse," Kai says.

"Fact," I say. "But the way they loved one another was beautiful." Tears stab my eyes as emotion charges through me. I didn't realize I'd still be this hormonal so long after the... I purposely break that thought, unable to even say it in my mind.

I grip Kai's arm tighter, glad he's here. When he asked what Trent had said to make me go crazy on his ass that day in the cafeteria, I refused to tell him, much to his frustration, and he took that out on my body the next day when he yanked me into a different classroom.

But I couldn't say it.

Because he'd murder Trent without hesitation, and I'm not putting myself through this shit to protect him only to lose him over my douchey ex.

We drive for over an hour, and I'm content in Kai's arms, clinging to him while he peppers kisses all over my face. Drew watches us through the mirror, smiling, and I'm glad he approves.

"Where does Charlie think I am?" I ask, as Drew takes the next exit off the highway.

"He knows where you are. He just doesn't know Anderson is with us."

I stare out the window at unfamiliar roads, asking for the

umpteenth time where we're headed. But like all the other times, the guys remain tight-lipped.

We pull into the entrance to a private hospital a few minutes later, and I guess where we are. I bolt upright, my gaze bouncing between my brother and my boyfriend. "Oscar," I whisper, and Drew nods.

My heart is pounding behind my rib cage, and I clutch Kai's hand in an iron grip as we walk down the hallway toward Oscar's room.

"This is it," Drew says, stopping in front of room four hundred and eighteen.

"You want me to come in with you, baby?" Kai asks, and it's tempting.

"No. I need to do this alone." They explained in the elevator he's still in a coma. I look between them, not sure if they know this. "He took a bullet for me that night. He tried to hold Louis off so I could get away."

"We know," Kai says. "And we owe him."

"He's my hero," D adds.

"Mine too," I whisper.

Kai kisses me sweetly. "Take all the time you need. We'll be right out here." He points at a row of chairs against a side wall.

I gulp, nodding, as I curl my hand around the door handle and step into the room.

"Abigail!" Julie, Oscar's wife, rushes toward me enveloping me in a warm hug. "Oh, my sweet girl." She grasps my face in her small hand. "Oscar would be so happy to see you here." She takes my hand, pulling me over to the bed. "Honey. Abigail is here to see you, and she looks as beautiful as ever."

A messy ball of emotion clogs my throat as I stare at Oscar's prone body in the bed. He's got tubes coming out of both arms, and he's hooked up to a machine. The sheets are folded over just above his waist, and he looks so thin and frail in the bed. His face is a horrid ashen color, and he looks so old.

"You can talk to him," Julie says. "I don't know if he hears, but I like to think he does."

"Hey, Oscar." My voice cracks as I move closer to the bed, taking his hand in mine. It's warm to the touch, which is unexpected but reassuring. "I'm sorry it's taken me so long to visit, but my father locked me away at Parkhurst, and I only returned to town this week."

Julie looks at me aghast. I probably should've been more circumspect. Knowing Oscar, he hasn't told her much about the fucked-up goings-on at Chez Manning.

"He tried to save me that night," I tell her. "And I hate that he's here because of me."

"Oh no, honey." She rises, wrapping her arm around my waist. "Oscar loves you, and even if he doesn't survive this, I know he wouldn't have any regrets dying to protect you."

"What have the doctors said?"

"Not a lot. His body has healed, but his mind hasn't. They don't know how long he'll stay like this, and the longer it goes on, the more there is a possibility of brain damage."

I clutch her hand, hating to think of Oscar suffering like that. "Can I do anything? Maybe get a second opinion? And let me take care of his medical bills."

"You have already done so much for us, and I can't thank you enough."

I stare, perplexed at her, because I've done jack shit. There hasn't been time.

"I don't know what we would've done if you hadn't sent your young man and his friends to help. Drew, too, of course."

"I don't understand." My brows knit together.

"Oh. Oh." A light bulb appears to go off in her mind. "I just assumed you sent them."

"I would have if I'd been here. Oscar is more of a father to me than my father has ever been."

"He adores you." She squeezes my waist. "And given how you've all rallied round to help us, I can see why."

"What exactly did my friends do?"

"Drew transferred Oscar here after your father ended his employment and we lost our medical coverage. Then your boyfriend turned up at my doorstep with Sawyer and Jackson. Kaiden rented us a house two miles from here so we could be closer to Oscar. He even arranged for the girls to go to a new school temporarily, and he put far too much money into my bank account." Tears pool in her eyes. "Sawyer installed a new security system at the house, and Jackson came with me to purchase a new car because Oscar's car has gone missing."

"It looks like my brother and my friends have taken care of everything," I say, hardly able to talk over the lump in my throat.

"They have, and I'm so grateful." She glances at her husband with fresh tears in her eyes. "To spend every day here with him, knowing I have no other worries or concerns, is more than I could have hoped for. And it's all thanks to you."

I shake my head. "I did nothing."

"Don't you see that you did?" She presses a kiss to my cheek. "Those boys don't have an allegiance to my husband. Most of them don't even know him." She looks me directly in the eye. "Their loyalty is to you. They did this *for you*."

CHAPTER TWENTY-NINE

I leave Julie with her husband and slip out into the hallway. Drew and Kai have their heads bent together, and they're conversing in low tones. I hate to break up the renewal of their bromance, but my heart is fit to burst, and I can't contain it. Plonking myself down on Kai's lap, I wrap one arm around his neck and drape my other arm around my brother, pulling them both into me. "Thank you for what you did for him."

"You okay?" Kai asks, peering into my eyes.

"I'm okay. Sad, because I hate seeing him like that and I hate the thought he might not come out of his coma, or come out of it intact, but at least he's still alive."

"I called Rick while you were in there. One of his professors at Harvard is a neurologist. He'll talk to him and see if he can recommend someone to come and give us a second opinion."

I let go of my brother, wrapping both arms around Kai's neck. "I fucking love you." I dot kisses all over his face. "And you are so getting laid for this."

"Ugh." Drew scrubs his hands down his face. "I did not need to hear that."

"Suck it up, D. At least you don't have to listen to us doing the deed." I shudder, remembering the nights I heard Jane's screams all the way from my bedroom.

"Unless we get it on in the back seat." Kai waggles his brows, and I snicker at the look of abject horror on my twin's face.

"He's joking."

"Am I?"

"Gross." Drew stands, clamping a hard hand down on Kai's shoulder. "And just when I was starting to like you again, man." He shakes his head.

"My cock makes your sister happy," Kai unhelpfully supplies. "You should do a happy dance, dude."

"If you mention your cock and my sister in the same sentence again, I will pound your ass into dust."

Kai laughs, lifting me off him and placing my feet on the ground. He stands, circling his arm around my shoulder. "I'd love to see you try."

"Kai's a legend in the ring," I admit. "And he has quite the rep on the underground scene, or so I've been told."

"Who said that?" Kai asks as we walk toward the elevator.

"Xavier told me the night we went to the Grid." A pang of sorrow jumps up and bites me in the ass at thoughts of my bestie. Former bestie? I don't know.

Drew slams to a halt. "He took you to *the Grid?*" His jaw snaps, and his eyes scream murderous intent.

"He didn't tell you?"

"It seems, with you, Xavier kept most of it to himself."

That helps.

But I need to have a conversation with Xavier to find out for myself.

I've been avoiding him, sending all his calls to voicemail, because I'm trying to build myself up to it.

I'm terrified his confession could be the last straw.

The last string to snap.

The final break which destroys me completely.

"How do you know Sylvia will even speak to you?" Sawyer asks Sunday night, when we're convened in the warehouse for a catch up.

"I'll blackmail her into it if I have to," I calmly reply.

"How?" Kai asks.

"She was screwing her personal trainer last year behind Christian's back. I'll threaten to tell her husband if she doesn't cooperate."

Jackson chuckles, shoving his feet up on the table. "I've missed your devious nature."

"Only because you weren't on the receiving end of it," Kai says, his voice dripping with sarcasm.

"Do you mind?" Xavier eyes Jackson's feet like they are poisonous. "I eat off this table."

"Do I look like I care?" Jackson makes a drama of crossing his feet at the ankles.

"No problem, man," Xavier says, backpedaling as a slow grin spreads across his mouth. "I've also fucked on this table. Many times. Right about where your feet are."

Jackson slides his legs down so fast he loses his balance and the chair wobbles precariously, throwing him back. Sawyer grabs the chair before it crashes to the ground, rolling his eyes. "Children. Grow up. Or leave the room and let the adults talk."

Xavier flips him the bird. "You're just cranky because now you're picturing me naked being topped by some hot stud with a monster cock."

"Jesus fucking Christ." Kai buries his head in his hands.

"TMI, dude," I say, attempting to smother a snort of laughter.

It's almost impossible to hold on to my anger when Xavier is genuinely one of my favorite people in the universe.

"I have no words," Sawyer mutters.

"That's because I'm right," Xavier teases, rubbing his crotch and jerking his hips forward. "But you won't confirm it."

"All right. Comedy hour is over," Drew cuts in. "We've got assholes to take down and plans to make."

Everyone sobers up, but I'm glad for the light-hearted banter because it helps remind me who these guys are. "I need to bring something up," I say, clearing my throat and preparing to eat crow. Because Drew will go postal times a thousand when I admit this. "Because we agreed no secrets." I wet my lips and look my brother in the eye. "Don't get mad, but *IfollowedyouintothesexdungeonlastweekandIsaweverythingIshouldn't.*" I rush the words out fast before I chicken out of my confession.

"You what?!" Drew roars, slamming his palms down on the table.

"Back the fuck up there," Xavier says. "You snuck into *the* sex dungeon?"

"How many other sex dungeons do you know?" I raise my hand as he opens his mouth to speak. "Nope. Don't answer that. And, yes, I'm talking about the bastard sperm donor's depraved sex club in the basement of my house."

Xavier grins this massive grin, delighted I'm speaking to him again. But it's surface level. Because we still have shit to discuss.

"Why the hell would you go in there?" Kai asks, and the face he wears is almost identical to my brother's.

"Because I wanted to know why my twin was dressed up as if he was going out at midnight on a school night."

"Did nothing we discussed the last time we were here sink into that obstinate skull of yours?" Drew shouts, and I've never seen him so enraged. "Fucking hell, A!" He grabs fistfuls of his dark hair and starts pacing. "If they'd caught you in there…" He shivers uncontrollably.

"Well." I wipe my clammy hands down my jeans, trying to prepare for the second detonation. "I was just leaving *whencharliecaughtme*."

Drew storms around the room like a madman, racing to the wall and pounding his fists against it in a scary display of aggression. Xavier doesn't call him out on the damage he's doing because even he's a teeny bit afraid of Drew right now.

Jackson and I trade similar tormented expressions.

Kai gets up, walking to Drew, and they converse in low tones.

"What are they whispering about?" I ask Jackson, leaning into his ear.

"Fucked if I know," he says in a low voice.

"While they're distracted," I whisper again, pressing my mouth more fully to his ear. "You got any weed?"

"Is that a serious question?"

"Well, yeah, because I don't see you smoking it much anymore."

"I'm trying to cut back, but that doesn't mean I'm not packing." He slides a joint out of his back pocket, slyly passing it to me. "If you're caught with that, I'll deny all knowledge."

"It will be long gone before I'm caught." I just need something to take the edge off on nights when I'm bored and lonely in my bedroom.

"What are you two talking about?" Kai asks, dropping into his seat beside me.

I kiss him to distract him while I slip the joint into the pocket of my hoodie. "We were just wondering the same thing about you two?"

Drew is back in his seat, and while he appears under control, he still looks like he wants to throttle sense into me.

"We were comparing notes on how stubborn you are." Kai levels me with a stern look.

"We were comparing notes on how overprotective you are," I toss back with a fake sugary smile.

"We might as well call this meeting to a close," Sawyer says, crossing his arms and sighing impatiently.

"I'm finding it entertaining myself." Xavier scratches the side of his blood-red hair as he winks at Sawyer.

"You would."

"Enough," Drew snaps, pinning me with a frosty look. "Tell me and leave nothing out."

So, I do, and it doesn't take long for the jovial atmosphere to evaporate completely.

"Shit, A." Drew cradles his head in his hands, and his breathing is labored. Kai links his fingers through mine. "I never wanted you to see any of that."

"One part of me wishes I hadn't, but another part is glad I did, because now, I'm even more determined to take him down. And I think we need to add the order and Parkhurst to our list."

"Are you truly that insane or that naïve?" Drew barks.

"I'm not fucking naïve," I snap back. "Or insane. I'm fucking disgusted." I stand, bracing my palms on the table, and leaning across at him. "How are you not absolutely sickened at what is going on down there?"

"Trust me, I'm sickened!" he yells. "You think I wanted to be there?"

I remember his stiff stature. "I know you didn't want to be there, but how can you do nothing about it?"

"Because there is nothing that can be done, A. You don't understand how powerful these people are. They are virtually untouchable. And we must pick our battles. Father is our priority, and we can't lose sight of that."

"The girls were so young, D," I whisper, slumping back in my chair. "How can we turn a blind eye to that?"

"I'm only asking you to turn a blind eye to it for now," he adds, his voice dropping to normal levels.

"Who are those girls? Are they part of the elite too?"

"Some are."

"Why would the elite give their daughters over to other elite to degrade and abuse like that?" Kai asks. He's gripping the arms of his chair in a way that implies he's restricting his blood supply.

"Some do it for a short while as a punishment for disobedience," Drew says. "Others hand them over when they've exiled them from the family for any number of stupid reasons."

"Like?" I inquire.

"They have a medical condition, or they're not intelligent enough, or they refuse to abide by the traditions and rules." He drills a hole in the side of my skull. "Or they've tried to escape."

"Fuck." Kai hauls me over into his lap, and I drape myself around him.

"But most are girls they pull off the street," Drew continues. "Runaways and orphans, kids from foster homes. Girls, and boys, not likely to be missed. When they get older, they turn them into recruitment managers, paying them to find more young girls and boys to bring into the fold."

My nostrils twitch, and the scent of marijuana fills the air. I glance at Jackson, puffing frantically on a joint like it's the air he needs to breathe. Drew opens his mouth to say something, but Sawyer cuts him off with a sharp, pointed look.

"Who were those men because not all of them were local," I say.

"They are all high-ranking elite members, there by invitation. People Father wants to network with or manipulate. There are cameras all over the room, and they purposely capture men in inappropriate acts and then use it to blackmail them after. No one talks about it because they are too embarrassed, so more men fall into the trap."

"Are you saying Father uses the dungeon to blackmail members of the elite into doing his bidding?"

"That's exactly what I'm saying. You know how he operates. He finds weaknesses and exploits it."

"We'll never be able to defeat someone like that," Jackson says, frustration evident in the slump of his shoulders.

"Yes, *we will*." Determination surges through me. "We find his biggest weakness and exploit it until he's crushed with no way of getting back up again."

CHAPTER THIRTY

"Can we talk?" Xavier asks when the meeting breaks up.

"Yeah. Just give me a sec to say goodbye to Kai."

He nods, and I walk over to where Kai is lounging against the door, watching Sawyer half-carry Jackson to the car. "Is he okay?" I ask, because I've noticed something off about Jackson the past couple weeks.

"The anniversary of his sister's death is approaching," Kai confirms, pulling me into his arms. "He always goes a little off the rails."

"Can I do anything to help?"

Kai tucks my hair behind my ears. "There isn't anything anyone can do. It's just something he has to go through." He nuzzles his head into my neck. "I hate this part."

"Me too." I run my hand up and down his back. "I hate that we only get snatched moments here and there."

"We need to find something to bury your father with and fast."

"Hopefully, my conversation with Trent's mom will offer some leads."

"Anderson." Sawyer's tone is sharp. "We need to hit the road." He jerks his head in the car's direction.

I stretch up on my tiptoes, kissing him passionately.

"I love you," he whispers over my lips. "Be safe."

"Love you too." I hug him tight before letting him go.

"Call me later."

I bob my head. I look forward to his nightly calls as the highlight of my day. I blow him a kiss before waving at Sawyer and heading back inside to chat with Xavier. "You okay to wait for a few minutes?" I ask Drew as I pass by him. He has his nose buried in his cell, and his fingers are punching buttons as he taps out a text.

"I'm not in a rush, and I just messaged Charlie to say we're grabbing something to eat after the movie, so take your time."

I walk into the main room, and Xavier closes the door behind me, looking nervous as he wrings his hands together. "I was so worried you'd never speak to me again," he blurts. "I haven't been able to eat or sleep all week for fear I've fucked everything up."

"How could you do that to me?" I prop my butt against the edge of the table, folding my arms across my chest.

"I didn't have a choice," he admits, his voice wary. "When I first took the job, I thought it'd be a cakewalk, but then I got to know you, and I was smitten."

I purse my lips. "Attempting to flirt with me will not work."

He pushes off the wall, walking toward me. "I'm not flirting. I'm being honest. You're an easy person to love, Abby. I've told you that before, and it's true. You're even easier to like, and I knew I was in deep shit within the first week." His tongue flips against his lip ring in an obvious nervous tell. "But, as time went on, I convinced myself I wasn't really doing anything wrong."

"How'd you figure that?"

"Because Drew only wanted to protect you, and I was helping him to do that. I knew you'd be pissed when you eventually discovered the truth, but I hoped the fact I genuinely cared for you and that I didn't tell him tons of stuff would make it easier for you to forgive me." He stares at me pleadingly. "So, does it?" he asks, and I like his bluntness.

"I know both of you thought you were doing the right thing, but I needed you to be true, Xavier. You were the last one. The only one I thought I could trust one hundred percent. The only one who hadn't betrayed me." Pain slices across my chest. "But then I discovered that was just a lie. That you were just like everyone else."

"No, babe." Tentatively, he cups my face. "I'm not like everyone else. I'm your best friend. Nothing about what's happened alters that fact. Even if you can't forgive me. Even if you tell me to go away. I will always be your best friend. I will always care about you and ensure you're safe."

"Did you tell him about Kai and me?"

He shakes his head, dropping his hands from my face. "I didn't have to. He could see it for himself. But I would've told him if he hadn't figured it out because you were risking so much with Kai." I suck in a sharp breath. I'm pleased he's being honest with me, but that hurts too.

Stress seeps from his pores, and remorse is clear on his face. "I tried not to betray your confidence, and I told Drew the bare minimum because you deserved to be happy, and you *were* happy with Kai. So, I was doing everything I could to ensure he wasn't a threat to you. I only told Drew the things I felt it was important he knew. Only things that impacted your safety. I swear."

He rubs at a spot between his brows. "He went fucking apeshit on my ass after you told him about the Grid, demanding to know what else I'd kept secret, but I told him nothing, and he's no right to demand anything of me now."

"Why not?"

"Because I don't work for him anymore. I quit the morning after the shootout. When I discovered you were missing and none of those fucktards kept you safe." His nostrils flare. "Did the bastards tell you they kept me a virtual prisoner? I booked a plane ticket when Drew told me you were at Parkhurst, but they wouldn't let me leave." Frustration billows from his ears. "I didn't care about the shit they were telling me. I just cared about getting you out of there."

His eyes plead with me, and my lip wobbles as I grapple to contain my emotions. If Xavier had come to Parkhurst, he'd be dead now. He's smart enough to know that too, but he was still willing, and that speaks volumes. I want to hug the shit out of him, but I can't forget he was lying to me for months.

It's so hard to remain steadfast.

I mean, I've been able to put the other's deceptions behind me, so I should be able to do the same for Xavier. But it's different. In both a good and bad way. On the one hand, because he's my closest friend—besides Jane—it makes it easier to understand and forgive. But that's also the reason it's harder. He was, *is*, my best friend, so the betrayal runs even deeper.

But, then again, I felt the same way about Kai. And I'm giving him a second chance.

Xavier deserves the same opportunity.

"You understand you'll have to win back my trust?" I ask.

He nods his head vigorously. "I'll do whatever it takes. Just don't give up on me."

"You promise there will be no more secrets and lies?"

"I promise." His eyes radiate sincerity, and they're bright with hope and expectation.

I stop fighting it and wrap myself around him. His arms hug me in a warm embrace, and I shutter my eyes, clinging to my friend, praying we can find a way back to where we were. Because his friendship means so much to me. And I don't want to lose him from my life.

We hug it out, and then I pull back, eyeing him circumspectly. "Your deception hurt, Xavier. It hurt real bad. I'm surrounded by people I considered friends and family, and every person has betrayed me, but I've put those feelings aside for the others, so I'll do the same for you."

He reaches for me, and I step back, holding up a palm. "But it doesn't mean I forget or forgive. It means I'm giving you a chance to make it up to me, and if you fuck up, if you keep shit from me again, that is it for our friendship. It will be as dead as my father will be once we're through with him."

"You *are* staying in the car," I hiss, glaring at Drew. "She'll probably clam up if she sees you."

"It's not safe to hang around outside here by yourself."

I roll my eyes. Honestly, it's like talking to a brick wall. "You will be right out here watching, and there's no one around at this hour of night." I flap my hands in the air, gesturing toward the quiet street outside. "And Sylvia will not hurt me."

"You don't know that."

"She was one of Mom's best friends." I level him with a "get real" look. "She won't do anything to me." I stretch my hand out to him. "But if it makes you feel better, give me your gun." All the elite have a weapon in close possession, at all times. It was probably part of lesson one-oh-one at Parkhurst. Drilled into them from the time they were ten, when they first started going there.

He fishes a gun out of the glove box and hands it to me. I check that the safety is on before tucking it in the back of my black pants and opening the car door.

Drew tugs on my elbow. "Be careful."

I glance over my shoulder at him. "Sylvia is as harmless as a fly."

"I've learned to underestimate no one. You shouldn't either."

It's sage advice. "Duly noted. Now let me go before I miss her."

"I'll shadow you, but if there are any issues, text me."

"Got it." I press a kiss to his cheek. "Stop worrying."

He pulls my hand, lacing his fingers in mine. "You're all I have left, Abby. I can't bear the thought of anything happening to you."

"Nothing will happen to me. I know how to take care of myself, but I appreciate your concern." I kiss his cheek again. "Now chill out. I'll see you in a while."

I climb out of the car, shutting the door and watching as Drew moves it further along the road, pulling into the curb up ahead, where it's less conspicuous. I don't want to spook Trent's mom before I've explained, because I need to pump her for intel.

I wait outside the shrink's office for ten minutes before she shows. She spots me instantly. "Abigail?" Her voice sounds clear, which is unusual because she's usually strung out from drugs or booze or a concoction of both. I'm guessing she likes to show up for her therapy sessions looking like she's got a handle on things.

But I've been around her enough, heard Trent complain about her enough, to know it's not the norm.

"Hi, Mrs. Montgomery," I say, smiling as I approach her.

"I prefer Sylvia," she says, and that doesn't warrant an explanation.

"I was hoping you had a few minutes to go for a coffee," I say. "There are some things I'd like to ask you."

Her eyes dart around the area, her gaze turning suspicious. "The elite don't know I'm here," I say, answering her unspoken question. "Except for Drew." Her eyes widen in alarm. "He won't tell anyone about our meeting," I rush to reassure her. "He's trailing me purely to ensure I'm safe, and he means you no trouble."

"Is that the truth?"

I don't blame her for her caution. "Yes." I step closer, relieved when her shoulders relax. "You were one of my mother's best friends so that leads me to believe I can trust you. Can I trust you, Sylvia? Can I ask you about my mother and how she met my father and know that you won't relay that back to your husband or your son or my father?"

Fire dances in her eyes. "I would never betray any female in that way. And I avoid conversing with those men whenever I can help it." She presses her key fob, lifting her shoulder. "Come on. There's a coffee place off the beaten track a few minutes away. Let's talk there."

I thought I'd have to blackmail her into talking to me, but I can see that won't be necessary. Perhaps it's because she's sober, or maybe she's lonely, or she's waited for me to approach her about my mother, but whatever the reason, I'm grateful she seems willing to open up.

"I've overheard my husband and son discussing elite business," she says when we're in the car and en route to the coffee shop. "And I'm surprised Drew is here supporting you." She glances at me briefly. "Pleasantly surprised," she adds. "But surprised none the less."

"He has my back, and he wants to protect me." For the first time, I say it with conviction.

She squeezes my knee, smiling. "I'm glad you two are still close, and I'm glad he hasn't forgotten who he is. That he's looking out for you."

"We both want to know about our mother. We know she was planning to escape with Atticus Anderson and that our father killed her for it."

Tense silence engulfs us, and she grips the steering wheel tighter. "I heard about what went down in the ballroom," she says after a few seconds have passed, rounding the next bend. She looks me square in the eye. "I've been expecting you."

We don't speak again until we're at a small table tucked into the back of the unassuming coffee place. "Drew can join us if he likes," she offers after we've placed our order.

"Thank you, but I think it's best he keeps watch from outside. Just in case."

"Okay." She clasps her hands on top of the table, pinning her piercing blue eyes on me. It's hard to look at her face and not see the resemblance to Trent. "What do you want to know?"

"What happened to the child my mother was expecting? Because it was that pregnancy that sealed her fate and forced her into marriage to my father, right?"

"How much do you want to know, Abby? Because some of this won't be pleasant to hear."

The waitress sets our pie and coffee down, and I wait until she's gone before replying. "I want to know it all, Sylvia. Hold nothing back. I know how the elite work, and I doubt there's much you can say that'll shock me."

"That truly hurts to hear," she admits, placing her hand over mine. "Your mother fought so hard to protect you both so you wouldn't have to endure the things she'd endured, *we'd* endured." A shuddering breath leaves her lips as she stares off into space.

"What happened to the baby?" I ask, holding my breath in anticipation.

She shoots me a sympathetic look, squeezing my hand. "The baby was stillborn."

CHAPTER THIRTY-ONE

"I'd wondered if that was the case or if we had another sibling out there somewhere," I admit, feeling a pang of sorrow in my heart.

"Your father discovered the child was Atticus's, and he beat Olivia so badly she lost the baby."

Tears sting my eyes, and I swallow hard over the tormented lump in my throat.

He stole her baby from her too.

She squeezes my hand. "Your mother knew the baby had died because he'd stopped moving inside her, but your father refused to bring her to the hospital."

"It was a boy?" I whisper.

She nods. "She was only four weeks away from her due date, and that bastard locked her in her bedroom until she went into labor."

My hand shakes as I bring the mug to my lips, sipping the hot liquid, barely feeling it scald my raw throat as I contemplate the horror of living through that.

Knowing your husband killed your child and being forced to live with that until it was the time for the delivery must have been sheer hell.

And imagine going through that pain knowing there was no joyful bundle at the end.

A sob escapes my mouth, and I set my mug down, spilling coffee on the table.

Sylvia gets up, rounding the table and putting her arm around me. "I'm so sorry, Abby."

"He killed my babies too," I blurt, swiping at the hot tears coursing down my face.

"What?" Her shocked tone matches the mounting shock on her face as I explain.

"Oh my God, Abby. I'm so sorry he did that to you!" She lets me go, pulling her chair over beside mine and sitting down. Her arms encircle me again, and I accept her comfort willingly. "I should've done more for you." Genuine remorse flickers in her eyes. "Your mother would be so disappointed in me."

"We weren't your responsibility, and I know what those bastards are like. Father wouldn't have let you intervene."

"I tried, at the start, after your mother died. You probably don't remember, but you and Drew used to sleep over at our house every weekend." Her lips pull into a tight line. "It wasn't much, but I tried to do fun stuff with all of you, so you had some time to just be normal children, but your father eventually put a stop to it."

She grips the edge of the table. "I went to your house, to plead with him to reconsider and… Well, it didn't go as I'd planned." Her face is as white as the tablecloth.

"What did he do to you?"

She shakes her head, and her lip wobbles. "I can't talk about it. I'm sorry." Gulping down the dregs of her coffee, she pulls a flask from her purse and pours whiskey into her mug, uncaring who sees. She knocks it back, her hand trembling. "You must think so little of me," she says, shrugging in embarrassment.

"I know you've seen me at my worst," she continues, "but I tried fighting back, and eventually, Christian won. He broke me. Beat me down. Removed my fighting spirit. I watched my two best friends die after they attempted to escape, and I knew I was trapped. Christian took great delight in telling me how both my friends had been murdered, and he told me that would be my fate if I tried to do the same. So, I did the only thing I could."

She eyeballs me with her glassy gaze. "I checked out of life. I numb the pain and the reality, and it's only these weekly sessions when I let it back in, when I remember what my life has been like, when I accept the pain for the punishment of standing by and letting my husband turn my son into a monster just like him."

"You couldn't have done anything to stop it. I'm only beginning to realize how damaged they all are because of the stuff they've had to do at Parkhurst."

"I don't even know the half of it, and I'm disturbed," she says before seeming to collect herself. "I've missed seeing you at the house, but I'm not sorry your engagement to my son has ended. You deserve better."

"We didn't love one another, and I don't see how any marriage can work without love."

"You're right," she murmurs. "Love is the bedrock of any marriage. Without it, it's a daily struggle." She looks off into space. "I haven't believed in love in a long time."

I don't know what to say to that, so I say nothing, watching her under a sad veil as she stares out the window. After a couple minutes, she shakes off her melancholy, fixing me with a feeble smile. "We don't want to get sidetracked. I can't stay out too late, or he'll send someone to look for me. What else did you want to know?"

"How did my father come to be in Rydeville? Because I know he's not from here."

"Your father's adopted family moved into the area when we were fifteen."

"My father is adopted?"

"You didn't know?"

"He rarely talks to us, unless he wants something from us, and he never talks about his past. All I know is, his parents died in a plane crash when he was twenty-two."

"Your father was born to a junkie mother and her pimp. His mother overdosed when he was six weeks old and his father didn't want him, so he ended up a ward of the state," she explains. "He was in an orphanage for the first three years of his life when the Hearst family adopted him. They lived over on the West Coast someplace before Mr. Hearst's business interests brought him to Rydeville. They were from new money, and it was unusual for the elite to mix with new money, but your father is very charming, and he wormed his way into our circle at school."

I listen attentively, not wanting to miss anything.

"It was obvious he had set his sights on your mother, but Olivia was hopelessly in love with Atticus."

I guess there's no accounting for taste.

"If that's the case, how did my father charm her?"

"He didn't." Her eyes cloud over. "He manipulated the situation after his many attempts to woo her right out from under his best friend's nose failed. Your mother told Atticus what Michael was up to, but Atticus was an arrogant son of a bitch, and he gloated over the fact his friend was trying to steal his girl. He was secure in Olivia's love, and he thought that made them infallible. His arrogance was his downfall because it meant Michael got desperate."

"Why did he want Mom so badly?"

"Well, not only was she beautiful, smart, and kind, but she was the only girl from a founding family. Every guy at school wanted her, but she'd fallen for Atticus when she was thirteen, and her heart was always his." She pours more whiskey into her mug. "Anyway, Mr. Hearst Senior lost his business and his wealth, and it became a more urgent concern for Michael, so he planned things so Olivia would have no choice but to marry him."

"What did the bastard do?"

"It was senior year, and Christian, Atticus, and Charles were away on a football trip. Michael wasn't a good football player, and he never made the team, much to his disgust."

I can imagine that being a sore point for my father, because he likes to believe he's the best at everything and he hates losing to anyone, especially the other elite. He thinks he's so above everyone, and it's fascinating to learn he was at the bottom of the rung until his marriage elevated his fortune.

"We had planned a girls' night at my house. Michael showed up, persuading us to attend a college party with him. Your mother didn't want to go, but Emma and I were champing at the bit. We were both single, so we were keen to meet some older, college guys."

She chugs back more whiskey. "He drugged us and photographed us having sex with different guys." My stomach flips, and my mouth turns dry. "He didn't pimp Olivia out. *He* fucked her, without a condom, all night long and had someone photograph it. Things were different back then, and Olivia wasn't on birth control, because she was a virgin. It was a condition of the marriage agreement between her father and Atticus's father, and even though they were crazy about one another, Atticus respected her decision to wait for their wedding night. Or so I thought, because that's what Olivia had always told us."

She slumps in her chair a little as my cell pings with a message from Drew, checking in with me. I tell him I'm fine and slip my cell back in my pocket, reaching out to take the flask from Sylvia's hand.

"You need to drive home, and I won't have your death on my conscience."

"Death would be welcome at this point." Her tone is flat.

"Don't say that." I put the flask back in her purse, slanting a warning look at her.

She sighs, knotting her hands on her lap. "Michael sent the photographs to Atticus, and Atticus went ballistic. Then he found out she was pregnant with Michael's child, and in a fit of rage, he told his father, and his father immediately called off the wedding and informed Mr. Manning. Per the stupid elite traditions, it now meant Olivia had to marry the father of her baby, and Michael got his way."

"I don't understand something." My brows knit together. "Why didn't she tell her father she was drugged and raped?"

Her eyes drop. "Michael blackmailed her into keeping silent by using her loyalty to us. He told her he'd send our parents the photos of us having group sex with different men. It would ruin our reputations, and our parents would most likely have disowned us."

"But you were drugged and gang raped!" I protest, absolutely sickened.

"It wouldn't have mattered." She looks sad. "Your mother said nothing to protect us."

"I hate him. He's an evil, sick bastard, and he's got to be stopped!" I hiss, digging my nails into my thighs. I want to scream from the pit of my lungs.

"He's unstoppable. They all are."

Her voice is thick with resignation, but I refuse to believe it, because then it means we're doomed, and I'm not accepting that.

"Your mother was forced to marry Michael almost immediately, and it wasn't a happy marriage." Sylvia confirms what Drew and I have always known. "Once he had her, he stopped all pretense. He screwed around on her. He abused her—physically, verbally, and emotionally—and made her life hell. She wanted to hurt him, and she naively thought if he knew the baby wasn't his that he'd let her go, but he beat her to within an inch of her life, causing her to lose the baby and her sanity. She almost died giving birth, and there were complications which meant she suffered through a succession of difficult pregnancies and miscarriages in the years that followed."

She shifts on her chair, worrying her lip between her teeth, contemplating something.

"Whatever it is, I want to know."

She palms my face. "Your mother was a broken shell for years. Every miscarriage tore another little strip off her heart. She wanted to be a Mom so badly because it was all she had left. Plus, Michael wouldn't leave her alone until she gave him an heir. Every time she miscarried, he punished her, as if it was her fault." She visibly shivers, and my chest tightens at the thought of how he punished her.

Anger resurfaces and my determination strengthens.

"It didn't help that Atticus had married Emma by then and they'd had Maverick. Your mother sunk into a deep depression, and I think even Michael worried that she was past the point of no return, so he found a solution. A way to give him his heir and her the babies she so desperately longed for."

"What are you saying?"

"Your mother conceived you and Drew through IVF and via a surrogate."

"What?" I stare at her, shell-shocked.

Tears well in her eyes. "Your Aunt Genevieve carried you and Drew to full term."

"Oh, my God." Intense pressure settles on my chest. "Why didn't she tell me?"

"I can't answer that, love."

She glances at her watch. "I'm sorry to cut this short, but I need to head home before he sends someone out to search for me."

I struggle to snap out of it, remembering the other stuff I need to know. "Just a couple of other questions, please."

She eyes her purse longingly, and my heart aches for her. *How bad must it be that you need to spend every day high or drunk?* I used to think she was weak, but she's broken and destroyed because of things the elite have done to her. I wish I'd made more of an effort to speak with her when I was engaged to Trent and over at their house every second Sunday for dinner.

"You said Christian confirmed he murdered your two friends. Do you know if there's evidence we can use to pin my mother's death on my father?"

"I don't think so. Your mom died in a car accident. The brakes failed. I'm sure your father or my husband paid someone to tamper with them and keep their mouth shut. They also paid off whoever inspected the scene. They bribed the authorities to omit it in official reports. They think of everything, Abby. They always tie all loose ends. This is their job. If someone crosses them, they eliminate them without a second thought." She clicks her fingers. "They never leave a trail."

"But they did with Emma's murder," I say. "Do you know where my mother stashed the evidence proving my father killed her?"

A strange look appears on her face.

I frown. "What's that look for?"

"You mean proof that Michael got the pills found in Emma's stomach contents?"

"Yes." My frown deepens. "What else could I mean?"

"Your mother told me, but she wouldn't say where she'd hidden it. She believed it was safest if I didn't know, and she was right. After she died, Christian tried to beat it out of me, and when he realized I might be telling the truth, he put me through a polygraph." She squeezes my hand. "Your mother never stopped protecting me."

"And?" I encourage her to go on.

Air whooshes out of her mouth. "I'm not sure this makes much difference now, but she also told me she'd discovered that Atticus played a role in Emma's death."

All the blood drains from my face.

"Your mother had been having an affair with him on and off for a few years, after both of them were married. I didn't know until Emma discovered it and broke her friendship with Olivia. It was horrible, and I was caught in the middle. After Emma died, Olivia told me her and Atticus were planning to flee to Europe with all you kids. But a week before she died, she came to see me. She'd broken things off with Atticus after he'd let it slip."

"What happened?" I blurt.

"Your father drugged Emma and left her there to die, staging it so it looked like a suicide. When Kaiden found her, his screams brought Atticus to the scene."

"I know that." Kaiden admitted it to me a few months ago.

"Emma wasn't dead, Abby. When Kaiden found her, she was still breathing. Her pulse was weak, but she was still alive."

"Oh, my God." My heart is racing out of control. "What did Atticus do?"

"I knew the truth, because Christian taunted me with it. I'd been in agony for months trying to decide what to do with that knowledge, so when your mother showed up that day, full of the half-truths Atticus had told her, I filled her in on what had really gone down."

I bite on the inside of my cheek as I wait for her to tell me.

"Christian dropped by the Anderson house that day on Michael's instruction. Michael wanted to ensure Emma was dead, so he got Christian to go over to discuss something with Atticus. The door was open, and he could hear screaming, so he slipped inside the house.

Atticus doesn't know he was there. He doesn't know he saw, or that he told me, and you can't breathe a word about this, Abby. You can't tell Kaiden. If this gets out, Christian will kill me. And if he finds out you know, he'll kill you too."

I'm visibly conflicted, because Kai and I have agreed no more secrets, and this could be the worst one of all. But even if I walk away now, I'll have to tell Kai his dad is involved in his mother's murder. That truth will destroy him. Plus, she's already said enough to place me in danger, so I might as well get all the facts.

"I won't tell anyone. I promise," I lie, because I can't make a call like that on the spot. I will need time to assess it before deciding what to do.

She scrutinizes my face, and seeming happy with what she finds, she tells me. "Kaiden found his mother alive. For all intents and purposes, he saved her life. But Atticus was still in love with your mother, and he saw an opportunity. He got the kids out of the way, and he returned to Emma and put a pillow over her face, suffocating her until she stopped breathing."

CHAPTER THIRTY-TWO

"Abby." Drew snaps his fingers in my face. "You still with us?" He peers into my eyes with concern and sympathy. "Yeah, sorry. I just zoned out there for a bit."

I said goodbye to Sylvia after she dropped her last bomb, and we came straight to Xavier's warehouse, so I could update everyone at once without having to repeat myself. I blurted out the truth about Emma's murder to Drew because I needed to tell someone. He was as shocked as I was, but he agreed we need to wait and find the right time to tell Kai.

Kai deserves to know the truth even if it'll devastate him. But we can't tell him yet because he'll go after his father, and we need Atticus gunning for our father, to help keep him distracted, while we figure out a way to take him down once and for all.

Also, this knowledge is dangerous, and telling others puts everyone in danger.

"Babe." Kai forces my gaze to his. "If there's more, you need to tell us."

"There's not," I lie, hoping he'll forgive me.

"You've been in a bit of daze the whole time you've been speaking." He rubs his hands up and down my arms. "You're worrying me."

Eh, yeah. That's because I'm going to have to break your heart with news of how your mother really died. Plus, I've realized we are out of options vis-à-vis my father. Even if we find out where Mom stashed that evidence, it's of no use now. We can't pin this murder on my father when he wasn't the one who ultimately killed her.

Sure, he's an accessory and there was intent to kill, but that's not enough to put the bastard behind bars for life.

But I can't figure out why he didn't say anything back in the ballroom when Atticus threw out that allegation.

I have another light bulb moment.

Christian never told my father.

Holy fuck.

I slump back in my chair, and my brain hurts trying to figure it all out. *Why can't they just be your common garden variety villains? Why do they have to be criminal masterminds playing so many angles it makes my head spin?*

"Abby," Kai snaps, gripping my forearms. "What is going on?"

"My head is spinning from all this," I honestly admit. "My dad stole a baby from my mom too, and I've just found out my aunt grew us in her womb, and she never fucking told me even when she was sharing other secrets on her deathbed. Excuse me for zoning out for a while." My tone is cutting on purpose because I need to deflect him, and pushing his buttons usually works.

"C'mere." He opens his arms, but I glare at him.

"Come. Here." His eyes challenge me to continue disobeying him, and I wouldn't want to disappoint him, now would I? I cross my arms and narrow my eyes at him.

He hauls me into his lap unceremoniously, growling as his arms clamp down around me. "I know you're hurting, so I'll forgive you for that."

"I'm starting to understand how you feel about being betrayed," Drew admits.

"You have no clue how that feels because this is the tip of the iceberg compared to how I've been treated." That shuts them all up. "I'm tired, and Charlie will wonder where I am. We need to go."

Kai tightens his arms around me, and I know he doesn't want to let me go. Not like this. But we don't get a choice. Besides, I need to be away from him because guilt is doing a number on me, and I'm terrified he'll burrow his way into my head and figure out I'm hiding stuff from him.

"Another thing," Drew says. "They've called an emergency meeting at Parkhurst. We're leaving tomorrow night."

"What emergency?"

He shrugs. "I don't know until I get there."

"But it's five days until Christmas," I add.

"We'll only be away for two days, and we'll be back by then," he assures me.

Not that I'm in any rush for it to arrive. Christmas dinner is taking place at our house and the Barrons and Montgomerys will be in attendance.

Naturally, I'm looking forward to it about as much as a hole in the head.

"Okay."

"I want you to stay with Kai while we're gone," Drew says. "He'll keep you safe."

"Charlie will never go for that."

"Which is why he won't know." Drew winks conspiratorially at me. "I'm sure you can come up with some plausible explanation that will ensure Mrs. Barron's silence."

I smile for the first time in a few hours. "I think I can work something out."

"I'm remembering why we were such good friends, Manning," Kai drawls, smirking at my brother.

"Just keep that in mind," Drew says, jabbing his fingers in Kai's direction. "And look after my little sis."

I pay the driver, grabbing my purse and my weekend bag from the floor before climbing out of the backseat of the car. The door to the house swings open and Kai appears in the doorframe. His eyes never leave mine as I walk toward him, drinking him in from head to toe. He's wearing a tight-fitting black shirt rolled up to his sleeves, showcasing those tatted, muscular arms I love so much. My eyes travel south as I quicken my pace with the sound of tires squealing behind me as the Uber driver peels it out of there. Kai's dark jeans hug his muscular thighs in all the right places, and I'm imagining being on my knees in front of him, running my hands up and down his toned flesh as I take him between my lips.

He licks his lips, and his eyes flash with heated desire and dark promise having guessed where my mind has gone. Goose bumps sprout all over my sensitive flesh, and my core pulses with need. Dumping my bags on the ground, I race the last few feet and fling myself into his arms.

Our mouths collide in a battle of lips, teeth, and tongue and he lifts me up, hauling me into the house without breaking our kiss. My skin is on fire under my wool dress and tights as I wrap my legs around his waist, grinding against his massive erection.

"Fucking need you, babe," he murmurs against my lips, sitting me up on the table in the hall and spreading my legs apart. He wastes no time removing my coat, tossing it to the floor along with my ballet flats. His lips continue to devour mine, and I'm moaning and squirming on the table as I fumble with his belt buckle.

"The others?" I pant as his lips leave my mouth to trail a path down my neck.

"Upstairs. They won't come down," he rasps, lifting my hips and yanking my tights down as I pop the button on his jeans.

He tears his lips away to tug his jeans down, and I arch a brow as his cock springs forth.

"Going commando, huh?"

"Easy access," he says, grinning as he rolls a condom on. He places his palms on the wall on either side of my head and crashes his lips against mine. He kisses me deeply, ravishing me with his wicked tongue, as one hand slides up my thigh, brushing against my pussy. A guttural moan leaves my lips, growing louder as he pushes my panties aside and shoves two fingers inside me. "You're fucking drenched."

"I've missed you." I nip at his bottom lip, grabbing hold of his ass and spreading my legs wider. "And I need you now."

The sound of lace tearing echoes through the hallway as he rips my panties off and plunges inside me in one swift thrust. He fucks me mercilessly, pounding into me as his lips continue to make love to my mouth. The table shakes, emitting screeching sounds as it slams against the wall with every thrust of his hips. I wrap my legs firmly against his waist, lifting my hips slightly so he's hitting just the right spot.

He pumps his hips faster, his muscles strain, and the vein in his neck pops as he gets closer. His fingers rub frantically at my clit, and I scream as my climax roars through me the same time he releases with a loud grunt.

Dropping his head to my shoulder, we stay locked in position while our heartbeats return to normal levels.

When he lifts his head, the adoration on his face surprises me. He leans in, kissing me softly, completely at odds with the way he's just roughly fucked me. "You're fucking perfect, babe. You know that?" He rubs his thumb along my lower lip, and I suck it into my mouth.

"Fuck." He claims my lips in a hard kiss before pulling back. "As much as I'd love to go for round two, I doubt the others are keen to hear that a second time."

"Is it safe to come out yet?" a familiar voice asks from behind the living room door, and I slap Kai's chest.

"You said they were upstairs!" I hiss, jumping down and snatching the ripped remains of my panties.

Kai smirks. "Oops. My bad." He grabs the balled-up lace from my hand, stuffing the shreds in the pocket of his jeans as he fixes them in place. I tug up my tights and slip my feet into my flats while glaring at him. He reels me into his arms. "Don't be mad that I'm so crazy about you I couldn't wait until we got upstairs."

His words melt me on the spot, as Xavier calls out again. "Hello! Still waiting."

I slide out of his arms, opening the living room door as Kai puts sneakers on and goes outside to grab my bags. "Hey."

Xavier wraps his arms around me without hesitation before jerking back, grinning. "You reek of sex." He winks. "Naughty girl." He glances at Kai as he comes back inside. "Although, if the hottie was mine, I'd jump his bones the second I got here too."

Kai flips him the bird. "Keep your sexual innuendos for Hunt. He appreciates them more," he drawls.

"Stop stirring shit," Sawyer says, appearing behind Xavier.

"How come you're here?" I ask Xavier.

"Sawyer and I are investigating your father's childhood. Trying to see if we can find out which orphanage he was in and get the inside track on Mom and Pop," he explains. "I'll crash here for a few days until my flight." All the guys are going home for Christmas. Kai refuses to go to his father's house, so he's going to Sawyer's place for a few days.

"Great. Hopefully, there might be something there, because he's very cagey when the subject of his past crops up."

Sawyer looks at me. "You get away okay?"

"Yep." I brush past them into the living room, flopping down onto the couch. "I told Mrs. Barron I was going out of town to purchase a special wedding present for Charlie and swore her to secrecy, claiming I wanted it to be a surprise." Kai scowls like he always does when mention of Charlie or the wedding arises. Not that I blame him. He's handling it far better than I would if the roles were reversed.

"I think this is yours," Jackson says, looming over me and holding out his hand. A piece of flimsy lace wafts through the air as he lets go of a scrap from my panties.

I send daggers at Kai, and he chuckles.

"Your screams were so loud I thought he was killing you," Jackson adds, his voice slurring a little.

"Lauder." Kai's good humor evaporates, and he pins his friend with a warning look.

Jackson smirks, taking a puff of his blunt. "If you don't want us commenting, don't fuck her in public."

Kai's fists knot at his sides, and I'm expecting him to take a chunk out of Jackson, but he ignores him, focusing his gaze on me. "Are you hungry?"

"I could eat."

He holds out his arm, and I take his hand, letting him pull me up and lead me away.

"Why is he drunk and high at lunchtime on a Wednesday?" I ask as we walk toward the kitchen, lowering my voice so the others don't hear.

"Today is the anniversary of his sister's death. It's not a good day for him."

"Oh." I'm deep in thought as Kai steers me into the kitchen, lifting me up and placing my butt on the island unit. "We should do something to try to distract him."

"Like what?" Kai asks, bending down as he opens the refrigerator.

I shamelessly ogle his ass as he plucks items from the fridge. "I could make homemade pizzas, and we could watch some funny movies, maybe?" We can't go out, in case someone sees me with them, and it's like the frigging Arctic outside, so shooting some hoops or going swimming is out, leaving few options.

Kai shuts the refrigerator with his hip, bringing several packages over to the counter and dumping them beside me. He spreads my legs, positions himself between them, and wraps his arms around my neck, smirking. "Were you just checking out my ass?"

"Guilty." I grin, resting my hands on his shoulders. "You know you have a fucking amazing ass. I won't pass up an opportunity to drool."

He smiles, hauling me against his chest and hugging me. I rest my head on his shoulder, feeling unbelievably content. "I love that you're back here," he says, running his fingers through my hair. "I wish I could wake up beside you every day like before."

I ease back, cupping his face. "I wish that too." I peck his lips. "And we'll have that again. It's the only thing keeping me going."

I make a variety of homemade pizzas while Kai argues with Xavier over which movies to watch. Sawyer has to basically bribe Jackson into coming out of his room to join us.

The atmosphere is tense and conversation feels forced, because it's obvious Jackson is in a bad place. He's sprawled across one couch, smoking a joint while sipping on a beer. I force a few slices of pizza on him, hoping the food will soak up some weed and booze.

Kai and I called dibs on the other couch, while Sawyer and Xavier occupy the two leather recliners. They bitch and argue nonstop during the movie like an old married couple, and the thought brings a smile to my face. "What are you thinking?" Kai whispers in my ear, running his fingers up and down my arm, sending a flurry of tingles cascading all over my body.

He's spooning me from behind, and I can feel the evidence of his arousal digging into my ass. "We should set them up," I whisper back, subtly nodding in their direction.

"I'm not getting involved in that shit, and neither are you." He grasps my hips, pulling them flush with his boner, and heat floods my body.

Feeling eyes on me, I whip my head around, meeting Jackson's dark gaze. His eyes drift to my chest and lower, to where Kai has a firm grip on my pelvis. Weird tension crackles in the air, and I shift uncomfortably, pulling my eyes from Jackson and refocusing on the movie even though I can't even remember the name.

"You okay?" Kai whispers.

"Peachy," I lie.

The odd tension doesn't leave. If anything, it gets worse, and I feel Jackson's attention on us even though I avoid looking in his direction.

He's in a funny mood. Lashing out with crude and hurtful remarks that we all purposely ignore. Deep-seated anger surrounds him like an invisible cloud, emitting hazardous vibes. I know it's all wrapped up with his sister, but I've never seen him like this, and it's unsettling. I'm used to Jackson being the laid-back flirtatious stoner, and I'm not sure I like this version of him.

When the movie ends and Kai asks if I want to go upstairs, I nod eagerly, keen to exit the toxic energy in the room.

I drop my handbag on the bedside table and my other bag on the floor, shrieking as Kai lifts me from behind, dusting kisses all along my neck and grinding his arousal into my ass. He lifts my dress from behind, prodding my ass with one finger through my tights. "I want to take you here," he whispers, sliding his finger up and down my ass crack.

I shiver all over. We haven't done that although he's voiced his desires previously, and he's played with my hole during sex which I've enjoyed. I don't know when we'll be alone again, so I nod. "Okay."

He spins me around, his eyes dancing with excitement. "You sure?"

I worry my lip between my teeth, smiling shyly at him. "Yeah. I trust you."

He has me stripped and writhing naked underneath him in next to no time. His magic tongue is doing the most amazing things to my body, and it doesn't take him long to bring me to orgasm. He flips us around, placing me on his lap. "Ride me, baby."

I lower myself down over his hard length, moaning loudly as he fills me up. It's so intense like this, and I like to savor the sensation, bouncing gently on top of him. Of course, that doesn't last long, and he grips my hips, slamming me up and down on him, urging me to go faster. I oblige, because in the bedroom, Kai is king, and he knows a hundred different ways to make me fall apart in the best way.

He lifts me up off his cock, plunging his fingers into my pussy unexpectedly, pumping his fingers in and out a few times, before situating me back on his cock. I resume the pace he likes, swirling my hips as I slam up and down, grinding my clit on his dick.

His fingers trek around to my ass, and he spreads my cheeks, causing me to whimper in anticipation. He slides one finger into my puckered hole. "Breathe, baby, and relax. Concentrate on riding me, and just relax your muscles."

I do as he says, groaning at the intense feeling as he pushes his finger in deeper and starts sliding it in and out.

The door slams open, and I scream, halting my movements as I whip my head around. Kai discreetly removes his finger from my butt, and his hips still.

Jackson is standing in the doorway, framed by the light in the hallway behind him. His eyes blaze with need as he takes in the scene before him.

Butterflies scatter in my chest, and I may have stopped breathing. I'm frozen on top of Kai, staring at Jackson as he drinks his fill. His eyes linger on my bare breasts, and his eyes darken with lust. He smooths a hand over the bulge in his sweatpants, and my heart rate accelerates.

Warm fingers brush my face as Kai moves my face around to his. His gorgeous brown eyes are like molten chocolate as he stares at me, watching my pulse beating erratically in my neck and my chest heaving. He runs his hands up my body, roughly kneading my breasts without breaking eye contact. I'm very much aware that Jackson is in the same position in the doorway and that Sawyer or Xavier could come along at any moment.

Kai's gaze drills into mine, and I suck in a breath as I spot the question in his eyes. My heart thumps wildly behind my rib cage, and my body temperature elevates a few notches. His cock jerks inside me, and I instinctively grind my hips, whimpering as my channel grips his walls. He grabs my chin, bringing my face down closer to his, asking again.

Peering into his eyes, I nod.

He pulls my mouth down to his and kisses me. "You sure?" he whispers over my mouth.

No.

Yes.

I don't know.

"Yes," I whisper.

I sit back up on his lap, gently moving my hips and keeping my eyes locked on Kai's as he turns his head in Jackson's direction.

"Come in, and lock the door behind you."

CHAPTER THIRTY-THREE

"Ride me, baby," Kai commands, as the door shuts and I hear the lock being turned. "Show Lauder how good you fuck me." Kai points at the tub chair in the corner. Every nerve ending in my body is on high alert as I sense Jackson moving across the room toward the chair.

Kai grips my hips, watching me carefully, and I move up and down on top of him, gyrating my pelvis and taking him deep as I fuck him. Movement from the corner of the room behind me sends shivers of excitement dancing along my spine.

Jackson has watched Kai grope me before, and I've seen him jack off previously, but this is the first time we've welcomed him into our bedroom as a voyeur. It will most likely be the first *and* last time, as I know Kai is only doing this because his best friend is in pain and he needs the release.

"You trust me, baby?" Kai asks, still scrutinizing me closely.

I confirm with my eyes, continuing to bounce up and down on top of him as the rustling of clothing dropping to the floor sends liquid lust straight to my core. I grip Kai's cock tight inside me, causing him to cry out.

"Fuck, baby. That feels so good."

"What's she's doing?" Jackson asks, his voice sounding closer.

"Her cunt is hugging my cock real tight," Kai confirms, and my pussy clenches as if on cue.

"Fuck him, beautiful. Fuck him hard," Jackson says, placing the chair at the side of the bed where he has a better view. Kai grabs onto my hips, thrusting up inside me as I move up and down on his cock, my breasts jiggling and shaking with the motion.

Jackson leans back in the chair, spreads his thighs, and grabs hold of his naked erection, pumping his cock in measured strokes as he watches me grind down on top of Kai. A loud moan leaves my lips as so many sensations wash over me.

"Take me into your mouth, baby," Kai says. "Show him how good you suck cock."

"Oh my God." Their dirty talk is turning me into a writhing mess on the bed.

There's no mistaking the lust-drenched look in Jackson's gaze as I move off Kai's cock and kneel in between Kai's legs. Taking his dick in my hand, I curl my fingers around his impressive length, pumping him from root to tip in a few quick strokes. Guiding his cock into my mouth, I suck him off the way he likes it, running my tongue along the underside before nibbling along the front and pushing into his slit, licking the bead of precum gathered there. Then I take him fully into my mouth, opening wider so he can push in farther, and I slide my lips up and down his hot length.

Kai grabs the back of my head, cursing and moaning as he fucks my mouth while Jackson jerks his cock harder and faster, while his eyes roam my body. I stare at my boyfriend while I blow him, meeting his lust-drenched gaze as he shoves his cock deeper into my mouth.

Kai growls, and there's a popping sound as he pulls his dick from my mouth. "I don't want to come yet."

I lie flat on my back as he climbs over me. Jackson is groaning, and the sounds of his hand sliding along his cock elevate my already heated arousal to new heights.

I didn't think I'd enjoy having someone watch, but I do.

Feeling his eyes on me as Kai thrusts inside me sends an added thrill rushing along my sensitive skin.

Kai sits up straighter, pulling me upright, clasping his hands behind my back and holding me steady as he pumps into me, and it's so intense at this angle. My hair tumbles over my shoulders as I throw my head back, moaning, while rocking my hips against his. He pulls my lips to his and kisses me deeply. "You okay with this?" he asks, breaking the kiss, and I love that he's making sure I'm comfortable.

"Are you?" I ask, peering into his eyes.

He nods, and I see the truth staring back at me.

And I get it.

Jackson needs this tonight, and Kai's being a good friend.

But it's also about exerting his claim. His control.

Kai is confirming I'm completely his, so Jackson is under no illusion about what we feel for one another.

Kai continues to thrust inside me, kissing along the column of my neck, down to my collarbone, and lower to my tits. He draws one tender nipple into his mouth, sucking on it hard as he pinches and twists my other tit roughly.

It's the only way I can tolerate him touching them. I bury my emotions behind the pain, and that's how I want it.

Jackson grunts, and the leather squelches as he moves around in the chair.

Kai pushes me flat on my back again, pivoting his hips and pulling one of my legs up onto his shoulder as he pounds into me. His fingers move to my clit, and he rubs me in jerky motions, sending every cell into my body into a state of heightened bliss as pressure builds.

"Fuck!" Jackson groans, and I turn my head to look at him while Kai continues his skillful ministrations.

Jackson's heated eyes lock on mine as he furiously pumps his cock, and watching him jerk himself off while my boyfriend is fucking me is so incredibly hot. Jackson throws his head back, his eyes shutting as a guttural moan filters through the air. Cum spurts from his cock, splashing all over his toned abs as he releases on his stomach.

My pussy walls clench, my orgasm growing closer, and Kai curses, drawing my attention back to him. Little beads of sweat dot his brow, and the look in his eyes is one of possessive intensity as he lifts my other leg onto his shoulder, tilts my hips up, and slams into me.

I explode, screaming out his name, my body spasming as the fiercest orgasm sweeps through me, turning my limbs to liquefied jelly.

Kai pulls out, fixing a look in Jackson's direction. Jackson nods, grabbing a handful of tissues from the bedside table and cleaning himself up before pulling his clothes back on. He's at the door when Kai calls to him. "It was a onetime thing."

He turns around, lounging against the wall. "I know."

"And we don't speak of it. Ever. To anyone." The threat is blatant in Kai's tone.

"I would never." Jackson looks to me. "That was seriously hot, beautiful, but you know I respect the fuck out of you. No one will hear about this from me."

"Thank you," I pant.

"Okay. Cool." Kai pulls me up into his arms, holding me against his chest, and I can tell he just wants him to go now.

Jackson has his hand on the door handle when he turns around one final time. "You're so fucking lucky, man." He eyeballs Kai. "She's everything. Don't mess it up."

The door snicks shut, and I look up at my boyfriend. "You good?"

He slaps his hard-as-granite cock against my hipbone. "Not yet, but if you're tired—"

"I'm not." I slide my hand down the gap between our bodies, wrapping my fingers around his shaft. "That was hot, and I'm not done with you yet." I grip his cock more firmly, sliding my hand up and down his length.

Kai runs his hand down my spine before his fingers move to my ass. "You still up for this?"

All the tiny hairs lift on my body and adrenaline courses through me as I nod. I'm glad he knew not to go there with Jackson in the room, because that would've been pushing it too far.

Kai pulls away, walking to the drawer on the bedside table and taking out a small tube. Removing the condom from his dick, he tosses the rubber in the trash. Then he liberally applies lube to his cock, sliding his hand up and down his hard erection, and my tongue sticks to the roof of my mouth as I gulp nervously.

He climbs back on the bed, still lubricating his cock, and liquid warmth gushes from my pussy as I clench in anticipation. He claims my lips in a searing-hot kiss that curls my toes, pulling my body in flush to his. He kisses me for a while, his hands roaming the contours of my body until I'm putty in his hands. Then he positions me on all fours, yanking my hips up and pressing my head down into the comforter while he situates himself behind me.

His slick fingers move up and down my ass crack before he pushes two fingers inside, pumping them in and out of me slowly.

"Oh, fuck." The sensation is so strange but not unpleasant.

Kai's fingers probe and massage the walls of my ass, and then he spreads my ass cheeks, and I squeal as his wet tongue presses against my hole. He spreads me wider, and his tongue pushes in farther, and pressure is already building. Alternating with his tongue and his fingers, he works my puckered hole until it feels like I'm ready to combust.

His cock presses against my entrance, and my body tenses again. "Relax, babe." Sliding his hand underneath me, he rubs at my clit before plunging his fingers into my welcoming pussy while he carefully eases into my ass. I'm panting as he inches in farther, my body firing on all cylinders as his touch hits me in several places. "Okay?" Kai asks when it feels like he's all the way in, his voice strained.

"I'm good," I rasp, feeling overwhelmed at the sensation of his cock and his fingers inside me at once.

Kai fucks my ass slowly at first, and then he picks up his pace, finding a rhythm with his fingers as he alternates his thrusts between my ass and my pussy. The sensations flooding my body are out of this world, and I exist on an alternate plane.

I come apart first, screaming from the top of my lungs as the most intense, most powerful climax literally rips through me, tearing my body apart before sealing it back together.

Kai shatters, roaring as his cum fills my ass. I can feel the warmth trickling down my legs when he pulls out, and then we collapse on the bed in a tangle of sweaty, exhausted limbs. Kai pulls me into his body, wrapping his arms around me protectively. "Was that good, baby?"

"That was more than good," I truthfully admit, grinning. "It was hot as fuck." I'm still smiling as I press my ear to his chest, listening to the comforting beat of his heart, letting it lull me to sleep.

I'm expecting it to be awkward the next morning with Jackson, but it isn't. He acts normal. Like he wasn't in the room watching our most intimate moments. And I appreciate that. I know he's doing it to ensure I'm comfortable and that I don't regret letting him into our bedroom.

Jackson is gorgeous, and seeing him jerk off while watching Kai and I fucking was one of the most erotic moments of my life, but it was most definitely a one-off.

I love Kai.

I'm *in love* with Kai.

And I don't want to share any aspect of our relationship with anyone else.

We're naked, wrapped around one another, later that night, in bed, supposedly watching a movie when Kai clears his throat, capturing my attention. I prop up on one elbow, tracing my fingers along the tattoos on his chest as I wait for him to spit it out. He mutes the TV. "I've been thinking."

"Oh, oh," I joke, and he slaps my ass.

"I'm being serious."

"Okay." I plant a sober look on my face.

"What if we took off? You and me? We have enough money to disappear."

I place both hands on his chest. "I know we do, and it's not like I haven't thought of that, but they would never stop looking for us."

"We could move around."

I kiss him. "God, I love that you want to do that. I honestly do. But it wouldn't work. They would catch up to us, eventually. Do you want to be looking over our shoulders for the rest of our lives? And could you leave everyone behind and never see them again?"

He pulls me into his arms. "I'd do it for you."

Emotion bursts out of me. "Fuck, I love you." I kiss him hard. "I love you so much, but we both know we can't leave." I sigh in exasperation. "He would take it out on our loved ones, and I couldn't live with myself if anything happened to them because we selfishly ran."

"It's not selfish to want a normal life." He weaves his fingers through my hair.

"But it is to run when we know others will pay the price."

He rests his head atop mine. "I know you're right. I'm just so frustrated. We need to find that evidence."

Guilt slams into me. I don't know how to tell him the truth about his mother's murder. If there will ever be an opportune time. But I've decided he needs to know sooner than later, and I'll tell him when he returns after Christmas.

It's risky because I'll have to find a way of stopping him from going after his father.

But I won't hold on to this secret indefinitely because he has a right to know.

CHAPTER THIRTY-FOUR

Unfortunately, our time together goes way too fast, and before I know it, Drew is texting me telling me to get my ass back to the Barrons'.

It kills me saying goodbye to Kai and the guys, and I have a physical pain in my heart, fighting tears, as the Uber takes me away from them.

I plant a fake smile on my face when I arrive back at the Barrons', telling Elizabeth I've ordered a custom-made watch for her son, with a personal engraving I designed, and it'll take a few weeks to be delivered. I remind her to keep it a secret, and she promises Charlie won't know I was gone these past two days.

Charlie is in great form when he arrives back, grabbing me into his arms and kissing me thoroughly. I panic for a minute, hoping he can't taste or smell Kai on me, and all that does is exacerbate my guilt.

I feel sick kissing Charlie, and I can't do it for much longer.

The following morning, it's as if a switch has flipped, and he's cold and dismissive at the breakfast table.

I see little of him the next couple of days as he leaves each day, only returning in the early hours of the morning.

I'm bored out of my skull and practically climbing the walls in frustration. The ballet studio is closed for Christmas, and I don't have any space to dance here. I pound the treadmill in their home gym for a couple hours each day, but that's the height of my excitement, because I've already smoked the joint Jackson gave me. I can't concentrate long enough to watch a movie or read a book because I'm nervous about dinner at my father's tomorrow, especially with Charlie's fluctuating mood swings.

When Christmas morning dawns, I try my best to enter into the spirit of things, but it's hard to remain cheery when I'm dreading dinner and I'm pissed because Kai didn't answer my call last night. I know he's in New York, at the Hunt residence, by now, and Sawyer mentioned they host a lavish Christmas Eve party, but surely, he could've found five minutes to call me.

I've decided Charlie has the male equivalent of PMS because he's floating on cloud nine this morning, and all seems to be forgiven. He hasn't let me out of his arms, and he lavished me with ridiculous presents I didn't need, including a fabulous deep-red dress that swings out from the waist and rests just above my knee. He begs me to wear it to dinner, and I'm guessing he's trying to one-up Trent, because he's never bought me a dress with matching shoes and jewelry, and he wouldn't have picked out something I'd like. The dress has a high neckline which covers my bigger bust and slim straps. It's elegant but understated, and it's something I would have chosen for myself.

I'm happy to wear it if it keeps Charlie happy. And if he wants to rub Trent's nose in it, who am I to stand in his way? I welcome any opportunity to stick it to my ex.

I both hate and love seeing glimpses of the old Charlie, because it reminds me of the boy who was one of my best friends, and guilt assuages me for faking things with him while I'm sneaking around behind his back.

But I remind myself I have no choice.

The first big surprise lands the minute we walk into the formal dining room at Chez Manning when my father introduces me to his fiancée.

I blink several times, and tug on my ears, sure I must be mistaken as I look over the willowy blonde draped across his arm. She's younger than him but not too young, which is surprising given what I now know about the elite's penchant for younger girls. Charlie squeezes my waist, and I snap out of it.

"I apologize for my rudeness," I say, extending my hand toward her. "But I'm a little taken aback. My father has never mentioned you."

Drew does a slicing motion across his throat behind the bastard's back, and I know I shouldn't push his buttons, but I'm on edge today, and that's when my snarky side usually comes out to play.

"Well, I've heard all about you," Patrice says, smiling broadly, revealing a set of perfect teeth. "And I'm looking forward to getting to know you better. I know I can't replace your mother, but I'm hoping we can be friends." Her green eyes sparkle with expectation as my stomach flips over.

"You can't replace my mother," I say with a tight smile. "And you shouldn't want to." I take a sip of my champagne, eyeing her over the rim. "Not if you value your life."

Father almost chokes on his whiskey, and Patrice fusses over him. Charlie steers me away over to the other side of the room. "What the hell is wrong with you?" he asks in a low voice so only I can hear.

"If he wants me to act polite, he could at least give me some warning!"

"You know everything you do reflects on me," he says, twirling a lock of my hair and subtly pulling on it. "So be on your best behavior. Today is important."

"Why?" I eye him suspiciously.

"It just is." He tucks me in under his arm as Sylvia, Trent, and

Christian arrive. Sylvia and I exchange knowing looks and purposely avoid conversing too much as we wait to be called for dinner. I'm surprised Shandra isn't here, but I'm guessing she had plans with her family. Trent glares at me and Charlie, and I snuggle into Charlie's side, pawing at him and somehow resisting the urge to flip Trent the bird.

Dinner is a tense affair, and I'm fed up being bored, so I decide to liven it up a little. "So, Patrice. How did you and my father meet?" I ask, as we are waiting for our dessert to be served. Charlie tenses on my left while Drew tenses on my right.

"Oh, we work together."

"You work at Manning Motors?"

She shakes her head, and her blonde hair sways with the motion. "I work in the legal department at Parkhurst."

Figures. She must be a blue blood.

And it's clear she's the perfect trophy wife.

This must be another box he needs to tick.

"How lovely," I drawl, lifting my glass to have it refilled.

"She'll have a water," Charlie says, placing his hand over the glass before the waitress can top it up.

"You don't get to decide that for me!" I eyeball the waitress. "More champagne, please."

Drew pinches my thigh hard, and I count to ten in my head. I smile at the confused waitress. "Actually, I'll just have water. Thank you."

Father sends a proud smile in Charlie's direction while Trent loudly chuckles. "You poor bastard." He points at Charlie. "You've no idea what you're in for. You sure you still want to go through with it?"

"Trent." Christian sends a warning to his son, and Sylvia and I lock eyes at the same moment with the same inner thought. *What is he implying?*

"I know it's a foreign concept to a cold, ruthless bastard like you, but I love Abby and she loves me. There is nothing to reconsider."

Although I'm fucking furious with Charlie, I press my body into his, smiling as he kisses my temple.

After dinner, Father ushers us all into the burgundy living room. I frown as I spot the projector and screen that's set up in the room. The drapes are closed, and the only light in the room is from a few lamps scattered around the vast space.

"What is this?" Charlie asks, and I notice the tick pulsing in his jaw.

"What would Christmas be without a few choice home movies?"

All the color drains from Charlie's face. "No," he barks out. "I didn't agree—"

"You sure you want to continue that sentence, son?" Dad puffs out his chest, challenging Charlie.

"Charles?" Charlie's dad steps forward, sending him an inquisitive stare. It's clear neither of the Barrons knew about this.

I have a real bad feeling. Drew pins me with worried eyes, and I know he's sensing the same.

"Well?" Father asks, leveling a harsh look at Charlie. The bastard extracts his cell. "You want me to call it all off?"

Charlie clears his throat. "That won't be necessary."

Father nods, pride and relief shining in his eyes, before he turns a hate-filled look at me. Acid crawls up my throat, and butterflies invade my chest.

"Mom. Can you and Lillian step out of the room, please," Charlie says, exchanging a silent communication with his father.

"They can stay." Father smirks.

"I'd rather they didn't." Charlie stares at his mother, gesturing toward the door. She looks to her husband, and he nods, and she ushers her daughter out of the room with a perplexed expression on her face.

"You might want to sit down for this, Abigail." The bastard smirks again, his eyes lingering on my chest briefly.

Drew and Charlie both stiffen, and I fight a bout of nausea. "I'm fine to stand."

"Very well."

I want to charge him and wipe that smug smile off his face. I glance at Charlie as my father moves to the projector. "I know you know what this is."

His jaw tightens, and his muscles strain against the sleeves of his dress shirt. "You have no one to blame but yourself. Just remember that."

My stomach drops to my toes, and I brace myself for it.

But absolutely nothing could've prepared me for what appears on the screen.

The bastard has the volume turned up loud, and our collective moans ring out around the room. My cheeks inflame, but it's not from embarrassment although I'm completely humiliated watching the replay of the other night in Kai's bedroom on a screen large enough to show every thrust and every touch in detail. No, I'm consumed with murderous rage as I watch the man who fathered me attempt to break me again.

The recording starts at the part where Jackson is jerking off, just before he leaves.

"Turn it off!" Drew shouts.

"We're just getting to the best part," the bastard says. The video fasts forward, and I cringe as I watch Kai maneuvering into my ass.

Christian's loud laughter rings out around the room, and I'm sickened at the sight of the telltale bulge in his pants. Sylvia's glazed eyes peer at me, with a hint of sadness, and her "get numb" strategy is looking more and more appealing. Trent looks ready to fly across the room and murder me.

"You did this," I hiss under my breath, glaring at Charlie.

"No," he grits out, averting his eyes as Drew races toward the projector. "You did this to yourself."

"How did you get that footage?"

"I planted a camera in your purse."

"You unimaginable bastard."

"All you had to do was stay away from him." He stares at me, his nostrils flaring, knuckles clenching, muscles bulging. "How could you lower yourself to do that with Lauder watching? I thought you had more class, but perhaps Trent is right, and you're nothing but a whore."

I slap him across the face, uncaring if I've sealed my death warrant. "I would rather be Kai's whore than your wife." I yank my ring off my finger, throwing it across the room as Drew shuts down the video.

"You really shouldn't have done that," Father says, glaring at Drew. His gaze jumps to me. "Retrieve your ring, and put it back on your finger. Now."

"Fuck. You." I flip him the bird, jutting my chin up defiantly. "You will have to fucking kill me before I'll marry him."

He stalks toward the projector, shoving Drew out of the way, pinning him with a look loaded with the promise of retribution. "Oh, there'll be killing all right if this wedding doesn't go ahead," he says, pushing a button on the machine. "But it won't be your life I'll take."

A new image appears on the screen, and my dinner threatens to reappear.

"No!" I scream, staring in horror at Kai. He's stripped to his boxers while strapped to a chair with his head lolling from side to side, and every inch of his body is bloodied and bruised.

CHAPTER THIRTY-FIVE

Someone yanks Kai's head up, and a sob rips from my throat at the sight of his bloody face. His left eye is completely shut, the skin on his lid swollen and multicolored.

"I fucking hate you!" I rush toward my father, but Drew intervenes, jumping in front of me and pulling me back. I thrash about in his arms, legs and arms flailing as my tortured cries ring out around the room. "I will fucking kill you, you bastard! You leave him alone!!" Angry tears stream down my face, and I'm pumped full of adrenaline and rage. I'm primed to explode, and I want to unleash my anger on my father.

"Control her!" Father snaps at Charlie.

"Give her to me," Charlie demands of Drew.

"Fuck off." Drew steps back, keeping a firm hold of me. "Calm down, A," he whispers in my ear. "You're no use to Kai like this."

His words sober me up, and I rein my anger in.

"Patrice, darling." Father turns to his fiancée with a fake adoring look on his face. "Would you retrieve that ungrateful bitch's ring?"

"Of course, sweetheart." She looks unruffled as she walks to the corner of the room where I flung the ring and picks it up.

"I'll take it." Charlie steps forward, taking it from her.

He reaches for me, and I cringe away from him. Drew tightens his arms around me. "Back off, man."

"Can't do that, I'm afraid," he says as there's a knock on the door.

"Perfect timing," Father says. He levels a stern look at Charlie. "Hit her if you have to, but keep her restrained."

"Kai!" I scream as he's carried into the room by Benjamin and Maurio. He's still strapped to a chair, and his injuries look so much worse in the flesh. My heart pounds, and my lungs scream for air as I struggle to hold back tears.

I can tell it takes great effort to lift his head up, but he does. "Abby," he rasps in a hoarse voice.

I thrash about in Drew's arms, needing to go to him. "Let me go."

"Not yet," Drew whispers in my ear. "Keep it together, A. Please. You need to keep it together for Kai."

Again, my brother's words calm me down, reminding me of all that's at stake. Father can end Kai's life with the click of his fingers.

I know I alone have the power to save him, so I've got to set my emotions aside and bring my A-game.

"What do you want?" I ask when I've gotten myself under control. I deliberately avoid glancing at Kai, because I won't be able to rein my emotions in if I keep looking at him.

I want to stab my father a million times over for what he's done to him. I'll add it to the list of all the things he needs to pay for.

"What I've always wanted." Father stalks toward me, and I shuck out of Drew's arms, standing my ground as the bastard walks right up to me. He grips my chin painfully. Charlie steps up behind me, dropping his hands to my waist. "You married to an elite and your shares in Manning Motors transferred to me."

"I'll do it, and I won't fight it this time. I promise. Just let Kai go. Please."

He pinches my chin, stretching my neck as he tilts it up. "You're just like all women. Ruled by your emotions." He narrows his eyes. "But you have inner strength, and it's why you keep pushing back. You're not as easy to break as most women. That might make me proud, if you weren't trying to fuck with my plans and ruin my reputation."

He lets go of my chin, but my reprieve is short-lived. He slaps me across the face, and Drew pulls me back, shielding me with his body. "You hit her again, and I'll put a bullet through your skull."

The bastard laughs. "I think not, son. Or have you forgotten the things you've done?"

"You don't get to hurt my sister," Drew snarls. "You can do your worst to me, but you won't put your hands on her again or you can look for a new heir because I'll put a bullet through my heart before you can stop me."

Silence descends for a few beats until he says, "I will deal with you later." Father's threat sends chills down my spine. "Come here, Abigail, unless you want me to kill the punk right now. I know Trent's only dying for an opportunity to pay him back."

I step forward quickly, and the bastard chuckles. "You make it too easy."

"I told you I'll do what you want. Just let Kai go."

"Abby." Kai stirs in his chair, attempting to lift his head again. Pain makes mincemeat of my heart as I look at my broken and battered boyfriend. "No," he murmurs. "No deal."

"Stop, Kai," Drew says. "Don't make this any harder on her."

"If I let the punk go today, there's nothing to stop you from running off with him," the bastard says, "and while I can increase security, you're a cunning cunt, and I know you'd continue sneaking around with him, so I need something more."

"I give you my word."

He cranks out a laugh. "Your word means shit."

"I told you she was a lying, cheating whore," Trent supplies.

"Quiet!" Father snaps, and Trent shuts up.

"What are you saying?" I work hard to keep the panic from my voice and my face.

"You will marry Charles today. Here. The minister is on his way."

My head spins, and my stomach lurches violently in protest, but I maintain a cool exterior, nodding my consent because I don't trust my voice to say the words.

"No, Abby!!" The chair shakes as Kai tries to move. He looks at me through his one open eye, pleading with me not to do this. "Don't do it."

"I have to. I don't have a choice. Not if I want to keep you alive."

"You can't trust him," Kai pants. "He'll kill me, anyway."

"He won't." Charlie pulls me over to his side. "It was part of the deal we made. I know what your death would do to Abby, and I need my wife to be present, not locked in grief."

"Deal?" Charles Barron Senior steps forward. "What deal are you talking about, son?"

"Your son has the smarts you weren't born with," Father says, stepping in front of Charlie's father. "Did you honestly think you'd get away with partnering with my enemies behind my back?"

Charles looks at Charlie, his face aghast. "What have you done?"

Charlie's face hardens. "You were the one who told me love was worth fighting for." Charlie looks at me momentarily before looking back at his father. "I did what I had to do for the woman I love."

"You fool!" Charles shakes his head. "She's in love with another man!" He points at Kai. His head slumps again, and I know he's struggling to stay conscious. "She will never love you! Whatever you've done has all been in vain!"

"She will learn to love me."

"God." Charles shakes his head. "I thought we raised you to be smarter than this."

"I am smarter *than you*." Charlie squares off with his dad. "Your plan would've gotten Mom and Lillian killed! You sided with the wrong team, Dad. But it's okay. I've cleared up your mess."

"You stupid boy. You've no idea what you've done."

"The only stupid one around here is you." Father shoves Charles in the chest. "Your son will succeed where you failed because he does what is necessary to make things happen. You had a choice, Charles, and you made the wrong one."

Dad whips a gun out of the back waistband of his pants, presses the muzzle to Charles Barron's head, and pulls the trigger.

Sylvia screams as Mr. Barron falls to the floor on his back with a resounding thud. His glazed eyes stare up at the ceiling, and blood trickles from the bullet hole in his head. My hand shakes as I cover my mouth and glance at Charlie. His Adam's apple jumps in his throat, and the vein in his neck throbs wildly, but outwardly, he looks like witnessing his father being murdered in cold blood has had no effect.

"Maurio. Clean up that mess before the minister gets here." Father summons his bodyguard with a click of his fingers. Maurio and Benjamin drag Charles's dead body from the room while we watch in silence.

"Now. Back to business," the bastard says, like he hasn't just murdered a man in front of us. I'm shaking all over and working hard to disguise it. Charlie tightens his grip on my waist, and I want to push him away because he makes my skin crawl, but Kai's life is hanging in the balance, and I can't risk pushing anyone's buttons.

Father picks up some documents on top of the coffee table, removing a pen from his inside jacket pocket. "You just need to sign on the dotted line, and she's all yours."

Charlie takes the papers and starts reading through them.

"There's no need to go over it again," Father says. "It's like we agreed. The shares in Manning Motors that transfer to you when Abby turns eighteen will automatically be reassigned to me. And when you graduate, you are both free to leave Rydeville provided you settle somewhere in the US and you continue to fulfil your duties to the elite and the order within Parkhurst."

He sends a scornful look in Kai's direction. "I won't harm the delinquent or your mother and your sister." He stares Charlie in the eye. "Provided you remain married to my daughter and she does nothing to damage the Manning reputation."

Charlie flips through the pages and, seemingly happy, puts his scrawl on the last page. Ice replaces the blood flowing through my veins when there's another sharp knock on the door.

Father strides to the door and opens it with a flourish. "Mr. Wittington." He shakes his hand. "It's so good of you to agree to do this today of all days."

"Anything for you," Mr. Wittington says through gritted teeth, and I wonder if he's someone the bastard is blackmailing. "Who's the lucky couple."

"We are." Charlie laces his fingers through mine, stepping forward.

"Congratulations."

"Abby, no!" Kai calls out in a tortured voice. "I'm begging you. Don't do this."

I turn to Father. "Let him go now."

"I will free him when you are married."

"Father, please." It's bad enough I have to do this, but I don't want Kai watching.

"Just shut up, and do what you're told."

"He's lying, Abby," Kai croaks. "Do not do this."

"Kaiden. This is the only way I can protect you and keep you alive," I choke out, trying to wrest out of Charlie's hand so I can go to him. But Charlie wraps his hand around my wrist in warning, and pain punches me from all sides. I would give anything to touch Kai one final time, but Charlie will deny me if I try anything, so I'll just have to make do with my words.

I might pay for this later, but it's not against the rules. "Please don't ask me not to do this, Kai, because I'm doing it to save you." A sob rips from my throat and tears sting my eyes. "I love you, Kaiden. You have my whole heart, now and always."

He straightens his spine, biting down on his lip as pain wracks his body, pinning me with his one good eye. "I love you too, Abby. So much. And I'm not giving up."

"How touching." Sarcasm drips from my father's words. "I knew I was right to have an insurance plan."

Terror has a vise grip on my heart as I stare at Charlie. *What else has he done?* But he looks as confused as I am. "Don't you want to know what it is?" he mocks.

Christian roars out laughing. "You're a sick, evil bastard, Michael. It's why I'll follow you to the end of time."

"Can we cut the amateur dramatics and be done with this?" I plead, because I'm close to my breaking point.

"You want kids, right, Abigail?" he asks, throwing me off course.

"Yes." My tone is wary. "Why?"

"If you want kids, you'll have to stay married to Charlie."

I have no idea where he's going with this.

"Why?" Drew asks, folding his arms as he slants a look at the bastard. "What did you do?"

"Abigail has long proven she's one of those women who needs to be controlled because she's not capable of making wise decisions for herself, so I discussed some options with the doctors at Parkhurst while she was a guest there and made an informed decision on her behalf."

The look on his face is downright evil, and a shiver works its way through me as I piece things together.

How tired and emotional I've been.

The pulling sensation in my stomach, aching abdominal muscles, and bloody discharge that I attributed to the abortion.

"No!" Intense pain presses down on my chest, and I'm struggling to get enough air into my lungs. I bend over, almost crippled in pain.

"What did you do?" Charlie asks in a lethal tone.

"Relax, son. She can still give you an heir, but she won't be able to carry any of your babies because the doctors performed a hysterectomy on her, and she no longer has a womb."

The dam breaks, and tears pour down my cheeks.

"You twisted bastard," Kai growls, finding a resurgence of energy from somewhere as he rises, thrashing about in the chair, attempting to snap the binds around his arms and legs.

Benjamin stalks toward him, punching him in the face, and I scream. Kai slumps in the chair, out cold, and while I hate to see him like this, it's for the best. At least this way, he won't have to watch as I'm forced into marrying another man.

"I had a right to know this," Charlie says through gritted teeth.

"They had already performed the procedures before you and I began working together, but it'll be fine. Thanks to the fertility treatment, the doctors removed fifteen healthy eggs. They are frozen and will be ready whenever you decide to have children. You can conceive via IVF with a surrogate, like we did."

He grins at Drew and I, thinking this is the first time we've heard this.

"There are additional benefits. Your wife won't get fat, and you can fuck your surrogate as often as you want because you'll own her too." He shrugs. "And if she opposes you, like Olivia's bitch of a sister did me, you can have fun taking what you want for the hell of it."

My tears have dried, and I'm just numb inside now.

This is the worst violation of all.

He has taken everything from me.

My mother.

My freedom.

My breasts.

The babies that were growing in my womb.

The love of my life.

And now this.

I will never feel a child moving inside me.

Never enjoy the wonder of pregnancy.

Never experience what it's like to birth a baby.

Whatever is left of my humanity crawls away, and darkness sweeps through me. My veins solidify as anger coats every tissue and nerve ending in my body. Resolve whips through me, and I vow he will pay.

I'm done playing this game by everyone else's rules.

I'm done hiding behind all the men in my life.

To beat my father, I have to join him in the game.

He believes in keeping your enemies close.

Up till now, I've wanted justice. I've wanted to see him rot in jail, paying for his sins for the rest of his life.

But I've changed my mind.

Now, he must die a slow and painful death.

One inflicted by me.

I will torture him and make it painful and prolonged, and I'll enjoy watching him suffer. Breaking him down. Destroying him in the way he's tried to destroy me.

But he has always underestimated the women around him.

It's time to show him he's underestimated me for the last time.

I straighten up, swiping my thumbs under my eyes. Taking

Charlie's hand, I drag him over to the shell-shocked minister. "I'd like to start the ceremony now."

"Good girl, Abigail." Father takes Patrice's hand, and they come to stand beside us. "All you need to do is obey. I will stick to my side of the bargain, provided you do the same with yours. Patrice can help you." He grabs her ass and squeezes. "She knows how to be a good submissive."

"I would be happy to help." She smiles, and I return it. It's far easier than I expected.

Only Drew, Charlie, and Trent are naturally skeptical, but they say nothing.

Drew, because he's pragmatic and he knows this must happen.

Charlie, because he wants me too much to question it too deeply.

And Trent, because he wants to see me suffer, and he knows after today's confrontation that I don't want to marry Charlie.

The minister clears his throat. "Are we ready to begin?"

We nod. "Very well." He looks down at the book open in his hands. "Dearly beloved, we are gathered here today…"

TO BE CONTINUED.

Would you like to read a special bonus deleted scene featuring Abby, Kai, and Jackson in a steamy threesome? Copy and paste this link into your browser:

https://smarturl.it/TBbonusscene

Come join the Rydeville High Elite Spoiler Group on Facebook to discuss all your theories and vent with like-minded readers! Copy and paste this link into your browser:

https://www.facebook.com/groups/RHESpoilerGroup

The third and final book in Kai and Abby's romance is releasing in early October 2019.

COMING 2020

Jackson and *Sawyer* are both releasing next year. These will be interconnected standalone titles. Subscribe to the author's romance newsletter or follow her on Facebook for all the latest information in relation to the Rydeville High Elite series.

ABOUT THE AUTHOR

USA Today bestselling author **Siobhan Davis** writes emotionally intense young adult and new adult fiction with swoon-worthy romance, complex characters, and tons of unexpected plot twists and turns that will have you flipping the pages beyond bedtime! She is the author of the bestselling *True Calling, Saven,* and *Kennedy Boys* series.

Siobhan's family will tell you she's a little bit obsessive when it comes to reading and writing, and they aren't wrong. She can rarely be found without her trusty Kindle, a paperback book, or her laptop somewhere close at hand.

Prior to becoming a full-time writer, Siobhan forged a successful corporate career in human resource management.

She resides in the Garden County of Ireland with her husband and two sons.

You can connect with Siobhan in the following ways:
Author website: www.siobhandavis.com
Author Blog: My YA NA Book Obsession
Facebook: AuthorSiobhanDavis
Twitter: @siobhandavis
Google+: SiobhanDavisAuthor
Email: siobhan@siobhandavis.com

BOOKS BY SIOBHAN DAVIS

KENNEDY BOYS SERIES
Upper Young Adult/New Adult Contemporary Romance
Finding Kyler
Losing Kyler
Keeping Kyler
The Irish Getaway
Loving Kalvin
Saving Brad
Seducing Kaden
Forgiving Keven
Summer in Nantucket
*Releasing Keanu^*
Adoring Keaton*
Reforming Kent*

STANDALONES
New Adult Contemporary Romance
Inseparable
Incognito
When Forever Changes
Only Ever You
No Feelings Involved
Second Chances Box Set

Reverse Harem Contemporary Romance
Surviving Amber Springs

RYDEVILLE HIGH ELITE SERIES
Dark High School Romance
Cruel Intentions
Twisted Betrayal
*Sweet Retribution^*
Jackson*
Sawyer*

ALL OF ME DUET
Angsty New Adult Romance
Say I'm The One *
Let Me Love You*

ALINTHIA SERIES
Upper YA/NA Paranormal Romance/Reverse Harem
The Lost Savior
The Secret Heir
The Warrior Princess
The Chosen One
The Rightful Queen*